Praise for
Babylon 5:
Dark Genesis: The
Birth of the Psi Corps

"A solid, stand-alone novel . . . A fascinating spotlight on the enigmatic, deadly telepaths."
—*USA Today* (recommended reading)

"*Dark Genesis* is the kind of rare tie-in book that equals, or even bests, the franchise whose world it borrows. If you've heard the ravings of *Babylon 5* fans . . . then this book is for you. You'll get a glimpse into the world they enjoy so passionately."
—*Cinescape Online*

Published by Ballantine Books:

CREATING BABYLON 5 by David Bassom

Babylon 5 Season-by-Season Guides by Jane Killick
#1 SIGNS AND PORTENTS
#2 THE COMING OF SHADOWS
#3 POINT OF NO RETURN
#4 NO SURRENDER, NO RETREAT
#5 THE WHEEL OF FIRE

BABYLON 5 SECURITY MANUAL

BABYLON 5: IN THE BEGINNING by Peter David
BABYLON 5: THIRDSPACE by Peter David
BABYLON 5: A CALL TO ARMS by Robert Sheckley

The Psi Corps Trilogy by J. Gregory Keyes
BABYLON 5: DARK GENESIS
BABYLON 5: DEADLY RELATIONS
BABYLON 5: FINAL RECKONING

Legions of Fire by Peter David
BABYLON 5: THE LONG NIGHT OF
  CENTAURI PRIME
BABYLON 5: ARMIES OF LIGHT AND DARK
BABYLON 5: OUT OF THE DARKNESS

Books published by The Ballantine Publishing Group
are available at quantity discounts on bulk purchases
for premium, educational, fund-raising, and special
sales use. For details, please call 1-800-733-3000.

Book III of
Legions of Fire

Out of the Darkness

By Peter David

Based on
an original outline by
J. Michael Straczynski

A Del Rey® Book
THE BALLANTINE PUBLISHING GROUP • NEW YORK

A Del Rey® Book
Published by The Ballantine Publishing Group
TM & copyright © 2000 by Warner Bros.

www.randomhouse.com/delrey/

Library of Congress Catalog Card Number: 00-106076

ISBN 0-345-42720-3

Manufactured in the United States of America

First Edition: November 2000

10 9 8 7 6 5 4 3 2 1

Hiller of the planet Mipas had always been an enthusiast about Earth history. He wasn't alone in that regard; many of the residents of Mipas shared the interest. Earth history had become something of a fad. But Hiller specialized in one particular aspect of Earth activity and culture, and that was the great art of mountain climbing.

It was a practice that was virtually unknown among the Mipasians. Not that there was a lack of mountains on Mipas; far from it. There were several particularly impressive ranges, including some that rivaled those scaled by the immortal Sir Edmund Hillary, someone for whom Hiller felt a particular closeness thanks to the similarity in their names.

However, no one on Mipas had ever displayed the slightest interest in endeavoring to scale any of these peaks. All in all, Mipasians weren't an especially aggressive race—they preferred to live their lives peacefully and avoid the notice of the more aggressive and bellicose races that populated the galaxy.

Hiller, though, felt the urge to tackle the mountains.

They seemed to taunt him, their peaks shrouded in cloud and mystery. It was said that gods resided up there. Hiller didn't lend much credence to that theory, but nevertheless he simply knew that, sooner or later, he was going to have to try to find out for himself.

"Why?" his friends would ask him. "What is this need? Why this driving ambition to clamber up the side of a protruding geographic formation, at great personal risk?" Hiller would always give the exact same response. He would toss off a salute with one tentacle and declare, "Because it's there." He was rather proud of that quote, having come across it in his studies.

1

Now Hiller was on the verge of accomplishing his most ambitious feat. He was in the midst of essaying a climb up . . . the Big One. The Mipasians had never bothered to name their mountains. This one was dubbed the Big One for convenience' sake, simply because it was the biggest mountain around. Many days had Hiller climbed it. Many times had he nearly fallen to his death, dangling by the tentacles before continuing his long, slow, and oozing way up the side. And finally, after many perilous days and nights, he had nearly reached his goal. He had broken through the clouds, and was using a breathing device to aid in his ascent, since the air at the mountaintop was quite thin.

He felt giddy. A child's wonder possessed him, as he wondered whether he would indeed witness the surprised expressions of the gods, gaping at him, when he managed to reach the peak.

And then, as he stopped for a moment to rest, he heard something. It was a deep, sonorous sound that at first seemed to be coming from everywhere. It echoed from all the rock walls, its origin impossible to discern. Hiller looked around with frustration, then plunged a tentacle into his pack and extracted a viewer. Mist and clouds hovered all around him, but the viewer could easily punch through and give him a clear idea of what, if anything, lay in the vicinity.

He activated the viewer and again wondered if he would find the gods waving at him. How amazing—and amusing—would that be?

After a few moments, he began to discern shapes. They were coming from the north . . . no. No, not quite. They were coming from overhead and descending quickly, horrifyingly quickly. Two of them, no, three, perhaps four. It was impossible to be certain. What he did know, though, was that they were getting closer.

The mountaintop began shaking in sympathetic vibrating response to the powerful engines that were propelling the objects through the sky. Pebbles, then larger rocks began to fall, and at first the full significance of that didn't register. As even bigger rocks tumbled around him, though, he suddenly realized that he was in mortal danger.

He started scrambling back down as quickly as he could, having spotted a cave on the way up that might provide shelter. But it was too late, and he was too slow. A massive avalanche fell upon him and Hiller lost his grip. His tentacles flapped about in futility, and suddenly the mountainside where he had been clinging was gone, and he was falling, unable to stop himself or help himself in any way. Gravity had taken over, pulling him down. He hit a protruding cliff and tumbled off it, hearing things break inside him and not wanting to think about what they were. Then he landed hard on an outcropping.

For just a scintilla of a second, he thought he actually might be able to survive. Not that he had the slightest idea how he was going to get down off the mountain, considering that he was already losing feeling below his neck. But he reminded himself that it was important to worry about one thing at a time.

However, the entire issue became academic as the gigantic pile of rocks tumbled around and upon him. He let out a last shriek of protest, frustrated that something so unfair and capricious was happening at the moment of what should have been his greatest triumph.

Fortunately, the rock slide left his head unscathed. Unfortunately it wasn't quite as generous with the rest of him. His body was crushed, the pain so massive and indescribable that his mind simply shut down, unable to cope.

And so as it happened, from his vantage point on the ledge, Hiller was able to see the cause of his death with his own eyes. They were huge ships, smaller than the gargantuan cruisers he had seen on news broadcasts, but larger than the one-to-one fighters that were so popular with the local military.

The style, however, was unmistakable.

"Centauri," he whispered. Whispering was all he could manage, and even then it would have been incomprehensible to anyone who was listening.

The Centauri ships moved off at high speed, heedless of the damage they had already left in their wake. Amazingly, the clouds seemed to part for them, as if with respect. Each ship possessed four curved fins, jutting at right angles to one another, knifing through the sky. He was able to see, far in the distance on the horizon, one of Mipas' largest cities. The ships were going right for it. The velocity with which they were moving was staggering. One moment it seemed as if they were near the mountain; the next they were practically over the metropolis.

They wasted no time at all. Their weaponry rained death down upon the city. Hiller watched helplessly, his body dying all around him, his vision becoming dark. Because of the distance involved, he saw the flashes of light that indicated that the city was being fired upon, and some seconds later, the sounds would reach him faintly, like far-off thunder.

It made no sense. Why would the Centauri attack Mipas? They had harmed no one. They were neutral. They had no enemies, nor did they desire any.

As the world faded around him, his mind cried out to the gods who had not chosen to present themselves, "Why? We have not hurt them! We never could, never would hurt them! What possible reason could they have?"

And then the words of his friends reverberated through his brain just as that organ shut down for good. His final neurons and synapses answered his own question with another—one that made ironic sense:

"Why climb a mountain . . . ?"

**EXCERPTED FROM *THE CHRONICLES OF LONDO
MOLLARI—DIPLOMAT, EMPEROR, MARTYR, AND
SELF-DESCRIBED FOOL.*
PUBLISHED POSTHUMOUSLY.
EDITED BY EMPEROR COTTO.
EARTH EDITION, TRANSLATION © 2280
Excerpt dated (approximate Earth date)
May 14, 2274.**

It is with some degree of shock and personal disappointment that I must conclude that I am losing my mind. I know this because, for the first time in . . . well . . . ever, I must admit . . . I actually felt sorry for Mariel.

Mariel, for those who have trouble keeping track of all the many players in these diaries, is my former wife. She is also the current wife of our inimitable—thank the Great Maker, for if he were capable of being imitated, I think I would have gone mad sooner—prime minister, the noble Durla. It has never surprised me that Mariel attached herself to him. She has that way about her. Mariel attaches herself to individuals of power in the way that the remora affixes itself to the stork.

For a time she was with Vir Cotto, my former attaché and current ambassador to Babylon 5. Fortunately enough for him, he lost her in a game of cards. I was shocked at the time. Now, in looking back, I can only wonder why I thought of it as anything less than Vir's good fortune.

More recently, I was walking past the rather elaborate quarters Durla keeps for himself in the palace these days. Back when he was simply Minister Durla, the minister of Internal Security, he maintained his own residence elsewhere. Since being made prime minister, he has relocated to the palace itself. This is an option open to whoever holds the rank, but most have not chosen to avail themselves of it. Durla, however, is not like most others. He immediately took up residence in the palace and, in doing so, sent me a very clear message, that I shall never be rid of him. That he has, in fact, set himself a goal that is no less than that of becoming emperor.

5

Not that he would admit it, of course. There are moments when he directly challenges me, but he always does so subtly, then backs off as rapidly as he can. For someone with such power and dominance, he is really quite craven. It sickens me.

I wonder why it sickens me. I should be thanking what I foolishly refer to as my lucky stars, for if he had a core of genuine mettle inspiring him, then he would be unstoppable. Durla, however, remains a bully even to this day, and bullies are cowards. He may have gone quite far in our society, but no matter how far one goes, one cannot avoid bringing oneself along.

So . . .

I was walking past Durla's quarters, and I heard what seemed like choked sobbing emanating from within. Ironic that after all this time, I still carry within me some vague aspect of the gallant. There were guards on either side of me, as there so often are. My aide, Dunseny, was also walking with me. Dunseny, the aging-and-yet-ageless retainer of the House Mollari, used to be quite a bit taller than I was, but he had become slightly stooped with age, as if his body felt obliged to make some concession to the passing years. He actually noticed the sound a heartbeat before I did. It was the slowing of his pace that drew my attention to it.

"There seems to be a problem," I observed, hearing the sounds of lamentation. "Do you think it requires my attention?"

"I do not know, Highness," he said, but he did so in a way that basically carried with it the word "Yes."

"We can attend to it, Highness," one of two guards who stood at Durla's door offered.

"You?" I said skeptically. "You attend to things by shooting them. That is not a criticism, but merely an observation, so please take no offense. Far be it from me to offend someone who shoots things. However, I believe I can handle this on my own."

"On your own, Highness?" the other guard asked.

"Yes. On my own. The way I used to do things before others did them for me." Offering no further comment, I entered without knocking or ringing a chime.

Passing through the entryway, I found myself in an elaborately decorated sitting room, filled with statuary. Durla had acquired a taste for it. I felt more as if I were walking through a museum than a place where people actually dwelt. On the far side of the sitting room there was a high balcony that offered a spectacular view of the city. I had a not dissimilar view from my own throne room.

Standing on the balcony, leaning against the rail, and looking for one moment as if she intended to vault it, was Mariel. Normally her face was made up quite exquisitely, but in this instance her mascara was running copiously. The smeared makeup left trickling splotches of blue and red on her cheeks that gave her entire face the appearance of a stormy sky at daybreak.

Upon seeing me, she gasped and made a vague effort to try to clean herself up. All she did was make it worse, smearing the makeup so grotesquely that she looked like some sort of painted harridan from a stage drama. "I'm . . . I'm sorry, Highness," she said desperately, her efforts to pull herself together failing miserably. "Did we have . . . I wasn't expecting a visit from . . ."

"Calm yourself, Mariel," I said. I pulled a cloth from the inside of my gleaming white jacket and handed it to her. As an aside, I cannot tell you how much I despise the traditional white of the emperor's garb. Michael Garibaldi, my erstwhile associate on Babylon 5, once referred to it as an "ice cream suit." I do not know exactly what he meant by that, but I doubt it was flattering. I could not blame him, though; there is little about it that I find commendable.

"Calm yourself," I said again. "We had no appointment. I was simply passing by and heard someone in distress. There are so many distressed individuals out there," and I gestured toward the cityscape. "I cannot attend to all of them. But at the very least, I can help those who are within these four walls, yes?"

"That's very kind of you, Highness."

"Leave us," I said to my guards. Dunseny, ever the soul of proper behavior, good tact, and common sense, had waited in the corridor.

"Leave you, Highness?" They appeared uncertain and even suspicious.

"Yes."

"Our orders from Prime Minister Durlà are that we are to remain by your side at all times," one of them said. I would record here any distinguishing characteristics he exhibited, for the sake of reference, but I cannot. My guardsmen were something of a homogenous lot. The aforementioned Mr. Garibaldi called them the "Long Jockey Brigade," I believe. I am no more conversant with the term "long jockey" than I am with "ice cream suit," but I will say this: Mr. Garibaldi certainly had a colorful way of expressing himself.

"Your adherence to orders is commendable," I said.

"Thank you, Highness."

"However, you overlook two things. Prime Minister Durla is not here. And I am. Now get out, before I command you to arrest yourselves."

The guards glanced at each other nervously for a moment, then wisely hastened into the hallway. I turned my attention back to Mariel. To my surprise, she actually seemed to be smiling slightly. Even laughing softly. " 'Arrest yourselves.' Very droll, Highness."

"With all that has passed between us, Mariel, I believe 'Londo' will suffice."

"No, Highness," she said simply. "I believe it necessary always to remember your station and mine."

A remarkable attitude. "Very well. Whatever makes you more comfortable." I took a few steps around the room, arms draped behind my back as if I were on an inspection tour. "So . . . do you wish to tell me precisely why you are so upset?"

"I see little point, Highness. It's nothing. A passing mood."

"Has Durla been abusive to you in any way?"

"Durla?" The thought seemed to amuse her even more than my passing comment had, moments earlier. "No, no. Durla, in point of fact, is not really here enough to be considered abusive. He is busy these days. Very busy." She looked down, apparently having suddenly taken great interest in her hands. "I do not begrudge him that. There is a great deal for him to do."

"Yes, yes. Destabilizing the region and sending our world spiraling toward certain destruction can be very time-consuming, I should think."

She seemed surprised by my tone. "He is your prime minister. I would think he carries out your wishes and desires. He serves Centauri Prime, and you *are* Centauri Prime."

"Yes, so I hear. The emperor is the living embodiment of Centauri Prime. A quaint notion. A grand custom. I think I like the sound of it more than I do the practice." I shrugged. "In any event, Durla does what Durla wishes. He no longer consults with me, or even needs me." I looked at her askance. "Or you, I should think. Is that the reason for the tears? That you miss him?"

"Miss him?" She appeared to consider that a moment, as if the thought had never before entered her head. If she was feigning contemplation, she was doing a superb job. "No," she said thoughtfully. "No, I do not think I miss him . . . as much as I miss myself."

"Yourself?"

She made to reply, but then stopped, as she appeared to reconsider her words. Finally she said, "I think of where I intended my life to be, Highness. I had plans, believe it or not. There were things I wanted to do when I was a little girl . . . not especially reasonable, all of them, but I . . ." She stopped and shook her head. "I apologize. I'm babbling."

"It is quite all right," I told her. "In all the time that we were married, Mariel, I do not think we actually spoke in this manner."

"I was trained to say all the right things," she said ruefully. "Speaking of one's disappointments and shortcomings—that wasn't deemed proper for a well-bred Centauri woman."

"Very true. Very true." And I waited.

Again, I must emphasize that I bore no love for this woman. I looked upon this interaction with a sort of detached fascination; the way one looks with curiosity at a fresh scab, impressed that such a crusted and nauseating thing could appear on one's own body. In speaking with Mariel, I was—in a way—picking at a scab. Then, since she didn't seem to be volunteering any information, I prompted, "So . . . what things did you wish to do? As a young girl, I mean?"

She half smiled. "I wanted to fly," she replied.

I made a dismissive noise. "That is no great feat. A simple ride in—"

"No, Highness," she gently interrupted. "I do not mean fly in a vessel. I wanted . . ." And the half smile blossomed into a full-blown, genuine thing of beauty. It reminded me of how it was when I first met her. I admit it. Even I was stunned by her beauty. I did not know then, of course, the darkness that the beauty hid. But who am I to condemn others for hiding darkness?

"I wanted to fly on my own," she continued. "I wanted to be able to leap high, wave my arms, and soar like a bird." She laughed in a gentle, self-mocking way. "Foolish of me, I know. I'm sure that's what you're thinking . . ."

"Why would I consider it foolish?"

"Because such a thing isn't possible."

"Mariel," I said, "I am the emperor. If you had asked anyone who knew me—or, for that matter, if you had asked me directly—what the likelihood was of such a thing coming to pass, I would have thought it to be exactly as possible as your fantasy. Who knows, Mariel? Perhaps you will indeed learn to fly."

"And you, Highness? Did you indeed dream of becoming emperor?"

"Me? No."

"What did you dream of, then?"

Unbidden, the image came to my mind. The dream that I had not had until well into my adulthood. But it's a funny thing about certain dreams: they assume such a state of importance in your mind that you start to believe, retroactively, that they were always a part of your life.

Those powerful hands, that face twisted in grim anger. The face of G'Kar, with but one eye burning its gaze into the black and shredded thing I call my soul, and his hands at my throat. This dream had shaped, defined, and haunted my life for, it seemed, as far back as I could remember.

"What did I dream of?" I echoed. "Survival."

"Truly?" She shrugged those slim shoulders. "That doesn't seem such a lofty goal."

"I had always thought," I said, "that it was the only one that mattered. I would have placed it above the needs of my loved ones, above the needs of Centauri Prime itself. Now . . ." I shrugged. "It does not seem to be such an important thing. Survival is not all that it is reputed to be."

There was a long silence then. It was very odd. This woman had been my enemy, my nemesis, yet now it seemed as though she were another person entirely. Considering what I had faced, considering those who desired to bring me down . . . the machinations of one young Centauri female didn't seem worth the slightest bit of concern.

Not so young, actually.

I found myself looking at Mariel, really looking at her for the first time in a long time. She was not decrepit by any means, but her age was beginning to show. I wasn't entirely sure why. She was older, certainly, but not that much older. She seemed . . . careworn somehow. She looked older than her years.

"Strange," she said slowly, "that we are talking this way. With all that has passed between us, Lond—Highness—"

"Londo," I told her firmly.

"Londo," she said after a moment's hesitation. "With all that we have been through . . . how odd that we would be talking here, now. Like old friends."

" 'Like,' perhaps, Mariel. But not actually old friends. For I shall never forget who I am . . . and who you are . . . and what you did to me."

I wondered if she would try to deny that she had endeavored to kill me fifteen years earlier. If she would bleat her innocence in the matter. Instead, all she did was shrug, and without rancor in her voice say, "It was no worse than what you did to me."

"Next thing, you will tell me that you miss me."

"It is impossible to miss what you never had."

"That is very true." I looked at her with even more curiosity. "You have not told me why you were crying. That is, after all, the reason I came in here. Was it indeed because you miss 'yourself'?"

She looked down at her hands with great interest. "No. Someone else."

"Who?"

She shook her head. "It does not matter . . ."

"I wish to know, nevertheless."

She seemed to consider her answer a long time. Then she looked over at me with such melancholy, I cannot even find words for it. "I appreciate the time you've taken here, Londo . . . more than you can know. But it really, truly, does not matter. What is done is done, and I have no regrets."

"Whereas I have almost nothing but regrets. Very well, Mariel." I rose and walked toward the door. "If, in the future, you decide that there are matters you wish to discuss . . . feel free to bring them to my attention."

"Londo . . ."

"Yes?"

"My dream is childhood foolishness . . . but I hope that you get yours."

I laughed, but there was no trace of mirth in my voice. "Trust me, Mariel . . . if there is one thing in this world I am certain of, it is that, sooner or later, I will get mine. And sooner, I think, rather than later."

— *chapter 1* —

Luddig wasn't a particularly happy Drazi.

He did not like the building to which he had been sent. He did not like the office within the building. And he most certainly did not like that he was being kept waiting in the office within the building.

Luddig was a first-tier ambassador in the Drazi diplomatic corps, and he had fought long and hard to get to where he was. As he drummed his fingers impatiently on the expansive desk he was sitting beside, he couldn't help but wonder why it was that things never quite seemed to work out the way that he wanted them to.

Seated next to Luddig was his immediate aide, Vidkun. They provided quite a contrast to one another, Luddig being somewhat heavyset and jowly while Vidkun was small and slim. Not that Vidkun was a weakling by any means. He was whipcord thin and had a certain air of quiet strength about him. Luddig, on the other hand, was like a perpetually seething volcano that tended to overwhelm any who stood before him with belligerence and bombast. As diplomats went, he wasn't particularly genteel. Then again, he'd never had to be. His activities were confined mostly to his office and occasional backdoor maneuvers.

It was one of those activities that had brought him here, to Centauri Prime, to the place called the "Tower of Power." It was an impressive and elegantly simple structure that, when viewed from the ground, seemed to stretch forever to the sky.

Luddig had not come here on his own, of course. It had been set up meticulously and scrupulously in advance. No one on the Drazi Homeworld had been aware that he was coming to Centauri Prime . . . well, not "officially" aware. He had brought Vidkun along primarily to have someone to complain to.

"This is how they treat Luddig of the Drazi!" Luddig said in disgust. He was one of those who chose to affect the popular Drazi habit of referring to himself in the third person. "An hour and a half we wait," he continued. "Waiting and waiting in this stupid room for this stupid minister." He cuffed Vidkun abruptly on the shoulder. Vidkun barely reacted. By this point in his career, he scarcely seemed to notice. "We had a deal!"

"Perhaps you should remind him of that, sir," Vidkun said with exaggerated politeness.

"Remind him! Of course Luddig will remind him! Drazi do not have to, should not have to, tolerate such poor attention to Drazi interests!"

"Of course not, sir."

"Stop agreeing!" Luddig said in annoyance, striking Vidkun once more on the shoulder. Since it was the exact same place, it left Vidkun a bit sore, but stoutly he said nothing. "You keep agreeing. It shows you are trying to mock Luddig!"

Vidkun tried to figure out if there was any conceivable way in which he could respond to the accusation. If he said it wasn't true, then he'd be disagreeing and thereby disproving the contention. Except he'd be calling Luddig a liar. If he agreed that was what he was doing, Luddig would shout at him that he was doing it again. Vidkun wisely chose to say nothing at all, instead inclining his head slightly in acknowledgment without actually providing any admission one way or the other.

Clearly Luddig was about to press the matter when, with miraculously good timing, Minister Castig Lione entered.

Lione was a tall man whose build and general look bordered on the cadaverous. He had such gravity about him that he could have used it to maintain a satellite in orbit, Vidkun mused. Then he noticed several of the black-clad youths known as the Prime Candidates following Lione, dropping back and away from the minister as he walked into his office. Vidkun came to the conclusion that Lione already did have satellites. They were the youth of Centauri Prime, and as near as Vidkun could tell, the best and the brightest. Their loyalty to Castig Lione was reputedly unyielding and unwavering. If Lione had told them to break every bone in their bodies, they would do so and do it willingly.

Vidkun did not, as a rule, like fanatics. If nothing else, they tended to be a bit too loud for his taste.

"Ambassador Luddig," said Lione, bowing deeply in respect. For a man of his height, bowing was no easy thing. Luddig should have appreciated the gesture. Instead he scowled even more fiercely. Vidkun rose and returned the bow, and got another quick physical rebuke from his superior. "To what," continued Lione, "do I owe this honor?"

"This honor." Luddig made an incredulous noise that conveyed contempt. "This honor. This treatment is more like."

"Treatment?" His eyebrows puckered in confusion. "Was there a problem with your arrival? My Prime Candidates were given specific instructions to provide you full protection in escorting you from the port. I cannot, of course, account for the reactions your presence might engender among our populace."

"It has nothing to do with that—"

Lione continued as if Luddig had not spoken. "In case you are unaware, all foreigners have been banned from the surface of Centauri Prime. That is how highly charged sentiments have been running. Fortunately, as a minister, I have certain . . . latitude. So I was able to arrange for your visit to our fair—"

"It has nothing to do with that!"

Lione blinked owlishly. "Then I am not quite sure what you are referring to."

"We had an arrangement!"

"Did we?"

"About Mipas!"

"Ah." Lione did an exceptional job of acting as if he had been unaware of what was getting Luddig so agitated. "You're speaking about the unfortunate, but necessary, attack on Mipas."

"Unfortunate but necessary how! Unfortunate, yes! Necessary . . . Drazi do not see that! Has Centauri Prime totally taken leave of senses? Or has Centauri Prime forgotten that Mipas is under Drazi jurisdiction!"

"Jurisdiction, yes. Curious how that happened, isn't it." Lione's calm, even lazy tone suddenly shifted. "Curious that the Drazi government paid so little attention to Mipas . . . until valuable minerals were found on it. Suddenly a world that was just beyond the outermost edge of the Drazi borders became Drazi property . . . when your government reconfigured the borders to allow for . . ." Lione actually chuckled, and it was not the most pleasant of sounds. ". . . to allow for the expanding universe theory. 'If the universe is expanding, Drazi territory must expand with it to keep up with natural law.' That was priceless, I have to admit. No one in the Alliance gainsayed you, simply because they were stunned by the sheer gall your people displayed."

"If Centauri Prime has issue with expansion of—"

Lione held up a hand, stilling the new torrent of words. "The Centaurum has no such issues. Expand territories all you wish. Reconfigure your borders and decide that you're entitled to take possession of the Vorlon Homeworld, for all we care. But Mipas, well . . ." and he shook his head sadly. "The fact is that our intelligence informed us that Mipas was acting in concert with, and providing aid to, certain insurrectionist factions here on Centauri Prime."

"Is lie!"

"Is not," Lione responded coolly. "The information we have received is quite definitive. Mipas was aiding those who would overthrow our beloved emperor and drive our prime minister out of office. Naturally, out of a sense of self-preservation, we had to take action."

Between gritted teeth, Luddig said, "We had an understanding."

"Did we?"

"Do not play games with Drazi!" Luddig warned. "Centauri Prime is as interested in mineral deposits on Mipas as Drazi! I know that! You know that! Everyone know that! We had arrangements!"

"And how much you must have enjoyed those arrangements, Luddig," said Lione. "Under-the-table payments made to you by certain Mipas officials. And you, in turn, pass those payments along to us. A token of respect; a tithe, if you will, to purchase our goodwill. And you succeeded for quite some time, Luddig. I commend you for your industry. And I commend you for the deftness with which you managed to cut yourself in to those payments. How much did you manage to keep for yourself? Ten percent? Twenty?"

"Do you think Drazi not take risks!" Luddig said hotly. "Luddig of Drazi has his own expenses, own concerns. Certain officials turn their own blind eye to 'under-the-table payments,' as you say. Money has to cover their eyes, too. It was beneficial arrangement for all."

"Yes, yes, I daresay it was. Just as this little arrangement exists with other governments, other 'officials' such as yourselves. Others who envelop themselves in cloaks of self-righteousness, more than happy to complain publicly about the Centauri, while you have no difficulty in private backroom dealings. I can smell the corruption in all the governments of your pathetic Alliance. The odor of hypocrisy permeates even the vacuum of space, Ambassador Luddig."

Vidkun watched in fascination as Luddig became so angry that the skin flaps under his throat stood out and turned pale red. "Luddig does not have to sit here and listen to this!"

"Stand if you prefer, then," Lione said lazily. "It does not matter to me." Then once again, his attitude shifted, from torpor to quiet intensity. "Understand this, Ambassador. We stand by the results of our investigation. And since we know that the Mipasians were acting with the insurrectionists, we can only assume that the Drazi were aware of this connection and approved of it. That, Ambassador, would mean that you are—rather than our silent partners—our enemies. We do not advise that you become enemies of the Centauri Republic. That would be most unfortunate for all concerned."

Vidkun had the distinct feeling that Lione was assuming Luddig would wilt under the implied threat. To Vidkun's surprise—and, if he had to guess, to Lione's surprise as well—Luddig did not come remotely close to wilting. Instead he was on his feet, breathing so hard that it was rasping in his chest. "You threaten Drazi?" he demanded.

"I threaten no one," Lione said.

But Luddig wasn't buying it. "You are! You violate Drazi interests! You renege on deal!"

"The deal, such as it was, was entirely unofficial, Luddig," Lione pointed out. "You said so yourself. If you wish to complain about it to the Interstellar Alliance—if you wish to try to roust your fellows from their stupor and bring them into full war with us—then you will have to go public with the terms of our little arrangement. That will not go over particularly well, I assure you, because it will bring not only your own government under scrutiny, but others as well. No one is going to want that."

"Maybe Drazi do not care about scrutiny or deals," Luddig shot back. "Maybe Drazi care about Centauri thinking they can do whatever they wish, whenever they wish, to whomever they wish. Maybe Drazi believe that Alliance is willing to overlook 'deals' or treat them as stopgap measures to full war that can no longer be avoided because of Centauri stupidity and arrogance!"

Lione did not answer immediately. Instead he contemplated what Luddig had said. He leaned back in his chair, the furniture creaking under his weight, and he interlaced his fingers while studying Luddig very, very carefully.

Then he smiled.

Vidkun felt his spine seize up.

"It seems, Ambassador, that we may have underestimated the . . . vehemence with which you will be pursuing your claim. Very well."

"Very well what?" Luddig's eyes narrowed suspiciously.

"I shall take your concerns to the prime minister and we shall see if restitution cannot somehow be arranged."

Luddig puffed out his chest with sudden confidence. "Yes! That is attitude Drazi want to see!"

"Excuse me a moment, won't you? No, no, don't get up. I have a small room designed for . . . private communications. Will not take but a minute." He did not rise from his seat so much as he seemed to uncoil.

The moment he walked out of the room, Vidkun turned to Luddig, and said, "We are dead."

"What!" Luddig scoffed at the very idea. "You saw! He spoke of restitution! He spoke of—"

"Ambassador, with all respect, what he spoke of doesn't matter. In these sorts of things, what is *not* said is often more important than what is. I am telling you, we are—"

"We are Drazi! And you are coward!" Luddig said angrily, stabbing a finger at Vidkun.

"Sir, I am no coward," Vidkun said, bristling.

"Yes! Your own cowardice stops you from seeing that Centauri do not wish to anger Drazi! You are not worthy of being aide to Luddig! A new aide will be required upon our return!"

Vidkun was about to argue the point further, protesting the accusations of cowardice, when the door opened and Lione entered again, stooping slightly to avoid the top of the door frame. "The prime minister wishes to see you, but his schedule simply will not allow for it today. Tomorrow, however, bright and early, he would be more than happy to discuss the matter. In the meantime, deluxe accommodations have been arranged for you at a facility nearby. We certainly hope that will suffice."

"For now," Luddig said noncommittally. "We reserve judgment until we actually see accommodations."

"Very prudent," Lione said agreeably.

As they headed down to street level, Vidkun's head was spinning. Every early warning system in his makeup was screaming at him that they were in mortal danger. But Luddig was so overwhelmingly confident, and Lione seemed so eager to please, that he was finding it harder and harder to believe that there was, in fact, any jeopardy. It might be, he thought bleakly, that Luddig was correct. Perhaps he was indeed a coward, and simply didn't have the proper mental strength to pursue a career in the diplomatic corps.

They walked out into the street, a pleasant sun beaming down at them, and a glorious day on Centauri Prime apparently lying ahead of them. There were passersby, casting glances in their direction, but there did not appear to be any problem. There were Prime Candidates forming a protective circle around them, but Luddig—chatting animatedly with Lione—didn't pay them any mind. He was calm, cool, and confidently secure that he had a complete handle on the situation.

"Kill the Drazi!"

The shout came from someone in the crowd, and it was suddenly taken up by others. What had appeared only moments before to be a benign, loose assemblage of people suddenly firmed up into a mob.

"Kill the Drazi! Death to outworlders! Centauri Prime over all! Death to enemies of the Great Republic!" These and other sentiments suddenly seemed to come from everyone, everywhere.

And the enraged Centauri citizens were advancing, coming in from all sides.

The Prime Candidates melted away. Suddenly the protective wall of bodies was gone.

Luddig's accusation no longer registered in Vidkun's mind. He was beyond cowardice. He was terrified. The infuriated Centauri were moving toward them with one mind, and there was nowhere to go, nowhere to run. Then suddenly a strong hand was on his arm, pulling him away. The last thing he saw was Luddig going down beneath the clubs and fists of the crowd. Luddig was screaming, and it wasn't a particularly brave-sounding scream. It was high-pitched, and plaintive, and rather pathetic.

Someone held him. Vidkun let out a yelp and turned to see the face of the man who was about to kill him.

To his surprise, there was no anger in the expression of the Centauri man who had yanked him away from the crowd. The Centauri's long, black/red hair was high and swept up. His face was very angular, his chin coming almost to a point. It was his eyes that caught Vidkun the most, though. There was intensity, at least in one of them, but . . .

Then the world seemed to whirl around as someone else pulled at him, and just as quickly as he had been in the midst of danger, Vidkun was being thrust back into the Tower of Power. He staggered, looking around at his saviors: the very same Prime Candidates who had deserted them moments before, leaving them to the mercy of the mob. The red-haired Centauri was no longer in sight.

Vidkun thought he heard Luddig screaming once more, but then the scream was cut short by a sound like a melon being crushed. The expressions of the Prime Candidates never wavered. They simply stood there, like automatons.

"To my office," came a voice, the voice of Lione. Vidkun was still in shock and offered no resistance as he was escorted back upstairs. Moments later he was seated opposite Castig Lione. He couldn't help but notice that he had been seated in the chair closer to the desk: the one that Luddig had been sitting in.

Lione was shaking his head with a great air of tragedy. "How unfortunate. How very, very unfortunate," he intoned. "To think that such a thing would happen. But there are random acts of violence everywhere . . ."

"Random?"

"Yes."

"Acts of violence?" He was having trouble processing the words. He had to fight to bring his full faculties to bear upon the situation.

"Yes. Here the two of you were, walking the streets of Centauri Prime, and a lone madman attacked and killed your superior. We tried to stop it, of course."

"A . . . lone madman?" He felt a pounding in his head, as if his brain were shouting at him to pull himself together, and match what was being said with what had happened.

"Yes, of course. There's only so much protection even the most dedicated guards can offer in the face of such . . ." He shook his head. "Very likely, it was the work of the rebels and saboteurs. They were endeavoring to discredit the Centaurum, and such actions are taken to reflect poorly upon this government in the eyes of others. In any event, it is pointless to dwell upon it. My guards dispatched the madman. Justice was done, and it's important that we put the whole unfortunate business behind us."

"You ordered it!" Vidkun was trying to rally. "You ordered the assault! The mob! You!"

"Mob!" Lione sounded shocked. "I saw no mob. Nor, I would suggest, did you." Then he smiled and reached into his pocket. Vidkun automatically flinched, bracing himself for some sort of weapon to be drawn, but Lione instead simply pulled out what appeared to be a credit chip and extended it to Vidkun.

Vidkun took it, looking at it blankly. "What is this . . . ?"

"Access to a private account that Luddig set up. He thought we did not have right of entry to it. Luddig apparently thought a number of things that were in error." He shrugged. "It was where he was siphoning payments from the various worlds . . ."

"Worlds?"

"You don't seriously think that Mipas was unique, do you?" The very notion appeared laughable to him. "No, no . . . Luddig had a number of 'clients.' There are quite a few worlds out there in which the Drazi maintain interests. Interests that stem from tradition . . . and from profit.

"Everyone is interested in protecting his or her interests, Vidkun. Luddig, unfortunately, is no longer capable of protecting his. You are. His interests . . . have become your interests. And very likely his position . . . presuming you are canny enough, judicious enough, and . . ." He cleared his throat and indicated the credit chip with a nod. ". . . generous enough to make things happen. If, that is, you are interested in doing so."

He stopped talking for a moment, and it seemed to Vidkun as if he was waiting for Vidkun to say something. But the Drazi did not speak. Something warned him that it would be wiser not to.

Lione's lips thinned into a death's-head smile.

"You could, of course, take a more aggressive stance," he acknowledged. "Try to rally the Alliance against us. Endeavor to prove your case. Anger a good number of people; upset a number of agreements that are understood amidst more people than you would truly believe possible. You could do all that. I have to admit I would not advise it. But it is a way you might go."

Vidkun found the nerve to speak. "And if I indicate that is what I am going to do . . . then I, too, would suffer an accident."

Slowly Lione shook his head. "That would be a foolish position for me to take. You could agree to anything I say . . . then once you are off-world, safely beyond concerns for your own life and limb, you might say and do anything you wish. Threats are extremely unreliable. What I am endeavoring to point out is that cooperation is far more to your advantage. It will benefit you. It will serve your needs. You do have needs, I assume. You are still quite young. There are things you want to accomplish, goals you wish to achieve. A quiet understanding will get a great deal that rabble-rousing and accusations will not."

"And in the meantime, you will attack more worlds, as you did Mipas . . ."

"Mipas was a threat. If you believe nothing else I tell you, believe that. We acted in self-defense, nothing more. You seem a reasonable person. How can any reasonable person condemn us for that? That is indeed the entire point of the barter system which Luddig so deftly oversaw. The moneys paid are an act of good faith. We do not ask for it; it is offered freely. Even if we were not paid, we would still not attack. Assorted worlds have these arrangements with us at their behest, not ours. They misunderstand the Centauri mind-set. We are not out to destroy others, no. No, not at all. Our intention is simply to make certain that no one ever attacks us again. We are not bullies. We just desire to show that we are strong. You do see the difference, do you not?"

"Yes. Yes, I do," Vidkun said slowly.

"That is good to know, considering that Luddig apparently did not see the difference. We do not take well to threats. But cooperation . . . that is different. And there are many who are most anxious to cooperate with Centauri Prime." He sat forward and, in doing so, almost seemed capable of bending from the hip and leaning over the entire desk. "I am hoping . . . that you are one of those. For your sake. For ours. For the sake of the continued interests of the Drazi Homeworld. To all of that, Vidkun . . . I'm sorry . . . *acting Ambassador Vidkun* . . . you hold the key."

Vidkun nodded slowly in acknowledgment.

"The prime minister would still like to meet with you tomorrow," Lione told him. "Are you amenable to that?"

Once more Vidkun nodded. He thought about Luddig, beaten to death by the crowd. And he thought about the contempt with which Luddig had addressed him, the way that Luddig had made him feel.

"I believe I am," Vidkun said. "And I believe . . . I should inform my government of the tragic circumstance that led to Luddig's passing. It is . . . commendable how quickly you were able to dispose of his assailant."

Lione inclined his head in acknowledgment of the compliment. "We of Centauri Prime are only concerned with doing what is right."

— chapter 2 —

Twenty years . . .

Delenn was very likely as aware of the passage of time as any other person alive. Always in the back of her mind lurked the knowledge that her beloved husband, her soul mate, John Sheridan, the man who had virtually reconfigured the way of the galaxy, had only twenty years to live. That had been the price of survival on Z'ha'dum. If she could go back in time, if she could prevent any one moment, it would be that one. An impressive priority, considering some of the horrific things she had witnessed in her time, some of the disasters that had occurred to those whom she loved.

Twenty years to live . . .

The enigmatic being named Lorien had brought John Sheridan back from the dead through means Delenn had never fully understood. What she *had* understood, though, was that the "fix" was only temporary. That after a mere two decades, Sheridan would simply shut off, like a light.

Twenty years to live . . .

That's what she'd been told . . .

. . . fourteen years earlier.

Once upon a time, she had been able to put such considerations out of her mind, sometimes for days on end. Lately, though, not a day—sometimes, it seemed, not an hour—passed without her dwelling on it.

Despite her closeness with her husband, though, despite the deep bond they shared, she was able to keep her concerns from him. Occasionally he would notice that she seemed preoccupied, and would remark upon it. She would easily deflect his comments by saying that she was thinking about David, their son. At twelve years of age, he was growing into something that was an impressive combination of mother and father. Remarkably, David seemed to possess elements of both their personalities. He was fully capable of being a young hellion, tearing about their home on Minbar with a definitely Human enthusiasm and abandon, much to the chagrin of his mother, the amusement of his father, and the utter frustration of his teachers.

On the other hand, when faced with studies, David consistently rose to the occasion with such facility that his teachers wondered just how much he could accomplish if he applied himself fully.

Outwardly he appeared Human. The color of his hair had shifted over time. He had gone from being towheaded to dark-haired, and he tended to wear it long. This annoyed his father, whose old military instincts kicked in. Every so often, he would extol the virtues of a short haircut, but David seemed to pay such critiques no mind. Curiously, his eyebrows retained their light color, but the dark eyes beneath remained evocative of his mother.

He did, however, possess his father's charisma. That much was unmistakable. Nor was his charisma limited to its effects on Humans; Minbari women—grown women—would do double takes when he passed, looking him up and down appreciatively while he winked at them or came up with some bon mot that always prompted gentle laughter or looks of amusement.

This tendency was something that drove his mother to distraction . . . particularly when David's father would watch such exhibitions and grin approvingly. Only when he noticed Delenn's silently annoyed gaze did John Sheridan quickly try to cover his paternally proud smile.

Six years to live . . .

That thought would come to her at times such as now, when Sheridan was openly agitated about something. She desperately wished that he would set aside his burden as president of the Alliance. She had pointed out on any number of occasions that "president" was an elected office, for a particular term, and that it might not be a bad idea if Sheridan considered pushing more strongly for an open election, to find a replacement. Sheridan did consider it, but every time he tried to follow through, the other member races saw it as some sort of desire on his part for a vote of confidence. Naturally they gave him that vote with gusto and enthusiasm, and inevitably some other disaster would occur that would keep John Sheridan firmly in office.

It was as if the Fates themselves were conspiring against them, making sure that they would never know a time of peace.

Six more years to live . . .

At night in their bed she would whisper to him, *"Let's run away,"* and some nights he would actually seem to reflect on it. In the dead of night, he would speak of laying down his burden, of spending his remaining years in peace. And then the dawn would come, and the John Sheridan of the nighttime would disappear, replaced by John Sheridan, man of responsibility. Consequently, it pained her when so much as an hour, even a minute of his day caused him aggravation. But she had no control over it. All she could do was sympathize and be there for him, for counsel, for support . . . for sanity.

This was one of those times.

"They're *idiots*!" Sheridan raged.

They were in his office, except he wasn't in it so much as stalking it, like a caged animal. With them were the only two individuals in the entire galaxy he appeared to trust completely: Michael Garibaldi and Citizen G'Kar of Narn.

Neither of them truly worked for Sheridan. Once upon a time, Garibaldi had been Sheridan's chief of security. Those days were long past, and his responsibilities as a businessman occupied much of his time. His latest journey to Minbar was actually more of a stopover on his way to some other appointment. From the look on his face, Delenn suspected that he might very well be wondering whether the impromptu visit had been such a good idea.

G'Kar was another story altogether.

It was hard to believe that the tall, proud Narn had once been someone so insolent, so bellicose, that Delenn had literally had to bend him to her will via gravity rings. Since that time, G'Kar had become—there was no other way for her to say it—a creature of destiny. It was as if he knew that he had an important part to play in the grand scheme of things, and he was serenely and securely accepting of that role. Delenn couldn't help but suppose that it did, in fact, show some consistency. If G'Kar was an enemy, he was implacable. If, however, he was an ally, there was none more devoted.

On one occasion, Sheridan had referred to G'Kar as "the

king's hand." This was a reference that completely eluded Delenn, and she had said as much.

"Ancient kings had men known as their 'hands,' " Sheridan had explained to her. "They would go out into the field and do the dirty work. The things that the king could not, or would not, get involved in. The hand was the most trustworthy and dependable of the knights."

"That is interesting to know, Your Highness," Delenn had said with open amusement, and bowed deeply. Sheridan had rolled his eyes, wondered out loud why he ever bothered to tell her anything, and taken the gentle ribbing in stride.

He wasn't in stride at the moment, though. His frustration had reached a boiling point and nothing that either G'Kar or Garibaldi could say would calm him. Wisely, then, they chose to say nothing, and instead allowed Sheridan to vent.

And vent he did, his neatly trimmed grey beard bristling as if it had a life of its own.

"I thought this was going to be it. This was going to be the one. Was there any planet more benign, less threatening, than Mipas?" He didn't give them time to answer. Instead he started ticking off responses on his fingers. "Bricarn 9. Shandukan. Harper's World. The list goes on and on! All helpless. All useful to the Centauri war machine, either for positioning, or raw materials, or even just sending a message to the Alliance that the Centauri are a force to be reckoned with. A message that the Centauri themselves thrive upon, becoming bolder with each unanswered strike! But every damned world they go after is a border world, far out at the edge of their interests, and making no move against the Centauri!"

"They're quite carefully selected, for maximum impact with minimal risk," G'Kar squeezed in, as an opinion.

Sheridan nodded vehemently. "Exactly. And the risk remains minimal because certain factions in the Alliance keep refusing to go up against the Centauri! Every time the Centauri take an aggressive action and succeed with impunity, they're that much more emboldened to keep to their course! A course that, over the past year, has brought us closer and closer to a costly, full-blown war!"

" 'Cost' probably has a good deal to do with it," a grim

Garibaldi commented. "Not that I can prove it, you understand, but I suspect there's some serious greasing of palms going on."

"There are many who are happy to overlook long-term ramifications in return for short-term profits," G'Kar said. "It's been a pattern throughout history."

"Is that how it works, then?" demanded Sheridan. "Throughout history, the strong allow the weak to suffer so that they can obtain selfish goals?"

"Of course," G'Kar said reasonably. "Where have you been hiding?"

"That was the past," Sheridan insisted. "We're supposed to have advanced. We're supposed to have learned. Learned that you cannot allow thugs and monsters to have their way." He stopped at the window and gazed out as if he were trying to look past the Minbari horizon. As if he could spot Centauri vessels cruising around in the depths of space, looking for new prey. He shook his head, and when he spoke again he sounded discouraged and frustrated. "You would think that if we'd learned anything from the Shadow War, it was that even the most benevolent of races can become despotic, if they're allowed to exercise their might unchecked. Yet here we are again, facing an enemy who is building up strength, weaponry, and confidence, and the pacifists in the Alliance would have us do nothing."

"They don't think it affects them directly," Delenn finally spoke up. "The problem, John, is that your efforts with the Alliance have been too successful in other areas. Through the treaties you've overseen, the crackdowns on trade piracy, the assorted economic models you've introduced . . . through all of that and more, you've helped bring about an unprecedented sense of prosperity and economic stability throughout the system. When people are satisfied with their financial situation, when they want for nothing . . . it is difficult to get them to leave their comfortable homes and hurl themselves into the depths of space to fight wars. They have so much, they are not willing to risk losing it."

"If they can't get off their asses to fight the Centauri, they're sure as hell going to lose it," Sheridan said flatly. He leaned against his desk and shook his head, looking more discouraged and frustrated than Delenn could recall seeing him in years. "They keep being 'encouraged' to look the other way. They believe that if they simply let Centauri Prime take this world or that world, that it will be enough to placate them. They think things are going to settle down. They don't understand that it isn't going to happen unless we *make* things settle down . . . and that won't happen for as long as the Centauri think that they can walk all over us!"

Six more years. And this sort of irritation was all he had to look forward to, day in, day out? Delenn could not recall a time when she more despised Londo Mollari.

"I've spoken to the Brakiri. The Dubai. The Gaim. And on and on, a list almost as long as the list of worlds that have fallen to the Centauri," Sheridan continued. "No one wants to get involved. They come up with reason after reason why it's not a good idea, and you're right, Delenn, it all boils down to the same thing: It's not their problem." He shook his head. "If we had simply waited around until the Shadows were ready to attack Babylon 5, it would be a seriously different galaxy out there. These damned pacifists . . ."

"Since when is peace bad?"

The youthful voice startled Sheridan out of his frustrated diatribe. They all turned toward the speaker, even though they all already knew who it was.

David Sheridan stood there, leaning against the door frame and smiling in that infinitely self-possessed manner that only adolescents could summon with facility.

"And here he comes . . . the great agitator," Garibaldi said with the air of someone who had been down the same road any number of times.

"Hey, Uncle Mikey."

Garibaldi emitted a pained howl, as if he'd just been stabbed through the heart. He staggered across the room, then suddenly lunged and snagged an arm around the back of David's neck. David let out a howl of anything other than anguish, as Garibaldi yanked on his long hair and snarled, "No 'Uncle Mikey'! I hate 'Uncle Mikey'! You *know* I hate 'Uncle Mikey'!"

"I'm sorry, Uncle Mikey!" David howled, choking on his own laughter.

"Punk kid. Get a haircut."

Garibaldi shoved him free, turned to John Sheridan, and

chucked a thumb at the teen. "You got a punk kid there with no respect for his elders, including his beloved godfather."

"Tell me about it," Sheridan commiserated.

"David, I thought you were at your lessons with Master Vultan," Delenn said.

"I was. Vultan decided it was time to take a break."

"Meaning that he took his eyes off you for half a second and you were gone."

David shrugged noncommittally.

Delenn let out a sigh that was a familiar combination of love and exasperation. "He's your son," she said to Sheridan.

"How reassuring," G'Kar remarked. "There were those rumors . . ."

"Your sense of humor, as always, is not appreciated, G'Kar," Sheridan said with mock severity.

"True comic visionaries rarely are during their lifetime."

"A few more remarks like that, and I'll solve the 'lifetime' problem for you," Sheridan warned with that same feigned gravity.

"Sounds like you folks are all having a good time kidding around with each other," David observed wryly. "Kind of interesting, considering that when I came in everything sounded pretty damned grave."

"Language," Delenn said reflexively.

"Sorry. Pretty goddamned grave."

She looked heavenward for strength.

"You wouldn't, by some chance, be trying to change the mood in here simply because I'm around?" inquired David.

The adults looked uncomfortably at each other.

"It's all right," he continued, clearly not interested in waiting for an answer. "I was actually standing outside the last few minutes."

Garibaldi pointed at David and said to Sheridan, "That boy has a future in surveillance. Let me take him back to Mars and train him for a few years. You won't recognize him."

"If his hair gets much longer, I won't recognize him in any event," Sheridan commented.

"You didn't answer my question, Dad," David said, clearly not about to let his father off the hook. "You're angry with the pacifist factions who don't want to get into a full-blown war with the Centauri. What's wrong with pacifism? I mean, look at the Earth-Minbari war. Thanks to the aggressiveness of the Humans who fired on the Minbari, killing Dukhat, and the Minbari responding with pure rage, *there* was a needless interstellar war that cost millions of lives."

Delenn flinched inwardly. David *would* have had to bring that up. The fact was that it was Delenn herself who had made the fateful decision to attack the Humans, even as she had cradled the still-warm corpse of Dukhat. *They're animals!* The words, screamed in an agonized voice barely recognizable as her own, still rang in her head. But David had never learned that. It was a secret that she kept buried deep in her, a moment that she could never forget, no matter how much she wanted to.

"And then," continued David, unaware of his mother's inner turmoil, "the entire Human Homeworld would have been wiped out if the Minbari hadn't suddenly surrendered. The reasons were complicated, but the result was the same: a peace movement. So obviously, those who seek peace are right some of the time. When do you decide it's the right time for peace . . . and when it is time to go to war?"

"It's not an easy question," Sheridan admitted.

"Well, actually, it is an easy question. The answer's the tough part."

Sheridan glanced at Garibaldi, who had just spoken, and responded wryly, "Thank you, Michael, for that reassuring clarification."

"No problem."

Delenn stepped forward, and resting a hand on her son's shoulder, said, "It depends whether one is in a situation where a movement of peace is viewed as a benefit for all concerned . . . or merely a sign of weakness."

Sheridan nodded in confirmation. "There are some who use peace, not as a tool, but as a weapon. Something to distract or forestall opponents while they move forward with their plans for conquest."

"And how do you know when that's the case?"

"You have to look at the whole picture," Sheridan said. "You don't examine one action, or even a couple of actions. You look at everything they've done throughout their history, and get a clear idea of where they've been. Based on that, you can determine where they're most likely to go."

"In the case of Londo and the Centauri," Garibaldi said grimly, "where they're going to go is anyplace they want to. Right now they're the six-hundred-pound gorilla."

"The what?" David looked at him blankly.

"The gorilla. It's an old joke. Where does a six-hundred-pound gorilla sit? Answer is, anywhere he wants. Get it?"

"Kind of." David hesitated, then asked, "What's a gorilla?"

Garibaldi opened his mouth to respond, then closed it and sighed. "Never mind."

Easily turning his attention away from the joke that had left him puzzled, David said, "Londo . . . the emperor . . . you think that's what he wants to do? Go everywhere . . . anywhere . . . he wants?"

"I don't know. I don't know the man anymore," Sheridan said. He looked to G'Kar. "What do you think, G'Kar? You haven't been saying all that much. What's your opinion on Londo's intentions?"

"His intentions?" G'Kar shrugged. "I could not tell you for sure. But there is one thing I do know for certain: Londo Mollari is one of the most tragic individuals I've ever met."

"Tragic?" Garibaldi snorted. "Look, G'Kar, I once liked the guy. And then he went power mad, and now he sits there on Centauri Prime playing all sides against each other. And yeah, okay, I'll be honest . . . losing Lou Welch to those high-haired bastards didn't exactly endear me to the whole Centauri experience. I've heard them say, in their rhetoric, in their histories, that the emperor is the living incarnation of Centauri Prime. If that's the case, I have some major issues with the incarnation, because it means he's the living symbol of a planet that's gone straight down the tubes. So I don't exactly see, G'Kar, why I'm supposed to shed a tear for him and think of him as a tragic figure."

"Shed tears or not, as you see fit," G'Kar said with a shrug. "I know I shed none. Why should I? He was responsible for mass drivers being used against my people. For the deaths of millions of Narns. Do you know what would have happened if not for Londo Mollari?"

There was a pause. "What?" inquired David.

"Very likely the exact same thing," G'Kar told him. "It is my

belief that Londo became swept up in circumstances that were
beyond his control . . . perhaps even beyond his understanding.
And by the time he did understand, it was too late. I believe he
had hopes and dreams for his people, but only in the most
ephemeral of terms . . . and others transformed those hopes into
a harsh reality that he never contemplated in his wildest dreams.

"That, Mr. Garibaldi, is the tragedy of Londo Mollari: that he
never had the opportunity to become that which he might have
been had the vagaries of fate not caught him up. Do not misunderstand," he added hastily. "As I said, I shed no tears for him. In
many respects he brought it on himself, and there were times he
might have been able to stop it. Then again, perhaps not. We will
never know. But whether he is pitiable or not, whether he is
someone with whom we empathize or not, is beside the point.
He remains a tragic figure nonetheless."

Sheridan was shaking his head and looking over at Garibaldi.
"And here you said he wasn't talking much. See what happens?
Now we can't shut him up."

"I won't burden you with my opinions if it's a problem, Mr.
President," G'Kar said archly.

Sheridan waved him off.

"So what do we do, John?" Delenn said. "We remain stymied."

"We stay the course, that's all," Sheridan told her reluctantly.
"I'm not going to unilaterally order the White Star fleet to attack
Centauri Prime. I have to present an example for the Alliance,
and what they do *not* need is an example of a leader who func-
tions without giving a damn about the opinions and desires of
his constituency. The Alliance refuses to pull the trigger. I can't
go forward without them, so we remain together and stationary.
And we hope that once the Alliance does come to its collective
senses, it's not too late."

"That certainly seems the only way to go," Garibaldi agreed
reluctantly. G'Kar simply nodded noncommittally.

Sheridan then gave Delenn a significant look, and she understood immediately what he wanted. "David," she said, "why
don't we go for a walk?"

"Dad wants to be able to talk without having me around,
right." Despite the phrasing, it wasn't a question so much as an
affirmation.

"Nothing gets past you." Sheridan chuckled, but there was edginess in the laugh.

"Fine." David shrugged with feigned indifference and allowed Delenn to lead him out.

"He's a sharp boy, and he's growing up fast," said Garibaldi. "We probably could have kept talking in front of him."

"Let's let him be just a kid, at least for a while longer."

"I wouldn't say he's ever been 'just a kid,' Mr. President," G'Kar said.

"That's probably true." Sheridan seated himself back behind his desk. The back-and-forth with David had taken some of the ire out of his voice, but he was still clearly not happy with the situation. "The thing I find most disturbing about this is the business with the Drazi. One of their own people was murdered, and they simply let it go."

"The word on ISN was that it was a lone nut acting without the government's knowledge or consent," Garibaldi said. "They're even suggesting that it's a private group of saboteurs who're working to bring down the Centauri government by staging acts of violence designed to foster war with the Alliance. The new Drazi ambassador backed it up. Not that I necessarily believed it for a second . . ."

"You were wise not to," G'Kar said. "It was, in fact, the organized actions of a mob, performed with the full cooperation of the local authorities and Minister Lione's pet troops, the Prime Candidates. They tore the poor devil apart. His assistant was hurried away. I saw his picture on the same ISN broadcast that Mr. Garibaldi saw; he's the new Drazi ambassador. It seems his predecessor's misfortune was his own good luck."

Garibaldi looked at him suspiciously. "You're acting like you saw this as an eyewitness."

G'Kar said nothing.

Garibaldi looked from G'Kar to Sheridan. "Someone want to tell me what's going on? I mean, there's no way G'Kar could have seen it. A Narn on Centauri Prime? Impossible. They've banned all off-worlders . . . and even when off-worlders were welcome, Narns never were."

"I have ways," G'Kar said with great mystery.

"Mind telling me what they are?"

"I cannot, in good conscience, do so," G'Kar informed him.

"And you?" He turned expectantly to Sheridan.

But Sheridan shook his head. "I don't know, either. G'Kar hasn't told me."

"And you find this acceptable?" Garibaldi was openly incredulous.

"I'm learning to deal with it," Sheridan said.

"He is John's foot," Delenn, who had just reentered, said.

"His what?"

"Hand," Sheridan corrected her. "It's an old title . . ."

"Look, I don't care if he's your hand, your foot, or your lower intestine," Garibaldi said. "I don't like secrets being kept. Not among us. Not after everything we've been through together. Because secrecy under such circumstances leads to sloppiness, and the next thing you know, someone decides they're going to be a hero and they get themselves killed."

"That," G'Kar said, sounding not a little regretful, "is an occupational hazard for being a hero."

"And for being a martyr," Garibaldi reminded him, "I hope you're not aiming for that status for yourself."

"Why, Mr. Garibaldi . . . I didn't know you cared." He sounded more amused than anything else.

Sheridan turned to Delenn. "David squared away?"

"He's back with his teachers. He said he still doesn't understand who decides when peace is the right thing to do."

"What did you tell him?"

"I looked him right in the eye and said, 'I decide. And if I'm not around, your father decides.' "

"Really. And what did he say to that?"

"He said, 'As long as Uncle Mikey doesn't.' "

"I'll kill him," said Garibaldi.

This generated a booming laugh from Sheridan. Delenn loved hearing him laugh, because he did it so infrequently. With all his responsibilities, all the stress upon him, she wished that he could laugh more often. He needed to desperately. And she needed it, too.

Six more years . . .

Some days it seemed as if it was going to pass in an eyeblink. Other days . . .

Other days it felt as if it was going to be an eternity.

EXCERPTED FROM
THE CHRONICLES OF LONDO MOLLARI.
Excerpt dated (approximate Earth date)
March 30, 2275.

My concern about my memory grows.

Things that happened many years ago . . . these are clear to me. I can remember every word that was spoken, every nuance of every moment from ten, twenty, thirty years past. I can remember exactly what it felt like to run as a child, to fall and skin my knee. The twinge of the pain can be re-created in my mind with utter clarity.

I cannot remember what I had for dinner last night.

I have had to drink rather heavily in order to maintain some of the more sensitive entries in this journal, because I have not wanted my . . . associate . . . to be aware of some of the things I write. The problem is that I think it's starting to take its toll upon me. That and age . . .

. . . and the mirror.

I look in the mirror and I see reflections of a man I do not recognize . . . and yet, unfortunately, do. The image of me in my dreams . . .

My dreams . . .

Durla and *his* dreams. Now there is a subject . . .

It takes a great deal of effort for me to recall what happened at a ministry meeting yesterday. Durla was there, that I recall. He was in one of his wild-eyed moods, speaking once more about dreams that had come to him, images in those dreams, and he was presenting blueprints and descriptions of new and greater weapons.

The others looked upon his work and marveled at Durla the Visionary. That is what they call him: the Visionary. One of the greatest seers in the history of Centauri Prime. When he was elevated to the office of prime minister, he started claiming that he had been guided by his dreams for years. When he was a mere member of my personal guard, such statements would have garnered laughter. Now . . . now the others make appreciative noises and exclamations of amazement, and speak of the exciting time in which we live, that such a prophet walks among us.

It is ridiculous. Nonsense.

Except . . . those things that we produce tend to work. Or at least our scientists are able to make them work. The Centauri Republic is being crafted in Durla's image. Odd. It gives me a strange feeling of nostalgia. I see his designs for weapons, for ships . . . and I get the same chill I did when I saw the Shadow ships crossing the skies over Centauri Prime. Black and fearsome things they were, and to look at them was like staring into the very heart of madness. I wonder about these dreams, and their origins, but it is pointless to inquire. Durla would not understand, nor would he care.

No, two things occupy Durla's thoughts: his endeavors to build up our military might, and his desire to bring down the saboteurs who continue to frustrate and thwart him. They have done so in small ways and have not been able to truly stop the progress. For every munition factory they manage to destroy, there are five others. They can no more stem the tide than a coral reef can impede the ocean. But they are a presence and an irritant nonetheless, and Durla continues to be angered by their activities.

These matters will come to a head sooner rather than later, I fear. I do not like to think about whose head they may come to.

My memory . . .

I saw a lovely young woman walking the corridors the other day. I spoke to her, smiled at her, feeling for a moment like the Londo of old. Then I realized that she was Senna, the young woman whom I took as my ward some years ago. I had not seen her in quite some time. She remains without husband, and without interest in acquiring one. Instead she occupies herself by acting as an occasional nursemaid for some of the children of Centauri ministers and such. She is quite popular with them, so I understand.

Dinner!

Dinner the other night was with Vir. I recall now. I do not remember what we had . . . but he was there. Senna was there, too. They spoke quite gregariously with one another, I seem to remember. One would have almost thought I was not there at all.

Sometimes I think I am not.

— chapter 3 —

Milifa, of the house of Milifa, burst into Durla's office, unable to contain his excitement. "Is it true?" he asked before Durla could open his mouth. "Is what I've heard true?"

Durla leaned back and smiled. Milifa was a man who virtually radiated strength. Remarkably charismatic, powerfully built, he was the head of one of the most influential houses in all the Centaurum. Even his excitement was carefully channeled, his dark eyes crackling with intensity as he said again, "Is it true?"

"Are you going to give me breathing space to tell you, my friend? Or will you simply keep asking?"

Milifa took a step back and a deep breath. "Do not toy with me on this, Durla. I warn you."

Virtually any other person who spoke the words "I warn you" to Durla would have been subject to harsh treatment. But from Milifa, Durla was willing to take it. "Yes. It is true," he responded.

Milifa sagged with visible relief. Durla had never seen the robust aristocrat so emotionally vulnerable. Even on the day that Milifa's son, Throk, had been killed, Milifa had managed to keep his rawest emotions in careful check.

"Four . . . years," he said incredulously. "*Four years* since the safe house of the Prime Candidates was destroyed. Four years since my son and his friends died at the hands of those . . . those . . ." He trembled with barely contained fury.

"I cannot apologize enough, old friend," said Durla, "for the length of time it has taken us to apprehend one of these subversives. It is, frankly, an embarrassment. I do not know any other way to put it."

"An embarrassment, yes. Perhaps," Milifa said sourly, "your

36

duties as prime minister have atrophied the skills you so adroitly displayed when you were minister of Internal Security."

"That is neither here nor there," Durla told him. He rose from behind his desk and came around it, clapping Milifa on the back. "He is being questioned even as we speak. Do you wish to come and see?"

"Absolutely," Milifa said. "After waiting four years to see the face of one of these bastards, I have no intention of waiting a moment longer."

Durla was pleased to see that the questioning was already under way. He was not, however, pleased to witness its lack of success.

The subject was strapped into an oversize chair, his feet dangling a few inches above the floor. He was rail thin, narrow-shouldered, and unlike most other Centauri of Durla's acquaintance, his hair was something of a mess. His head was lolling from one side to the other, as if attached to his shoulders by only the slimmest of supports.

Several members of the Prime Candidates were there, as well, looking particularly grim. Durla recognized one of them as Caso, a close friend of Throk's. Caso had suffered, to some degree, from survivor's guilt. A lung illness had kept him home in bed the day that the other Prime Candidates died in the explosion; had Caso not been bedridden, he would have died with the others.

"What is the vermin's name?" Milifa asked, standing just behind Durla.

"Lanas. Rem Lanas," Durla told him grimly. "He was found trespassing in one of our . . ." He paused, and then said, ". . . medical facilities, on Tumbor 2. He had counterfeit clearance identification on him. Quite well crafted, I might add. He was in the midst of endeavoring to rewire certain circuits that . . . if left unchecked . . . would have caused the facility to blow up. Fortunately, all he managed to do was trip an alarm. Our security systems have become increasingly sophisticated over the years."

"That is a fortunate state of affairs," Milifa said, "considering the alternative is leaving yourself open to being continually preyed upon by slime like . . . like this." His voice dropped lower on the last several words. He stepped forward and practically stuck his face into Lanas'. "Are you the one, slime? Are you the one who was responsible for killing my son?"

Lanas looked up at him without really seeing him.

"What's wrong with him?" demanded Milifa.

"Truth drugs, no doubt. Sometimes they take a while to reach full effect." Durla looked to Caso for confirmation. Caso, over the years, had apprenticed with some of the best interrogators in the Centaurum and had become quite skilled. He had personally requested the opportunity to handle the questioning of this latest subject, in the name of his departed friend. "How much longer, Caso?"

But Caso looked surprisingly uncomfortable. "Actually, Prime Minister, they should be at full effect by now. Before now, in fact. But he has been resisting all of our initial questions."

"Resisting?" Durla was astonished. "Are you certain you have administered them properly?"

"Positive, Prime Minister," Caso answered stiffly.

"And yet he resists? Increase the dosage."

"That may not be wise . . ."

Durla, feeling the quiet smoldering of Milifa next to him, said tightly, "On my authority. Do it."

Caso bowed deeply and put together another dosage. Moments later there was enough truth drug pumping through Lanas' veins to send a dozen Centauri pouring out every secret they'd ever held, all the way back to childhood.

Rem Lanas' eyes remained glazed. It was as if he was withdrawing completely into himself.

"I checked the records on this man," Caso said. "He was a worker on K0643."

"Was he now," Durla said. The excavation on K0643 had proven to be one of Durla's only unqualified disasters. He had been certain that there was some great source of weaponry there, but the entire excavation had been destroyed. There were wild rumors that techno-mages had somehow been involved . . . fleeting glimpses of them, but accounts of their numbers ranged from three to thirty. No one seemed sure of anything. He wondered if Lanas had been one of the workers who had been questioned. He leaned forward, and said, "What is your name?"

"Lanas. Rem Lanas." His voice was thick and distant.

"And are you part of an organization?"

Lanas' head teetered in affirmation.

"And what," Durla said with clear urgency, "is that organization? Tell me about it. Who is the head?"

"Minister . . . Durla."

A confused look passed among the Centauri in the room. Durla could feel Milifa's gaze boring through him, and he felt a faint buzz of danger. "Yes, I am Prime Minister Durla," he said, trying to discern whether the confused Lanas might simply be addressing him directly. "Who is the head of your organization?"

"Minister Durla," Rem Lanas said, this time with more conviction.

The blood drained from Durla's face.

But Caso looked suspicious, and said, "What is the nature of this organization?"

"Employment . . . workers . . . for excavation purposes . . ."

Durla put his face in his hands, partly out of frustration and partly to hide his relief. Such an absurd misunderstanding could have led to a world of trouble if left unchecked. "The Committee for Centauri Advancement," he said.

"Yes . . . organization . . ." Rem Lanas told them. He was half smiling, but it was such a disassociated look that it was clear he was thinking about something else completely.

Durla looked to Milifa, who seemed less than amused. "It's the association I created for the purpose of organizing Centauri workers for—"

"I do not care," Milifa said flatly. "I want to know about the bastards who killed my son. If he's one of them, I want all their names."

Durla nodded and turned back to Rem Lanas. "I am speaking of a terrorist organization. An organization created for sabotage. You are part of such a group, yes?"

Lanas nodded his head.

"Now we're getting somewhere," Durla said, smirking. Caso nodded approvingly. "How many people are in it?"

"All of them," Lanas told him.

"Don't spar with me, Lanas," Durla warned, becoming increasingly annoyed. He glanced up at Caso. "How is he able to do this?"

"I'm not sure," Caso said, looking a bit worried. "He should be unable to hold back anything. It should just all be spilling out of him."

"Lanas . . . who is the head of the organization?" Durla asked.

"The head?"

"Yes."

"The head . . . is our leader."

"Yes. His name. What is the name of the head of the organization?"

And his reply made no sense at all. "No. What is the name of the man on second base."

"Who?" Durla said, utterly flummoxed.

"No. Who is on first."

"What? "

"What is on second."

Durla felt as if he were losing his mind. In a harsh whisper he demanded of Caso, "This is gibberish. What is he saying?"

"I don't know!" Caso replied loudly.

"Third base," Rem Lanas intoned, as if by rote.

Durla was up off his chair with such force that he knocked it over. Caso was about to speak when an angry prime minister grabbed him by the front of his shirt and slammed him back up against the wall. "This is *idiocy*!" he said tightly. "What sort of game is this?"

"It's n-not a game!" Caso stammered, his veneer of Prime Candidate indifference wavering under the infuriated onslaught of the most powerful man on Centauri Prime. "It . . . it must be a fail-safe . . ."

"Fail-safe? What sort of—"

"Something planted in his mind. Imprinted. So that if he's being questioned or probed, instead of breaking through to the core of what we want to know, his mind automatically reverts to this nonsense. It becomes a loop that we can't get past."

"That's impossible!"

"No. It's not. I've . . ." He licked his lips nervously. "I've heard techno-mages can accomplish such things . . ."

"Now it's techno-mages!" Milifa bellowed. "Drugs! Children's stories about techno-mages! What sort of government are you running here, Durla!"

Durla rounded on him, suddenly not caring just how powerful

a house Milifa ran. He pointed a trembling finger at Milifa, and said, "The kind of government that could strip you of name, rank, and property with a snap of my fingers! So watch yourself, Milifa, and show some respect for who and what I am, before I make you less than who and what you are!"

Milifa, wisely, said nothing, but the set of his face made it clear he was not happy.

Durla, for his part, felt shamed. And the notion that this scrawny no one was playing games with him and shaming him in front of a long-standing ally infuriated him beyond reason. "Forget the drugs," he told Caso. "Now . . . now we chat with him in the way we used to do these things."

Minutes later, Rem Lanas was upright and spread-eagled, his arms tied to the walls on either side of the cell. Durla stood several feet away, the lash in his hand crackling with energy.

"Prime Minister." Caso sounded respectful but nervous. "The drugs in his system may impede his understanding if another element, such as extreme pain, is introduced into—"

"Then we shall give his system a chance to work the drugs out." He saw Milifa nod slightly in approval, took a step back and swung his arm around expertly. The lash slammed across Rem Lanas' back, shredding his shirt in a second. Lanas screamed, his eyes going wide, his body spasming.

"You felt that, didn't you," Durla said in a low voice. "Didn't you, Lanas."

"Y-yes," he managed to say.

"No one can endure more than forty lashes of that nature," Durla continued. "I do not suggest you be the first person to try."

"I . . . don't want to die . . ."

"At last, truth," Durla noted with satisfaction. "We don't care about you, Lanas. We want those in charge."

"In charge . . . of what?"

Durla did not hesitate. He swung the lash again, and again. Ten cracks of the lash crashed across Lanas' back, and each time the prisoner howled, until it seemed to Durla he could not remember a time when screams were not ringing in his ears.

"That," he said, "is eleven."

But Lanas didn't hear him, because he had lapsed into unconsciousness.

"Bring him around," Durla said to Caso.

Caso did so with brisk efficiency. Durla could see it in Lanas' eyes: When he came to, for a moment he didn't realize where he was. Perhaps he thought that what he had experienced was some sort of tortured dream. When he looked around, however, he realized the all-too-real nature of his predicament.

"Ask him who killed my son," Milifa demanded. "Was he himself responsible? Someone else?"

"Is your mind clear enough that you can answer the question?" Durla asked. Lanas glared up at him. "You see, we've figured out that when you lose control over your ability to keep information secret, you have some sort of . . . what was the word, Caso? Fail-safe. A fail-safe in your mind that prevents you from being forthcoming. It is my assumption that if you have possession of your faculties, then your free will holds sway once more. Employ that free will now. Save yourself."

"Tell me who killed my son," demanded Milifa.

Lanas seemed to notice him for the first time. "Who is your son?"

"Throk of the House Milifa."

"Oh. Him."

"Yes, him."

"He was the first."

"The first what?" Durla said. "The first victim of your organization?"

Rem Lanas took in a slow, deep breath. "Do you know who I am?" he asked.

"You are Rem Lanas."

"Beyond that, I mean." The pain in his voice appeared to be subsiding. And then, before Durla could reply, Lanas did it for him. "I am nothing beyond that. I am a nobody. A no one. I drifted . . . from one thing in life to the next. Used by this person, by that person. I have been a victim for as long as I can remember. No pride in myself, in my heritage, in my people. But I have been a part of something . . . that has made me proud . . . for the first time in my meager existence."

"So you admit you are part of an organization!" Durla said triumphantly.

"Freely," said Lanas. He looked like nothing. He looked like a weakling. But his voice was of iron. "And if you think that I am going to turn over those people who have helped to elevate me, for the first time in my life, to a creature of worth . . . then you can think again. And you, Durla . . . you think . . . you think you are in charge. You think you know everything. You know nothing. And by the time you do . . . it will be too late for you. It's already too late."

Durla suddenly felt a chill in the air. He brushed it off as he said, "If you know so much about me, why don't you tell me?"

"Because you would not believe. You are not ready. You likely never will be."

"Enough of this!" Milifa said, fury bubbling over. "Tell me who killed my son!"

"Your son . . ."

"Yes! Throk of the—"

"House of Milifa, yes. Your son . . ." He grinned lopsidedly. "Your son walked into his little hideout with a bomb in his hair. My understanding is that he realized it at the last moment and died screaming 'Get it out, get it out!' Very womanish, from what I've been told . . ."

Milifa let out a howl of agonized fury and grabbed the lash from Durla's hand. Durla yelped in protest and tried to grab it back, but Milifa was far bigger than he and utterly uncaring, at that moment, of Durla's high rank. He stiff-armed the prime minister, shoving him back. Caso caught Durla before he could hit the ground.

Milifa's arm snapped around, and he brought the lash crashing down on Rem Lanas. Lanas made no attempt to hold back the agony as the scream was ripped from his throat.

"Milord!" Caso shouted, trying to get the whip away from him, but Milifa, blind with fury, swept it around and drove Caso back. Any attempt to snatch it from Milifa's hand would simply have met with violence.

"Tell me—who!" And the whip snaked out.

"Who's on first!" shrieked Lanas, and the words were now pouring out of him, running together, bereft of any meaning. "What's on second, I don't know, third base . . ."

*"Tell me! **Tell me!**"*

"Get the guards!" Durla ordered Caso, and the young Prime

Candidate did as he was instructed. Milifa was paying no attention. Four years' worth of anger, of rage, poured from him all at once, focused entirely on the helpless individual before him. Over and over he struck, and each time he demanded to know who was responsible for his son's death, and each time Rem Lanas cried out nonsensical comments about third base. Except he did so with progressively less volume each time, even the screams having less force.

The door burst open and half a dozen guards poured in, Caso bringing up the rear. They converged on Milifa, and he swung the lash to try to keep them back. But they were armored, and although they proceeded with caution, proceed they still did. Within moments they had Milifa pinned to the ground, the lash torn from his grasp. His chest was heaving, his face flushed, his eyes wild. "Tell me!" he was still shouting, as if he had lost track of the fact that he was no longer beating his victim.

Lanas' head was slumped forward. Durla went to him, placed his thumb and forefinger under Rem Lanas' chin. The head fell back. And he immediately knew what Caso confirmed only a moment later: Lanas was dead.

"Idiot," he murmured, and then his voice grew along with his frustration. "Idiot!" This time he turned to Milifa, who was being held on the floor by the guards, and kicked him savagely in the side. Milifa let out a roar of indignation, but Durla spoke right over it. "*Idiot!* He was our first, best lead in years! Years! And because of you, he's dead!"

"Less . . . than forty lashes . . ." Milifa started to say.

"It didn't matter! The threshold of pain isn't an exact science! Forty was the maximum! But look at him! He wasn't particularly robust! What in the world made you think he could endure that sort of sustained punishment!

"But no, you didn't think!" and he kicked Milifa again. "You just cared about your pathetic son!"

"How *dare* you!" Milifa managed to get out.

"How dare you interfere with an official interrogation! How dare you think that you can withstand my anger! Get him out of here . . . no! No, on second thought, shove him over there!" and he pointed to a corner of the cell. The guards obediently tossed him over into the indicated corner and stepped back. "You can stay here and rot . . . along with the corpse of your new best friend!" and he indicated the still-suspended body of Rem Lanas. "I hope you two will be very happy together!"

He stormed out, allowing the guards to follow and close the door behind him. The last thing the angry prime minister heard was Milifa's enraged shout of protest, before it was cut off by the slamming of the cell door.

— *chapter 4* —

Durla was impressed to see that Castig Lione had made it to his office suite before he arrived there. "Tell me it's not true," Lione, trembling with suppressed rage, said immediately.

Durla considered it mildly amusing that the conversation echoed the one he'd had with Milifa, so very recently. "That depends," he said calmly. With Milifa locked away and his fury at Lanas passed, Durla was actually able to handle himself with a considerable amount of sangfroid. "What are you referring to, precisely?"

"Do not fence with me—"

"And do not forget your station, Lione!" Durla warned. He was still calm, but there was definite menace in his tone. "Do not forget who is the power on Centauri Prime."

"Oh, I have known that for quite some time," Lione shot back.

Durla's eyes narrowed. "What do you mean by that?"

"You have put Milifa into prison! Do you have any idea how many friends the House Milifa has? How powerful he is! You need the support of the main Houses . . ."

"I have the support of the military, Minister Lione," Durla said. "The generals respect my roots. And they respect my long-term vision. They have helped to execute my inspirations, developing the technologies that will lead us to bury the Alliance. They have as little patience for effete, mincing heads of Houses as I do. They know that conquest comes from military might, and they know that only I have the strength of will to bring Centauri Prime to its true destiny."

"The Houses remain the foundation of your power, Prime Minister. If that foundation crumbles . . ."

"Why should I care what is below me, when my destiny is that which is above me?"

Lione leaned on a chair without sitting, and shook his head. "Madness," he muttered.

But Durla was studying him, like a small creature of prey sizing up something larger than he, trying to decide whether or not he could bring it down. "I have not forgotten your comment. Who is the power of Centauri Prime, as far as you are concerned?"

Lione regained his composure. "Why, you are, Prime Minister."

"Now you are the one who is fencing. What did you mean?"

"You do not desire candor, Prime Minister."

There was a deadly silence in the office for a moment. And then Durla said, "Lione . . . we go back quite a ways. Do not, however, assume that that lengthy relationship has weakened my resolve or ability to do what I feel needs to be done if I am being defied. Do not further assume that the fact that you head the Prime Candidates gives you a power base that is comparable with mine. If I were so inclined, I could order the military to annihilate every single one of them. The streets of Centauri Prime would flow with the blood of your precious Candidates, and parents might mourn, but otherwise life would go on."

"You would never do such a thing," Lione said.

Durla smiled thinly.

Suddenly the door opened and one of the most massive Centauri that Lione had ever seen walked in. He had to stop in the doorway for a moment, turning sideways slightly, in order to enter. Pure charismatic energy seemed to crackle around him. His neck was so thick that it seemed as if his head were jointed directly into the top of his torso. Furthermore, he had cut his teeth so that small fangs projected over his upper lip.

"Minister . . . you remember General Rhys. He's been overseeing a number of our construction projects on assorted fringe worlds. He also did a superb job leading the recent strike forces on Mipas and other worlds. General, it is good to see you."

General Rhys bowed deeply. But as he did so, he never took his eyes off Castig Lione.

"General," Durla said quite conversationally, as if discussing the weather. "I'd like you to do me a service, if you don't mind."

"Whatever you wish, Prime Minister."

"That sword hanging at your side . . . is it merely ceremonial?"

"Intended for ceremony, but it carries a killing edge, Prime Minister."

"Good. Kindly draw it and decapitate Minister Lione if he does not answer to my satisfaction."

Lione started to bark out a laugh, then the laughter choked off in his throat as smooth metal rasped against the scabbard, and he found the blade poised right against his throat. Rhys was holding it quite steady, not wavering in the slightest.

"You . . . you're insane," Lione whispered. Then he gasped as the blade edge pressed ever so slightly. That alone was enough to cause a trickle of blood to start running down. A small stain of pinkish red liquid . . . his blood . . . tinted his white collar.

"Look into my eyes, Lione," said Durla. The degree of calm in his tone was absolutely frightening. Lione found himself unable to look anywhere else. "I will be able to tell if you are lying. I have become quite sensitive to attempts at duplicity. One does not reach my station in life without acquiring that ability. Lie, and I will know. Now tell me . . . who do you think is the true power of Centauri Prime?"

"You."

"Ah ah ah," Durla said scoldingly, and Rhys—without having to be told to do so—pushed the blade ever so slightly more against Lione's throat. The minister gasped and sat bolt still, as even the slightest breath would cause the blade to drive into his throat on its own. "Did you think that I was joking? I am not. I do not joke. Ever. This is your last chance, Minister: Who is the true power of Centauri Prime?"

In truth, Durla was fully prepared for Lione to answer that it was the emperor. Durla was perfectly aware that there remained a handful of holdouts who believed that Londo Mollari still mattered in some way, shape, or form to the business of Centauri Prime. It was a quaint notion, of course. Truthfully, he would be surprised if it turned out that Lione was among those benighted few, but anything was possible.

What he was not expecting was the answer that Lione gave:

"The Lady Mariel."

For just a moment Durla's lips twisted in anger, and he was about to order General Rhys to dispatch Lione for good and all. If nothing else, it would prove to the other ministers that no one was immune to the ire and retribution of the prime minister.

But something in Lione's look stopped him, and he realized with a sort of bleak horror that Lione absolutely believed it.

"Mariel? My wife?"

Lione let out a slow breath. Clearly he thought he was as good as dead. That being the case, there was no point in withholding exactly what he believed, what he thought. "We are not fools," he told Durla with a nervous sneer. "Your obsession with her was known to all. Did you think that I was unable to tell? That none of us would figure it out? And then you wound up acquiring her in some pathetic game. What a startling coincidence."

"It was no coincidence," Durla replied hotly. "If you must know, Lione, the woman was attracted to me. Vir Cotto had no desire to try to hold on to her, since all she spoke of was me, and he was more than happy to see me secure her."

"Oh, was he now. And how very convenient for him. The chances are that he played you for a fool."

"Impossible. Cotto is nothing."

"He was in a position to give you that for which you hungered. He must have been *something*."

"He is nothing, I tell you. The Lady Mariel wanted me . . ."

"Let us say that she did. The reason is obvious. She wanted to be able to manipulate you. She was a spy in my employ, Durla, or have you forgotten that? I know just how much information that woman was capable of acquiring. She likely learned of your fixation with her and decided to use it to her advantage. Women, after all, have no power in our government. What better way for a clever and ambitious woman like Mariel to gain influence than by sinking her claws into a man who would accede to her every whim."

"Mine is the vision, Lione," Durla stated flatly, his considerable aplomb beginning to erode. "Mine is the direction for Centauri Prime . . ."

"Right, right. Your dreams, from which you garner impressive scientific developments. How likely is that, Prime Minister? As opposed to the thought that they are being fed to you by your beloved wife, who in turn is acquiring them from contacts she has managed to cultivate. We all know you dote on her, fawn on her. She is your sense of self-worth, your inspiration, your image, all rolled into one. You are nothing without the Lady Mariel."

"I had already achieved greatness before she ever became my wife," Durla reminded him. He was barely managing to keep himself from leaping across the room, grabbing the sword, and dispatching Lione himself.

"You achieved it in the hopes of impressing her. How pathetic a life is that?"

For a long moment, Durla said nothing. He fought mightily with himself not to betray a shred of the emotion roiling within him. Then, in a hoarse, choked voice, he said, "General Rhys . . ."

Lione braced himself for the killing stroke.

"Thank you for your assistance. Wait in the outer office please."

If Rhys was at all disappointed that he was not going to have the opportunity to lop off Lione's head and thereby provide some excitement to what was otherwise a fairly dull day, he did not show it. Instead he simply sheathed his sword, bowed slightly, and walked out.

Minister Lione sat there, clearly not quite knowing what had hit him. When Durla slowly came around to him, he automatically flinched as he saw a hand move toward him. But all Durla did was pat Lione on the shoulder, and say, "I appreciate your candor." He touched the pale, reddish liquid on Lione's throat. "You'll probably want to have that looked at." Then he walked out, leaving a dumbfounded Lione to wonder what had just transpired.

The Lady Mariel was most surprised to see her husband. He strode into their sumptuous quarters unannounced and unexpected. He had not been around much lately during the day; indeed, he had not been around that much at night, either. It was a situation that offered both pluses and minuses. Not having him around was, of course, rather nice, due to the fact that she did not love him. Oh, she feigned it masterfully. Then again, it wasn't hard to fake something when someone else desperately wanted to believe in it.

But if she wasn't a party to his goings-on, it made it that much more difficult for her to get information for her beloved Vir.

Vir, who was back on Babylon 5, putting the information she fed him to good use. She didn't know for sure, but she would not have been surprised if her wonderful Vir was somehow involved with the rebels who were causing so much trouble for Durla and his plans. This, of course, was something she would never let on to Durla. First, it would mean betraying the incomparable Vir, and second, her own duplicity would become known. It would mean death. Her death would be unfortunate enough, but Vir's death—*that* she simply could not risk. He was too glorious, too magnificent.

Not for the first time, she wondered why she felt that way about him.

Some part of her understood that she had not always embraced such depth of feeling for Vir. On some level, she knew the change had simply come over her, and she could not comprehend what had prompted it. Ultimately, though, it made no difference. Her Vir was her Vir, and that was all. However she came by her feelings, she knew they were honest and true, and every time she was with Durla, only her thoughts of Vir sustained her. At those times, things didn't seem as bad as they were.

"My husband," she said quickly. She had been carefully braiding the long lock of hair that was the fashion with her generation. She did not rise from the chair where she sat, in front of the makeup table. Instead she stayed where she was and watched herself in the mirror as she meticulously continued creating the braid. "Would you forgive me if I did not get up?"

"I will try not to allow it to put a strain on our marriage," he said, in an oddly stiff tone. "You look lovely today."

"And you, strikingly handsome, milord husband," she responded. She knew he liked it when she addressed him in the formal manner, and used it whenever she thought he might be in an expansive mood. It was usually enough to get him talking and spilling choice nuggets of information. "To what do I owe the honor of this appearance?"

He regarded her thoughtfully for a moment, and then said, "Do you love Vir Cotto?"

She allowed the question to appear to catch her off guard. In truth, she had anticipated his asking that at some point. Indeed, the Lady Mariel made it a point to try to anticipate as much as possible, so that—should the eventuality transpire—she would be able to react with a carefully crafted reaction and response.

At least, that was the theory.

"Vir Cotto," she said. "The ambassador? From Babylon 5?"

"Your previous lover," Durla said. There was a slight edgy sharpness to his tone. "I'm sure you have some familiarity with him."

"Yes, of course. But do I love him?" She knew full well that Durla fancied himself a true student of psychology. Often had he boasted to her of his ability to simply gaze into someone's eyes and, by that method, determine the veracity of what they were about to say. So she had long known that the only way she could glide past a potentially awkward situation such as this would be to look him right in the eyes and lie with confidence.

The thing was, the best way to get through the lie was to use as much of the truth as possible. "To be perfectly candid, my love, Vir was simply a means to an end. I used him as a means of establishing diplomatic contacts in order to supply information to Minister Lione. Certainly you must have known that. You were aware that I was in Lione's employ."

"Yes. I was aware of that," he replied slowly. She continued to braid her hair. "You have not directly answered the question, though."

"I thought I had," she said carelessly. Once more she met his gaze, and this time she said flatly and with no lack of conviction, "No. I do not love Vir Cotto. I love only you, my great visionary."

It was the hardest thing she had ever said. Because the truth was that she did love Vir Cotto. The passing of years, the marriage to Durla . . . none of that had altered her thinking. Vir continued to be her sun, moon, and stars. She had agreed to the sham of Vir's "losing" her to Durla, had pretended that she had always secretly harbored a fascination for the prime minister, all because Vir desired it. She wanted to help Vir, to serve him in any way she could.

She hadn't lied about her original purpose for associating with Vir. Things, however, had changed. She had come to realize the full wonderfulness that was Vir Cotto. One treasured day, with a sudden burst of clarity, as if her previous life had been merely a dream, she abruptly had understood that Vir was the only man for her in all the universe.

She never doubted for a moment that, sooner or later, something would happen to Durla. Something nasty. Something final. Until that time, she would play the dutiful wife and think of Vir and provide him with whatever information she could garner. Because that was what Vir wanted.

Durla nodded and smiled at her affirmation of her love for him, as she had suspected he would. "You know of my dreams . . . my great visions," he said.

"Of course I do. Everyone on Centauri Prime does."

"Believe it or not, my love . . . in my dreams . . . it is you who comes to me."

"Me?" She laughed. "I am most flattered."

"As well you should be. It is not every woman who can serve as inspiration to the prime minister of Centauri Prime." He was walking slowly around her, his hands draped behind his back. "However . . . there are some who mistake this 'inspiration' that you provide me."

"Mistake? How?"

"They think that you control me. That I have some sort of . . ." He rolled his eyes and shook his head. ". . . some sort of obsession that unmans me in your presence."

"Ridiculous," she said vehemently, even as she finished braiding her hair. "You are Durla, prime minister of Centauri Prime. You answer to no woman."

"You know that. I know that. But they," and he pointed in the nebulous direction of the all-present "they," "they believe differently. And I fear that I must do something about it."

"I will support whatever actions you decide to take, beloved." She turned in her seat and smiled her most glowing smile.

He hit her so hard that he knocked her clear out of her chair.

Mariel fell back, striking her head on the floor. She lay there, stunned, feeling the blood welling up from between her teeth and trickling down from her nose. Her lower lip was already swelling, and her upper lip had gone numb.

She tried to stammer out something, anything, and then Durla hauled her to her feet. She tried to push him away but he was far too strong, and then he swung his hand around and struck her again. Her face reddened where he slapped her, and then he backhanded her and she went down again. Her lungs seized up with a coughing fit, and she spat out blood.

"There," Durla said.

"There?" She couldn't believe it. "Wha—what did I do? How did I displease you . . ."

"You haven't. Unfortunately we live in a world that is shaped by perception," he said sadly. "If the others think that I am un-manned by you . . . that I let you manipulate me in any way . . . then it can have a very negative impact on me and my fortunes. Even though it is not true. Therefore we need to make clear to any and all who are interested that I am my own man."

He kicked her in the stomach while she lay on the floor. She doubled up, curling almost into a fetal position, and then, with the side of his boot, he struck her in the face. Mariel, sobbing, rolled onto her back, her legs still curled up. She felt something small and hard in her mouth. She rolled it around on her tongue. It was a tooth. She spit it out and it made a faint *tik tik* noise as it bounced across the floor.

"Yes," he said with satisfaction. "Now any who see you will know that Durla is no woman's servant. No woman's slave. You may be my inspiration . . . but I have no compunction about treating you in the same way that I would treat the lowliest of the low. I do not play favorites. For you see, nothing, and no one, is more important than Centauri Prime. And only if I am strong can I help our beloved world attain its true destiny."

"Vir," she whispered, very softly, very hoarsely.

He hadn't quite heard her, because she said it just under her breath, and while he was still talking. "What did you say?" he inquired.

"Dear . . . I said . . . dear . . . please . . . don't hurt me . . . any more . . ." She didn't even recognize her own voice because it was so choked with pain.

"I need the full backing of all the ministers for the full military program that we have planned," he continued. He crouched next to her, and he spoke as if from light-years away. "Picture it, Mariel. Picture powerful warships, poised, ready. Needing only the final go-ahead from me to sweep across the galaxy like a black cloud of strength, reordering all the known worlds and uniting them under our rule. But it can only happen if the Centaurum is fully committed. To me. No hesitation, no reservation, no signs of weakness. I can take no chances that anyone think me soft. You understand, don't you?"

"Yes . . . I . . . I do . . . I . . ."

"Good."

Then he really began to hurt her.

And the thing that kept going through her mind was, *Vir . . . Vir will help me . . . he will save me . . . Vir . . . I love you . . .*

— *chapter 5* —

Vir Cotto felt the world spinning around him, and he sagged to the ground, staring up in disbelief.

He was just outside the palace. The sun was hanging low in the sky, the rays filtering through the haze as the twilight approached. As a consequence, there wasn't much light with which Vir could make out the head on the pike in the garden. But there was just enough light to see, and the head was just familiar enough to recognize.

Rem Lanas stared down at him lifelessly. And yet, even in that lifelessness, there was accusation. *Why weren't you here for me,* he seemed to say. *Why didn't you help me? Why didn't you save me? I trusted you, became a part of your cause . . . and this is what happened to me . . . because of you . . . you . . .*

He hadn't expected such a sight. He had been told to wait in the garden, that someone would be along to escort him in for his meeting with the emperor. But he'd been caught completely off guard.

He wasn't sure how long Rem's head had been up there. The weather had not been kind to it.

Then a bird landed on it. To Vir's horror, it pulled experimentally at Rem's cheek, trying to dig out what it apparently thought was a particularly appetizing bit of flesh.

"Get away!" yelled Vir, and he clambered up on a stone bench. "Get away! Get *away!!!*"

The bird ignored him, and Vir, who was gesticulating wildly, suddenly lost his balance. He stumbled backward, struck his head, and lay there, unmoving.

He had no idea how long he lay there, but when he finally did open his eyes, he found that night had fallen. He wondered how he could possibly have just been left in the one place, unseen by anyone, for such a period of time.

Then he felt heaviness in his chest, and a distant buzzing of alarm in the back of his skull. Suddenly he began to feel as if someone had clubbed him from behind. Probably, he reasoned, some sort of residual pain left over from falling and hurting himself.

With effort, he looked up at Rem Lanas' head atop the pike.

It was gone.

His own head was there instead.

It looked rather comical in its way, and he would have laughed had he actually been able to get the noise out. Instead, though, there was simply an overwhelming desire to scream at the hideous sight. However, he couldn't get that to emerge either. There was just a repeated, strangulated coughing.

He turned and tried to run, tried to shout for help . . .

. . . and there was someone there in the shadows.

The darkness actually seemed to come alive around him as he stared, transfixed, at the being—no, the creature—that was moving slowly out of the shadows toward him. It fixed him with a malevolent glare, as if it had already destroyed him somehow and he simply wasn't aware of it yet. Vir knew it instantly as a Drakh, a servant of the Shadows. But he reminded himself that the average Centauri had never seen a Drakh, and the last thing he should do was blurt out what was on his mind.

"Shiv'kala," the Drakh said.

The word brought back awful memories. Years earlier, at the behest of the now-dead techno-mage, Kane, he had spoken that name to Londo. The mere mention of it had gotten Vir thrown into a cell. Later on, working in conjunction with another techno-mage, Galen, he had come to realize that the name belonged to one of the Drakh. Immediately he understood.

"You . . . are Shiv'kala," he said.

Shiv'kala inclined his head slightly in acknowledgment. "Names," he said, "have power. Power, however, cuts both ways." When he spoke, his voice was a gravelly whisper. "You mentioned my name once. Do you remember?"

Vir managed to nod.

"When you did so, it drew my attention to you. Why did you?"

"Wh-why did I . . . what?"

"Why. Did you. Mention. My name?"

Once upon a time, Vir would have panicked at a moment such as this. Confronted by a dark, frightening creature of evil, he would have been reduced to a trembling mass of disintegrating nerves.

That Vir, however, was gone.

Gone, but not forgotten.

Outwardly he was all terror and wide eyes, hands trembling violently and legs buckling at the knees, causing him to sink to the ground in stark-staring terror.

Inwardly, his mind was racing. For he was seeing this entity before him not as some overpowering, terrifying monster, but rather simply as a member of another race. Granted, an incredibly formidable race. But he had been responsible for the destruction of a long-lost Shadow vessel that the Drakh had craved. He had seen Drakh warriors killed before his very eyes. He knew they were not invincible.

They had limits.

And the question posed him by Shiv'kala revealed some of those limits.

In a way it was remarkable. A bare half-dozen years ago, the mere mention of Shiv'kala's name had struck a chill within him. Now he was facing down the owner of the name, and he was analyzing him with methodical precision.

The sight of his own head on the pole had been a nice bit of theatrics, but that had been sufficient to tell him that he was no longer in reality. He was in some sort of dream state, into which the Drakh had inserted himself.

But the Drakh was asking him questions.

Which meant the Drakh didn't know the answers. After all, if he knew the answers, then why bother to ask at all? To try to "trick" him for some reason? What would be the point of that?

So even though the Drakh clearly had some sort of advanced mental abilities, they were hardly limitless. They were apparently able to broadcast into someone's dream state, and were probably capable of receiving transmissions. But they were not readily capable of reading minds. Or, at the very least, they couldn't read a mind that wasn't cooperating.

Furthermore, Shiv'kala had waited quite a few years to come

to Vir and start asking why his name had been bandied about. That indicated to Vir that their range might be limited, as well. Again, at the very least, it was limited where other species were concerned. Shiv'kala had had to wait until Vir was within reasonable proximity of the palace.

Why?

Because, as much as Vir's stomach churned just contemplating the notion, the fact was that the royal palace of Centauri Prime had become little more than a Drakh stronghold, a cover for the Drakh power base. Although Vir had strong suspicions that their true center of power was somewhere else on Centauri Prime.

But he had no desire to let the Drakh know that he had discerned so much, so quickly. Beings of finite power they might be, but there was no underestimating the ability of the Drakh to destroy him at their slightest whim. The only reason they had not done so by this point, he decided, was that they did not perceive him as a direct threat. If they *did* decide he posed a threat, however, he didn't stand a chance.

All of this went through his mind in less than a second, and by that point he was already back on the ground, "crumbling" at the mere sight of the formidable Drakh. He could tell from the Drakh's expression that Shiv'kala was by turns taken aback, appalled, and amused at the sight of this great, groveling oaf.

The thing was, he had to give some sort of answer that would throw the Drakh off track. He couldn't take the chance that Shiv'kala might figure out his connection to the underground. The only way to make sure of that was to present himself as a simple tool, a harmless foil who was about as capable of causing damage on his own as a wafting feather might be.

And the best thing of all was that he could tell reasonable amounts of the truth, which would be all the easier to sell to the Drakh. If there was one thing that Vir excelled at, it was sincerity. He wore sincerity as comfortably as other Centauri wore high hair.

"I . . . I was told to," he stammered out.

"By whom?"

"By . . . by . . ." He licked his lips. "By a techno-mage."

"Ahhhh . . ." Obviously it hadn't been the answer the Drakh

was expecting, but neither did it seem to surprise him. "A techno-mage. And where have you encountered a techno-mage?"

"Back on Babylon 5. I first met them when I was serving Londo." The words were tumbling over each other. It wasn't really that long ago—a minor part of a lifetime, really—that Vir Cotto had been a bumbling, tongue-twisted, and perpetually anxious young man. Vir remembered that Vir-that-was almost nostalgically. At the time, life had seemed hideously complex.

He remembered quite clearly the man he had been, and had no trouble at all summoning the Vir from years gone by. He took that much younger Vir, slipped him on like a comfortable overcoat, and impersonated him with tremendous facility. "Londo, he . . . he wanted the techno-mages' blessing and . . . and . . . and . . . and . . ."

Shiv'kala nodded, and moved his hand in a slight clockwise motion as if to indicate to Vir that he should get on with it.

". . . and he sent me to them to tell them he wanted to suh-suh-see them!" Vir continued. "I thought that would be the end of it. But it wasn't. No. No, it wasn't. Because they came to me, and told me to walk into the palace and say your . . . that name. Why? Why would they do that? Please, tell me . . ." And he started to sob. It was amazing to him how easily the tears came. Then again, considering everything he had been through, all the horrors he had witnessed, perhaps the impressive thing was that he was ever able to *prevent* himself from crying.

He reasoned that the best thing to do was allow the Drakh, all unknowingly, to fill in the gaps himself. Shiv'kala, as it so happened, promptly did so.

"We have our suspicions" was all the Drakh would offer, although he did add, "You would be wise, Vir Cotto, not to meddle further with magic workers. You are merely a game piece to such as they, to be discarded at will. Do you know us?"

Vir shook his head fiercely.

Shiv'kala glanced upward in the direction of the head. "Do you know him?"

Vir looked back up, and he saw that the head of Rem Lanas was back in lieu of his own. As appalling a sight as Rem's head had been up there, he had to admit that it was better than his.

"His . . . his name is Rem Lanas," Vir managed to say, making the response seem far more of an effort than it was. "I . . . met him on Babylon 5. We had drinks."

"You have met a great many people on Babylon 5, it seems."

"I . . . I . . ." He tried to find something to say, and finally settled on, "I have a lot of free time on my hands."

The Drakh either didn't register the response, or didn't care that it had been made. Vir couldn't help but feel that Shiv'kala was assessing him right then and there, trying to determine whether Vir was indeed going to be a problem.

"You do know," Shiv'kala said softly, "that this is all a dream. It is not happening."

"I had been kind of hoping for that to be the case," Vir told him.

"Be aware of one thing . . . we know of the predictions of the Lady Morella."

This caused Vir to freeze where he stood. Even though he was dreaming, even though he felt no normal sensations, he was still certain he could sense his blood running cold. "Morella?"

"Londo mentioned 'predictions' once," the Drakh said. " 'Both of us, protected by visions, protected by prophecy,' was what he said."

Vir remembered the exchange all too well. It had been in the cell that Vir had occupied for the high crime of mentioning Shiv-'kala's name—at the urging of a techno-mage, that much at least had been the truth.

"I sought clarification from him as to what he meant. He was . . . less than forthcoming. At first. But we can be most persuasive. He told us of how the Lady Morella made predictions, stating that one of you would succeed the other to the throne of Centauri Prime. Since he is still with us . . . that leads us to believe that you will be the next ruler."

"It's just a prediction. It means nothing."

"Perhaps. But be aware, Vir Cotto . . . should it come to pass . . ." And the Drakh's mouth twisted into something approximating a smile, the single most horrific thing that Vir had seen in the entire encounter. "Should it come to pass . . . there is much that we can offer you."

"I . . ." He gulped. "I appreciate the thought."

"Our power is great. You can benefit by it . . . or be destroyed.

The choice, for the moment, is yours. In the end, it may or may not remain so."

And then he stepped back into the shadows, which seemed to reach out to claim him.

Vir stood there a moment, steadying the pounding of his hearts . . . and then he noticed that the shadows were continuing to stretch . . . toward him. Even though he knew it was a dream, even though he was certain he was not in any real danger . . . nevertheless, he did not like in the least what the shadows portended, and he was loath to let them touch him. He backed up, and he bumped up against the pole on which he had seen his own head. He looked up involuntarily and let out a yelp of alarm.

Senna's head was there instead of his. It stared down at him, eyes glassy. And then the impact of Vir's thumping against it caused her head to topple off. The head fell, spiraling, and tumbled into Vir's arms even as he tried to do everything he could to avoid it.

And then, despite everything he'd been through, despite his being fairly inured to terrifying hardships, Vir found himself frozen, utterly paralyzed, unable to cope with what he was seeing.

He started to cry, tears running down his face, but without any heat. As grotesque and grisly a sight as it was, he clutched the head to him and the sobs crew louder.

And the head spoke to him. "Vir . . . Vir," came Senna's voice, impossibly, from the severed head. Then Vir was being shaken, and suddenly he opened his eyes, and the tears were very real and hot against his cheek.

Senna was looking down at him, her head securely back on her shoulders.

He remembered the first time he had seen her, more than a decade before, when Londo had taken her under his wing. There was no longer anything childlike about her. This was an adult woman, polished and intelligent, who looked as if she was already anticipating how she was going to respond to something you had not yet thought of saying.

She was dressed in a blue-and-white gown that was both simple and elegant. She had been wearing it the last time that Vir had seen her, about six months earlier, during a dinner with Londo that had quickly evolved into a rather pleasant evening.

She had, in fact, salvaged the evening, because Londo had spent much of it getting quietly drunk—which was something Vir had not often seen Londo do. Drunk, yes, but quiet? Never.

She had been witty, charming, entertaining, and utterly captivating.

He had also heard from her from time to time during the interim, although usually it was about more . . . business-oriented matters.

"Vir . . . Londo sent me to fetch you . . . and you were here, and . . ."

"I'm all right, I'm . . . I'm all right," he said quickly, clambering to his feet. He glanced around automatically. Even though he knew that there would be no sign of the Drakh—that, indeed, the Drakh had most likely never physically been there—he found that he was peering into the shadows to see if any of them moved. "I saw . . ." Then he caught himself. He certainly didn't want to tell this young woman what he had experienced. There was no need to risk alarming her.

"You saw what?" she asked.

Slowly he pointed to the head of Rem Lanas, perched atop the pole.

"He was . . . one of yours?"

His head snapped around at those words. He saw it then, in her face, in her eyes . . . she knew.

"Not here," he said firmly, and tugged her arm. He started to pull her out of the garden, and she offered no resistance, but then he stopped, and said, "Wait . . . Londo will be waiting . . ."

"If he waits a few minutes more, nothing will happen," Senna said, and with that they departed. The unseeing eyes of Rem Lanas watched them go.

EXCERPTED FROM
THE CHRONICLES OF LONDO MOLLARI.
Excerpt dated (approximate Earth date)
September 9, 2275.

They wanted me to do something. How gloriously ironic is that?

The House heads were clamoring to see me. They were up in arms because Durla has jailed one of their own. They wanted to know what I am going to do about it, not only as emperor, but also as the head of a House myself.

They all clustered outside my chambers, a flock of clucking birds, and at first Dunseny brought them in one at a time. But finally, at my instruction, he led in the entire group of them. Initially they comported themselves nobly, speaking in the sort of stately and pompous manner that I've come to expect. But soon one complaint tumbled into another, until they were all bleating about their situation. They tell me that, if this is allowed to continue, it is going to mean the end of the entire social and class structure of Centauri Prime. It will terminate life as we know it, everything that Centauri Prime is supposed to stand for and respect.

It is truly amazing.

Shadow ships darkened our sky . . . the Shadows themselves were given aid and comfort here on Centauri Prime . . . creatures who were the purest incarnation of evil ever known to this galaxy. That was not enough to be an end to life as we know it on Centauri Prime.

Nor was life as we know it threatened by Cartagia's mad reign, during which time the supposedly brave House leaders trembled in hiding, lest they truly lose their heads.

And now . . .

Well . . . truth be told . . . the life that we have come to know and cherish on Centauri Prime, the goals for which we have fought so diligently . . . these actually are in jeopardy. Not for the reason that the House heads claim, though. The heads

64

of the Houses live in the uppermost branches of the tree that is Centauri Prime. When one is that high up, it is difficult to perceive that the true problem is root rot.

It took me a little time to discern exactly what has them so up in arms. Most interesting: Milifa, the father of the late and unlamented—except by him—Throk, spoke challengingly to our prime minister. One does not do so if one expects to live to a ripe old age. Milifa apparently forgot that, and is now imprisoned.

A rather foolish move, that.

Tikane came before me, of the House of Tikane. And there is Arlineas, and Yson, and a host of others. Persons who, after hiding in fear from the rampage of Cartagia, feel a greater sense of safety under my more "benevolent" rule. They have also been supporters of Durla, helping to smooth the way to his assuming the office and power of prime minister. I believe they are regretting that decision, and are hoping that I will rectify it for them.

"The Houses, Emperor," Tikane told me with a vast degree of pomposity, "are the underpinnings, the backbone, of your strength." The others nodded in accord.

My strength.

My strength.

What know they of my strength?

It is Durla who runs things, and I . . . I have been fighting political battles and games for as long as I can remember. For a time I thought that I was truly winning . . . except in this sort of game, to win is to lose. Durla feeds on this sort of business, the way a fire feeds on oxygen. The only thing I take comfort in is knowing that even Durla is deceived. He deludes himself into believing that he knows what is occurring . . . but he does not. He has no idea that he himself is a tool, of . . . others. Were I to tell him, of course, he would not believe me. He is far too taken with his own sense of self-importance.

Then it was Arlineas who spoke, and he looked a bit concerned. I have no idea how long I must have simply sat there, staring off into space, lost in my thoughts. Next to Arlineas was Yson—small in stature, but looming in charisma—who, as was his custom, said nothing. Very rarely did he speak. As a result, on the few occasions when he did, his words carried with them far greater importance.

But it was Arlineas who spoke. "Highness, are you—" he said tentatively.

"I hear you," I answered him softly. "I hear everything."

"Then certainly," Arlineas said, "you have heard the stories of the massive fleet buildup. Individual workforces, operating independently of each other, each assembling different parts of the whole, but no one person truly knowing its capacity—"

"Or purpose," Tikane said. "No one person except Durla . . . who now has virtually declared war on the Houses." The others crowded together, all bobbing their heads in agreement. "What does this say to you, Highness?"

"What does it say to me?" I replied. For the first time in a long time, I felt something other than lethargy running through my veins. "It says to me that you and your ilk were more than content to allow matters to progress to this state, when it suited your needs and egos. Durla has made no secret of his intentions. How many of you nodded dutifully and applauded his grand vision. And Vallko . . . Vallko, standing in the Great Square, preaching of Centauri Prime's great destiny, which any fool can see means nothing less than the annihilation or subjugation of every other world. How many of you shared his prayers to the Great Maker and sought the Great Maker's blessing for the very endeavors you now decry."

"We are simply concerned for the general well-being of our world, Highness," Tikane protested.

"Your own well-being, you mean. You reap what you sow."

They looked at each other in puzzlement. "We are not farmers, Highness," Arlineas pointed out.

I shook my head. "Never mind. I did not expect you to understand. But," I continued with renewed strength, "if you do not comprehend that, then this might serve instead. Something a Vorlon once said . . ."

"A Vorlon?" There were immediate looks, one to the other. Most of them had never had the opportunity to see a Vorlon, even one inside an encounter suit. I, of course, had not only extensively been in the presence of a suited one . . . but I was present that amazing day when Kosh Naranek, the Vorlon ambassador, emerged from his suit. Others reported visions of a great winged being, and I . . .

I saw nothing.

Actually, that is not entirely accurate. I saw . . . light. An overwhelming brilliance. But it was shapeless, amorphous, and indistinct. For a moment, it seemed as though I perceived a hint of something, but that was all.

Sometimes I have wondered whether what others saw was some sort of mass delusion . . . or whether I was simply not deserving of the experience.

"Yes. A Vorlon," I said. "Understand, he did not say this to me directly, but to another. However, things have a habit of being passed around. And what he said was, 'The blizzard has already begun. It is too late for the snowflakes to vote.' Do you comprehend that, gentlemen?"

There were slow nods from all around. They understood all too well. They were not, however, happy about it.

"So . . . you will do nothing?" Tikane said. "You will simply allow Durla to do as he wishes?"

"Have you heard nothing I said?" I demanded. "He operates now using the power that your support provided him. He has grown beyond you. To him, you are all simple ground-dwellers. He no longer looks to the ground. He looks to the stars that he desires to conquer, and he has the backing of the military. And the people adore him . . . him and his ministers of religion and education and information. You, who have so much, cannot begin to comprehend how much those who have nothing appreciate such things as jobs and building toward a future of conquest. Since they have nothing, they consider it quite appealing, the prospect of taking that which others possess.

"You cannot stand against that, and I do not suggest you try."

"Then what do you suggest we do, Highness?" Arlineas demanded.

I sighed deeply and put a hand to my head. "I suggest you leave. My head hurts rather profoundly, and I would be alone."

They were not the least bit happy to hear that, but my personal guards did not particularly care about the feelings of the noble lords. They were escorted out. The last one to go was Yson, and I felt his rather malevolent gaze upon me even after he was out of the room.

"Leave me," I told my guards. They bowed and obeyed, closing the great doors behind them. The doors of my prison.

I rose from my throne and walked slowly across the room. Every movement these days feels labored and painful. In the past, at least my aches had been courteous enough to confine themselves to what is left of my soul; now they have actually intruded into my joints. *Most* inconsiderate.

I stood upon the balcony, holding tightly to the railing. I looked into the distance . . . and saw something that was most unexpected. There, walking across a field, were Vir and Senna. I had been wondering where Vir was; I had sent Senna to bring him to me, and yet there they were, walking away, speaking with each other like two old friends. Or . . . more than that?

Then something else caught my eye, on another balcony, to the right and one level up. I knew it well; it was the residence and offices of Durla. The fact that he had acquired accommodations higher than my own was, I had always felt, a not-so-subtle message from him to me.

What I saw now, though, was not Durla. It was Mariel, and she looked simply awful. She was bandaged, as if she had taken a great fall. I did not have a chance to get a good look, however, because she spotted me looking up at her . . . and immediately darted back inside.

It was never like her to be clumsy. Then again, age begins to tell on all of us, I suppose.

"What make you of that?"

It was Shiv'kala. As always, I had not heard his entrance at all. Even after all these years of our . . . "association" . . . I still had no clear idea of how he achieved his comings and goings. I used to think upon it for extensive periods of time, scrutinizing the walls from which he emerged to see if there were hidden passages and such. If so, I never managed to detect them.

"Of them?" I pointed to Vir and Senna, mere specks in the distance. "How kind of you to care about my opinion."

"I have always cared, Londo."

I turned and looked into the face of the creature I hated above all others. If nothing else, his unchanging nature was aggravating. My face, my frame, reflected every minute of every day of my life, and not in an especially flattering manner. Shiv'kala, for his part, looked exactly the same now as he had then. "You say 'I' rather than 'we'? I had always thought you spoke on behalf of the Drakh entire."

"You have never truly understood me, Londo," Shiv'kala said. "Believe it or not, you have had no greater protector or friend than me."

"I will opt for 'not,' if it is all the same to you."

Shiv'kala looked at me with what seemed to be a perverse sort of paternal disapproval. "You have not been the best of servants, Londo."

"I grieve for my lapses."

"You do no such thing. Your little rebellions have been numerous, and usually ill timed. That you have survived them has been largely due to my sufferance. Fortunately enough, in recent years they have been fairly nonexistent."

Something about the way he said that caught my interest. "Why 'fortunately enough'?"

"Because," he said evenly, "matters will be coming to a head. And now would be a most unfortunate time to be . . . problematic."

I chuckled softly. "Are you not concerned that saying such things may provide a temptation for me to do exactly what you fear?"

"Fear?" The notion appeared to amuse him. "We fear nothing, Londo, least of all you. However, I have invested a good deal of time in you. The notion that the time was wasted would be displeasing to me."

"Of course . . ." I said, understanding. "You are concerned that I will be motivated by the complaints. That I will attempt to interfere in the plans of Durla, your chosen one."

"Any 'attempts' you make will be just that. You cannot stop this, Londo, any more than . . ."

"Than that vessel, *Excalibur*, was able to stop your plan to eradicate humanity?"

We both knew precisely what I meant.

"You grow old, Londo," he said after a time of silence. "You grow old . . . and tired. I can help you, you know."

"Oh, can you."

He stepped in close to me. Once I would have trembled inwardly. Now I was simply bored.

"We have our methods," he said. "You need not be a slave to your body. Options can be offered you . . . if your actions suit our desires. You can be young and strong again."

"I was never young," I told him, "and if I had ever been strong, I would not have allowed myself to get into this situation in the first place. I am not interested, Shiv'kala, in anything you might have to offer."

"When you are on your deathbed, you might have something else to say."

"You are likely right. And it will probably be something like this . . ." and I put my hand to my throat and produced a loud *"Aaaackkkkkk!"*

He looked at me very oddly, did the Drakh. "You have a curiously odd-timed sense of humor, Emperor Mollari."

"I have learned that life is short, Shiv'kala, and one must find one's amusements where one can."

He looked out toward Vir and Senna. I could not help but feel that he was studying them in the same manner that I might examine an insect before I step on it. "You have not answered my question, Londo. What make you of that?"

"What do I make of two people walking?" I shrugged. "It means nothing."

"Sometimes that which means nothing means everything."

"You speak like a Vorlon."

It was a passing, offhand remark. I thought nothing of it. But the moment the words passed from my lips, a massive jolt of pain surged through my skull. I dropped to one knee, refusing to cry out . . . a resolve that lasted for perhaps three seconds before a scream was torn from my throat.

Shiv'kala stood above me, looking down at me with that same crushed-bug expression. "Never," he said coldly, "say that again."

"Never . . . never . . ." I managed to get out. Then the pain ebbed, just like that, and I sagged to the floor, on my hands and knees, trying to prop myself up and stop the room from spinning wildly around me.

"And never forget who I am . . . what you are . . ."

"Never," I said again.

As if he had forgotten that I was there, he looked back out in the direction of Vir and Senna. "Cotto has been made a tool of the techno-mages. Are you aware of that?"

I shook my head, which was a mistake, because it made the room spin utterly out of control. My left elbow gave way and I crashed to the floor. Shiv'kala did not appear to notice.

"At least he has been in the past. Perhaps they were utilizing him again that day he was wandering the palace and almost came upon me. Well, Londo . . . what one group can turn to their advantage . . . another can, as well. And this we shall do . . . when the time is right."

"Don't hurt him," I gasped out from the floor. "He . . . is harmless."

"Hurt the next emperor?" He seemed astonished at the thought. "Unthinkable. He is our insurance, Londo. In case you become too troublesome, or decline to remain malleable . . . you can be disposed of, and Vir instituted in your place. And I strongly suspect that he will be far more compliant than you have ever been."

"I have . . . complied . . ."

"On most things, yes. On some, you have not. There should be no exceptions. It is not for you to pick and choose. It is for you to obey."

"Obey . . . yes . . . I will . . ."

"See that you do," he said, and I could feel the temperature dropping significantly. "Otherwise Vir will step in where you leave off. If you do not desire such a happenstance . . . then do nothing to bring it about."

"I shall do nothing." The pain was beginning to subside, but the lack of control, the sense of humiliation . . . these were wounds that stabbed far more deeply, and would never depart.

I waited for the response—some retort, some threat, some . . . thing. But there was nothing. I looked up. He was gone.

I rose on unsteady legs and, as I leaned against the wall, I realized somewhat belatedly that I should have asked him if he knew the circumstances of how Mariel had come to be injured. For a moment, a demented moment, I thought that maybe Durla had done that to her. But then I realized that such a thing could not possibly be. He adored her. He doted on her. Amusingly, there were many who believed that she was the true strength behind the prime minister. I, of course, knew that it was the Drakh. But that was information that I had no choice but to keep to myself.

I have read back on what I have just written. My eyes are tired, and I feel myself growing fatigued. Vir and Senna came back later in the evening, and there seemed to be something in their eyes when they looked to each other . . . but they also appeared distracted, as if they had seen something that was bothersome to them .

. . . but I am an old man, and prone to imagining things.

What I have not imagined, however, is the concern expressed by the heads of the Houses. I do not care especially about their personal worries. Whatever ill fortunes befall them, they have more than brought upon themselves.

My memory of late continues to fade in and out, but occasionally I have times of starkly lucid clarity. And the extensive discussion of great vessels, fleets . . . these things, however, have caught my attention. Perhaps, despite whatever my "master" may desire, I shall see precisely what is going on, in detail. I likely cannot stop it; I am a mere snowflake, dressed appropriately for that status. However, I can at least provide a bit of slush, and see if Durla slips on it.

— chapter 6 —

Senna had never seen Vir looking so shaken. He kept glancing over his shoulder as they retreated from the area of the palace. "Vir, calm down . . . you're moving so quickly, I can barely keep up . . ."

"I feel like we're being watched." They were the first words he'd spoken since she'd found him on the ground in the garden, and they were said with such intensity that she didn't even try to argue. Instead she simply quieted herself and followed him until they seemed to be far enough from the palace that he was satisfied.

She looked around at the hill where they had come to a halt, overlooking the city, and unbidden, tears began to well in her eyes. Vir, turning toward her, saw them and instantly became contrite. "I'm sorry," he stammered, charmingly vulnerable in his discomfort. "I shouldn't have been so abrupt with—"

"Oh, it's not you." She sighed. Even though she was wearing one of her more formal dresses, she nevertheless sank to the ground with another heavy sigh. "This place used to be . . . well . . . a teacher of mine and I used to come here."

"I had lots of teachers," Vir said ruefully. "I don't especially feel nostalgic for any of them. They had very little good to say about me. Do you ever see your old teacher?"

She looked heavenward at the clouds that wafted across the darkening sky. They were tinged bloodred, which was symbolic somehow. "Every now and again. Up there."

"He's a pilot?" Vir asked, totally lost.

She smiled sadly and shook her head. "No, Vir. He's dead. Long dead."

"Oh. I'm sorry."

"So am I." She looked Vir up and down appraisingly. "He

71

would have liked you, I think. Because you're doing something about . . . about all of this."

"You mentioned that before. I'm not entirely sure what you're talking ab—"

Her gaze danced with amusement. "Don't try to lie to me, Vir. You're not very good at it."

With a heavy sigh he sat next to her. "Actually . . . I've not only gotten very good at it, I've gotten very *very* good at it. Which, on some level, kind of depresses me." He looked at her thoughtfully. "But not with you. You see right through me."

"As does the emperor, I suspect," she told him, and when Vir blanched visibly, she went on. "I don't know for sure. We've never actually spoken of it in so many words. I don't think he'd dare, for some reason."

"I can take a guess at the reason," Vir said darkly.

She wondered what he meant by that, but decided not to press the matter.

He seemed aware that he had said something better off not pursued, so he shifted gears. "I . . . did have some suspicions. All those times you would contact me, send me those chatty messages about something or other that Londo had said . . . and invariably, it was information that was helpful to me in my . . . endeavors. The thing is, I didn't know whether you were acting as Londo's mouthpiece, oblivious to what was going on, or whether you truly comprehended how the information you were passing along was being used."

"I see." The edges of her mouth twitched. "So you're saying you couldn't decide whether or not I was a blind fool."

"No! I . . . I wasn't saying that at all!"

She laughed quite openly this time. "Don't worry about it, Vir. You have a lot on your mind, I'm sure." At that he just stared at her, and began smiling. "What?" she prompted.

"I just . . ." He shook his head wonderingly. "You have a really lovely laugh. I never noticed that before about you." He seemed to shake off the digression and instead settled back down to business. "So all those messages you sent . . . they were actually at Londo's behest, because you felt you were aiding in the resistance movement."

"Partly."

"Partly?"

"Well . . ." She shrugged. "The truth is . . . I admire someone like you."

"You do?" He was genuinely curious. "Who is he?"

It took her a moment to understand his question, and then she laughed even more loudly. "You're so literal, Vir. Not really someone 'like' you. You. I liked communicating with you. I liked reminding you that I was around. Because what you do is so admirable.

"There are those who have a vision for this world that will lead us down a fiery path to total destruction. They pursue that path out of self-aggrandizement and ego and obsession with power. You, and others, try to stop them out of a pure sense of altruism. You care so much about helping others that you would risk your lives in order to do it."

"Not just *risk* lives," Vir said, glancing off toward the palace. From this distance, in the growing darkness, it was no longer possible to see the head that had been placed atop a pole.

She understood. "He *was* one of yours, then."

Vir nodded. "We have . . . all of us . . . certain 'safeguards.' A techno-mage aided us in conditioning our minds to resist truth drugs and such. But nothing is fail-safe. When I heard that Lanas had been taken, I immediately arranged a visit here, in hopes of being able to do something . . ."

"That was foolish."

He looked at her in surprise. "That . . . seems a bit harsh . . ."

"Yes. It is. It's also reasonable. Showing up here, timed with the capture of one of your people . . . you're drawing undue attention to yourself. You haven't fooled me, Vir; you've 'created' a persona for yourself, of a tongue-tied, fumbling bumbler—to convince others that you present no threat. You've done a superb job of acting."

"It's been less acting than you would think," Vir mused ruefully.

"Whatever the case . . . the masquerade has garnered you a certain amount of latitude. Despite the timing of your arrival, many will be willing to write it off as coincidence. You wouldn't exactly be the person they consider most likely to oversee an attempt to halt our world's military buildup.

"But all you need is for one person—the wrong person—to make the connection, and the next thing you know, you're

the one whose resistance to truth drugs is being tested." She
frowned. "You have to think of more than just yourself, Vir.
People are counting on you. All of them," and with one sweeping
gesture she took in the entirety of the city, "are counting on you,
even though they don't know it. The emperor, though he can't
say it, is counting on you." She hesitated a moment, and then
added, "And I'm counting on you."

Vir looked at her wonderingly. He had seen her on any
number of occasions, they had spent time together . . . but it was
as if he was truly seeing her for the first time. "I . . . won't let you
down," he said, and his voice was hoarse.

Senna had used her attractiveness, her vivaciousness, all as
ploys to get people to talk to her. She had been particularly successful with the Prime Candidates, who vied for her attention
because she was perceived as a potentially valuable acquisition.
Indeed, the late and unlamented Throk had gone so far as to push
for a marriage, a move that had been blocked by the emperor and
was eventually rendered moot by . . .

"You were the one," she said suddenly. "The one who blew up
the Prime Candidates' safe house. The one who killed Throk."

He looked away. The move spoke volumes.

She said nothing more for a time, and then she reached over
and rested a hand atop his. "It must have been very difficult for
you, Vir."

"It wasn't me," he said tonelessly. "It was someone . . . I don't
know."

"But I thought . . ."

"We're in a war, Senna. We all become people we don't
know . . . and wouldn't want to know . . . and in times of peace,
people we would very much like to forget. I want to forget the
person who killed him . . . very much."

She nodded, understanding, and then his hand twisted around
and squeezed hers firmly. She interlaced her fingers with his,
and she felt the strength in them, but also a faint trembling.

Senna had no idea what prompted her to do it, but she leaned
over, took his face in her hands, and kissed him. She had never
before kissed anyone sincerely. Reflexively he tried to pull back,
but then he settled into it, enjoying the moment, kissing her
back hungrily. There was nothing sexual in the contact; the need
was far deeper than that. When they parted, he looked at her

in amazement. "I . . . shouldn't have done that . . ." he began to apologize.

"In case you didn't notice, Vir, I did it," she said softly. She even felt slightly embarrassed, although she knew she shouldn't. "At the very least, I initiated it."

"But I'm . . . I'm old enough to be your . . . your . . ."

"Lover?" She was startled at her own brazenness. She couldn't believe she'd said it. At the same time, she was glad she had.

He looked at her for a long moment, and this time he was the one who initiated it. Her lips, her body, melted against his. When they parted, he took her chin in one hand and studied her with both tenderness and sadness.

"Another time, perhaps," he said. "Another life. I can't obligate someone else to me when I'm traveling down a road so dark, I can't even guess at the end."

"I could walk down that road at your side."

"You need to keep your distance. Because the road tends to branch off . . . and if I walk out on one of those branches, and the branch gets cut off behind me . . . I can't take you down with me. I couldn't live with that knowledge . . . for whatever brief period of time I was allowed to live, that is."

It was difficult for her to hear, but she knew he was right. Or, at the very least, she knew that what he was saying was right for him, and that nothing she could say or do would dissuade him.

"Are you sure Londo knows? About me, I mean," Vir suddenly said, switching gears. "And he's told no one?"

"If he had told someone . . . anyone . . . do you think you would still be at liberty?" she asked reasonably.

"Probably not. I'd likely be up there with poor Rem. How many more, Senna? How many more good and brave men are going to die before this business is over?"

"There's only so much you can do, Vir. You must do your best, whatever that may be, and pray to the Great Maker for strength in dealing with the rest."

"I just wish I knew," Vir said grimly, "whose side the Great Maker is on. Durla and his allies believe just as fervently as I do that they are acting in the best interests of Centauri Prime. We can't both be right."

"Perhaps," she said thoughtfully, leaning back, "you both are."

He looked at her in surprise. "How can we both be?"

She seemed surprised that he had to ask. "Isn't it obvious?"

"Not immediately, no."

"You have a destiny, Vir. I can tell just by looking at you."

"All creatures have a destiny," Vir said dismissively.

"Yes, but you have a great one. It's plain to see. The people of this world are going to need you in ways that you cannot even begin to imagine. And perhaps the Great Maker desires the actions of Durla because he has plans for you. And those plans include your being forged into the man who will guide Centauri Prime to its future. But you can only become that man by battling the plans of a truly great enemy . . . and Durla has been selected for that purpose."

He stared at her. "You're saying that people are fighting, dying . . . that millions may be annihilated, if Durla has his way . . . all so that I can eventually pick up the pieces?"

"That's one way of putting it."

"It's not a good way, and I can't say I'm especially thrilled with the idea. It makes the Great Maker sound insane."

"Why should he not be?" Senna challenged. "After all, he made us in his image . . . and look at the terrible things we have done, as a race. Are we not insane?"

"That," Vir said, "makes a horrifying amount of sense."

They walked through the corridors of the palace, chatting agreeably about matters of little to no consequence. It was a rather pleasant change of pace from what they had been dealing with before.

At one point, Vir made a joke that Senna found particularly amusing, so much so in fact that she was seized with laughter, then had to stop and compose herself. Vir stopped, too, grinning amiably, and Senna took his hand in hers.

"Well, well! Looking quite friendly, are we?"

Senna and Vir stopped and turned. She still held his hand.

Durla was walking toward them with his customary swagger. Next to him was a woman that Senna could only assume to be Mariel. It wasn't possible to be sure, however, because she was wearing a veil. This was extremely odd: the only women who wore such things were the legendary telepaths who had once accompanied the emperor wherever he went. That, however, was a custom that had ended with the death of Emperor Turhan. Cartagia, proclaiming that he did not want women around who could peer effortlessly into his mind, had ordered them all killed. They were the first casualties of his bloody reign, and most certainly not the last.

Despite the fact that she was veiled, Senna could sense Mariel's gaze upon her, boring right through her. She reflexively released her hold on Vir's hand, doing so almost guiltily.

"I have known the lady Senna for quite some time," Vir said calmly . . . almost too calmly. "She is much like a beloved niece to me." Senna nodded in confirmation.

"Of course," Durla said with a polite smile. "Oh, and Senna, you of course remember Mariel. She is much like a beloved wife to me. Say hello, Mariel."

"Hello." Her voice was so soft as to be almost inaudible.

"Move aside your veil, dear. It is difficult for them to hear you."

"I . . . do not wish . . ."

"I did not ask you what your wish was in the matter," he reminded her in a voice so sharp that it made Senna jump. She looked to Vir, who somehow was maintaining a look of polite curiosity, but nothing more. "Move aside your veil so that you can greet our visitor properly." He looked at Vir apologetically. "She is being rude to you, perhaps out of some residual resentment over your losing her to me. But I do not tolerate rudeness. Do I, Mariel." It wasn't a question.

"No, husband. You do not," she said. And she put a hand to her veil and moved it aside so that Senna and Vir could see her face.

Senna gasped. She regretted doing so instantly, but it was an involuntary reflex, for Mariel's face was battered and bruised.

Vir gripped Senna's upper arm, also by reflex. He was holding it so tight that it hurt.

"What . . . happened?" Vir managed to get out.

"She is very clumsy, our Mariel," Durla said in a voice dripping with solicitousness. "She tripped over her own words." It had the sound of a remark that Durla had been rehearsing, in preparation for a question that he was longing to answer with smug arrogance.

"I must be more cautious in the future," Mariel admitted, and now she was looking to Vir. Her gaze flickered between Vir and Senna, and Senna saw in those eyes hurt that she could not even imagine.

Vir started toward Durla, and suddenly Senna knew beyond any question that if she did not do something, Vir would be upon him. There was no upside to such a confrontation. Durla had been a trained soldier. That had been some time ago, true, but the training remained. He might be a formidable foe. But if Vir, carried by burning rage, did manage to overwhelm Durla and beat him senseless, as was undoubtedly his intent, then his pretenses would be forever shredded. Senna might wind up proving uncomfortably prescient in her concerns over Vir being imprisoned and drugged up, even before the night was over.

Immediately Senna doubled over in "pain," crying out loudly enough to attract Vir's attention before he had managed to take more than a step or two. He looked at her, confused. "What's wrong?"

"Some sort of . . . of sharp cramp. Please. Would you . . . be so kind as to help me to my room?"

As this occurred, Mariel replaced the veil. Durla was looking at Senna with what seemed boundless compassion. "Attend to her, Vir. I have known her for quite a while, as well. I knew her back when we all called her Young Lady. Quite a woman she has grown into. Yes, attend to her, Vir, by all means. I have a dinner with my ministry to attend."

"Perhaps . . ." Vir had barely managed to gain control of himself, and when he spoke it was in a voice that was vaguely strangled. "Perhaps . . . the lady Mariel should . . . should be resting . . . do you think?"

"Oh, no," Durla said dismissively, "no, not at all. When one acquires a trophy such as the Lady Mariel, one is always eager to display her, even when she is feeling less than her best. And she is more than willing to accommodate my desires. Are you not, my love?"

"As . . . you say, my love," Mariel said, sounding like one already dead.

"There, you see? Enjoy the rest of your evening," Durla told them cheerfully. "And have a care with Senna, Ambassador . . . she is very precious to all of us."

Senna was holding Vir's forearm in a grip of iron. She surprised herself; she had no idea she was that strong. But desperate moments tended to prompt acts of equally desperate strength.

Durla headed off down the opulent corridor, the light seeming to dim as he passed. Mariel cast one more glance back at Vir and Senna, but the veil blocked any hint of her expression. Senna had a feeling that she could guess.

"That . . . bastard!" Vir spat out. "How . . . how could he . . ."

"I'll tell you how," Senna said with confidence. "She is his one weakness."

"His what?"

"His weakness . . . or at least she is seen as such. That's what I've heard from some of the chattier members of the Prime Candidates. And apparently he wishes to send a message to any and all concerned that he has no weaknesses at all."

"Naturally. Because if he'll treat someone he loves in that manner, then what mercy will he show for those he considers opponents?"

"None."

Vir was nodding in grim understanding. Clearly he wanted to say more, but he seemed to catch himself. That was probably wise. If there was one thing Senna had come to understand, it was that in many ways, the palace had ears everywhere. She didn't quite understand the how and why of it . . . but she definitely knew the truth of it.

"Should we tell the emperor?" she asked tentatively.

"Londo?" Vir laughed in grim recollection. "He divorced her. She tried to kill him. He's not going to give a damn about what happens to her. He'd probably have a good laugh over it . . . and that's something I don't think I could stand to see. Better that we don't bring it up." He looked in the direction that Mariel had gone, and there was tragedy in his face. "I never thought he would . . . if I'd known, I'd never have—"

"You'd never have what?" she asked with genuine curiosity.

"Nothing," he told her after a moment. "It doesn't matter."

Privately she resolved to mention Mariel's "condition" to Londo in Vir's absence. Out loud, she said, "Vir—"

"I said it doesn't matter. What's done is done, and can never be undone . . . no matter how much we may wish it." He squeezed her hand gently, and said, "Let's go have dinner with Londo. It's best not to keep the emperor waiting any longer than we already have."

EXCERPTED FROM
THE CHRONICLES OF LONDO MOLLARI.
Excerpt dated (approximate Earth date)
September 23, 2275.

For the first time in a long time, I had fun today. I totally disrupted Durla's meeting . . . gave him a reminder of just who was in charge, for all the good that will do . . . and then had some excitement that resulted in a most unexpected reunion.

I am worn out from it and won't go into detail. Tomorrow, maybe. Hopefully even my occasionally faulty memory will suffice to hold on to the recollection until the morrow.

In case it is not . . . I shall jot down the phrase that will most stick in my mind, simply because Durla's expression was so priceless. The look on his face, as he spat words from his mouth that did not match the expression. "Emmmperor," he said, dragging out the first syllable as if it would go on forever. "How . . . pleasingly unexpected to see you . . ."

— chapter 7 —

"Emmmperor . . . how . . . pleasingly unexpected to see you . . ."

Even as he spoke, Durla felt all the blood draining out of his face. He composed himself quickly, however, and rose. Seated around the table were Minister of Development Castig Lione, Minister of Information Kuto, and Minister of Spirituality Vallko. In addition, there was also General Rhys, next to whom Kuto—in his loud and amusingly self-deprecating manner—insisted that he sit. "Far easier than dieting," Kuto had chortled, slapping his more than ample belly. Not that Rhys was fat. But he was large enough and broad enough that he made Kuto look small in comparison, which naturally pleased Kuto no end.

"I believe this is your first visit to the Tower of Power, if I'm not mistaken," Durla continued. "Welcome, welcome. Minister Lione has been kind enough to arrange for these particular facilities to be used for ministry meetings. Hopefully you will find them up to your standards."

Rhys was at the far head of the table, and he was already standing and offering his chair to the emperor. Londo, with the omnipresent Dunseny at his side, nodded in acknowledgment of the gesture and took the proferred seat. He glanced around the table, bobbed his head in greeting once more, and then sat there with a slightly vacant smile.

"Highness?" Durla said.

Londo still didn't respond until Dunseny nudged him slightly, then he seemed to come to himself. "Yes. Good to see me. And it is good to be seen. I felt that I had not been doing that sufficiently of late." He leaned forward, and said in a conspiratorial voice, "I raised quite a fuss on my way over, you know. People in the street pointed, whispered among themselves. 'Is that he?' they asked. 'Is that the emperor? I thought he was dead!' " Londo laughed at that rather heartily, until the laughter suddenly turned to a violent, racking cough. It took a full thirty seconds for it to subside, and during that time the ministers looked uncomfortably around the table at one another.

Finally Londo managed to compose himself. Dunseny solicitously dabbed at the edges of the emperor's mouth with a cloth.

Durla found it difficult to believe that the old retainer was still at Londo's side. Dunseny had managed to outlive every member of the House Mollari who had been there when he started with the family. He seemed thinner, greyer, but otherwise no less efficient in his duties and attentions. For a time Throk had replaced Dunseny, as a means of keeping a perpetual closer eye on Londo, but Throk had come to a bad end. At that point, Londo had firmly reinstated Dunseny, and Durla had decided to let the matter go rather than press it. Somehow it didn't seem worth the aggravation.

"My apologies, Ministers. Old age is not exactly a blessing."

"Then again, it's preferable to the alternative, Highness," Kuto said in his booming voice.

Londo shot a glance at him. "Is it?" he asked.

There didn't seem to be any ready response for this, and Kuto didn't try to make one.

Londo's gaze focused on Lione. "Minister . . . where did you acquire that scar on your throat?"

Lione automatically reached up to touch it, but caught himself. Without looking at Durla, he said, "A mishap, Emperor. Nothing more."

"Yes. Most unfortunate. I hear tell from Dunseny that there seems to be a virtual epidemic of clumsiness going on in the palace these days. Your wife, I hear tell, suffered such a seizure," Londo said, swiveling his gaze to Durla. "Odd. When I was married to her, she was the most graceful and coordinated of all the women whom I called wife. Curious that she would become so accident-prone. Perhaps the process of aging has been no kinder to her than to me, eh?"

There was something in his look that Durla definitely did not like. So he cleared his throat a bit more loudly than was needed, and said, "Highness . . . you still have not graced us with the purpose for your visit . . ."

"The purpose. Ah, yes. It is my understanding, Durla, that this meeting was being held to discuss the current state of readiness for the Centaurum's reclamation of our great and illustrious heritage—presumably, over the dead bodies of those who would stand in our way."

"May I ask who told you that, Highness?"

"Certainly. General Rhys did."

Durla, stunned, looked to the general. Rhys returned the look blandly. "His Highness asked," he said by way of explanation. "He is my emperor, the supreme ruler and commander of this world. If he asks me a question about the status of military readiness, naturally it is my obligation to respond truthfully."

"Ah. Pardon my surprise, General . . . you had not informed me that the emperor had asked."

"You did not ask, Minister."

Durla cursed to himself. That was typical of Rhys. He was a brilliant tactician and an utterly fearless fleet commander. But he had a streak of individuality that he flashed every so often, apparently for Durla's benefit. Technically, he had done nothing wrong. He was indeed obligated, through oath and historical tradition of his rank, to answer first and foremost to the emperor, with *no* obligation whatsoever to report those discussions to others . . . even the prime minister. If Durla made too much of an issue of his actions, it would reflect poorly on him.

"Highness," Durla said carefully, "these are matters of an extremely delicate and sensitive nature. In the future, I would appreciate if any inquiries you might wish to make on these subjects come through my office."

"Are you endeavoring to dictate terms to me, Durla?" Londo asked.

There was an undercurrent of danger in the tone that brought Durla up short. Suddenly he was beginning to regret that he had not taken steps to dispose of Londo ages ago. Granted, the military supported Durla. There was no question about that, and there was intense loyalty from those who remembered Durla from when he himself was part of the rank and file. They perceived him as one of their own. However, ranking and highly regarded officers—such as Rhys—continued to show respect for the position of emperor. Not even aberrations such as Cartagia had diminished the military compulsion to stand behind whoever held the highest rank in all of Centauri Prime. Durla had no desire to make Rhys and other higher-ranking officers, for whom Durla spoke, choose their allegiances. Because he had no real way of controlling how those choices would fall.

So he put forward his most ready smile, and said reassuringly, "Of course not, Highness. You are Centauri Prime. I would no sooner dictate terms to you than tell the sun which way to rise."

"Don't underestimate yourself, Prime Minister. I have little doubt that—if you thought you might succeed—you might easily decide that the sun should rise in the west so that you can sleep in."

This drew mild laughter from the others. Durla nodded amiably at the small joke made at his expense.

"We have quite a military industrial complex under way, Prime Minister," Londo continued. "Many papers are brought before me for my signature and seal. I have continued to sign off on them, as an indication of my support. For I believe, as do you—as do all of you—that Centauri Prime has a great destiny to pursue. Although I doubt I could put forth the matter so eloquently or enthusiastically as Minister Vallko."

"I am honored and flattered that you would think so, Highness," Vallko said. "I have always felt that our positions complemented each other. That you attended to the well-being of the bodies of our people . . . and I to their spirits."

"Well said, Minister, well said," Londo said, thumping the table with unexpected vigor. "And since the bodies of my people are involved in the work that you are doing, I wish to know where we stand."

"It is somewhat . . . involved, Highness."

"Then involve me."

Durla started to offer another protest, but he saw the firm, unyielding look on the emperor's face and abruptly realized that—most unexpectedly—things had become uncertain. He had to remind himself that there was really no need to keep Londo Mollari out of the loop. It wasn't as if he could do anything to thwart their efforts. The people's taste for conquest had only been whetted by strikes Centauri Prime had made against worlds at the outer fringes of the damnable Alliance's influence. There was already momentum involved, and there was no way that anyone, even the emperor, could stem the tide.

And, of course, he had no intention of doing so. Durla was

quite certain of that. This was merely an exercise in face-saving, that was all. When Centauri Prime achieved its destiny of conquest, Mollari wanted to be able to bask in the reflected glory. Understandable. Who wouldn't want to? But the people would know the truth, and the military—despite Rhys' knee-jerk compulsion—likewise would know it was Durla's vision that fired the Centauri movement. In the long run, Mollari's endeavors to attach himself to Durla's greatness would backfire. Durla was sure of that. He would be revealed for the posturing poseur that he was.

In the meantime, why risk alienating allies such as Rhys and those he represented just because he—Durla—was able to see through the emperor's pathetic maneuvering?

"Very well," Durla said simply.

And so he proceeded to lay out, in detail, all the up-to-date particulars of Centauri Prime's military buildup. All the outposts, operating under varying degrees of secrecy, that were assembling the Centauri fleet that would sweep out among the Alliance worlds and spread the ultimate dominance of the Centaurum.

"So we are not rushing into this," Londo said slowly, once Durla was finished providing the specifics.

"Absolutely not, Emperor. The initial strikes that we have made served a twofold purpose. First, we were testing the will of the Alliance members, and frankly, we are less than impressed. They have grown complacent in their prosperity and their sense of peace. To them, our attack on Narn was an aberration, a distant memory at best. We have managed, through a carefully orchestrated campaign of publicity and information, planned by Minister Lione and well executed by Minister Kuto . . ." and he gestured toward the pair, who nodded gratefully, "to associate those days—in the minds of the Alliance—with the reign of the mad emperor Cartagia. You, Highness, are seen as a very different animal."

"Certainly a less rabid one, I would hope," Londo said with a hint of irony. "So I am perceived as a comparatively benign, harmless ruler. An interesting epitaph, I suppose. 'Here lies Londo Mollari: a harmless enough fellow.' "

This drew a laugh from Kuto, who promptly silenced himself when he noticed that no one else was joining in.

Picking up after the momentary quiet, Durla continued, "We have further managed to pave the way, through backroom dealings, for key representatives of key governments to be . . . accommodating . . . to our attacks on assorted worlds. Furthermore, in launching the assaults, we have been testing the versatility and effectiveness of the vessels that we have assembled thus far. We are pleased to report that the tests of these prototypes have met with overwhelming success."

"Excellent." Londo nodded. Dunseny's head was likewise bobbing in agreement.

"There were a few places where ship performance could be improved." General Rhys spoke up. "Questions of maneuverability, and proper distribution of energy resources in weaponry. Problems that made no difference against small worlds that are relatively helpless . . . but could loom large when it comes to battles against the more powerful members of the Interstellar Alliance."

"We are attending to that, Highness," Lione quickly assured him. "I have scientists, technicians, going over all the specifics cited by the general and his board of advisers. Nothing is being left to chance."

"I have found, Minister, that 'chance' usually has its own feelings as to just what is being left to it, and has a habit of inserting itself into matters at its whim." Londo scratched his chin thoughtfully. "And it will come to a direct challenge to the Alliance, yes? I understand the reasons for concentrating on smaller worlds . . . but I cannot say I embrace it enthusiastically. It seems . . . beneath us, no? Considering what it is we wish to accomplish."

"The hard fact, Highness, is that the Alliance's attacks and strictures reduced us, militarily and technically, to a state of infancy," Durla said. Rhys looked as if he was bristling slightly, but he said nothing. Durla continued, "To that end, we must relearn how to walk before we can run. There is really no choice in the matter."

"But it is merely a temporary condition, Highness." Vallko spoke up. "Nothing is more firmly written in the book of fate than that the great Centauri Republic will hold the stars in its palm."

The words, to Durla's surprise, seemed to jolt Londo slightly. "Is there a problem, Highness?"

"No. No problem," Londo assured him quickly. "Just . . . a reminder . . . of an image I saw a long time ago. A vision . . . of just that. I think perhaps, Vallko, you are indeed correct."

"Of course he is correct, Highness," Durla said flatly. "Our timetable calls for, at most, another two years before a full fleet has been assembled. A fleet that will more than satisfy all the requirements put forward by General Rhys and his advisers. A fleet that will cover the known galaxy as comprehensively as grains of sand cover a beach." His voice began to rise as he became more and more taken with the impending realization of his vision. "When the time is right, we will launch a multistage assault on the Homeworlds of many of the Alliance governments, taking the war to them directly." He saw heads bobbing around the table, and Londo's gaze was fixed upon him in fascination. "If we strike hard enough, we can immobilize them, and pave the way for full-scale assaults on their holdings that will leave them powerless against further Centauri aggression."

"The only problem," Vallko said with a touch of caution, "remains Sheridan. This is a man who faced both Shadows and Vorlons, and caused them to back down. There are some who say he is more than Human."

"With all respect, Vallko, we are definitely more than Human," Durla reminded him. "That makes us more than a match."

But Vallko's worries were not so easily dissuaded. "It is said he cannot die. Or that he is already dead."

And from the end of the table came a whisper from Londo. " 'You must not kill the one who is already dead.' "

Confused looks were exchanged around the table. "Highness?" Dunseny prompted.

Londo looked up at Dunseny and forced a smile. "Just . . . remembering old voices, Dunseny. At my age, I am pleased I can remember anything. Then again, you are older than I am by far, and you never forget anything. Why is that?"

"Because, Highness, at my age, there are fewer things worth remembering."

The exchange drew an appreciative chuckle from the ministers.

"Sheridan is just one man," Durla reminded them, bringing the conversation back on track. "Let us not forget that he was involved with three great campaigns in his life: the Earth-Minbari War, the Shadow War, and his assault on his own Homeworld. Let us also not forget how each of those disputes was ultimately settled," and he ticked them off on his fingers. "The Minbari surrendered; the Vorlons and Shadows voluntarily stood down and departed from known space; and his prime nemesis on Earth, the president, was considerate enough to commit suicide. Sheridan has never been in a position where he faced an enemy who would not back down. That is not the case here. Who here would back down from him? Which of you would tell me that—if faced with John Sheridan demanding your surrender—you would willingly do so?"

It was Rhys who spoke immediately. "Death first."

There were agreeing nods from around the table.

"He will be facing a very different creature when the full might of the Centauri Republic is unleashed upon him," Durla said.

"The people do not feel that way," Kuto said.

Durla turned and gaped at him. "The people? The people do not?"

"I am not saying they do not support you, Prime Minister," Kuto said quickly as the gazes of the others fell upon him. "But Minister Vallko is correct. The people rejoice in our achievements and call out their support publicly . . . but privately, my research says, they still fear Sheridan."

"We cannot have that!" Durla replied. "This is an alarming comment on the state of the Centauri mind . . . and it must be addressed at once. *At once!* Kuto—arrange for a public speaking display. Immediately, do you hear me! Lione, Vallko, assist him!"

The other ministers were caught off guard by the sudden change of mood in the room, the abrupt way that Durla's attitude had shifted. But they hastened to obey his orders. Londo said nothing, and merely watched silently.

Within moments, Durla and Londo were standing at a balcony on one of the lower floors of the Tower of Power. There were no windows in the Tower, which added to the mystique of the place. There was, however, the one balcony, which Durla had insisted upon for just such an occasion. The Tower had been well placed, for there was always a crowd of people around the base, just going about their business.

When Durla spoke, his voice boomed throughout the entire city, thanks to a multitude of hidden speakers. Not only that, but his oversize holographic image appeared throughout Centauri Prime, carrying his word far and wide. People on the other side of the world were jolted from their sleep by the unexpected intrusion of Prime Minister Durla. Londo, although at his side, was mysteriously absent from the projection. Only Durla's image loomed large, which he felt was as it should be.

"It has been brought to my attention," Durla's voice echoed throughout the assemblage, all eyes below turning up toward him, "that as Centauri Prime returns to glory, there are many of you who fear reprisals from John Sheridan. Many who think that this man, who formed the Alliance, presents a threat to our world! That our recent, successful endeavors to expand our holdings will be met with resistance, and that we—as many others have—will surrender to President Sheridan, simply because he will ask us to! And why not? The Minbari surrendered. The Vorlons surrendered. The Shadows surrendered. Why not we?"

And he received exactly the answer he was hoping for. Someone below shouted, "Because we are Centauri!" Immediately others took up the shout.

"Yes! We are Centauri!" Durla announced, receiving a resounding cheer in return. "And in those instances when we choose to exercise our might, we will achieve nothing less than victory! Victory at all costs! Victory in spite of all terror! Victory, however long and hard the road may be, for without victory there is no survival!"

"Victory!" the people in the street shouted.

"We shall not flag or fail!" Durla continued. "We shall go on to the end. We shall fight in the void; we shall fight on planets; we shall fight in hyperspace; we shall fight on the Rim. We shall fight with growing confidence and growing strength in space; we shall defend our Homeworld, whatever the cost may be. We shall fight in the asteroid fields; we shall fight in the nebulae; we shall fight among the stars—*we shall never surrender!*"

The roar that went up was deafening, and seemed to go on forever. Durla drank it in, a virtual sponge for the adulation he was receiving. He stepped back in off the balcony to receive the congratulations from the other ministers.

"Well done! Very well done!" burbled Kuto, and the others echoed the sentiments.

Only Londo seemed to have any pause. "And tell me, Durla . . . what do you think the reaction of Sheridan will be when he hears this speech of yours? How do you think he will react? Are you not concerned that he may be moved to strike first?"

"No, Highness, I am not," Durla answered firmly. "If he and his precious Alliance have not attacked because of our deeds, they will certainly not attack because of words. They will perceive it as saber rattling, nothing more. But our people—our people will know it for what it is. They will know and remember, and when the time comes . . ."

"They will know that we will never surrender," Londo said.

"That is exactly right, Highness."

"Let us hope—for your sake, if nothing else—that President Sheridan sees it the same way," said Londo.

The shouting continued, and Durla was only slightly soured to note that although many bellowed for him, the name of "Mollari" was being shouted with equal enthusiasm. But then he contented himself by recalling that the people in the square were truly only a fraction of the populace. Everywhere else it was Durla, and only Durla. And that was as it should be. Let the people call out for Mollari along with Durla, if it pleased them. Eventually they would come to realize who truly ran things.

Once upon a time, Durla felt as if no one would ever recognize him for his own achievements and his intrinsic greatness. Those days, however, were long past. He could afford to be generous, to share the wealth of the people's adulation. For the moment. Mollari looked weaker with every passing day. Certainly he had his robust periods, but his cough was becoming more and more pronounced. It was indicative of something deeper, more damaging to the emperor's health. But for some reason, Mollari seemed disinclined to seek out medical attention. And Durla certainly was not going to push the matter.

The shouting grew louder and louder. "Highness, they call for us," Durla said, bowing low in a gesture that was slightly mocking. "Shall we go back out and satisfy their worship?"

"I have never had any desire to be worshipped, Prime Minister," Londo said with a touch of amusement. "But if it will please you . . ." and he gestured that they should go back out onto the balcony. They stepped out and waved once more to the crowd. The people cried out almost as one, shouting their names, praising them to the skies so that the Great Maker himself would take note.

And that was when the shot rang out.

EXCERPTED FROM
THE CHRONICLES OF LONDO MOLLARI.
Excerpt dated (approximate Earth date)
September 24, 2275.

I did not hear it at first, because the shouts of the crowd were so deafening. Instead what I felt, rather than saw, was a sharp sensation across my forehead. I put my hand up to it to see what it could be, and when my hand came away it was tinged pink with blood. Then there was a sound, that of a ricochet, or of something striking nearby, and then a second.

I've been shot, I thought, and for a moment I felt—not concern or fear—but instead an almost giddy sense of accomplishment. So long had I been haunted by the image of G'Kar with his hands at my throat, I was almost resigned to it. If I was to die at the hand of an unknown assassin, then I had managed to thwart destiny. It was cold comfort to be sure, but given the comfort I had received of late, "cold" was almost a warming trend.

Before I could think or feel anything else, I was being hauled backward by my personal guards. Durla was likewise being hurried away from the balcony, General Rhys himself ducking Durla's head for him to make certain he was not hit. Below, the people were still cheering; they had not yet figured out what was happening.

"The emperor's been shot!" one of the guards cried out.

And then Dunseny was standing directly in front of me. He was saying loudly and firmly, in that no-nonsense tone that only the very old can successfully carry off, "Step aside. Let me see him." Amazingly, the guards halted in their ushering me away, and Dunseny inspected my forehead with clinical expertise. "He hasn't been shot," he announced sourly, and it was hard to tell whether his tone of voice was from annoyance at those who had pronounced me injured, or because he was aggrieved to discover it wasn't the case. He had a cloth out and was dabbing at the bleeding, which was already trickling off. "No burn marks," he said expertly. "It's a cut. A blast must have hit above or nearby him, chipped off a small piece of the building, and the flying debris cut across his head. See? It's stopping already."

"I am not surprised," I growled. "Blood circulates up there for the brain, and I have not been making many demands upon it lately."

General Rhys was already barking orders both to my guards and to his own security people. Although his authority extended only to the latter, everyone was attending to every word he uttered. "Get down there! Find the shooter or shooters! The emperor and the prime minister will stay here until the area is secured!"

"The crowd is huge, General, how will we—" one of his security staff began.

Rhys gave him a look that could have sliced him in half. *"Move!"* he bellowed with such force that his voice alone almost knocked the man off his feet.

The next hour was very confused, with mixed and conflicting reports being fed to us every few minutes. Durla, the other ministers, and I returned to the room where the briefing had been held, and there was great speculation among all of them as to who or what was responsible for this atrocious assault upon my sacrosanct person. The consensus seemed to be that the Alliance was behind it—Sheridan in particular. I did not believe it for a moment, and said so. "Sheridan may be many things," I told them flatly, "but an assassin is not one of them." They accepted my opinion with polite attention, but I suspected that they believed they knew far better than I about such matters.

Dunseny, meantime, expertly bandaged the wound on my head, although it was such a pathetic thing, really, that he needn't have bothered. I can only assume that he found that activity preferable to simply standing there and letting me bleed.

General Rhys disappeared, presumably to oversee the search-and-destroy mission personally. When he returned, he did not simply enter the room. Instead he virtually exploded into it, pushing the sliding doors aside since, apparently, they did not move quickly enough to suit him. "We have him," Rhys said without any preamble, and then added, "A more bizarre set of circumstances we have never seen." He turned, and shouted, "Bring them in!"

When I saw who was being led into the room, I was stunned.

Brought in side by side were Yson of House Yson, and another individual. Yson, burly and taciturn as always, was glaring. But no one was noticing; it was the person beside him who garnered all the attention.

"G'Kar?" I barely recognized my own voice. I didn't know whether to laugh or cry. "G'Kar?" I said again.

"The emperor remembers my name. I am flattered," he said.

Kuto was immediately on his feet. "Immediately," though, may be too generous a term. It took him long moments to thrust himself to standing as his bulk fought gravity and won, but just barely. "What a magnificent day!" Kuto called out, apparently creating the release for the press even as he spoke. "Yson, one of our own nobles, fought to stop a vicious, bloodthirsty Narn from shooting and killing our beloved emperor!"

"No."

It was a young voice that had spoken, and then I saw that a number of the Prime Candidates had crowded in at the door. Clearly they had been in the midst of a struggle. Their hair was disheveled, and some of them had torn clothing. In the forefront was one I thought I recognized. But I could not remember his name if someone had put a gun to my head. I knew because, after all, someone practically had just done so, and his name still was not forthcoming.

"What do you mean, Caso?" asked Lione, graciously supplying the missing piece of information for me.

Caso pointed at Yson. "He was the one who was shooting. The Narn was trying to stop him."

"What?" Durla sounded horrified. "A Narn saved our emperor? And . . . *this* Narn?" The notion that a Narn might have had a hand in preserving my life must have seemed for him to go against the natural order. Imagine, then, his even greater astonishment when Yson himself spoke up.

"Not him," Yson said with great annoyance. "I wasn't shooting at the emperor. I was shooting at you, Durla."

One of the guards stepped forward. He was carrying a phased plasma gun. "Yson used this, Highness," he said, proffering it to me, as a hunter would deliver a trophy.

"I . . . I don't understand," Durla said. To my delight, he was stammering. It was a joy seeing him coming so close to losing his composure completely. "Caso . . . you claim that you saw it all?"

"Not all, Prime Minister," said Caso. For some reason, the others seemed to be tossing him unkind looks, but Caso did not let it perturb him. Or if it did perturb him, he did not let it show. "We were close enough to hear the first shot, despite the din of the crowd around us. We fought our way through, and there discovered that Yson was struggling with his weapon, a red-haired Centauri in the process of trying to yank it from his hands."

"A red-haired Centauri? But then how did the Narn—"

"He has a name, Durla," I interjected, sounding far calmer than I actually was. "Considering you apparently owe him your life, you could at least do him the courtesy of using it."

Durla looked ready to argue the point, but apparently decided it was not worth it. "How did . . . Citizen G'Kar . . . become involved? And where did he come from?"

"He . . . *was* the Centauri. It was apparently a holographic disguise of some sort. Whatever device was generating it was broken during the struggle, and the disguise dissipated."

Durla's eyes went wide. "A changeling net," he whispered. "They are illegal!"

"Arrest me," said G'Kar.

Slowly Durla rose from his seat. He was trembling with barely contained rage. "Oh, I will do more than arrest you! I will have you executed for . . . for . . ."

"Saving your life?" G'Kar was merely amused. I was not surprised. After all that G'Kar had endured in his life, it took far more than the ire of a Centauri politician—even a highly placed one—to give him pause. "Execution might not be such a terrible fate," he continued, sounding philosophical. "The fact that it took me as long as it did to dispatch this . . . person," and he indicated Yson with a nod, "is a bit embarrassing. I can only attribute it to the deleterious effects caused by extended use of a changeling net. Don't worry. Given time to recover, I'm certain that I will be sufficiently strong to take on anyone in this room if so inclined."

"I will have you executed," Durla said, reining himself in, "for trespassing on Centauri Prime. Alien races are forbidden . . . or had you forgotten?"

"I forgot completely," G'Kar replied. "I wore the disguise only because I wanted to have hair. Tall hair."

Great Maker, I'd missed him.

"You wore the disguise to spy on us! You are a trespasser and a spy! For that alone, your life is forfeit."

"But it is not that alone, Durla," I said. I rose from my chair. My legs felt slightly unsteady, and I took a moment until I was certain that I could endure the simple act of standing. "That must be factored in with the debt that is owed him by you . . . and by me. Perhaps Yson's intent was to dispense with you, but I could just as easily have fallen within his target. Correct, Yson?"

Yson looked at me with utter scorn. "Durla is power mad. He has nothing but contempt for the Houses. For the traditions of Centauri Prime. But you . . . you are worse. For there is nothing worse than a weak emperor."

Slowly I nodded.

Then, in one motion, I turned and pulled on the ceremonial sword that General Rhys had in his scabbard. I admired the hissing noise it made as it slid out. Yson's expression of disdain was still on his face as I turned and swung my arm as fast as I could. The blade was as sharp as it sounded, and I was pleased to see that my arm still had some strength in it. Yson's sneer was frozen even as his head slid from his shoulders and thudded to the floor.

No one said a word.

I pointed the sword at G'Kar. His one eye glittered at me.

"Are you free for dinner?" I asked.

── *chapter 8* ──

David Sheridan could see the eye, looking at him, and it seemed far less fearsome than when it had first appeared.

He still could remember exactly the first time that he had noticed it. He had just turned twelve, and had fallen asleep after a long day of celebration. In his dreams, he had been running, just running, across a great Minbari plain. He wasn't doing so out of fear, or pursuit. He was running simply for the pure joy of running, of feeling the youthful energy channeling through him, feeding him as if there was an endless supply that would carry him through an eternity of sprinting.

Finally he had stopped. It wasn't out of a need to catch his breath, but because he felt as if he should stop, because he was *supposed* to catch his breath. Then again, this was a dream, after all, and he was the one who set the parameters.

And then, for no reason he could discern, the world around him started to go dim. It was as if a total eclipse had suddenly and inexplicably sprung into existence. He looked up at the Minbari sun that had provided warmth and comfort for as long as he could remember.

The sun looked back down at him. A single great eye had taken up the entirety of it, and it was peering at him in silence.

He stared at it, transfixed. It blinked once, then again, and then it addressed him.

Hello, little sun, it said.

The scream had begun within the dream, but reached its completion when David sat up in bed. Unfortunately Minbari beds were upright slabs, and as a result David fell forward and hit the floor. He lay there, gasping, clutching the cool tiles, soaked with sweat and looking around as if afraid that the eye might still be upon him. Even though he knew that it made no sense, he ran to the window and looked to the moon, but found no eye peeking back.

Nevertheless he did not go back to sleep. He stayed there at the window, unmoving, waiting to watch the sun rise so that he could make sure for himself that the sun was as it usually was. He wasn't disappointed, for the sun shone that morning in all its normalcy, washing away the last dregs of that heart-stopping dream.

But he had not forgotten it. That would have been impossible . . . because every so often, the eye returned. Not very often; just from time to time, as if it was checking on him.

As terrifying as he had found it that first time, it became less so with each subsequent exposure. The eye never did anything harmful or threatening. It just watched him, occasionally saying a couple of well-chosen, nonintimidating words. He asked one of his teachers about it and was told that it undoubtedly represented either his mother or his father, or perhaps both. It was, they said, a subconscious desire to know that—when he was at his most vulnerable—his parents were watching over him and keeping him from harm. From then on, David gradually relaxed to its presence, seeing it not as a threatening image, but as a symbol that all was right with the world.

This particular night, the eye had returned, after an absence of many months. It did so, however, in a very odd way. David was dreaming that he was having dinner with himself. The "self" seated on the other side of the dining table appeared a few years older, and he possessed a look of quiet confidence. What was particularly odd was that he had a hair crest that was evocative of the Centauri. David couldn't for the life of him figure out why his older self looked like that.

"Do you like it?" the older David asked. "I'm not sure if it's me or not. What do you think?"

Young David shrugged.

"Good. No opinion. Not thinking," older David said. "Not thinking is what you'll want to do." And then his forehead blinked.

David stared more closely, having at first accepted the unreality of the moment without question. But now he was struck by the oddness of the fact that the elder David had a third eye. It was nestled serenely smack in the middle of his forehead, and it was staring at him. He recognized it instantly.

"That's my eye," he said.

There was a sudden rush of wings, and David jumped slightly. A bird, a crow of some kind, perched atop the elder David's head. He didn't seem to notice the weight.

"Does it offend you? If so, it can be plucked out," said the elder David. And then the crow stabbed its beak down and snatched out the eye from his forehead. David gasped as the orb was swallowed up effortlessly, and then the crow, or raven, or whatever it was, flapped its wings and took off.

"Are you all right?" he asked urgently.

More plates of food materialized in front of the older David. "Fine," he said. "See?" He pointed . . . and the eye was back. "It will always be there," he said. "Always. Waiting. Loving you."

The eye stared at him, stared through him, and David felt vaguely uncomfortable, but he couldn't quite determine why.

"Dammit!"

It was his father's voice, explosive and angry, and it was enough to snap David to full wakefulness. He blinked against the darkness, but saw that there was light filtering through the window. It was early morning.

His father had stormed past David's room, and for a moment David thought that his father was angry with him. But he continued walking, and behind him David heard his mother moving, as well. She said in a soft but rushed voice, "John, hush! You'll wake David!"

"That's the least of my concerns, Delenn," he retorted, but he lowered his voice nevertheless. They continued to speak, and G'Kar was mentioned, but he couldn't make out what they were talking about.

The timing of the sudden jolt couldn't have been better. The dream was still fresh in his mind, much more so than if he'd woken up on his own. He stepped down off his bed, reached for a robe, and pulled it around himself. Then he padded noiselessly down the hall, following his parents' voices.

Finding them presented no difficulty. They were in his father's main office, and he could tell from the way his father's voice came from one side of the room, then the other, that his father was pacing.

"We have to do something about this," Sheridan was saying. "We can't just let G'Kar sit there in Centauri hands!"

"It's not that simple, John . . ."

"Yes. It is. We go to the Alliance, or the Narns specifically, and say—"

"And say what?" There was a sharpness, a hardness in her voice that hadn't been there before. "That G'Kar was captured while on Centauri Prime? They will ask why . . . a reasonable enough question. After all, the Centauri have made no secret of the fact that off-worlders are forbidden. And you will tell the Alliance . . . what? That G'Kar was there because you and he had a tacit understanding that he was supplying you information about the Centauri? That he wasn't telling you how he was acquiring this information, and that you were not inquiring? That your 'hand' was caught in the cracker jar?"

Despite the seriousness of the moment, Sheridan laughed shortly. "Cookie jar."

"Who cares?" she retorted. "John, G'Kar knew the risks, as did you. You accepted those, as did he. And now he is dealing with the consequences, as you must."

"And I'm going to deal with them by getting him out. Fine, I won't go to the Alliance. I'll get him out myself."

"You'll be killed."

"It won't be the first time."

"How dare you."

Crouching, David peeked around the edge of the door frame. His father had stopped in his tracks and was staring at his mother. She was much smaller than he was, yet at that moment her anger was so great that it seemed to fill the room. *"How dare you,"* she repeated.

"How dare I? How dare I what?"

"How dare you recklessly and foolhardily throw away your life on a hopeless mission just to satisfy your ego."

"This has nothing to do with ego," he protested.

Before he could continue, she cut him off. "Yes, just as when you went to Z'ha'dum," she said, and clearly the very recollection of it was difficult for her. David had heard mention made of that dead world several times, and he knew that his father had journeyed to it. There were even tales that he had died there, but that was nonsense, of course. After all, there he was, clearly alive. "And at the time you went," she continued, "you were 'only' the commander of Babylon 5. We were not married. You had no son. You had no Alliance of which you were the president. You were young and cloaked with the banner of righteousness, and no doubt you thought you would live forever. None of those have been, or are any longer, the case. You have responsibilities to me, to David, to the other races in the Alliance."

"And my responsibility to G'Kar?"

"He is where he needs to be. They are not going to hurt him. Vir already passed that information along to us. He has been given humane, if Spartan, accommodations in the palace itself."

"And he's not being allowed to leave!"

"John . . . perhaps he is not supposed to," Delenn suggested reasonably. "Perhaps circumstances have conspired to put G'Kar right where he is supposed to be. Londo is cut off there, surrounded by many destructive forces. My guess is that, on that entire planet, he had not one ally on whom he could utterly depend. G'Kar is now that ally. Who knows what poisons have been whispered into Londo's ear. Who knows what dark forces may be shaping his thinking?"

"And you're saying G'Kar can undo that." He sounded skeptical.

"I'm saying he might be able to. He certainly has a far greater chance of doing so by being there. Those two . . . G'Kar and Londo . . . they are bound by fate, John. They circle each other, like binary stars."

"Binary stars," Sheridan reminded her, "allow no life between them. Their gravity wells crush whatever planets might start to form."

"Yes," she said. "I know. And that may well be the case with G'Kar and Londo, as well. They may well be destined to crush all life between them with the intensity of their will, until nothing is left. Perhaps not even them."

"Is that supposed to make me feel better somehow?"

"No. It is simply supposed to be a statement of what I believe. Unless my beliefs are no longer of importance to you."

He sighed heavily. "Of course they're of importance to me." He embraced her, holding her so tight that David thought he was going to break her. "It's just . . . when I think of G'Kar in that place, surrounded by enemies . . ."

"This is G'Kar we're talking about. He thrives on that sort of situation. Sometimes I think he's not happy unless he's surrounded by enemies. And he may be able to make a difference, John. He might very well be of far more service there than anywhere else."

And then David jumped—as a loud voice came from behind him. "And what have we here?" In an instant he was on his feet, turning at the same time. As a result he tripped himself up and landed hard on his own backside.

Master Vultan, his occasional teacher and frequent source of frustration, was standing right behind him, arms folded. "Spying, are we?" he asked in a stern voice, his bearded chin bristling with indignation. It was difficult for David to tell just how genuinely annoyed Vultan really was.

Determining the annoyance level of his parents, however, was no problem at all. When Delenn and Sheridan emerged from his office to investigate what the noise was about, they both stared down at their son and frowned. "How long were you hiding there, David?" his father demanded.

"Since you woke me up with your shouting," David replied.

This got Sheridan a dirty look from Delenn, which he did his best to ignore. "You shouldn't be hiding there, listening in on other people's conversations," Sheridan told him.

"You're right. Next time I'll find a better place to hide," he agreed, standing and dusting himself off.

His mother was not the least bit amused. "David . . . your actions were inappropriate."

He sighed heavily, and said, "I'm sorry, Mother." He was far slower to employ his sharp and ready wit on his mother. He just couldn't help but feel that he was far less likely to get away with it than he was with his father. He had a feeling that, secretly, his father was amused by his son's rebellious streak. That certainly made sense; after all, John Sheridan had practically written the book on rebellion. "I'm sorry, Father," he continued. "But when I heard you mention G'Kar . . . well, I've always liked him, and I hate to think about him being in trouble."

Sheridan sighed and seemed less irate than he had moments before. Now he just looked sad. "So do I, David. Your mom, too. But she's right: at this point, it's G'Kar's play. We have it on reliable authority that he is in no danger. On that basis, he may very well be able to do a lot of good, working from the inside, as it were."

Vultan looked from Sheridan to Delenn and back. "Are neither of you going to punish the boy? He eavesdropped. Certainly that behavior cannot be tolerated."

"You're absolutely right," Sheridan said firmly. "David: extend your left hand."

David immediately did as his father dictated. John Sheridan stepped forward sternly, looked down at the outstretched hand, and then slapped it once lightly on the knuckles. "Let that be a lesson to you," he said gravely.

"I shall never forget it, Father," David replied seriously.

Vultan rolled his eyes and shook his head in exasperation. "That child," he informed them, "doesn't need a teacher, or parents. He needs a keeper."

The moment he said that, something cold clutched at the base of David's neck. He trembled, and the look on his face caught his mother's attention. "David . . . what's wrong?"

Sheridan saw it, too. "What's the matter, son?"

"I don't know," David confessed. "Just the oddest feeling, that's all. It's like . . . like . . ."

"Like someone just stepped on your grave?" Sheridan suggested. "That's what my dad used to say when he'd get that look on his face."

"Yeah. Something like that," David agreed.

"I do not like that phrase," Delenn said curtly. "Please don't use it again."

"All right," Sheridan said, clearly not quite understanding his wife's reaction, but not wanting to argue. He turned his attention to David's teacher, and said, "Master Vultan . . . I think that David might be a bit starved for attention. I confess I've been somewhat preoccupied lately, and the boy has had to resort to tactics such as this just to get a crumb of attention. It's not right. If it's all the same to you, I think his mother and I would like to spend the day with him."

"As you desire," Vultan said, looking not the least bit upset over the prospect. He turned on his heel and departed, his long robes swishing softly on the polished floor.

"Go get washed and dressed, David," his father said. "Perhaps we'll take a shot at climbing the Mulkeen Heights today. Best view on Minbar, so I'm told."

"Okay, Father," David said. Then, recalling how disconcerted he'd felt just a short time ago, he quickly embraced his parents before running off down the hallway.

"He's your son," Delenn said, shaking her head as she watched him go.

"So you keep telling me," Sheridan remarked. "Part of me thinks you keep on saying so because you're hoping to establish some sort of alibi." Then he turned serious once more. "Do you really think G'Kar will be okay?"

"Vir is certain. The situation under which G'Kar was taken was quite unique. It's Vir's opinion that Londo is watching out for him."

"And Vir's opinion can be trusted?"

"I think so, yes. Don't you?"

He gave it a moment's thought, and remembered Garibaldi's description of the events surrounding that last visit to Centauri Prime . . . the one that had resulted in the death of Lou Welch. Michael had been uncharacteristically taciturn about the affair, but had managed to convey—through fewer words rather than more—that Vir Cotto had a handle on things. Sheridan even suspected, although he couldn't prove it, that Vir was somehow involved with the occasional acts of "terrorism" that the Centauri tried to ascribe to the Alliance.

So Sheridan said finally, "Yes, I think it probably can. It's hard to believe, considering how Vir used to be, that he is now one of the most dependable of all the Centauri."

"We've all changed, John, from what we used to be. Look at you . . . and me . . ." and she playfully pulled at his beard while running her fingers through her long black hair. There were a few tinges of grey in it.

"You're saying that we all have more hair?" he said. "Well, there's worse fates." Then, once again, he turned solemn. "We have more hair . . . but G'Kar has one less eye. And he lost it on that world where he is right now. If things turn ugly there, he could lose the other . . . and far more."

"That is the downside," she admitted. "On the other hand, there is always the bright side. Do you remember that urn?"

"Urn?" he asked, not certain what she was referring to.

"The vase," she prompted. "The one Londo gave us . . ."

"Oh! Yes. The last time we saw him. The one we're supposed to give David on his sixteenth birthday . . ."

She nodded. "With the waters from the palace river locked in its base. I found it in storage recently. It reminded me of how Londo was that day . . . the last day we saw him. He seemed so desperate just to have even the slightest hint of friendship . . . from us . . . from anyone . . ."

"And you think G'Kar will provide him that."

"We can only hope. Do you think that we should give the vase to David early? Before his sixteenth birthday?"

"Nah," Sheridan decided. "Let's honor Londo's request. The man who dropped that vase off was the closest thing to the Londo of old that I could recall. I miss him. There's no telling how this entire Centauri situation is going to play out. But on David's sixteenth birthday, whatever the outcome, he'll at least get a sense of the Londo Mollari that we once all knew."

— *chapter 9* —

The catacombs beneath the capital city were considered by many to be little more than a myth. Ostensibly, the great Emperor Olion had constructed them, centuries earlier. Olion, so legend had it, was absolutely paranoid over the notion of his people turning against him. So he had the catacombs constructed as a means of escaping any pursuit. Supposedly he was the only person aside from the actual creator of the catacombs—whom he subsequently had assassinated—to know the layout of the maze. The catacombs led from the city to the outlying regions and provided a handy means of getting in and out unseen, if one were so inclined, not to mention eluding pursuit.

But it was all the stuff of legend. The entrances certainly no longer existed. And even if they did exist, the tunnels would be so overrun with vermin that they would be virtually unpassable.

Years ago, however, when he was a young man looking for fossil remains of primitive Centauri cultures, Renegar—a heavyset lad even at that tender age—had literally fallen into myth.

Renegar had embarked on a one-man excavation on the outskirts of the hinterlands. The ground had given way, and he had fallen through into the catacombs of lore. When he had picked himself up, dusted himself off, and managed to push aside the mounting feelings of panic, he actually found himself rather taken with the place. True, the vermin population wasn't particularly appreciated, but the prospects of exploration proved too enticing for him to pass up.

Having almost no friends, and parents who displayed little interest in his comings and goings, Renegar wasn't about to share with anyone his new and exciting discovery.

He brought sounding equipment and other locator devices that hadn't existed centuries ago when the catacombs were first built. Over the course of many years, he managed to map the place rather thoroughly . . . aided and abetted by the occasional explosive device. Rock falls and other natural "disasters" had blocked some of the paths, and Renegar quickly discovered that the judicious use of explosives could be tremendously helpful. The key word was "judicious," of course. The first time he tried, he nearly blew himself to kingdom come. Necessity became the mother of invention, and his familiarity with explosives and excavation came to serve him well in later life.

The catacombs, as well, found new purpose.

Renegar made his way to the meeting area with sure, steady steps, his knowledge of the catacombs by now so ingrained that he no longer needed the maps he had taken such pains to create in his youth. A rodent ran across his foot, and he kicked it out of the way. It was fortunate that such creatures didn't bother him, else he never would have been able to last in his exploration of the caves.

"Renegar!" The whisper came from up ahead, and he recognized the voice instantly. "Is that you?"

"Of course it's me. Who else would it be?" he asked grimly. He climbed over one more rise and came around a corner to discover the others whom he had decided—insanely, he sometimes thought—to trust not only with his life, but the future of his world.

Vir, naturally, was among them. So was Dunseny. There were far more people Vir had managed to enlist over the years, but no one, with the exception of Vir, knew everyone who was a part of the rebellion. That was probably wise, Renegar mused, but he couldn't help but feel that it put a massive amount of strain on Vir himself.

The strain was beginning to show. Vir was looking more tired, even a bit more despondent, than he usually did. But there was still an air of grim determination about him, as if—having decided upon the course he must follow—he had resolved that he would see it through to the end, no matter what.

"You saw?" Vir said without preamble, and Renegar knew precisely what he was talking about.

"How could I not see? That damnable Durla was everywhere. Is it true, though? That someone tried to kill them both? The emperor and Durla?"

"Durla, for the most part. The emperor was simply at the wrong place at the wrong time," Dunseny said.

"That might well summarize his life," Vir commented ruefully. Then, in a more businesslike tone, he added, "But it's not going to end there. Durla will never let it end there. If one House head endeavored to dispose of him, he's going to fear that all of them may form an alliance against him."

"You're saying he's going to declare war on the Houses?" asked one surly-looking but forceful fighter named Adi.

"Without a doubt. And that can only benefit us."

"How?" The question was echoed around the group, but it was Dunseny who answered.

"The House heads have resources. The military may back Durla, making his power unassailable, but the Houses have their own resources, ranging from personnel to weapons. Not only that, but there are key military personnel who owe ancient allegiances to the Houses, which supersede any way they may be beholden to Durla. In battling the Houses, in challenging the House heads directly, Durla may be sowing dissent within his own support system."

"He won't realize the danger if he thinks he's above them .... which he does," Vir said. "It's the oldest danger in the world: arrogance becomes the enemy's undoing."

"Yes . . . including yours."

They turned to see who had spoken, and there was a collective and startled gasp from all of them.

A grey-skinned creature stood in the shadows.

Renegar immediately went for his weapon, and the voice boomed again from the monster. "It's too late. Whatever you do to me is of no consequence. Since I have seen you, I will commune with my brethren, and they will in turn seek you out. I've seen all your faces. You're finished. But first . . ." The creature paused dramatically. "I'm going to sing a few show tunes."

The others looked at each other.

"Juuuust me . . . and my shaaadow . . ." the creature from the darkness began.

"Tell me I'm dreaming," Adi said.

Vir was watching the entire scene with a severe lack of amusement. "Finian," he said sternly. "What sort of foolishness is this? I recognize your voice; I know it's you."

At that, the creature slumped to the ground in front of the incredulous group. It was at that point that they were able to see the wound that gaped in the back of its head, thick liquid coagulating around it. Clearly the thing, whatever it was, was dead. Then all eyes shifted as Finian, the techno-mage, stepped into view. "Did I scare you?"

"Yes," Vir said flatly.

"Good." This time it wasn't Finian who spoke, but rather Gwynn, another techno-mage who seemed to have taken an interest in the events that occurred on Centauri Prime. Finian, as always, maintained something of an open manner, with his round face and blue eyes that seemed incapable of any sort of deceit. Of course, that alone provided reason enough not to trust him.

As for Gwynn, her attitude was as imperious as ever. She looked at them as if she were observing them from a great height that made their concerns seem childish and irrelevant. Renegar didn't trust either of them. As a general rule of thumb, trusting techno-mages wasn't an especially advisable pastime.

"You have every reason to be scared," Gwynn continued. "We found him wandering the catacombs. He had a bit of an . . . accident. Rocks, even boulders, can come loose around here at the most unexpected times. If they strike unexpectedly enough, and with sufficient force . . ." She shrugged. "The results can be tragic, as you see."

"What is it?" Adi said, looking at it wonderingly.

"That," Vir told him, "is a Drakh. One of the creatures I told you about. Told all of you about," he said, raising his voice. Not that anyone was having trouble hearing him, his voice echoing there in the tunnels. "The creatures who brought a plague to humanity. The ones who are operating behind the scenes here on Centauri Prime. And, I believe, the ones who are truly responsible for the 'visions' that our beloved prime minister is always talking about."

"What's it doing down here?" Renegar demanded.

"We are not sure," Gwynn said evenly, "but he may or may not have followed you, Renegar."

Renegar turned deathly pale. "Impossible," he spat out. "He couldn't have known to follow me . . ."

"Perhaps not," Finian agreed. "He may have simply stumbled

upon the catacombs on his own, and heard people talking. But I don't think so. I think the Drakh observe everyone, all the time . . . and something about Renegar's actions caught this one's attention."

The others looked accusingly at Renegar. He stepped back defensively. "I didn't know!"

Voices began to be raised in anger, but Vir shouted them down. "No one is blaming you, Renegar," he assured his fellow rebel.

"Then maybe someone should be," Gwynn responded. "This is not a game, Vir."

"Don't you think I know that!" Vir shot back at her. "I had one of these damned things in my head, Gwynn! I know what they're capable of!"

"Then know that you were most fortunate that we intercepted this one," Finian said. "We believe that although they have the ability to communicate telepathically with one another, it doesn't happen instantaneously. There is a procedure involved in which they sort of 'agree' to commune en masse. It takes some effort and preparation, and I doubt this one had the time to engage in it. As far as the Drakh are concerned, this fellow will simply have dropped off the face of the planet. They will keep an eye out for him, put their feelers out, and try to locate him. We will make certain that they do not succeed."

"We cannot keep covering for you, however," Gwynn said.

"We haven't been asking you to," Vir pointed out. "It's not as if we've been needing you to hold our hands. We've been doing fairly well on our own. We've managed to impede Durla's war machine . . ."

"Not enough." Again, it was Dunseny who spoke up. In quick, broad strokes he described all that he had heard at the briefing in the Tower of Power.

Vir was pacing by the time Dunseny was finished. "It's obvious that nothing short of total domination is going to satisfy Durla."

"Durla and the Drakh who support him," Finian said.

There were nods from all around. "It's clear what we have to do," Renegar said. "What we've been doing up to now is fine, as far as it goes. But we have to go further. We have to take on the

Drakh, head-to-head. We have to drive these creatures off the face of Centauri Prime!"

There were shouts of agreement, but then Vir's voice carried over theirs once more. "If we take on the Drakh head-to-head, we'll be wiped out."

"You took them on," Renegar said. "You told me yourself. You blew up that death station that the Shadows left behind."

"Yes. I did," Vir confirmed. "And I got lucky. The majority of the Drakh weren't around when it happened; if they had been, the station would have been left intact. The problem is, the Drakh are *always* around on Centauri Prime. They're watching Londo, they're watching Durla, and they're watching me. Their agents and influence are everywhere.

"Plus, we still don't completely know what their influence over Londo is. There are too many pieces we don't have, too many things that aren't ready."

"We're ready for freedom!" Renegar asserted.

"But we're not ready for suicide," Adi said.

"Coward!"

"I'm no coward." Adi wasn't so easily riled as to react to insults. "I'm just not an idiot, either."

"He's right," Finian said, "as is Vir. You still don't have enough raw power backing you up, and you dare not confront the Drakh directly without it. You will have only one chance to do so, and if you are not fully prepared, they will annihilate you."

"So what do we do?" Renegar demanded.

"We do," Vir told him, "exactly what we've been doing. We prepare things slowly, methodically."

"And get killed?" Renegar replied. "The way Rem did?"

There was dead silence at that. The loss of Rem Lanas was still a gaping wound.

"Maybe," Vir finally said. "Or maybe we're ready when the time is right."

"The more time passes, the more ships Durla gets into place, the more the odds skew in his favor," Renegar said.

"Not necessarily," Finian said. "Your attacks on the construction efforts slow them . . . while you continue to convert individuals or groups over to your cause. At the very least, you sow seeds of suspicion, so that when the full Drakh influence is revealed, the people will come flocking to your cause."

"Also, the Drakh will become overconfident," Gwynn said. "The closer the fleet comes to completion, the more sure they will be in their conduct. You see . . . they have no glory of their own. They bask purely in the evil of the Shadows. The Shadows were far greater than their servants, but if the Drakh believe they are attaining the Shadows' purpose, they will assume an air of invincibility."

"And that will be a mistake," Vir said. "Besides . . . we need their resources."

"What resources?" Adi asked.

"Don't you see?" Vir smiled in grim amusement. "The Drakh on this world . . . they aren't the only ones. The entire foul race has contaminated everything good and noble there ever was about Centauri Prime. We don't just want to stop them. We want to obliterate them. We want them to pay for Rem Lanas . . . for corrupting every office and every official of importance in our world, up to and including the emperor.

"They, through puppets such as Durla, are constructing engines of destruction. We impede the creation of those engines because we need time to build up our own assets. But ultimately, the fleet will be completed. It's inevitable . . . but it's also desirable . . ."

"Of course," Adi said, understanding. "Because once it's completed, we can use it against the Drakh themselves."

"Yes," said Dunseny. "They think that the fleet will go up against the Alliance . . . when in fact they're aiding in the creation of the very fleet that's going to be used to assault the Drakh."

"Exactly." There wasn't much light in the cavern, but what there was danced with almost hellish glee in Vir's eyes. "If we are patient . . . and thorough . . . and build up our forces . . . we will be triumphant. It *is* possible to take the long view. Once I met a servant of the Shadows. I told him that I longed to see his head on a pole and that, if it happened, I would wave to him like this." And he demonstrated, waggling his fingers in a manner that almost seemed comical. "It took several years . . . but that was exactly what happened."

"But how long can we sustain this?" Renegar asked. "Because if we are not careful, it'll be our heads up on poles, just as happened with poor Lanas."

"We will sustain it as long as is necessary," Vir told him firmly. "Remember, there are more, many more in our little movement. And we will get the job done. We have our connections. We will continue to get information, and use it well. But if we rush into anything, we'll be carried along in the tidal wave of events . . . and get swamped. We have to ride the crest of it and, in that way, stay above it."

"But we have techno-mages on our side," Renegar pointed out. "The two of you have stayed mostly in the background. Your disposing of this," and he nudged a toe into the body of the Drakh, "is something of a departure. Either you stay away or, when you do show up, you utter a few cryptic comments. But otherwise, for the most part, you keep to yourselves."

"That is because you are not our pawns," Finian told them. "You do as you wish, when and where you wish. We are, however, not averse to watching your backs every now and again." He indicated the fallen Drakh. "Case in point."

"Do not presume that we always will, though," Gwynn warned. "Your boundless enthusiasm is a disincentive. Plus, we have our own affairs to consider. So I suggest you do not try our patience . . ."

"For you are subtle and quick to anger?" Vir asked. When Gwynn nodded, looking a bit surprised, Vir explained, "Londo once told me that a techno-mage said that to him, many years ago."

"It has not changed," Finian said.

Clearly deciding that the conversation needed to head off in another direction, Vir said firmly, "All right . . . here's what we'll do, then. All of you know people at different levels in the Houses. Talk to them. Feel them out. Get eyes and ears into any of the Houses where we don't have contacts. Durla is going to come down on them even more harshly than he has before. He's going to feel the need to either beat them down or eliminate them completely. We have to let them know that there is an alternative. That they do not simply have to roll over.

"In addition, our strikes at key construction points will continue. Siphoning the materials through deliveries at Babylon 5 has been an exercise in caution, but I've been using the station as a clearinghouse for the individual components of the explosives, so no one has been associating it with the completed devices."

The conversation went on for some time, Vir laying out the groundwork for how their resistance movement was going to continue to survive. The techno-mages stopped talking, simply listening and—remarkably—even nodding on occasion. Finally Vir said, "All right . . . are there any questions?"

"Yes. I have a question," Renegar said.

Vir looked at him expectantly.

"Are we going to win?" he asked.

Without a moment's hesitation, Vir replied, "Yes. And not only are we going to win . . . but the Drakh are going to lose. You've seen the face of the enemy," and he pointed at the fallen creature. "It's nothing unbeatable. They can be hurt. They can die. And if that's the case, then we can injure them and we can kill them. And we will. However many it takes in order to rid Centauri Prime of this . . . this cancer that's eating away our soul. That's what we'll do with our underground movement."

"Considering where we're meeting," Adi said, looking around, "I'd say 'underground' is definitely the right word for it."

This resulted in something very unusual for one of their clandestine meetings: a roar of laughter. For just one moment, they had a feeling of what it would be like to meet, not as coconspirators or desperate freedom fighters, but simply as men enjoying each other's company. Renegar wondered whether they ever would have that opportunity, to live relatively normal and unassuming lives. And he said as much.

Vir looked at Renegar skeptically and responded. "Renegar . . . if you had a normal and unassuming life . . . you wouldn't know what to do with it."

Renegar thought about that, then nodded. "You are very likely correct. But . . ." he added, "would it not be nice . . . to have the opportunity to find out?"

To that notion, Vir had no response.

EXCERPTED FROM
THE CHRONICLES OF LONDO MOLLARI.
Excerpt dated (approximate Earth date)
September 24, 2276.

Note to historians: Although naturally the Centauri year is different from an Earth year, we have taken the liberty of adjusting the date and having it reflect a parallel passing of time, vis-à-vis Earth time, due to Londo's passing reference to his anniversary with G'Kar, so as to avoid confusion for our Earth readers. We at the Centauri Historical Society are aware of the late emperor's fondness for inhabitants of Earth, and feel that he would approve of our efforts to minimize anything that might leave those readers in a quandary. For chronological purists among you, we thank you for your indulgence.

G'Kar stood at the door, in the same way that he always did. Straight, tall, looking directly ahead. And I, seated on the other side of the table, gestured for him to enter just as I always did. "One would think," I told him as he walked across the room, "that after all this time, you would see no need to stand on ceremony."

"Ceremony, Highness, is all we have. Without it, you are merely an oddly dressed Centauri in clothing that picks up dirt all too easily."

"You know what I like about you, G'Kar? You make me laugh."

"You did not laugh just now."

"So I didn't like you as much. Sit, sit." He never sits until I tell him to. I think he considers it a sort of odd game. "So . . . how was your day today, G'Kar?"

"The same as it was yesterday, Londo, and very much—I suspect—the way it will be tomorrow. Unless, of course, you decide to have me executed today."

"Why today?" I asked. I signaled for the wine steward to bring me a new bottle, and he went off to fetch it.

"Why not today?" he countered. "Sooner or later, my amusement value will reach its end, and then . . ." He shrugged and made a throat-cutting gesture.

"Is that how you think I see you, G'Kar? As only having 'amusement value'?" I shook my head, discouraged. "How very tragic."

"Of all the tragedies in your life, Londo, I truly think that my opinion in this instance rates fairly low on the scale."

"True. True." There was a silence then, the comfortable silence of two old acquaintances. I do not know if, even now, I dare use the word "friend." The new bottle was brought, glasses were placed in front of us, and the wine was poured. G'Kar raised his glass and sniffed its contents with a delicacy that provided an amusing contrast to his rough-hewn exterior.

"This," he announced, "is actually a good vintage."

"Is not all my wine of good vintage?"

"Not of this caliber," he said. "To what do I owe the honor?"

"It has been a year," I told him. "A year since you saved my life and came under my protection. A year since we began our weekly dinners together. I am surprised. I would have thought the date would be seared into your memory."

"There is a great deal occupying my mind at the moment, Londo," he said. "My apologies. This significant date must have been squeezed out of its proper place of importance. So if we are to celebrate this anniversary, does that mean you will be letting me go?"

"Why would I want to do that?" I asked. "Allow my most excellent friend, G'Kar, to simply depart? No, no . . . I am afraid I cannot, if for no other reason than that it would reflect poorly in the eyes of those who watch me most carefully."

"Because I am a potential tool that might be used in the event that the current situation deteriorates."

I hated to admit that he was right but, of course, he was.

"True enough," I said slowly. "My prime minister and his associates have made it clear to me that you will be allowed to live only if you do so here, under my protection. If I permit you to leave, it will seem as if I am granting you permission to violate the laws of Centauri Prime. Laws that ban visitors, that ban changeling devices. I cannot be seen as being lenient on criminals."

G'Kar had finished his wine. The steward moved toward him to refill the glass, but G'Kar, as usual, placed a hand over it to indicate that he wanted no more. "Why can you not?" he asked. "Be lenient, I mean. Certainly a quality such as mercy would be highly valued. Particularly when one considers the brutal actions taken by some of your predecessors. The people of Centauri Prime would likely regard it as a pleasant change of pace."

I laughed curtly at that. "It is a nice theory, G'Kar. But people do not want a change of pace, pleasant or otherwise. They want no more and no less than what they are accustomed to. Believe it or not, there are still those who believe Cartagia was the best emperor we ever had. That he harkened to a day when billions feared the Centauri because we were unpredictable. There are many who believe that I will indeed let you go, and they will eagerly use such a decision to undermine my authority . . . to undermine me. As fond as I am of you, G'Kar, I consider your freedom too high a price to pay for a crisis of confidence that could cost me my throne . . . and, of greater significance, my life.

"But you know, G'Kar . . . all of this is very much beside the point. We should ponder other matters. A new topic!" I announced, and I tapped my spoon repeatedly on my goblet as if I were addressing a crowded room of revelers.

While we had talked, food had been laid out for us, and it smelled excellent. I started to eat hungrily, having had very little over the course of the day. G'Kar, as always, ate little to nothing. It was completely beyond me how he managed to maintain the energy to function, considering the small quantities he consumed.

"What new topic would that be, Londo?" he inquired.

I allowed a moment to finish chewing my food. It would hardly have been dignified to send vegetables spewing out of my mouth like a multicolored fountain. "I think you should choose this time, G'Kar. I have done so the last few times. And they have been stimulating chats, to be sure, but I think it time that you seize the bull by the reins."

"The what?"

I waved dismissively. "An Earth saying. It is of no importance."

"No, that might be an interesting topic," G'Kar said. "Your fascination with all things pertaining to Earth. I have never quite understood it. You research them, you quote from them. Their achievements pale compared to those—laudable or otherwise—of the Centauri Republic. They are a relatively minor species. At least, they started out that way.

"Yet the Centauri saw something in them. Some spark, some potential. You must have. If not for the Centauri, after all, the Humans would not have acquired the jumpgate technology. Or at the very least, they would have lagged far behind in acquiring it. It might have taken them decades, even centuries more, to become a true power in the galaxy." Interest glittered in his one normal eye. "What was it about them, Londo? I have to admit, I didn't see it, nor did any of my people. What was the fascination?"

I chuckled. "It was a little before my time . . . a hundred years or so, you understand. So I cannot exactly tell you firsthand. But . . . I have been doing some reading. Comments, letters, correspondence from the emperor and the ministers at the time, that sort of thing."

"And what have you discovered?"

I leaned forward and gestured to G'Kar that he should do likewise, as if I was concerned that someone would overhear. He leaned closer.

"They thought," I said, "that the Humans would annihilate themselves."

"Really."

I nodded. "They saw the Humans as an opportunity for quick profit. And they thought that the Humans, once they had acquired the advanced technology, would move too quickly for their own good. My predecessors anticipated that there would be struggles and wars within the then-primitive Earth Alliance. Centauri Prime would secretly fund both sides, benefit from all concerned and—once the Humans had more or less obliterated themselves—the Great Centauri Republic would step in and pick up the pieces. It was a simple way to expand our control with no risk to ourselves, and nothing but profit to be had. It seemed the perfect arrangement."

"But it did not work out that way."

"Not exactly. They didn't wind up destroying themselves. Instead they managed to hang on long enough to offend the Minbari, and wound up almost being wiped off the face of existence. We predicted a war, yes . . . but the wrong war. They tripped themselves up, as we thought they would, but what a foe to do it with!" I laughed softly at the thought. "They wanted our help, you know. Wanted us to help them against the Minbari. If we had, the Minbari would have turned on us just as quickly. We knew we would not have had a chance against them. What would have been gained?"

"Did you not feel you owed it to them, as a race? If not for your giving them the technology, they would not have encountered the Minbari and gotten themselves embroiled in a war."

"Nonsense," I said firmly. "Responsibility only goes so far."

"Does it?"

He was watching me. I hated it when he watched me like that. "What is that supposed to mean?"

"If you do something to set events into motion, you owe something to those whom you have affected. You gave them the flame. They then burned themselves. You had a responsibility to try to tend to the wound . . ."

But I shook my head. "No. We gave them the match. It was they who chose to light the flame. It was purely their responsibility, wasn't it."

"Was it?"

"Bah!" I said in disgust. "We always get to this at some point or other. 'Yes, it is, no, it isn't.' No debate or discussion. Just rephrasing my question as another question. And then we go no further."

"So one who is given the match and chooses to light it . . . is owed no aid from anyone? No succor? Whatever the consequence or outcome, it is his responsibility and his alone to deal with?"

"That is correct, yes."

"And what of you, Londo?" His voice suddenly turned sharp, his manner alert. "You were given a match by the Shadows, were you not? By their agents? And you used that match to light a flame that wound up bringing a torch not only to my world, but also ultimately to your own. Yet now you want my aid to overcome that which you have thrust yourself into."

"Your aid? I have no idea what you're talking about."

"I do not know entirely myself, Londo." There was something about him, something that seemed to say that I could hide nothing from him. He exuded confidence. I almost envied him. "But there is something. *Something* you want of me. Something you are . . . saving me for. That is why I have been here for a year—that and no other reason. You could have me executed with impunity. You could find a way to allow me to depart, if you really wanted to. Instead you keep me here for your own purposes. I think you know what they are."

"Oh, really. And what do you think they are?"

And that cold confidence seeped over from him. It seemed to drain something from me as he said, "I think . . . you want me to help you escape. Not out that door. Not off this world. I think you want me to help you escape through the only way that will allow the pain to stop. To the only place where no one can ever touch you or hurt you again. I do not think, though, that you are ready for that. Or perhaps you feel that it is not a judicious moment. And so you wait. And we chat. And we have dinner. And we play at having polite discussions about matters both consequential and inconsequential, when the only thing you really wonder about is: Is now the time? Is there more that I can do? Should do? Or should I ask my old friend G'Kar to do . . . what I myself cannot or will not do?"

Suddenly it was very, very cold. I felt it down to my bones, my blood . . . my very being. Whatever warming attributes came from the wine were gone.

"I think you should leave now," I said.

G'Kar inclined his head slightly, in deference, and rose. The guards were immediately at his side. What nonsense. As if they could have stopped him if he endeavored to attack me. He looked at one in curiosity, and said, "You are new. You are new to the guard . . . but I have seen you before. Where?"

The guard looked at me, seeking my permission to reply. I nodded absently, and he looked back to G'Kar. "My name is Caso. I was a member of the Prime Candidates."

"Of course. You were there that day, a year ago. You saw me stop the shooter. You are no longer a Prime Candidate?" He shook his head. "Why?"

He said nothing, but it was I who answered. "Because it was felt," I told him, "that he was wrong to reveal that you had saved Durla and me. The others pressured him to state that you yourself were involved, or even masterminded it. That way there would have been no reason not to dispose of you. And Durla is not pleased with the idea of being beholden to a Narn—any Narn—much less you."

"But you stuck to your principles," G'Kar said approvingly to Caso.

"I simply held to the truth," Caso told him. "It was not a difficult decision."

"Oh," G'Kar said, glancing at me, "you would be amazed how difficult a decision that can be sometimes."

Caso escorted him out then, leaving me with a bottle of wine that was not sufficiently full, and a soul that was not sufficiently empty, for what I needed to do.

— chapter 10 —

Reality and fantasy were blurring for Durla. He was standing on a high cliff on Mipas, overlooking the ships that prepared to plunge into battle, and he could not recall for sure whether what he was seeing was really happening, or merely another of his visions.

"Magnificent," he said, and the wind carried his words away so that no one heard, save himself. Even so, the fact that he himself had heard it was enough.

Mipas was only one of the worlds where Centauri war vessels were being gathered, but it was a pivotal one, since it was within close proximity to the Drazi Homeworld. Fortunately, Minister Castig Lione had done a more-than-admirable job of greasing the right palms and making certain that the right people in the Drazi government asked all the wrong questions, thereby making sure that none of the Drazi would look too closely at what was going on. They knew Mipas was a hub of industry, but the Centauri insisted—with most convincing vigor—that the facility was simply being used as a construction project for the Centauri government to keep its populace gainfully employed.

And it was true that, at this site and at others like it, the Centauri had labored long and hard. And now the fruits of those years and years of labor were coming close to paying off. The ships looked so ready for battle—so powerful, that even sitting on the ground as they were, relatively helpless, they still appeared formidable.

It was, without question, the largest fleet that any one race had in its possession. Its creation had not come without cost, and it had required long years of experimentation and dedication.

"Magnificent," he said again. He wondered abstractly whether he had forgotten every other word in his vocabulary.

But it *was* magnificent, there was no denying. The ships were stretched all the way to the horizon, ready to leap into the air at his command. Not only that, but many already were up and flying. The sky was alive with activity, hundreds of ships, passing in perfect formation.

He stood there, arms stretched wide, and he could practically feel power from the ships themselves flooding into him. He felt as if he could, with a mere wave of his hand, send other worlds spiraling into oblivion. With his mighty fleet backing him up, he could shatter planets at his merest whim.

"Soon . . . very soon, sir," General Rhys said at his side. "Another two, three weeks . . . and we will be ready. At your hand, and your hand alone, will we strike."

It sounded good. Indeed, it sounded superb. "My hand," Durla said, sounding enchanted with the notion. "My hand will reach out. My hand will crush the Alliance worlds. They will not be able to stop us. Nothing can stop us."

And suddenly Mariel was at his side. She was smiling and perfect and glowing with that glorious inner light which, for some reason, he never saw when she was with him under other circumstances. "Sheridan can," Mariel said firmly. "He can stop you."

"Never!" Durla shouted.

"He stopped the Shadows. He stopped the Vorlons. He can stop you."

"I will eliminate him! Obliterate him! I—"

"I love you, Durla, you above all others," Mariel said. "And Sheridan shall be delivered into your hands. Sheridan and also Delenn."

"How?" Durla's eyes were wide in wonder. "How will you do this?"

"The son. The son is the key. Once you have the son, the father and mother will fall into line. He was born for one reason and one reason only: to become Sheridan and Delenn's greatest weakness. They will sacrifice themselves in order to save him. They will think, in so doing, that it is only themselves who are to be sacrificed, but in fact they will be sacrificing Sheridan's Alliance, as well. He has tried to create something greater than himself. He has not quite yet succeeded. He does not realize that once he is gone, his Alliance falls apart. When the Alliance worlds are assaulted by this mighty fleet you have created, they will turn to Sheridan for guidance, and they will find him gone. They will turn to each other and find only races that have let each other down. It will be glorious. It will be chaos. And it will be the end of the Interstellar Alliance."

"And I need do nothing?"

"Nothing." Mariel smiled. "Durla . . . do you know what you are?"

"Tell me."

"You are the greatest leader, the greatest thinker, the greatest Centauri who has ever lived. In the future, all will sing songs and say prayers to you. The actions you take in the coming weeks will grant you immortality. None will ever forget the name of Durla. You will be like unto a god."

"A god," he whispered.

"Even the Great Maker himself will pale in envy at the praise that will be sung to you. For the Great Maker possesses the abilities of a deity, which aid him in all that he would create. You, Durla, are a mere mortal . . . yet look at what you have managed to bring into being, through the sheer power of your will."

The sky was now so thick with ships that the stars were not even visible. Every so often they managed to peek through, ever so slightly, but for the most part it was a solid blanket of fighter vessels.

"All this, you have done. And for all this, you will be rewarded."

She reached for him then, her lips against his . . .

. . . and he awoke with a start.

In the darkness of the room, Durla felt flushed, breathing hard. It was that disconcerting sort of sensation that one always experienced when waking up in an unusual place.

The facility in which he was housed wasn't especially plush or fancy, but it was the best Mipas had to offer. It was only one night, though; the next day he would journey to another of the worlds that the great Centauri Republic had taken, and witness the final stages of the construction there.

It was a glorious tour, a validation of all his work.

His work.

The more he pondered, the more his suspicious mind began to work. And then he heard a soft moan. He glanced over and saw Mariel lying next to him, tossing and looking less than comfortable. Perhaps she had likewise been dreaming. But her vision wasn't remotely as broad as his, which caused him no little aggravation. After all, she had always been present in his dreams—an avatar of greatness. Certainly it wasn't her fault that the Mariel of the real world could never match up to that of the imaginary.

Nevertheless, it was a keen source of disappointment.

He shook her awake, and she sat up with a start, blinking furiously. The blanket fell away, revealing the sheerest of nightgowns. Once upon a time, that sight alone would have been enough to inflame his blood. Now he barely gave it a glance. "Mariel . . . tell me what you think of me," he said.

She looked at him in confusion. "What?"

"Your opinion. Of me. I desire to know what it is."

"You are . . ." She licked her lips, still clearly befuddled, but game enough to try to reply. "You are my sun and moons, my stars, my everything. You are—"

"Stop it," and he grasped her firmly by the arms. "I need to know, because we stand on the brink of something great. On the brink of recapturing the lost glory of Centauri Prime. But it is important to me that you tell me what you think of this venture, and of me."

"Why . . . is it important?"

He took a deep breath. "It simply is. Now tell me. Am I a great leader? Will songs be sung about me?" When she didn't reply immediately, he shook her roughly and repeated, "Tell me!"

And suddenly her face twisted in fury, anger so palpable that he felt as if daggers were being driven into him through the ferocity of her gaze alone. "You desire to know what I think? Very well. I think you are mad. Insane. I think you are drunk with power. I think you tell yourself that all that you do, you do for Centauri Prime, when in fact you do it for yourself. I think you will bring death and destruction to our people. I think these 'great visions' you profess to have are nothing more than the delusions of a rotting soul making lengthy preparations for its own damnation. I think that if you have a shred of decency, you will halt this insane project before it goes any further. That you will refrain from bringing the wrath of the Interstellar Alliance down around our ears and instead work to create something good and prosperous and decent. Something that can stand as a symbol for a thousand years and say, *See here! We of the Great Centauri Republic accomplished this, and it benefited every sentient being everywhere.* And, Durla, if you persist in this course, then you will only lead others to destruction, and the only songs that you will inspire will be dirges. You wanted to know what I think? That is what I think."

It had all come bursting out of her in a rush, words spilling over themselves. She wasn't thinking rationally, or wisely. As had been the case with abused and downtrodden wives throughout the ages, she had been thinking at that moment about one thing and one thing only: to wound him. To get back at him in any way she could.

But always a woman of craft, intelligence, and deviousness, Mariel had suffered his wrath long enough. Before he could swing at her, she whipped the covers off her body and leapt from the bed with the force of a recovered predator. Something had at last awakened inside her, a sense of dignity, of self-worth, a growing ember of the respect she once held as a devastating lady of Centauri Prime.

Tonight she would get it all back.

Before Durla could untangle himself from the bedsheets, Mariel ripped open the bedroom door so hard that it slammed into the wall. She fled down the hallway, feeling him coming up fast behind her. Only a few more steps to go; she could just reach the other room in time. She grasped the handle of the door at the end of the hallway, pushed, whirled, and closed it, throwing herself against the door and locking Durla out. Forever.

As Durla pounded furiously against the door, Mariel leaned against it and felt the blessed wood at her back, taking the brunt of his anger for once. Across the room, there was a dark terminal. She stared at it, realizing that she was trapped here only as long as she allowed herself to be.

Mariel crossed the room, touched her fingers to the side of the terminal, and activated a call to Emperor Londo Mollari of Centauri Prime. She was taking him up on his offer of help. She was going home. And in a few moments, there would be nothing Durla could do to harm her.

— chapter 11 —

"Happy birthday, David!"

David Sheridan squirmed as his mother planted a kiss on his cheek. He wiped it off as quickly as possible, then howled in anguished laughter as Michael Garibaldi kissed him just as aggressively on the other cheek. "Uncle Mikey!" he managed to get out as he quickly wiped the drool from his face. "Oh, *yuck*!"

" 'Oh, yuck'? Is that all you have to say?" Garibaldi asked him in mock offense. "And after the terrific present I've gotten you?"

They were gathered in Sheridan's den, a more private room for study and contemplation. It boasted an assortment of mementos from earlier in the careers of both Delenn and Sheridan, and the room overall had more of an "Earth" feel to it. At least, that's what David was told. Having never actually been to Earth, he could only take his father's word for it.

"Present? Is it the trip? Finally?" David asked.

Delenn rolled her eyes, as if this were a subject that had been broached a hundred times before . . . and indeed, perhaps it had. "David, we said eighteen . . ."

"What is the big deal about eighteen?" he demanded. Knowing that his mother was a dead end, he turned to his father. "Dad, I'm sixteen now. Would you please tell Mom that she's being paranoid."

"You're being paranoid," Sheridan told her promptly.

"So you're saying I can go."

"No, you can't go. But it's your birthday, so I figured I'd humor you."

David sighed in exasperation. He turned to Garibaldi, his court of last resort. "Can you believe this? They won't put me on a shuttle by myself to go visit you on Mars. To go anywhere! What the hell is going on?"

"Language," Delenn said primly.

"Sorry. What the bloody hell is going on?"

"Attaboy," Garibaldi said.

"A reminder here, David," Sheridan said. "You're 'sixteen' on a technicality. Minbari years are shorter than Earth years. By Earth standards, you've still got a ways to go."

"Okay, fine. But I've also got some Minbari blood in me, so that should count for something."

"Yeah. Don't get too attached to your hair, for one thing," Garibaldi cracked.

Delenn, who was busy slicing the white-and-chocolate cake that had been brought in minutes earlier, shook her head. "You, Michael, are precisely no help whatsoever."

"Thank you."

"You're welcome. Here," and she shoved a piece of cake at him.

"Look, I gotta tell you, the kid's got a point, that's all," Garibaldi said. He took a bite of the cake, then said, "Who baked this?"

"I did," Sheridan said. "I figured it's never too late to try something new."

"Well, guess what. You were wrong." He put the cake aside as Sheridan scowled. "It's just that . . . well, the kid's sixteen years old and he's never so much as flown on a shuttle by himself? Aside from a trip or two to Babylon 5, he's spent practically his whole life on Minbar. He should get out, have a chance to see the galaxy. My God, when I think what I was up to when I was sixteen . . ."

"The imagination fairly reels," Delenn said.

"It's a different situation, Michael, and you know it." Sheridan lowered his voice and glanced at David, as he said to Garibaldi, "And I don't know if now is the best time to—"

"Discuss it," David interrupted. He had finished his piece of cake, his teenaged taste buds apparently not the least put off. "God, I can't think of the number of times I've heard that. When is it going to be safe to discuss things in front of me, huh? How sheltered am I going to have to be?"

Sheridan looked to Delenn, but she shrugged slightly in a What-else-can-we-say?" manner. "It's just . . . different," he said.

"How?" The question came from both Garibaldi and David.

"Because," Sheridan said patiently, "I'm the president of the interstellar Alliance. And the fact is that there are people out there—some of them outside the Alliance, some of them, I hate to say, part of it—who might well desire to put pressure on me any way they can. To say nothing of the numerous people I've piled up over the years who have individual grudges with me. And my son would be a terrific prize to acquire in that regard."

"Wow, you really are paranoid," Garibaldi said.

"And so are you. Don't you remember? It's one of the things I've always liked about you."

"And paranoia has its time and place," Garibaldi admitted.

"That being all the time and every place," Sheridan replied.

"True enough. But don't you think there should be some balance? Like I said, when I was sixteen—"

"You were already bumming around the galaxy, I know. Snagging rides wherever you could, exploring colonies, getting into trouble. And it made you the man you are today."

"God help us all," Garibaldi said cheerfully.

"The point is," Sheridan continued, "David isn't you. You could do whatever you wanted, get into whatever trouble you wished, with relative anonymity. David had the bad luck to be my son."

"I don't think of it as bad luck, Dad." David sighed. "I wish you wouldn't put words in my mouth."

"Sorry."

"He's got so many of his own they just kind of spill out all over the place into other people's mouths."

"Don't help me, Michael," Sheridan told him.

"The thing is, you're right about one thing," David said.

"One thing." Delenn laughed. "My, my. That's an improvement of one hundred percent over most discussions you two have, John. You should be proud."

"Don't help me, Mom," David deadpanned. He turned back to his father. "The thing is . . . you're the president of the Interstellar Alliance. To all intents and purposes, you're the most powerful man in known space."

"A bit of a high-flown description, but I'll accept that," Sheridan said.

"But why is it, then . . . that the most powerful man in known space . . . has the most powerless son?"

Sheridan looked down a moment and sighed. "David . . . I wish the situation were different. I wish we lived in other circumstances."

"We live in the circumstances that we make, Dad. You can't create a certain set of circumstances, and then moan about it and chalk it off to the doings of fate."

"He has a point, John."

"*Et tu,* Delenn?"

"I'm not saying that your concerns aren't valid. Just that his are equally valid. There is no easy answer," she replied.

"When is there ever?" He thought about it a moment, and then said, "Maybe when you're seventeen . . ."

"Forget it, Dad," David said impatiently. "Just forget it. I'll lock myself in my room and come out when I'm fifty, and maybe that will be safe enough." Before Sheridan could respond, David turned to Garibaldi. "Okay, so what is your present, then?"

"David, you raised the subject; we can't just let it drop," Sheridan said.

"You know what, Dad? It's my birthday. If I want to drop a subject, then I think it should get dropped."

Sheridan put up his hands in an attitude of submission, whereupon David looked back at Garibaldi. "So? My present?"

Garibaldi reached into his jacket and pulled out a PPG. He handed it to David, and said proudly, "Here you go."

David took it and turned it over reverently, feeling its heft. "Wow," he whispered.

Sheridan's face was so dark that it looked as if thunderheads were rolling in. "Michael," he said stiffly. "May we speak privately a—"

"Oh, calm down, John. David, pull the trigger."

"David, you will do no such thing!" Delenn snapped.

"Will you guys trust me? After twenty-plus years, you'd think I'd've earned that. David, point it over in that direction and pull the trigger."

Before his parents could stop him, David did as he was told. He braced himself and pulled the trigger.

There was not, however, any of the expected recoil. Instead an image instantly appeared, floating in the air, materialized there by a steady stream of light from the end of the "PPG." It was a scantily clad young woman, life-sized and in glorious holographic 3-D, performing a dance that could only be described as extremely suggestive.

A grin split David's face. "Wow! Who is she?"

"God, I wish I knew." Garibaldi sighed. "Happy birthday, David."

Delenn cleared her throat loudly. "Michael . . . I don't know that it's particularly appropriate . . ."

"If you're going to keep the kid nailed to Minbar, the least you can do is let him get a view of what's out there. Am I right, John?" He paused. "John?"

Sheridan was staring at the holograph. With an effort, he blinked himself back into the moment. "Oh . . . right."

"John!" Delenn sounded almost betrayed.

"Delenn, it's harmless."

"Harmless! It teaches him to look upon women as physical creatures, rather than complete beings of spiritual and . . ." Her voice trailed off as she watched the gyrations. She angled her head slightly. "Are those . . . real?"

"Absolutely," Garibaldi said immediately. "You can tell."

"How? No, on second thought, I don't want to know," she amended quickly.

"That's probably wise," Sheridan said judiciously. Then a thought struck him. "Oh! One other thing."

He crossed to a cabinet and opened it. David watched in curiosity as his father delicately removed an urn. Walking carefully, as if afraid he would trip and drop it, Sheridan brought it across the room and settled it on the table in front of David where his other presents lay. David looked at it skeptically. "It's an urn," he said.

"That's right."

"Well . . . that's nice," David said gamely. "I was figuring I'd finish off the evening by having myself cremated, so . . . now I've got someplace to put me."

Sheridan laughed, and Delenn told him, "This is not just any urn. It was a gift from Londo Mollari."

"Before he became an asshole," Garibaldi added.

"Michael!" Delenn scolded.

"Okay, okay, you got me. He was an asshole already."

"Michael!"

"Oh, come on, Mom, it's not as if you speak highly of him."

"Ease up on your mother, David. And Michael, please . . . for once," and he made a quick throat-cutting gesture before turning back to his son. "David . . . I know that we've made some less-than-flattering comments about the Centauri in general and their emperor in particular. And God knows Londo has made some incredibly bad choices in his life. Then again . . . we all have."

"Not me," Garibaldi said. "Not a single mistake."

"Single, no. Numerous . . ."

Garibaldi clutched his heart as if stabbed by Sheridan's comment. Sheridan returned his attention to David. "The fact is that Londo brought us this urn before you were born. He told us that the Centauri tradition dictates that this be given to the heir to the throne when he comes of age."

"Like a Christmas fruitcake?"

Sheridan blinked. "What?"

David chucked a thumb at Garibaldi. "He told me that there was only one Christmas fruitcake ever baked. And no one wanted it. So it gets passed around from person to person, throughout history, every Christmas."

"You're just a bundle of information, aren't you, Michael."

Garibaldi grinned. "Boy's got to learn sometime."

"Yeah, well, hopefully what he'll learn is to stop listening to you. The point is, David, that—at that time, at least—we were the closest thing to family Londo ever had. He felt a . . . a connection to you. You were a sort of surrogate son, I guess. He was reaching out to you and, in so doing, reaching out to us, as well."

"And then he spent the next sixteen years trying to conquer the galaxy."

"I don't know how much of that is Londo, and how much of it is his advisers," Sheridan said. "In any event, they'll never succeed. We have some intelligence-gathering facilities of our own . . ."

"And they're not what they once were," Garibaldi said.

Sheridan glanced at him in amusement. "You mean since you left the job, it's gone downhill."

But Garibaldi obviously took the comment quite seriously. "If you want to know the truth: yes. You're depending on what other worlds are telling you. Except I know that palms have been greased, that people have found it to their advantage to look the other way, and no one truly believes that the Centauri are capable of trying what I think they're going to try."

"Londo may be many things, Michael . . . but he's not insane. Attacks on individual border worlds are one thing. But if the Centauri get it into their heads to make a full-blown strike at the allies, they'll be smashed to pieces."

"Londo may not be insane, but that prime minister of his is a few anvils short of a chorus," Garibaldi replied. "The problem is that he's ignorant and arrogant. Ignorance you can deal with. You can outsmart ignorance. Arrogance you can likewise get around. Arrogant people, you can appeal to that arrogance and set them up for a fall. Ignorance *and* arrogance is a deadly combination. Now, if the other members of the Alliance want to stick their heads into the sand, that's their choice, of course. But I'm hoping that you, Mr. President, aren't turning into one of those, or letting a gift from sixteen years ago soften you in your concerns toward the Centauri. Because I'm telling you: They're a threat."

"Believe it or not, Michael, I haven't lost sight of that," Sheridan said patiently. "But I also haven't lost sight of the fact that, once upon a time, Londo Mollari was our friend. God willing, he may be again someday. And in hopes of that time . . . here," and he slid the urn closer to David.

David picked it up, turned it over. "The bottom part is sealed," he noted.

"Yes, we know," Delenn said. "It's supposed to contain water from a sacred river that ran in front of the palace."

"It's kind of okay," David allowed. He turned the vase over. For some reason it felt . . . comfortable in his hands. Even though it was the first time he had seen it, he felt as if it had always been his. "It's nice."

"Kind of okay? Nice? From you, David, that is high praise indeed," his mother teased him.

He hefted the vase once more, then glanced at the leftover cake. "Mom, is it okay if I have another piece?"

"My God, he likes it," Sheridan said, amazed. "Absolutely—"

"—not," Delenn told him flatly.

David's "Mom!" overlapped with Sheridan's slightly less anguished, but just as annoyed, "Delenn!"

"You know how I feel about gluttony," she said. "Be satisfied with what you have, David. The rest of the cake will be here tomorrow."

"I sure as hell know I'm not going to take any of it," Garibaldi piped up cheerfully.

"I don't recall anyone asking you," Sheridan told him.

David found that, the longer he looked at the urn, the more trouble he had taking his eyes off it. "Dad . . . would it be okay if I sent a message off to the emperor? To thank him?"

"I think that would be a very nice gesture," Sheridan said. "You may have to jog his memory a bit. He never had the opportunity to meet you, after all."

"Who knows?" Delenn said. "If the situation changes for the better—perhaps you will have the opportunity to meet the emperor face-to-face someday."

"And won't that be wonderful," Garibaldi said.

chapter 12

When General Rhys met the prime minister for breakfast, he found Durla to be in a fairly somber mood. "Is there a problem, sir?" Rhys inquired.

Durla was holding a roll, staring at it. Then he placed it down carefully and looked at Rhys. "General," he said after a moment, "my lady wife, Mariel, will not be continuing with us. I wish to have her returned to Centauri Prime as soon as possible."

"Is she feeling ill?" Rhys asked solicitously.

"You can say that, yes."

"Ah" was all Rhys said.

"I believe she wants to go home. This surveying of our fleet is too strenuous for her."

"Ah," he said again.

"Furthermore," Durla continued, "I think it best if she be kept to herself for a while. I am concerned about things she might say and do."

"What . . . sort of things?" inquired Rhys.

Durla looked at him darkly and seriously. "Unfortunate things. Things that, if they were spoken by just any woman, would be considered disloyal enough. But spoken by the wife of the prime minister? They could serve to undermine my people's faith in me. I will not have it, General. I will not be undercut by her."

"That's very understandable, Prime Minister," Rhys said judiciously. But he was more than capable of reading between the lines . . . and was wondering, in a bleak manner, why Durla wasn't insinuating that the woman simply succumb to an "accident" on the way home. It was not a suggestion, however veiled, that Rhys was looking forward to receiving. He was not quite certain how he would react to such a thing. He was a soldier, not an assassin.

The question, however, promptly became moot when Durla spoke again. "From whisperings I have heard, and things she has said . . . I believe the emperor has taken an interest in her fortunes."

"I thought the emperor despised her," said a surprised Rhys.

Durla shrugged, clearly mystified. "Who can possibly intuit the way in which the emperor's mind works . . . or even if it does work at all." He laughed heartily at his little witticism, but when the general offered little more than a slightly pained smile, he reined himself in. Instead, all business, he continued, "So make certain that she is kept to herself. I do not want her talking to others. I do not want her sending communications to others. She needs time, I think, to assess the current state of affairs and come to terms with them."

"As you wish, Prime Minister."

Durla smiled. "There are times, General, when I think that you alone fully understand my concerns."

"You wish to make Centauri Prime great again," Rhys said. "You see our future as a great monument. Naturally you must chip away at anything that is not in keeping with your vision."

"Yes, yes. Exactly." He let out a sigh, as if relieved.

Then he got up and walked over to the great bay window that overlooked the field. There, in the morning sun, the ships gleamed. Not as many as in his dream, no. But a considerable number nonetheless. Besides, his dreams always looked to the future, not to the present or the past.

In the distance, the construction facility was going full strength. It provided him further affirmation that nothing could possibly stop them. The future was in his hands.

His hands.

He looked over at Rhys. General Rhys, who, when he led the troops into battle, would cover himself with glory. General Rhys, who simply carried out the orders, but did not—should not—be the one making the final decisions.

It was remotely possible that, once the battle began, it would be Rhys who would be remembered. Despite the assertion of his dreams, that it would be Durla whose name would be celebrated, he nevertheless felt a degree of uncertainty.

He could see it now. *General Rhys led the attack, General Rhys launched the ships, General Rhys paved the way . . .*

There had to be a reminder of just who was in charge.

"General," he said abruptly, "I have given the matter some thought. Only one individual should have the final go-codes."

A flicker of uncertainty moved across Rhys' face. "Pardon, sir?"

"The final go-codes. The launch codes," Durla said matter-of-factly. "When all our ships have moved into position, the final encoded signal confirming the assault should come from me. Our fleet should answer to no other voice."

Slowly Rhys stood, uncoiling like a great cat. His gaze never left Durla. "Prime Minister," he said slowly, "with the greatest of all respect . . . those codes should also be in the hands of the fleet general."

"You mean yourself."

"Yes, I will be on site. You will not be . . . or at least, should not be, for you are too important to the future of Centauri Prime. Ideally, you should relay the go-order to me, and I in turn will inform the fleet . . ."

"Leaving the decision to strike, ultimately, to your discretion. I do not find that acceptable."

Rhys stiffened. "Prime Minister, I must ask . . . is there anything in my actions, or something in my conduct, that leads you to believe I am not trustworthy?"

"Not thus far," Durla said mildly. "But I do not intend to wait and find that I have misjudged. It is my vision, my dream that has brought us this far, General Rhys. It is my voice that the brave soldiers of our Republic are entitled to hear when they hurl themselves against our enemies in the Interstellar Alliance. And that is how it shall be."

Durla wondered just how much Rhys was going to object. He expected a fairly lengthy argument over it. He certainly hoped that he wasn't going to have to relieve Rhys of duty. He had proven too dependable an officer.

Fortunately, that dependability held up, for Rhys bowed slightly, and said, "If that is the prime minister's wish, then that is how it shall be."

"Thank you, General," Durla said, with a thin smile. He looked out once more at the fleet. "Marvelous, is it not?" He sighed. "To think that the foolish Houses of Centauri Prime thought I required their cooperation to create it. They did not realize how much could be accomplished in spite of them."

Rhys said nothing.

Durla turned back to him, feeling that the silence connoted disapproval of some sort. "Problem, General?"

"Since you are asking me, Prime Minister . . . I believe your lengthy campaign against the House heads, and the Houses themselves, has been . . ." He seemed to search for the right word. "Unfortunate."

"Indeed."

"Many are dead. Many more are in hiding. You have, I believe, not done yourself a tremendous service."

"Perhaps," he said with a shrug. "Then again, I have shown them that I play no favorites. They got in my way, General. Those who get in my way . . . tend to come off badly."

"I shall remember that, Prime Minister."

"See that you do, General. See that you do."

And at that moment, half the field blew up.

Durla couldn't believe it. Even as the heat rolled around him, even as the general pulled him away from the window so that no flying pieces of debris could injure him, Durla refused to accept what he was seeing. "It can't be!" Durla shouted.

"The underground," Rhys snarled. "This treasonous act is of little consequence, though, Prime Minister. Only a handful of ships . . ."

"And it could be more!" Durla howled. "Have your men search the grounds! Make certain there are no more explosives! And if you find anyone who might be a part of it, execute them!"

"Don't you wish them questioned?"

"No! I want them dead!" He thumped the wall in fury repeatedly. "I want them dead! Their leader, dead! Their allies, dead! All of them, *dead*! By my command, by my authority, anyone who is part of these saboteurs will die in as grisly a manner as is possible! Now go, General! *Go!*"

Rhys was out the door in an instant, and Durla looked back at the flaming wreckage—all that remained of half a dozen beautiful vessels.

He wanted someone to die for this. Immediately.

Well . . . if the dream was right, David Sheridan would shortly be in his hands. Which meant the father and mother would be, too. They could all die together, as payment for this atrocity.

That was how his dreams would want it.

— chapter 13 —

David lay back in his bed—or as "back" as the Minbari bed allowed him to be—and stared at the ceiling.

He had seen videos of Londo Mollari in action. The emperor had been addressing Centauri crowds in relation to some anniversary or something. David had been struck by the way the emperor had seemed bigger than life, somehow. He didn't speak so much as he had words explode from him. It was almost spellbinding to watch.

He would have liked to have the opportunity to talk to Londo. He could thank him for the urn. He would be interested to hear Londo's point of view regarding certain events he'd heard his father and mother describe. And he would love to ask just what the hell was going on with that hair.

Then he heard something.

It was some sort of rattling. David's eyes had grown accustomed to the darkness, so he wasn't entirely blind. He stepped down off the bed and looked around, listening carefully. There was silence for such a long time that he had almost convinced himself that he had imagined it. But then he heard it again, coming from the direction of the urn . . .

No. It *was* the urn. The urn from Centauri Prime was actually rocking slightly.

The first thing that occurred to him was that this was the beginning of a quake of some kind, but nothing else seemed to be affected by it. Then the next thing he thought of was that there was some sort of bomb inside the vase. But that made no sense at all. How could a bomb sit in a vase in his father's private study for sixteen years? No, that couldn't be it.

The vase's trembling seemed to have its origins at the base.

David crouched closer, trying to make out what could possibly be causing it.

And suddenly the urn cracked open.

Reflexively David ducked back, but he was far too slow. From the small pile of debris that had once been an urn, something small and dark moved so quickly that he couldn't even begin to track it. It came right at him, and he batted at it helplessly, swinging through the air and missing it. There was some sort of moistness at the base of his throat then, and he tried to pull at it. His fingers felt something disgusting and protoplasmic, and he yanked his hand away from it. A wave of nausea seized him. It was as if some sort of huge tumor had sprung into existence on him.

He felt something snaking down the front of his shirt, sliding across his chest, and he opened his mouth to scream. Even as he did so, he staggered about the room, knocking over books and furniture as he tried to shake the thing off.

It's me.

The cry for help died before it could be fully born. There was no hesitation for David; he recognized instantly just who and what was upon him now. It was as if David had found a piece of himself that had been missing for as long as he could remember.

"You?" he whispered.

Yes. It's me, little sun.

He felt as if his world were spinning out of control. He tried to tell himself that he was, in fact, asleep. That none of this was happening.

Do not deny it, little sun. I have come here to help you. You have been waiting for me all this time.

David grabbed at the thing on his shoulder, and immediately a jolt of pain ran through him. He fell to his knees, gasping, trying to call out, but he felt his throat constricting. He couldn't get anything out, try as he might.

Why do you fight me when I have come here to help you? The voice in his mind sounded hurt. *I have spent so many years reaching out to you, becoming one with you. Why would you try to reject me now, when you and I have been together for so long?*

"What . . . are you?" David managed to get out.

I am everything you have ever wanted. Far more so than your parents. Your father, with his rules and restrictions. Your mother, with her moral harping. They don't understand you. They don't know what you need . . .

"I need you . . . out of my head!" David grated. He made no further move to pull the creature off his shoulder, however. He had learned better than that. His mind was racing, though, trying to summon the strength to call for help, trying to determine any course of action that would get this thing off him.

You don't want to do that. You know you want my help . . .

"I don't!"

You do. You want your chance to see the galaxy. You want to be out, exploring. You have the same desire to be a part of the great interstellar flow of life that your father had . . . except his father gave free rein to his desires, and yours won't.

He stopped. On some level . . . on every level . . . the thing was making sense. He knew it to be true, and this thing knew it, too. What was more . . . the fact that it knew it was comforting to him somehow. He felt as if he was sharing with it—in a way that he wasn't able to with his parents.

And then he tried to shout at himself—inwardly—that that was exactly what the creature wanted him to think. That he was falling into some sort of trap, as if this thing, this monstrosity on his shoulder, were his friend . . .

I am not your friend. I am your soul mate. I know you better than your parents know you. I know you better than you know yourself. And I can give you what you want . . .

"I want you off me!" But for some reason he noticed that his voice sounded a little less heartfelt this time.

You want off this world. What is there here for you? You have no friends. Minbari regard you with suspicion because of your lineage. You have private tutors, and in the rare instances where you have classes with other youths, you are far smarter, and they resent you for it. Your parents invited several guests to your birthday. They were all too "busy" or had other plans. Lies. They did not want to be with you.

You are neither Human nor Minbari, fish nor fowl. There is no place for you on Minbar. You want to see other places, to explore other worlds. To learn the truth about other races through firsthand experience. That is what you want. And I can provide you with that.

For a long moment, David said nothing. And then he spoke one word.

"How?"

His mind, however briefly, however momentarily, was open to the possibility.

From then on, it was only a matter of time.

John Sheridan couldn't sleep.

That bothered him a good deal. He usually had no trouble sleeping. In fact, it was one of the few things he wasn't having trouble doing these days. Lately he had been feeling the aches and pains more sharply than he wanted to admit. His reactions had slowed, his physical prowess was diminished. He felt as if his very thought processes were slowing down. As if there were a vague haze slowly descending.

He had the disturbing feeling he knew exactly why. The words of Lorien echoed more and more in his mind these days, even as he felt certain aspects of himself starting to . . . to dim. He knew that Delenn had to be thinking about it. *Twenty years,* Lorien had said.

At one point, a year or so earlier, Sheridan had joked that they should move to the Drazi Homeworld. Since a Drazi year was equal to 1.2 Earth years, Sheridan had jokingly reasoned that it seemed a quick way to pick up an additional four years of life. Delenn hadn't smiled when he'd said it; instead she'd immediately gone off to be by herself. He knew from then on not to attempt to deal with the subject by making light of it. In fact, since that time he hadn't dealt with it at all, at least not where Delenn was concerned.

They had both known that Lorien wasn't speaking in exact numbers, but rather in rough approximations. In the final analysis, they really could only guess how much time Sheridan had left.

Well . . . that was as it should be, wasn't it? Everyone had a finite time, when you came down to it. If one was going to look at it from a morbid point of view, birth wasn't the beginning of life; it was the beginning of a slow, protracted death. So Sheridan—unlike others—had a general idea of how much longer he had. That wasn't really such a bad thing, was it?

"Yeah. It is," he said to no one in particular.

Restless, he walked down a hall, without really having a destination in mind. It was a surprisingly chilly night for Minbar, and he had his robe tightly drawn around him. Maybe it wasn't so chilly at that. Maybe he was just feeling the cold more.

"Stop it. Stop feeling sorry for yourself," he scolded.

For the longest time, he had thought the thing he was going to regret the most was not having the chance to grow old with Delenn. But he had come to realize that he was wrong about that. At least he'd had the chance to grow older, to experience that gradual, easy comfort that two life mates have with one another. He might not have had the chance to consume an entire meal . . . but at least he'd had a taste of it.

Losing out on the chance to see David grow up, however, was really going to be hard to take. His son was sixteen, barely on the verge of manhood. There was so much Sheridan could do for him, so many ways he could try to provide guidance. But he wouldn't be there to do it.

And grandchildren; he would never have grandchildren. He would never have the chance to bounce a small continuation of his bloodline on his knee, one that would still be growing up when the next century turned. And perhaps feel his own father's voice in the back of his head, saying, "Well done, Johnny. Well done."

He would just have to be satisfied with what the cards had dealt him. After all, if Lorien had simply left him there to die, then David would never have been born.

Yes . . . he would just have to be satisfied.

Unfortunately, being satisfied had never been Sheridan's strong suit.

He stopped in his tracks. The light was dim in the hall, but still he saw someone at the other end. At first he was sure it was an intruder, but then he realized that it was David. Sheridan had been thrown for a second; something about David seemed a little odd. His body posture, the way he was carrying himself, was subtly different. Sheridan couldn't begin to imagine why.

"David?" he said cautiously. "Are you all right? You're up late." With a touch of levity that sounded horrendously forced, he added, "Still flushed with excitement from your birthday party?"

David said nothing. He walked slowly toward his father, and

Sheridan realized that his son was fully dressed, in a loose-fitting shirt and slacks. He was wearing the new boots Sheridan had given him for his birthday.

"Are you going somewhere, David?" A hint of caution entered Sheridan's tone. He was becoming more concerned that something was awry. "David?"

David drew to within a foot of him, and Sheridan put a hand on his son's shoulder. He started to say, "David, what's wrong?" Then he felt a lump under David's shirt.

David's spine stiffened, his eyes going wide, as if Sheridan had just stuck a finger directly into his nervous system. "What the hell?" Sheridan said, and even as David tried to take a step back, Sheridan yanked at the neck of the shirt, pulling it aside.

An eye glared balefully out at him.

Sheridan froze in place, his jaw dropping. He had no idea what he was looking at, but the surreal horror of it paralyzed him for just an instant. It was at that moment that David's fist swung, and there was no doubting just whose son he was. It was a powerful right cross, and even if Sheridan had been prepared for it, it would have done him damage. As it was, Sheridan wasn't ready for it at all, and he hit the ground like a bag of wet cement.

David stood over him, staring down at his father's insensate form with utter dispassion. He wasn't even fully aware that he was responsible for his father's current unconsciousness, and even if he had been aware, he wouldn't have cared. He knew who it was who was lying on the floor, of course. But for all practical purposes, he might as well have been looking at a stranger.

He turned and headed toward the nearest landing port. There was a private port not far away at all. That, of course, was to accommodate all the various dignitaries who came and went, visiting his father. There were several shuttles kept ready at all times, in the event that the mighty president of the Alliance had to get somewhere quickly.

David approached the port and slowed when he found another Minbari approaching him. He was a member of the warrior caste, and David could see that he was a guard. It was clear from the Minbari warrior's calm demeanor that he wasn't expecting any trouble. He didn't even have his hands near his weapon. He obviously considered this detail more for show than anything else. Who, after all, could really sneak in through the port?

"Young Sheridan," the guard said. "Odd hour for you to be out and about. May I help you with something?"

"Yes. You may put your hands over your head." And as he said that, the "PPG" given him by Garibaldi was in his hands.

The guard had no way of knowing that it wasn't real. It was possible, of course, that the guard might drop and pull his own weapon fast enough that he could shoot down David Sheridan. The positive aspect of that was that he would have done his job. The negative—and it was a sizable one—was that he would have just shot and killed the only son of John Sheridan and Delenn. It wasn't an option he was particularly happy about.

Slowly the guard did as he was told.

"Lie down. Flat," David continued mildly. He projected nothing but utter confidence. "Don't move, if you want to keep breathing."

He kept his "weapon" leveled on the guard even as he walked up to him. He placed it against the base of the guard's skull and pulled the guard's own weapon from his belt. For a moment he considered using the fake PPG to try to club the guard into unconsciousness, but he quickly dismissed the idea; it would be much too difficult, thanks to the guard's Minbari bone crest.

Shoot him. Kill him, the voice from his shoulder said.

David held the newly acquired genuine gun firmly and aimed it squarely at the Minbari's back. His finger twitched on the trigger. But that was all.

David . . .

"No," he said firmly.

The voice seemed to laugh in understanding. *Very well, then. Render him helpless, if you are more comfortable with that.*

Within minutes, David had bound and gagged the guard using strips of cloth torn from the guard's clothes. With that attended to, he walked quickly over to one of the shuttles and climbed in.

He looked over the control board. He actually had a good deal of practical flying time. His father had seen to that part of his education, at least. He remembered the first time he had taken a vessel into orbit, his father sitting proudly at his side, complimenting him on his handling of the craft and telling him that it seemed as if he was born to do this.

And Sheridan had been right. David *was* born to do this. By Sheridan's own admission, it was David's birthright, and his father and his mother had denied it to him. Of what use was it to live his entire life on one solitary planet, when the stars called out to him?

He brought the systems on-line, powering up the shuttle. For the briefest of moments, he wondered just where he was going to go. But then he knew—without having to consider it any further.

He was going to Centauri Prime. That was where he belonged. He didn't know *why* he belonged there, but he knew he did.

Sheridan felt himself being hauled to his feet before he had fully recovered consciousness. He blinked in confusion against the light that was streaming in through the skylight overhead. It was early morning, and Sheridan couldn't for the life of him remember why he was lying on the floor in a hallway.

"John! John, what happened?" someone was shouting at him. No, not shouting—just speaking forcefully, and with great urgency.

Garibaldi was staring at him, extremely concerned, supporting him by holding his arms up. "Happened?" Sheridan managed to get out thickly. "I don't—" Then it came back to him with the force of a hammer blow, and Sheridan shook off the confusion in an instant. "David! Something happened to David! There was this . . . this thing!"

"John!" It was the alarmed voice of Delenn this time. She was barreling down the hallway, followed by a Minbari whom Sheridan recognized as the sentry from the port. "John, David was at the port last night! He attacked this man and stole a shuttle!"

"It wasn't David," Sheridan said. When he saw the perplexed expressions of the others, he quickly clarified, "It wasn't David in control. It was something else . . . this . . . this thing on his shoulder, I've never seen anything like it. It looked like a lump of clay, but with an eye. It was controlling him. It had to be."

They ran quickly to David's room. Sheridan cursed himself for honoring his son's request for privacy by having his room set far apart from that of his parents. If he'd been nearby, he might have heard something earlier on, and been able to intervene before matters got out of hand.

Sheridan and the others looked in dismay at the wreckage. Whatever clues they might have found seemed hopelessly lost. Everything was smashed to pieces.

Sheridan leaned against the wall, sorting through everything he had seen. "Where could it have come from?"

"If it's as small as you say it was, it could have snuck in through any part of the house," Garibaldi said. He looked around. "David didn't go without a struggle, I'll tell ya. He tried to fight that thing off."

Delenn suppressed a shudder as she picked up the pieces of the Centauri urn, which had apparently been shattered along with other objects in the room.

"We've got to find him," Sheridan said furiously. "I want word sent out to all the members of the Alliance . . ."

"That might not be wise," Garibaldi told him.

Sheridan looked at him incredulously. "How could it not be wise?"

"Because it's everything you've ever feared," Garibaldi said. "If you advertise to everyone that your son's disappeared, two things are going to happen. First, knowing that he's off Minbar, every bounty hunter, every crackpot, every nutcase is going to turn out in force looking for him. They'll want to snatch him and use him to exert pressure on you. And second, any nut and his brother can claim that they have him and start making demands. Sure, they won't be able to prove that they have him, but you won't be able to prove they don't. You go wide with this, I guarantee you'll solve nothing, and create a thousand headaches you can't even begin to imagine."

"What would you suggest, then?" Sheridan asked icily. "Where would we start looking?"

"Centauri Prime," Delenn answered.

They looked at her. "What?" Sheridan said.

She was holding up pieces of the urn, pieces from the lower half of it. "Londo said that this held water from a sacred river? It's dry. There's no sign of its ever having been wet, not the slightest aroma of mildew or any smell that would accompany stagnant water. There's no moisture on the cabinet that it was on when it broke, none on the floor."

"It could have evaporated," Garibaldi offered uncertainly.

"It could have. But I don't think so. I think that thing John saw was hidden inside here, in some sort of hibernation. Waiting, all these years, for us to give it to David."

It made sense.

It made horrific sense.

"He said we would always be friends. Do you remember, Delenn?" Sheridan said. His jaw constricted with mounting fury. "Remember what he said the day he gave it to us? That that day in our company meant so much to him. Well, now we know exactly what it meant, the bastard."

"What do we do?" Delenn asked.

"We go to Centauri Prime," Sheridan said without hesitation.

But Garibaldi shook his head. "You do no such thing. You don't know for sure that it was Londo."

"Are you defending him now, Michael?"

"No, I'm trying to make sure you don't rush into something half-cocked," Garibaldi said. "I'm as furious about it as you, but I've got more practice than you do keeping myself wrapped up. If David was taken from here, it was for one of two reasons: either they're just going to kill him as a means of revenge, or they've got plans for him. If it's the former, you can't help him. If it's the latter, those plans will certainly involve you, and you have to sit tight until you find out what their next move will be. His kidnappers will contact you. At that point, you'll know for sure that it's Londo, or whoever, and *that's* when you can plan your strategy."

"My strategy is already planned," Sheridan said tightly. "It starts with killing Londo Mollari. After that, I'll improvise."

EXCERPT FROM
THE CHRONICLES OF LONDO MOLLARI.
Excerpt dated (approximate Earth date)
November 29, 2277.

I cannot remember the last time I ran.

Not just ran. Sprinted. My personal guards actually had to run to keep up with me, and everyone we dashed past gaped at us. At me. And why should they not? My office is all about ceremony and posturing and maintaining dignity. The sight of the emperor charging down a corridor as if the hordes of hell itself were on his heels, well . . . I would have gaped as well.

I flung open the doors to Durla's private suite, the place that served him as both home and office. Durla was in a huddled conference with several of his ministers. Truthfully, I do not remember which ones. This has nothing to do with my recurring difficulties with memory. In this instance, I was simply so furious over the circumstances that had brought me here that I saw no one save for Durla.

He opened his mouth to make some oily inquiry as to why I had decided to grace him with my presence. I did not give him the opportunity to ask. "Get out," I snarled, and it was more than evident that I was referring to everyone but Durla.

And yet, incredibly, the ministers did not immediately leave. Instead they glanced at Durla, looking for confirmation. His. Over mine. The wishes of a prime minister over those of an emperor. Scandalous. Insanity. That such a thing could ever happen, and that I could be the emperor who had allowed matters to sink so low . . . it was a ghastly situation.

Trembling with rage, I said, *"Now!"* Just as I said that, Durla nodded, and the others rose and departed the room. I turned to my guards and said, "You, too."

"Highness, perhaps it may not be wise to—" one of them began.

"I am the emperor and you will do as you are ordered!" Whatever vestiges of pride and authority I might have had were obviously sufficient to get the job done, because the guards turned and walked out, leaving Durla and me alone.

"Is there a problem, Highness?" Durla inquired, unperturbed.

"Tell me how you did not do it," I said through clenched teeth.

"What 'it' would that be, Highness?"

He knew damned well, but if he wished to play his games for the few seconds longer I was going to allow him to live, so be it. "I have heard," I said, "that the son of John Sheridan is here. That you have kidnapped him. Yes? No?"

"No, your Highness."

"You deny that he is here?"

"No, I deny that he was kidnapped. Apparently he arrived here of his own free will."

"And why did he do this, eh?"

"Because we are Centauri Prime," he told me, "and it is our destiny to have all our enemies delivered unto us."

I could not quite believe what I was hearing. "What?"

"Highness," and he began to circle the room, and speak as if he were addressing a child. "His presence here is simply part of my grand vision."

"Not again." I had heard about his "vision" for Centauri Prime, and plans for the great Republic, all too many times.

"All this," and he gestured to the window that overlooked his balcony, "is because I envisioned it, Highness. When the great wave of Centauri vessels crashes upon the shores of the Alliance worlds, it will be the ultimate realization of my vision. I have willed it into existence. Because I have believed in it . . . it has come to pass.

"This is simply another example of the power of my belief. I believed that David Sheridan would come here . . . and he has. I must admit," and he leaned back against his desk, looking insufferably smug, "when Minister Lione informed me of young Sheridan's arrival, I was not the least bit surprised. Even Lione remarked upon how calm I was. Naturally. I could see it as clearly as I see you."

"And now that he is here, you will send him back, yes?"

"I will send him back, no," he told me. "You cannot be serious, Highness. This is the ideal opportunity to bend our greatest enemy to our will."

"You are insane! You would bring the might of the entire Alliance down upon us!"

"No. With his son's life at stake, Sheridan will bow to our will. It is inevitable. He cannot help himself. He is Human and, because of that, weak. In a way," and he laughed, "I almost feel sorry for him."

"Sorry for him? The Alliance fleet will bomb Centauri Prime back into the primordial ooze from which we crawled, and you feel sorry for him?"

"Yes, because he lacks the strength of dedication and commitment that even the lowliest of Centauri possess."

A door opened at the far end of the room before I could reply . . . and I gaped. I admit it. My jaw nearly hit the floor.

Mariel was there, emerging on unsteady legs. She was leaning against the door frame for support. There were faint discolorations on her face. Clearly she had been struck some short time ago. I knew that Mariel had not been seen as of late, but this . . . this . . .

I knew he had done it before. But now he had done it again, and what had seemed like an isolated incident became a pattern.

She had not heard me. I wondered if he had done internal damage to her. But she saw me and gasped, her hands automatically flying to cover her battered face. She ducked back into the other room, closing the door behind her.

Durla looked at me expectantly. He seemed to be wondering what other trivial matter I might bore him with at that moment. Forcing myself to speak clearly, levelly, I said, "You say . . . you have foreseen all this?"

"Much of it, yes."

"And have you foreseen . . . this?" And I drew back my fist and smashed him in the face as hard as I could.

It was likely a foolish move on my part, for Durla was an old soldier and still in battle-ready condition. I, on the other hand, had a flair for swords, but was older and much diminished. In a brief struggle, I might have been able to hold my own. In a prolonged fight, he could likely have done me great damage. Still, I was emperor, and there might still have been sufficient respect for the office to inhibit him from lashing out that aggressively.

None of that mattered. I struck him with no forethought, no care as to what might happen or how good an idea it was. All I knew, at that moment, was that I desperately needed to have my fist in direct contact with his face.

It was nice to see that I had not lost my punch, or at least was capable of recapturing it when the need arose. Durla went straight down, having been caught utterly unprepared. At that moment, I truly believe that I could have killed him with my bare hands.

And then the pain struck me.

— chapter 14 —

Durla had been caught completely flat-footed. He had to admit that he had come to underestimate just what the emperor was capable of, and being knocked flat by Londo Mollari was a decisive reminder.

His head struck the floor when he went down, and just for a moment the world spun around him. He saw Londo standing over him, raging, and his hands seemed even larger as they descended, clearly ready to throttle him. Just for a moment, the normally confident Durla wondered whether he could actually withstand a concerted attack from the infuriated emperor.

And then, just like that, the threat passed. Because the emperor pitched back, clutching at his head. If someone had driven a spike through his skull, the reaction could not have been more pronounced. From the floor, Durla watched, utterly stupefied, as Londo staggered back. His eyes were tightly closed, and he seemed for all the world as if he wanted to do anything rather than scream. But then the scream came, and it was very loud and laced with agony.

It was more than enough to alert the guards outside that something was up. By the time they pushed through the door, Durla was on his feet, looking down at the writhing form of the emperor.

For a moment he wasn't entirely sure what to say. It wouldn't do for word to get out that the emperor had been so angry with Durla that he had assaulted him. It was hard to determine just how much popularity the emperor still possessed. Durla did not for a moment doubt that the people had come to love their prime minister, but the affection for the office of emperor was historical, tried and true. They certainly seemed to adore their figureheads, and the attendant pomp and circumstance.

"The emperor is having some sort of an attack," Durla said quickly. "Have him brought to his quarters at once. Call a physician . . ."

"No!"

The word exploded from Londo as if torn from the depths of his dismay. And now Dunseny was at his side, propping him up. Londo's eyes were open wide as if there was agony still erupting behind them. "Highness, it's necessary," Dunseny said immediately. "I know your antipathy for physicians; you've not had more than the most cursory of examinations for over a decade. But in this instance . . ."

"In this instance," Londo managed to say, his voice still shaking, "I am still the emperor . . . and you are still . . . not." Whatever fit had taken hold of Londo seemed to be subsiding. "Help me up," he said in a vaguely commanding voice, and instantly several guards were at Londo's side, helping him to his feet.

One of them was Caso. Durla recognized him instantly. They exchanged a long look, then Caso helped the emperor to lean on his shoulders.

Durla had never been particularly impressed by Caso. He had struck Durla as faint of heart during the questioning of the traitor, Rem Lanas, and positively disconcerted upon the imprisonment of Milifa. When it had come time for Milifa to quietly die in prison, Caso had managed to absent himself to avoid taking part in that particular Prime Candidates function. His eagerness to clear the Narn, G'Kar, that day of the shooting, had not sat especially well with Durla, either.

Thinking of G'Kar and the prisons sent Durla's mind spinning in a particular direction, and he smiled faintly to himself. Without missing a beat, he turned to Londo, and said, "Highness . . . I hope you recover from your distress quite soon. And I shall remember our discussion for quite some time to come."

Londo was barely managing to lend any support to himself, but he still was able to summon enough strength to say, "I would strongly advise that you do so, Prime Minister . . . for all our sakes. Your treatment of young Sheridan, and of . . . others . . . shall not go unnoticed."

"No treatment shall," Durla replied, bowing slightly at the waist. His jaw was throbbing from where Londo had struck it, but he was not about to give Mollari the satisfaction of seeing him acknowledge it. "No treatment shall."

He waited until the room was empty, and then he turned and went into the adjoining chamber. Mariel was sitting there, looking very concerned, and when Durla entered she immediately stood. "What happened?" she asked breathlessly.

"The emperor," Durla said evenly, "tried to attack me. In this instance, I did not have to hurt him. He was most fortunate. And it was your appearance, I think, that set him off. That was not appreciated, Mariel."

"I did not know he was there, my lord Durla." She bowed slightly. "My . . . hearing is not what it once was. I sustained an injury . . . in my clumsiness . . . that has reduced my hearing acuity. It is being treated, however, and a full recovery is expected."

The words were very carefully chosen and he knew it. He did not smile, merely nodded slightly. "For the duration, you will have to listen more closely," he told her.

"Yes, my lord husband." When she saw that he was heading out, she said, "Where are you going, my lord . . . if I may ask," she added quickly.

"I am going to visit an old friend with whom I have had some disagreements," Durla told her. He smiled. "I'm going to see if there's not some way we can't see eye to eye."

"That's very considerate, my lord."

"Yes. It is," he agreed. And just as the door closed behind him, Mariel let fly a spit of contempt. It landed on the door and ran noiselessly to the floor.

"Leave me," Londo managed to say.

Dunseny looked at him uncertainly. They had brought him back to his inner sanctum and helped settle him into a leaning couch. The manservant had been fussing over him for some time now, trying to make him comfortable and all the time wheedling him about having a physician brought in. Londo would not hear of it.

"Are you certain, Highness?" Dunseny asked solicitously. "Might it not be wiser to—"

"It might be wiser to do as I say," Londo told them. "Now go."

Seeing no other real options, Dunseny and the guards departed as they were instructed to do. Caso, the last one out, cast a glance over his shoulder in obvious worry. Then the door closed behind him.

"Well?" Londo asked, once everyone was gone. "What are you waiting for?"

The shadows moved, as he knew they would. In a moment, an all-too-familiar form was standing several feet away from him.

"How dare you," Shiv'kala said.

"How dare I?" Londo seemed amused. "How dare I know you would be there? I am so sorry. Did I ruin your surprise? Your flair for the dramatic?"

"You know what Durla is to us. You know what we have invested in him. He is our future, Londo." After his initial anger, Shiv'kala seemed relatively calm. "Not just ours . . . but yours as well."

"Is that so?" Londo was about to say something more, but suddenly he was seized by a racking cough. Shiv'kala waited patiently for the hacking to subside.

"Yes, that is so. I must admit to you, Londo . . . I am somewhat disappointed in you."

"I shall try to hide my extreme dismay over letting you down."

"I have spent many years with you now, Londo. I have explained to you the Drakh philosophies, the Drakh teaching. Tried to make you understand why we do what we do. Yet at every turn, you seem unwilling to embrace all we can do for you, bring to you . . ."

"You mean in the way Durla has."

"We have approached Durla differently than we did you. But yes, he shares our vision."

"He has the vision you implanted within him."

"No," Shiv'kala said, sounding almost sad. "Londo, how little you understand your own people. We have simply worked with that which already existed. We have unleashed the greatness that was within him, just as we have tried to do with you. Not just you, but your people as well. The Centauri Republic will be great, Londo—with you or without you."

"I had been hoping it would be both." Londo seemed rather amused by the comment.

Shiv'kala circled him. "Believe it or not, Londo, throughout the years, I have been your greatest ally. When others felt you simply were not worth the effort, I stood up for you. I spoke on your behalf. I argued that you could be brought around. That the time and effort being spent on you was not in vain. Then an incident such as this one occurs, and it leads me to wonder if the other Drakh were not correct."

"Meaning that I have let you down, and so you will kill me for it?" He seemed to consider this. "I do not see the threat. Death holds fewer and fewer terrors for me with each passing day."

"You say that now, when your life is not threatened," Shiv'kala commented. "It is always simple to laugh in the face of death when it is not facing you. In time, you may change your mind. This much, however, is certain, Londo. You will never lay hands upon Durla again. You will not threaten him, nor assault him. Nor will you attempt to dispatch any agents or cat's-paws to do likewise, because we will find out. And the pain that was inflicted upon you via the keeper today . . . will seem as nothing. If you do not trust my word in any other matter, I suggest you trust it in this: You will not survive."

"No one ever survives," Londo observed. "One just gets progressively worse opportunities to die."

There was a respectful knock at the door. Londo glanced at Shiv'kala, but the Drakh had already blended in with the shadows of the room. "Come," he called.

The door opened, and two members of the Prime Candidates entered. They carried between them a silver tray, covered with a cloth, which they placed on the table next to Londo. He looked at it with bleary curiosity. "Yes? What is it?"

"Compliments of Ministers Lione and Durla," one of the boys said. Then they turned and departed while Londo leaned forward and looked with curiosity at the covered tray.

A bomb, possibly. Or some sort of trap. At that moment, however, Londo didn't particularly care. He pulled off the cloth and gasped.

An eye was sitting on it, looking up at him.

Except it was no normal eye. It appeared to be solid, with a red tint to it . . .

"G'Kar," Londo whispered. There was a note on the tray next to it. With hands trembling, he picked it up and read it.

"The noble Citizen G'Kar is being forced to send his regrets. He is feeling somewhat put out at the moment, and will not be able to join you for dinner in the foreseeable future. Instead he will be undergoing an intensive, rigorous 'training program' to make certain he remains in good shape. We trust our meaning has been made clear, and will not be forgotten."

Londo started to stand, as if to go charging to G'Kar's aid. "Where do you think you are going?" Shiv'kala asked calmly. That was not unusual. He was calm most of the time. Icy, like a frozen planet, and with about as much chance of displaying pity or mercy. "Certainly you are not considering helping your pet Narn, are you?"

Londo pointed in fury at the eye. "This was your idea, I take it?"

"No, actually. We probably would have thought of it . . . but the truth is that Durla conceived of it all on his own. It will not go well for the Narn, I fear. But he will not die. Durla would not want that to happen, for if he dies, then he cannot be a source of ongoing torment for you."

"Bastards!" Londo spat out, and he started for the door.

Then the pain came again. Londo got only a few steps before it overwhelmed him, like an ocean wave batters a sand castle to bits. Londo staggered back and sank into the cushions.

"Some quiet time for you now, Londo, I think," Shiv'kala told him, as if addressing an angry child. "A day or so to contemplate your actions, and why it would be most unwise to repeat those actions."

"Must . . . stop him . . ."

"You cannot," Shiv'kala said. "You cannot stop any of this. It has gone too far. Within days now, the fleet will be launched. Durla will see to it. He has prepared for it extremely well. And you cannot—will not—do anything to stop it, Londo. Otherwise I will make certain that Durla does indeed go too far in his . . . what was the phrase . . . 'training program' for G'Kar. And that will be the least of the recriminations that await you . . . all in retaliation for anything you might try to do, none of which could hope to succeed.

"The only thing you will succeed in doing is injuring yourself . . . and others. G'Kar, Senna, even that absurd Vir Cotto, for whom you continue to have foolish affection. All of them will know the punishments attendant in your failed attempts to stop the unstoppable.

"Have we made ourselves clear, Londo?"

"Painfully so, yes." He managed to nod his head.

"As I told you, Londo . . . believe it or not, we have been merciful until now. Do not, at any time, mistake mercy for weakness. We are not weak. We are Drakh. We are of the Shadows. Is that also clear, Londo?"

This time he didn't even bother to speak. He just nodded.

"I am pleased we had this opportunity to chat, Londo."

And then, rather unexpectedly, Londo managed to get out, "The boy . . . the Sheridan boy . . ."

"What about him?" If the Drakh had had an eyebrow, he would have cocked it in curiosity.

"Bringing him here . . . is insanity. Crossing his father, crossing Delenn . . . the Earth fleet, the Minbari fleet will be brought down upon us. Even you cannot possibly think that we can withstand such an assault. The Minbari fleet alone could level this world."

"Very likely. But such an action would only result in the boy's death, and Sheridan and Delenn will not risk that. They will come here, alone and unattended. We know this for a certainty. And when they come here, you, Londo, will oversee their execution."

"On what grounds?"

"On the grounds that they are responsible for sending the Shadows away. They will pay for that with their lives."

"And the boy?"

"We have plans for the boy. With his parents gone, he will 'escape,' and live to serve our interests."

"Your interests?" Then he laughed bitterly. "Oh. Of course. The keeper."

"In the vase that you left, yes. Had you forgotten about that?"

"I tried to. Unfortunately, I seem to remember all the things I would rather forget, and forget that which I really should remember. When I brought the keeper in the urn . . . I hoped . . . it was for the purpose of spying. That was all. Influencing his father and mother on Minbar, perhaps. I never thought that this . . ."

The Drakh leaned in close to him. "Never forget," he said, "who is in charge. It will go badly for you if you do."

And with that, he left Londo sitting alone in his room—in a pain-filled silence enforced by the keeper—trying to determine just how things could possibly go more badly than they already were.

EXCERPT FROM
THE CHRONICLES OF LONDO MOLLARI.
Excerpt dated (approximate Earth date)
December 3, 2277.

I had to call her.

I sat here, stewing for days, thinking about what I had seen . . . thinking about what that bastard Durla had done to Mariel, even knowing my protection extended to her after her return to the Palace. And I kept thinking to myself, *At least your hands are clean. For all your crimes, for all that can be laid at your feet . . . at least you have never treated a woman in such a manner.*

And then I thought about that some more, really thought.

I thought of Adira . . . my beautiful Adira. The dancer who elevated my past, haunted my present, and would never be a part of my future. When she died, I took certain . . . steps . . . which drove me down the dark road I currently tread.

I thought of Mariel, an appendage to that man, that monstrosity of a man. If I had never divorced her, she would not be in this position. I know, I know . . . to ensure her own future, she tried to kill me. But in a way . . . should I be entirely surprised? She observed the men in the society in which she was raised. My gender taught her the lessons to which she subscribed. If she was raised to be devious, to hold little regard for life . . . who am I now to condemn her? One who has led a stainless life myself? If I were not subject to coughing fits, I would laugh heartily at that.

I thought of Daggair, another wife of mine . . . eh. Well . . . I did not think of her too much. There is only so much guilt even I will feel.

And then there is Timov. Timov, whom I shunted away, for her own good. Making her believe that I do not, did not ever, truly love her. The thing is, she was a woman of boundless integrity and sharp wit. Had we ever truly been a team— Great Maker, the things we could have accomplished.

I felt the need to say this to her. To make her realize that I did truly value her. And—I have to admit it—to cleanse my own guilt, for in my own way I had abused her just as thoroughly as Durla had done Mariel. Abused her trust, abused her affection. I owed it to her, somehow, to make reparations for this.

Foolish. Foolish old man.

When my—small associate—freed me after a time of enforced "meditation," I resolved that I had delayed long enough. Too long, in fact. Years too long. I knew that she no longer resided on Centauri Prime but instead had relocated to one of the outlying worlds. It was not difficult for me to establish a real-time link with her. A woman whom I recognized as a longtime retainer to Timov answered my communiqué and looked most surprised indeed to see that she was being contacted by the emperor himself. She told me that her mistress would be right there.

Long minutes passed. I surmised that Timov was making me wait out of spite.

I was wrong.

When a wan and drawn woman appeared on the screen, for a moment I did not recognize her. There was none of the fiery robustness I had come to associate with the razor-sharp spitfire called Timov, but then I realized that yes, indeed, it was she.

She sat there, staring at me. Not saying a word. The only part of her that seemed to be truly alive was her eyes, and those blazed with the fire of inner vision.

"Timov," I said, surprised at the huskiness of my voice. I started to say, "You are looking well," but nothing could have been further from the truth, and we both knew it. So instead I cleared my throat and started to say her name again.

She cut me off curtly. "It's true. Are you satisfied? Obviously you're calling to see for yourself if whatever you've heard is correct. So . . . you're seeing. Good enough?"

"I have heard nothing," I said quite honestly. It may have been the most honest thing I'd said to her in years . . . if not ever.

"You haven't heard that I'm dying," she said with such contempt in her tone that it was clear she didn't believe it for a moment.

I have never taken quite as long to say a single, one-syllable word as I did at that moment. "No," I finally managed to get out.

"Mm-hmm." Still she did not believe. I could not blame her. "All right, then. Why, after all this time, have you called?"

"I . . ."

Everything I wanted to say to her flooded through my mind. But nothing came out.

She scowled in that way she had. "Londo . . . you chased me off Centauri Prime. You have treated me with disrespect that you would not show to your greatest enemy. You have exhibited contempt for me, you have—"

"I know, I know. I have done all these things. I know."

"I am the empress and have been dealt with as if I were the lowliest of slaves. And now, after all this time, what could you possibly have to say?"

"Why are you dying?" I managed to say.

"To annoy you. Anything else?" She seemed anxious to end the transmission, to do anything except talk to me, be anywhere except on a line with me. A hundred responses went through my mind, and only one emerged.

"I want you to know . . . I am sorry," I said.

She stared at me as if I'd lost my mind. The seconds passed like an infinity.

Then her eyes softened ever so slightly. "You should be. But not for what you imagine you're calling to apologize for."

"I'm afraid I—"

"You don't understand. But then you rarely took the time to understand, or even to consider your actions. You were impulsive the night you banished me from Centauri Prime." The effort of speaking took a great deal from her. She stopped to breathe, and I said nothing.

"I have been less impulsive and have had more time to speculate, given my current condition. Londo, I know about your dilemma."

"How could you possibly know?"

"Do you not remember Lady Morella? You asked her to tell you about your future."

"That was a private transaction."

"Mmm, everything important to a Centauri is a private transaction, hence everything important to a Centauri is open to public scrutiny. I'm your wife, Londo. Even in exile, I know almost everything you do.

"It comes with the territory." She did not say these words flippantly. In fact, her eyes burned brighter.

Ah, yes, Timov knew just as all empresses knew of their husband's good fortune and ill omens. I saw what she was saying now. She was implying that Lady Morella, previously a telepath somewhat stronger in psionic capability than the average empress, was granted special vision as the wife of Emperor Turhan.

Timov *knew.* As Lady Morella *knew.* I had to warn her. "It is very dangerous for you to speculate on these things. That is why you are kept in exile."

"I know that. You are surrounded in darkness, and it is a darkness I know better than to penetrate."

"I should go, Timov. I just wanted to call to say . . . many things. None of them expressible now."

"Good-bye, Londo," she said briskly.

I reached to cut off the transmission, and Timov abruptly said, "Londo . . ."

My hand paused over the cutoff switch. "Yes?"

"If you need me, call."

"I won't be needing you."

"I know," she said tartly. "That's why I made the offer."

The screen blinked off. And I knew at that moment that I would never see her again. But at least I had tried. Tried . . . and failed.

If I cannot achieve greatness, at least I can aspire to consistency.

— *chapter 15* —

Vir was hurriedly packing in his quarters on Babylon 5 when an urgent beeping at his door interrupted him.

"Go away!" he called.

"We need to talk," came a surprisingly familiar voice. And yet it wasn't entirely too much of a surprise. In fact, the main surprise for Vir was that it hadn't occurred sooner.

"Come," he called, his command disengaging the door lock.

Michael Garibaldi entered, looking entirely too calm. He glanced around. "Going somewhere?"

"Yes. You could say th—"

And then, before Vir could say anything further, Garibaldi was across the room. He grabbed Vir by the shirtfront and slammed him up against a wall, knocking over furniture.

"I don't think so," Garibaldi said, and he spoke with barely contained fury. "I think you're going to tell me exactly how you think your people are going to get away with—"

He stopped. There was a blade pressed up against his throat, the hilt gripped solidly in Vir's hand. And Vir was staring into Garibaldi's eyes with absolutely no trace of fear. Any resemblance to the Vir Cotto who first set foot on Babylon 5 was long gone.

"What I think," Vir said in a low voice, "is that you're going to get your damned hands off me. And then we will talk like the reasonable men I know that one of us is."

Very slowly, Garibaldi released his hold on Vir's shirt and stepped back, keeping the palms of his hands up where Vir could readily see them. "The only reason you got away with that," he said, "was that you were the last person I would have thought capable of doing it."

"That's how I get away with a lot of things these days," Vir told him. He slid the blade back into the scabbard that was hidden under his vest. He studied Garibaldi a moment. The former security chief was unshaven and glassy-eyed. "How long since you've slept?"

"Did you know about it?" Garibaldi demanded.

"About your not sleeping?" Vir was completely lost.

"About David?"

"David." It took Vir a moment to place the name. "Sheridan's son. What about him?"

"They have him."

Once again it took Vir a few moments to follow the track of the conversation . . . but then he understood. "Great Maker, no," he whispered.

"Great Maker, yes."

Vir walked around to the bar and promptly poured himself a drink. He held up the bottle to Garibaldi as an offering. Garibaldi took the bottle, stared at it a moment, then took a deep smell of the alcohol wafting from it before placing it back on the bar. "It's a good vintage," Vir said, slightly surprised.

"Maybe some other time . . . like when I'm on my deathbed."

"Tell me what happened. Tell me everything."

Something in Vir's voice must have convinced Garibaldi, for after only a moment's hesitation, he laid out the circumstances involving David's disappearance, in quick, broad strokes. When he mentioned the small lump of a creature on David's shoulder, Vir slowly nodded. "Drakh," he said.

"What? What about the Drakh?" Garibaldi said.

"Go on. I'll tell you in a minute."

So Garibaldi continued, and when he was finished, Vir simply sat there, contemplating his drink. "His parents are going out of their minds with worry."

"They have every reason to," Vir said. His eyes narrowed. "I think their friends are going a bit crazy, too."

"Sorry about . . . earlier," Garibaldi told him, gesturing to indicate his unexpected assault on Vir. "You said 'Drakh' before. Are you talking about the same Drakh who inflicted the plague on Earth?"

"The very same. That thing that you saw on David? Londo has

one like it on him. It's how they control you, or watch you, or something like that."

"Are you saying," Garibaldi said slowly, "that the Drakh are somehow involved with Centauri Prime? With this kidnapping?"

Vir took a deep breath and let it out. "Yes. They have been for some time. They control Londo. I suspect they control Durla, to some degree. I also have reason to believe that a Drakh was involved in the death of Lou Welch."

"You told me it was the Prime Candidates."

"It was. But the Drakh apparently helped." He shook his head. "The plague they inflicted on Earth is not dissimilar from the plague they've inflicted on my world as well . . . except on Centauri Prime it's more covert."

"I don't understand. Why didn't you tell me this sooner?"

"I couldn't take the chance," Vir admitted. "These are agents of the Shadows we're talking about. I was concerned that if you knew they were on Centauri Prime, you would tell Sheridan, Sheridan would tell the Alliance, and that would have been all that was needed for the Alliance to come down on my people, attack without hesitation. The Centauri, after all, were seen as a beaten people. The Drakh would have been something that you would have gone after . . . but Centauri Prime would have suffered. You would have killed the patient in order to annihilate the disease."

"And you're not worried about that anymore?"

"Why should I be?" Vir said reasonably. "They have David. I doubt Sheridan's going to order a strike on a world when it would ensure the death of his son."

"Pretty damned cold-blooded of you, Vir."

"I've had to make some pretty cold-blooded choices in recent years, Mr. Garibaldi. You get used to it." He sighed. "Perhaps I should have gone public sooner. By allowing them to dwell in the dark, I've let them fester and grow. But exposing them might well have meant the death of my people. With any luck, though, we'll be able to have it both ways now. We've mustered enough resistance that the Drakh can be revealed for what they are without it amounting to a death sentence for Centauri Prime."

"You told me to trust you," Garibaldi said, stabbing a finger at Vir. "You told me to let you handle things. To let the Centauri solve the problems of Centauri Prime. And I've been doing that. But it's no longer just the Centauri's problem. It's John Sheridan's problem, and Delenn's."

"I'll handle it."

"Vir!"

"I said I'll handle it," Vir repeated firmly. "I'm heading to Centauri Prime right now. I've spent years—years of planning and preparing, of risking my neck and the necks of others—and it's all coming to a head. The fact that David was taken is just further indication of that. The Drakh want vengeance . . . but more than that, they also want insurance. But all the insurance in the world isn't going to help them against someone they don't know is their enemy. Someone they think of as a patsy, a fool."

"I'm coming with you."

"Now *you're* the fool," Vir said. He walked over to Garibaldi and put a hand on his shoulder. "We'll get David back for you, Michael. But we have to do it our way."

"Who is we?"

"The Legions of Fire."

Garibaldi looked at him oddly. "What?"

Vir smiled thinly. "I've found Earth history as interesting as Londo does. There are all sorts of end-of-the-world scenarios, did you know that? And one of them—from your Norse, I think it is—describes the world ending when a giant fire demon, Surtur, sweeps the world with his sword and cleanses it of all evil. That's what the Legions of Fire are going to do, Michael. We're going to sweep Centauri Prime clean of the blackness that's been upon it for so long. We're going to expose the Drakh presence to the rest of the galaxy. That way, we can point to those who are truly responsible for the fate of Centauri Prime. Prove that it's the Drakh who should be blamed . . . and that this prolonged campaign of resentment and aggression has been aimed at the wrong people. That it should be stopped."

"And you really call yourselves the Legions of Fire."

"Do you have a better name?" Vir asked, mildly annoyed. "We could call ourselves 'Vir's Victory Squad' or 'Cotto's Crusaders,' but that might tip off who's in charge."

"No, no, it's fine. Legions of Fire. Fine." Garibaldi took a deep breath, steadying himself. "Vir . . . he's my godson . . . and Sheridan and Delenn are my best friends in the galaxy . . ."

"And believe it or not, I'm your second best friend," Vir said.

"I'll get the job done, and David home safely. You have my word."

"I didn't used to think that meant a lot," Garibaldi said, and then he shook Vir's hand firmly. "But now I believe it does."

By the time Garibaldi returned to Minbar, Sheridan and Delenn were gone.

— *chapter 16* —

Durla could not recall a time that he had wanted to cry tears of pure joy the way that he did at that moment. It was just as it had been in his dream. In fact, it was all he could do to make sure that he was not asleep.

There were ships everywhere. Everywhere. The skies above the spaceport were filled with them. The ground was likewise thick with ships preparing to take off.

They had come from all over, a few at a time, assembling on the only planet that seemed appropriate: the world designated K0643. The site of the failed excavation program had remained for him a stain on his otherwise perfect record. Now, however, he was prepared to erase that stain by using this backwater, nothing world as the jumping-off point for the greatest campaign in the history of the Centauri Republic.

The spaceport itself was nothing particularly wonderful. The buildings had been thrown together in a purely makeshift fashion. The command center, the barracks, all of them, shoddy construction. But they were serviceable, and that was the only important thing. All of the perfection of construction, all of the craft and abilities of the hundreds of workers who had brought this moment to fruition . . . that was what mattered.

General Rhys and all of his command staff were assembled, with last-minute checks being made, final preparations being completed. "The jumpgate has been fully tested and is on-line, General?" Durla asked.

Rhys nodded. "Absolutely, Prime Minister."

"No chance of sabotage?" he said darkly. "It will not go well for anyone, General, if anything should go wrong while ships are going through."

"I tell you, sir, it is impossible," Rhys stated flatly. "It cannot, *will* not happen."

"Well, then," and Durla nodded with approval. "That's heartening to hear." He looked around at the others, all waiting for his words. Surprisingly, he found himself thinking of his brother, the one whose death he had arranged out of a fit of jealousy. From time to time he had found himself wondering whether he had done the right thing. Now there was absolutely no question that he had. He had achieved the pinnacle of success, and if it was over his brother's dead body, well . . . so much the better.

"We all understand, then," Durla said. They all nodded. Naturally they did. And yet he couldn't help but outline the intent of the fleet again, simply because he loved the sound of it: the words, the plan, his own voice. All of it. "We intend to launch a multistage assault on the Homeworlds of ninety percent of the Alliance governments. The ten percent we are sparing are small and relatively helpless . . . and besides, we're going to need to get our new workers from somewhere, so we'd best leave a few worlds intact, correct?" He laughed at this, and the others quickly joined in. *They know what's good for them,* he thought grimly, and continued, "If we strike hard enough, fast enough, we can immobilize them and pave the way for full-scale assaults on their holdings. This plan of attack will leave them powerless against further Centauri aggression."

"Powerless," one of the captains echoed. "I like the sound of that." The others nodded in approval.

"We have," he said proudly, "over three thousand vessels at our disposal. They represent the result of almost two decades of slave labor. Oh, the Alliance has had its suspicions, the rumors have floated about. But in the end—an end which is coming quite soon—they were too lazy, and we, too clever."

"The Alliance does have more ships at its disposal," Rhys cautioned, clearly worried that his men might become overconfident. "The White Star fleet alone is a formidable one."

"True," Durla admitted, but then added, "however, we certainly have the single largest armada belonging to one government. We need not worry about intergovernmental disputes, or differences of opinion on the best way to attack. We will operate with one mind and one purpose, and in doing that . . . we cannot lose."

"Coordination is indeed going to be the key," General Rhys said. "Prime Minister, if I may . . ." Durla gestured for him to continue. "You all have been given predetermined points in hyperspace that will provide you access to each of your respective targets. Fail-safe points, if you will. You will stay on point until everyone is in place. Then we will launch full, simultaneous strikes on all the targets at once. You will attack military sites, the capitals, and communication centers, cutting off all the Alliance worlds from one another, instilling fear, and dividing them in panic. Since the Centauri fleet outnumbers any other single fleet, we will be able to hit our enemies in waves, one after the other, before the Alliance can organize its scattered members into any kind of cohesive force." He took a deep breath, and said, "On receiving the go-codes from the prime minister, you will launch your assaults."

There was a momentary confused look shared among the captains. One of them said, "Not from you, sir?"

"Do you not trust my judgment, Captain?" Durla demanded suspiciously.

"I did not say that at all, Prime Minister. It is just that, since this is a military operation . . ."

"And the military operation has been sabotaged repeatedly," Durla pointed out. "With all respect to yourselves, and very much to General Rhys . . . the one person I know I can trust is me. It has been my vision, my drive that has brought us to this point, and my words will launch the attack. Is that understood? Do all of you understand that?"

There was a chorus of "Yes, sir" from around the table.

Durla nodded in approval. "Then, gentlemen . . . to work."

As one, they rose from the table, filing out of the room and stopping only to congratulate the prime minister on his momentous achievement. At the last, General Rhys hesitated. "Prime Minister . . ."

"It will be a masterpiece of coordination, General," Durla told him. In his mind's eye, he could already see it. "I am coordinating with Minister Vallko. He is going to be having one of his spiritual gatherings at the great temple. There, I will address the people, and speak to them of our capturing the glory that is Centauri Prime. We will stand on the brink of history . . . and then I will transmit the go-codes. And the rise from the great blackness will begin."

General Rhys looked as if he were about to say something, but then thought better of it. Instead he simply said, "It has been an honor to serve under you, Prime Minister."

"Yes. It has, hasn't it."

He was right. It was just like in his dream, a dream made into reality.

Durla stood on a cliffside, and stretched out his arms as the ships roared to life and took off, one by one. And as each one swung by him, throbbing with power, they banked slightly in acknowledgment.

They bowed to him.

Just as everyone would. Sheridan and Delenn, who had by this point been informed of the whereabouts of their son, and were no doubt on their way to Centauri Prime. Once there, they would become public symbols of the humiliation that had been heaped upon the great Centauri Republic, and their fate would represent all the Alliance had to look forward to.

And Londo . . . well, Londo would probably decide that he had contributed all that he could to Centauri Prime. He would step aside willingly and name Durla as regent until such time that Londo's passing would ensure Durla's appointment as emperor. Then, of course, that time would come quite, quite soon.

The skies were so thick with ships that they blotted out the sun. It was as if night had fallen upon Durla. An endless night of glory, waiting to swallow him. And he fed himself to it willingly.

— chapter 17 —

"You should not have come here," Senna said as the small vehicle took them toward the palace. "Vir, this was not a good time . . ."

"I had to," he said as the Centauri Prime spaceport receded into the background. "I stopped receiving communiqués from Mariel. I lost track of where Durla's plans stood. I was . . ."

"Concerned for her?" Senna asked.

He nodded. "And not just for her . . . also for you, and Londo. And now apparently David Sheridan has been added to the mix. You knew about this?"

She nodded, looking grim. "It's a terrible thing. He simply showed up. No one knew he was coming, not even Lione, and he was most upset about it. The only one who did not seem surprised was Durla. Sometimes I think nothing surprises him."

"Oh, I think we can arrange a surprise or two for him," Vir said grimly. "Can you get me in to see Mariel?"

"He's put her into seclusion. She's not allowed visitors."

"So you can't."

She smiled. "I didn't say that."

Senna strode up to the two guards who were standing outside Durla's suite of rooms, and said firmly, "The emperor wishes to see you."

They looked at one another, and then back to Senna. "Why?" one of them asked.

"I have known the man for nearly half my life, and if there is one thing I have learned, it is never to ask why. Lately, he does not take well to that . . . if you know what I mean." And she put a finger to her temple and mimed a weapon being fired.

The guards hesitated a moment. Senna crossed her arms and

169

displayed her best look of impatience. "I do not think the emperor likes to be kept waiting."

Durla had ordered that a guard be kept outside his suite at all times. But Durla was not around, and Senna was well known to be trusted by the emperor. Somehow it seemed that ignoring the emperor's wishes, as relayed by Senna, might prove to have a negative impact on their life expectancy.

They bowed slightly to Senna and hurried off down the corridor.

The moment they were gone, Senna whispered, "Vir!" In response to her summons, Vir hustled down the corridor to her side. "The door is sealed," she told him. "So I am not quite certain how we can get in . . ."

Vir, looking utterly confident, pulled a small device from the interior of his jacket. He aimed it at the door, and it emitted a brief burst of noise. The door promptly slid open.

Senna glanced at the device appraisingly. "Where did you get that?"

"I move with an interesting group of people these days," Vir replied, and without another word walked into Durla's suite of rooms. Senna followed.

He took a few steps in and then stopped. There, on the balcony, looking out at the city, was Mariel. At least, he was reasonably sure it was she. Her back was to him. "Mariel," he called cautiously.

Mariel turned and looked at him, and it seemed as if she could scarcely believe what she was seeing. Nor could Vir entirely believe his eyes, either. The woman he had known, the vibrant, beautiful young woman, was gone. She had been replaced by someone whose face exhibited unending sadness, whose skin carried with it fading bruises that hinted of past atrocities.

"Vir," she whispered, and ran to him. She threw her arms around him, held him tightly, kissed him with such ferocity that he actually had to apply strength to separate her from him. "Vir . . . you've finally come to take me out of here?"

"Mariel, sit down."

"Vir!" She allowed herself to be guided over to a chair. "You don't know how long I've waited," she said. "Is it finally over? When do we leave? I do not care that I am still married to Durla, I will go with you, do whatever you want . . ."

She was speaking so fast, she was almost incomprehensible, and he gripped her firmly by the arms, kneeling so that they were on eye level. "Mariel . . . first things first. What is Durla doing? Where is he now?"

"I don't know," she said.

"What is his timetable? Where stand the ships he's been working on? How close to completion are—"

"I don't know, *I don't know!*" Her voice was rising, and Vir realized that she was rapidly coming to the end of her rope. "He doesn't talk to me anymore, doesn't tell me anything about anything! I don't know what his plans are, and I don't care anymore! I just want to be with you! The two of us, as it was always meant to be!"

"Vir, this isn't getting us anywhere. We should go," Senna warned him in a low voice.

"Vir, you can't." Mariel was clutching on to his arm, and all last traces of dignity, of strength, fell away from her. "Vir, you can't leave me here . . ."

"Mariel, it's not that easy. No harm will come to you, I promise, but I can't just take you out of here. We'll be noticed, we'll . . ."

"I don't care! Don't you *understand*, Vir? All that I have endured, I have endured for you! My love for you, it is boundless, it is endless. Please, Vir, I will do whatever you ask, whenever you ask! I have done nothing but dream of you, night after night. Whenever I was in his arms, it was yours I imagined. His lips crushing against mine, but I felt them to be yours and took comfort from that! You are my everything, my—"

"Stop it!" He felt as if what remained of his soul were being shredded. "Stop it, Mariel! You don't know what you're saying!"

"Yes, I do! I have heard it in my head, night after night, when I dreamt of you coming for me. It is all that matters, it is the only thing, it—"

"It's not real!"

He had not expected to say it. He had not wanted to say it. For years, the guilt he had carried within him had given him no peace, but he had still been sure that he would be able to contain the dark truth of what he had done. What was to be gained from telling her? Nothing. And yet when the words burst from him, he knew it was because his presence in her life was a lie, and he could not allow her to live it anymore. It was the only chance she had of divesting herself from the hellish existence that she currently endured. He had to try to undo the damage he had done to her.

She stared at him in confusion. "Not . . . real? What is not . . . real?"

"This thing you . . ." He took a breath and then turned to Senna. "Please . . . I need to talk to Mariel alone. Please."

Senna didn't understand, but she did not need to. "As you wish," she said, and she took Vir's hands in hers briefly and squeezed them. Then she walked quickly from the main room, the door shutting behind her.

Vir went back to Mariel, took her hands in his, and said, "You're under a spell."

"A spell." She repeated the words, but with no real comprehension.

"A techno-mage named Galen put it on you, at my request. I was . . . I was angry because I knew you had used me, to get in good with the other diplomats on Babylon 5. I knew you laughed at me behind my back. And I . . ." He looked down. ". . . I told myself that I had him do it to help the cause. So that I could bend you to my will, turn you back on the people who'd sent you to spy on me. But that was an excuse. I did it from petty revenge, and it was beneath me, and I've ruined your life, and I'm sorry. Great Maker, the words don't mean anything, but I am. I'm sorry."

"Vir . . ."

"Londo. Londo can help. He can grant you a divorce from Durla, and you can start over in a new life. We'll get you set up somewhere, I can—"

"Vir, it's all right."

He stopped talking and stared at her. "All right? How is it all right?"

"I saw. I saw the way Senna looked at you, and you at her. How she held your hand a moment before leaving. You think," and she laughed, "you think that I would not want to share you. That my love for you is so overpowering that I would be jealous of other women in your life." She stroked his cheek. "If you want both Senna and me, that is perfectly all right. Whatever makes you happy . . ."

"Mariel, I don't love you! Don't you see? I can't ever! Because any feelings you'd return for me were made for you by Galen!"

Her face flushed. "I don't know why you're saying these things. I know my mind! I know how I feel! No wizard put these thoughts into my head! You're just . . . testing me, that's it. Testing me . . . wanting me to prove my love to you, to—"

"No! I don't! It's—"

Suddenly the door at the far end of the room slid open. The guards were standing there, with Senna in between them.

"The emperor will see you now," Senna said gravely.

"He is not supposed to be in here!" one of the guards said.

"I heard her cry out," Vir said immediately. "I was outside and when I heard her cry of alarm, I thought that perhaps one of those saboteurs or someone like that was attacking Durla's wife. So I thought I would check, because there were, after all, no guards outside," he added pointedly. He bowed to Mariel, and asked solicitously, "Will you be all right, milady?"

Mariel, looking at him with limpid eyes, whispered, "I will prove my love."

Vir felt ill.

EXCERPTED FROM
THE CHRONICLES OF LONDO MOLLARI.
Excerpt dated (approximate Earth date)
December 25, 2277.

Vir looked ill.

At the very least, there were times when he had certainly looked better.

It is amusing the way things work out sometimes. There I was, speaking with Dunseny, saying to him, "You know what I desire more than anything? I would like to share a pleasant dinner with my old friend, Vir. Do you think that could be arranged?"

At that moment, in walked Senna with two guards. They stood stiffly at attention, as if they were awaiting orders. I had no idea what they wanted me to say. I looked to Dunseny, but he clearly had no better idea than I did. "Can I help you?" I inquired.

"We were told that you desired our presence, Highness," one of them said.

I didn't know what he was talking about. But I saw Senna standing behind them, nodding her head. Obviously this was some sort of childish prank and, to be honest, I thought it might prove amusing. I think I am someone very much in need of more childishness in my life. I found my head nodding in time to Senna's own. "Yes . . . yes," I said. "As a matter of fact, I would like you to bring me Vir Cotto."

The guards exchanged glances. "The ambassador to Babylon 5?"

"The very same," I said.

"I . . . believe I know where he can be found, Highness," Senna said. "He is actually here, in the palace."

I was astounded. Rarely do things work out for me as conveniently as that. "Escort him here at once!" I commanded the guards. As Senna led the apparently puzzled guards out, I turned to Dunseny; and said, "Have a meal prepared and brought up. Vir and I shall . . . chat . . ."

"At once, Highness," Dunseny said, and he went out to attend to my wishes.

174

The dinner was brought up mere moments before Vir arrived, escorted by Senna. "You will pardon me if I do not get up, Vir," I said. "My stamina is not quite what it used to be."

"Of course, of course," he said.

The food was laid out between us, and I gestured for everyone to leave us. Of course . . . I myself am never alone, but that is neither here nor there.

"So . . . Vir. What has brought you around?" I proceeded to eat heartily, displaying an appetite that was merely for show.

"Do I need an excuse to visit my Homeworld?" he asked. He wasn't touching any of the food in front of him. Perhaps he thought it was poisoned. If it were poisoned, I probably would have eaten it myself.

"Of course not. Of course not."

And we proceeded to chat. The conversation was strained at first, but as the time passed, the degree of comfort grew. He seemed guarded, even suspicious, and who could blame him really? After all, once before when we were together, I knocked him out and he wound up in a cell. For all he knew, this would be a repeat performance.

Really, it was not an important conversation, when one gets right down to it. Indeed, my memory is playing tricks on me. Much of what we discussed is gone from my head already. The drink, no doubt. However, there was one aspect that he seemed to find most . . . interesting.

"There is a Human work of literature that I stumbled over, Vir, that reminded me a bit of you and I."

"And what would that be, Londo?"

"The work of one Miguel de Cervantes. A book called *Don Quixote*. I'm in the middle of reading it, but it seems most fascinating. It is about a man with a most odd hobby. Do you appreciate odd hobbies, Vir? You have one or two yourself, I think."

He sat there for a moment, his face impassive. "We all have our hobbies, Londo, and each of them might seem odd to someone who doesn't participate in it."

"Oh, absolutely. But this fellow, this Don Quixote . . . I thought you might appreciate his particular hobby. I don't know why I did. But I did."

"And what would that hobby be, Londo?"

"He fights evil." I leaned forward. "He fights evil wherever he sees it. He even fights evil when no others see it. Even though he believes the odds to be hopelessly against him, he charges into battle against the forces of darkness. Many people in the book think him insane."

"Do they." There was no inflection in his voice.

"Yes. They do. But there is a handful of others . . . who do not."

"And who would these be?"

"One of them is his faithful squire—that is to say, assistant—Sancho. Sancho helps the intrepid Quixote on his missions, no matter how farfetched, because he wants to help Quixote recognize his dreams. To validate them. To fight . . . against the forces of darkness."

"Yes . . . you mentioned those," Vir said slowly. "I . . . think I understand."

"And that reminded me of you . . . and even us. I think that once upon a time, Vir . . . I was Quixote. I had dreams of greatness, of what the Centauri Republic should be. And you . . . you were my Sancho," and I laughed and shook a fist. "At my side, supporting me in my efforts while at the same time trying to get me to see the reality of what I was doing."

"And when Sancho tried to explain reality to Quixote . . . did he understand?"

"Not really," I admitted. "Interesting the parallels that can be drawn, eh? And now, you know . . . I think that the roles have turned. I think, in many ways, you are the new Quixote, yes? You see a world that you want to be better than it is, and you fight the good fight to make it that way. And that would make me Sancho . . . trying to assist you . . . to tell you what is what. To tell you when dark forces are encroaching, and when time is running out."

"I think . . . in that respect . . . you would be an excellent Sancho."

"Good, good." I paused and took a deep breath. "Would you like to know . . . one of the ways in which the good Quixote fought evil?"

"Very much, yes."

I quaffed more of my drink, and said, "Windmills."

He looked at me oddly. "Windmills? What are windmills?"

"They were tall structures . . . very tall structures, and things were made inside them. Very tall structures . . . that seemed ordinary . . . but Quixote saw them as something else. He saw them as giants, and he attacked them. Charged at them with a long stick. It was called 'tilting.' He tilted at windmills."

"So he was insane, is what you are saying."

"Ahhh, but that is the test, Vir, you see. To look at tall buildings and say they are giants is, of course, insanity. But to look at towering structures and say they *might* be giants, why . . . that proves you a man of vision. A man who can see things when others do not, and act accordingly. That way . . . that way you can be prepared to do what must be done." I emptied my glass, poured myself another. "You might want to read the book, Vir. Reading is one of your hobbies, yes?"

"Yes. One of them."

"You should read it, then, definitely. Because it might have a very dramatic impact on your other hobbies . . . very soon."

— *chapter 18* —

Their voices were echoing throughout the catacombs, and it took all Vir's lung power to shout them down.

They had gathered quickly at Vir's summons; indeed, they'd been prepared for it ever since Renegar had filtered the word out that Vir was coming to Centauri Prime. Even the techno-mages had managed to show up, although how they knew to come—and why they weren't spotted when they moved about on the surface of Centauri Prime—was pretty much anyone's guess.

"I don't understand any of it!" Renegar said in frustration. "Windmills and Coyote—"

"Quixote."

"Whatever it is! How does this relate to—"

"He was speaking to me in a code," Vir told them. "I'm positive."

"What sort of code?" Adi asked suspiciously.

"The kind of code that only two people who've known each other for years could get away with. He was being watched and couldn't say anything overt . . . but he was subtle enough that I got it."

"Or you were misreading it," Finian suggested. "You could have been hearing what you wanted to hear."

"No," Vir said fiercely. "I heard what he wanted me to hear, and he was doing it to help." He started ticking off points on his fingers. "He knows I'm involved with the Legions of Fire . . ."

"The what?" they chorused.

"You guys. Never mind that now. He knows that I'm tied in with the saboteurs. He was trying to tell me that Durla is on the verge of making his move. That the Drakh are present in large numbers on Centauri Prime. That if we're going to do something about it, we're going to have to do it now."

"We don't know that for sure," one of the others said. "Perhaps the thing to do is wait, to—"

"No," Vir said, stunning the others into silence. "You didn't see what I saw. You didn't see the look in his eyes, the desperation. He wants this stopped as much as we do. He knows that this insane plan of Durla's, this scheming by the Drakh, is only going to end in tragedy for all. We have to strike openly, publicly, and with finality. We have to turn over the rock that the Drakh are hiding under. It's the only way!"

"Londo might have been setting us up . . ." Renegar ventured. "If he's a tool of the Drakh, as you say . . ."

"Then why play games, huh? If he suspects that I'm involved with the underground, why not just tell the Drakh? Watch me disappear," and he snapped his fingers, "like that. You think the Drakh care whether I actually am a rebel or not? If Londo voices his suspicion to them, they'd obliterate me without giving it a second thought, just to play it safe. The fact that he hasn't . . . the fact that I'm still here, and not off in a dungeon being tortured or just being executed as a warning to others . . . that means something, I'm telling you! And the coded message he was sending me meant something, too! We have to stop them!"

"How?" That was, of course, the big question. It was Gwynn who had posed it.

Surprisingly, Vir had an answer.

"Now is the time," he said slowly, "to let everyone and everything know about the Drakh infestation on this world. Which means we reveal their headquarters. Londo has figured out where it is. I should have, too, to be honest. He kept talking about a tall structure that wasn't what it seemed . . ."

"The Tower of Power," Renegar said suddenly.

"Of course," Finian said, looking at Gwynn. "The structure with no windows. It makes sense."

"We've scanned it before, though, for signs of Shadow tech," Gwynn reminded him. "We came up with nothing."

"Probably because there was none when you first scanned it," Vir suggested. "Or so little that it was undetectable. No one could get inside, for a close scan, because the place is so closely guarded by the Prime Candidates."

"And it remains heavily guarded," Renegar pointed out. "If there are Drakh there . . . and we are going to expose them . . . how do you suggest we do it?"

"Simple," Vir said, with a surprisingly malicious smile. "We tilt."

—— chapter 19 ——

In his cell deep beneath the palace, his body aching with a world of pain, G'Kar heard something faintly that sounded a great deal like cheering. As near as he could tell, it was some type of a massive rally. He had heard sounds like that before, and assumed it to be some sort of religious meeting. They liked their religious meetings, the Centauri did. It was a way to bolster the spirit of a people whose main occupation seemed to be endeavoring to dash the spirits of others.

Still, every so often, whenever he heard such things, he wondered whether he was eventually going to be made the subject of one. He could see himself being pulled out on a cart or somesuch, to their great temple, bound from head to toe, being pelted by overripe fruit along the way. Once at the temple he would doubtless be subjected to assorted torture devices, hoping to wring a scream from him, as Cartagia had, before he died a hideous death. Curiously, he was certain at this point that he wouldn't mind such a fate. At least he would know where he stood. As it was now, the daily beatings and torments were wearing quite thin on him. The novelty was wearing off on his captors, as well; despite everything they had done, they had not been able to elicit the slightest sound out of him.

He wouldn't give them the satisfaction.

There was one thing he was at least grateful for: that John Sheridan had not done some damned fool thing, like sending someone to Centauri Prime in a vain effort to rescue him. Or even showing up himself. He knew Sheridan all too well, knew it was the kind of stunt he was likely to pull. But apparently he had not done so. He'd probably had the impulse, but cooler heads had prevailed. Thank G'Quan for that. The knowledge that

Sheridan and Delenn were nowhere near this insanity brought him some measure of comfort.

In their cell beneath the palace, Sheridan and Delenn heard something faintly that sounded a great deal like cheering.

"Sounds like they're having a party up there," Sheridan commented. They were the first words he had spoken in some time.

"Do you think it involves us?" Delenn asked. She noticed some sort of vermin crawling around in the corner of the cell, and did her best to ignore it.

Sheridan noticed where she was looking. Without a thought, he walked over and stepped on it. "You mean do I think he's going to trot us out, his prize prisoners, and lord it over us? Is that what I think?"

"Yes."

"Yeah, I think that's what he's going to do." Sheridan looked haggard, as did Delenn, and for good reason. Their captors had not been especially kind to them, depriving them of food and water, endeavoring to extract information about the Alliance's armed might. Neither of them had said anything to that point, and they had no intention of doing so.

Yet Delenn couldn't help but be apprehensive. The Centauri efforts at extracting information from them had, thus far, been fairly mild. She was sure they could do a lot worse, and she had said as much to Sheridan.

"My guess," he had replied, "is that their more 'efficient' methods wouldn't leave us in especially good shape. Perhaps not even very recognizable as ourselves. And they may want the option of maintaining at least a semblance of . . . I don't know . . . mercy. Having a mindless shell of President Sheridan speaking out on their behalf isn't going to convince many people."

It seemed to make sense to her, but nevertheless she couldn't help but feel that something worse was going to be forthcoming. And when they heard the crowd noises outside, she began to wonder whether or not this might be it.

She said something softly, and Sheridan looked at her. "What? What did you say?"

"Nothing."

"Delenn." He sighed. "People don't mutter things under their breath because they don't want to be heard. They do it because they do want to be heard."

"You should not have come here," she said finally.

"What?"

"When that monster . . . Lione . . . contacted us, told us that they had David . . . that we were to come here at once, directly, informing no one, or else they would kill him . . . I should have come on my own."

"Don't be ridiculous," he said.

But she wouldn't be dismissed. "It is not ridiculous," she informed him. "I should have come here as an effort to try to convince them of the insanity of their actions. Try to reason with them. But you should have remained behind."

"Send my wife to do something that I'm afraid to do?" He shook his head fiercely. "Sorry, Delenn. Call me old-fashioned, but it just doesn't work that way."

"Why?" she demanded, her ire rising. "Because you're a man? A Human male? How typical! You have to throw yourself into the heart of danger when every reasonable assessment of the situation says that you should stay behind. John, it was foolishness! You're the president of the Alliance, and you delivered yourself to our enemies! The Alliance needs you!"

"You're the one who should have stayed, Delenn! You could do the Alliance far more good than I could. I tried to talk you into staying behind—"

"I'm David's mother, in Valen's name!"

"Hah!" he said triumphantly. "Now who's being typically Human! And you don't even have as good an excuse as I do! We both know that, if it's the Alliance you're so concerned about, you were the logical one to stay behind."

"How can you say that?"

"Because you'd be around longer! I've only got a few more years left!"

And there it was.

Delenn suddenly felt the coldness in the cell more than she had before. She looked down and away from him, because she knew it to be true. He had acknowledged the terrible truth that had preyed upon her, and somehow made it all the worse.

"I'm sorry, Delenn," he said softly.

And she turned and thumped him on the chest. It didn't hurt, but it startled him. The fury exploded from her.

"You're sorry? *You're sorry!* Don't you understand anything, John? I know I should have remained behind! That I should have let you do this on your own! But I couldn't refuse to come and risk condemning our son to death, because he's the part of you that will live on! And I couldn't be separated from you because, with the dwindling years we have left to us, every day—every second—becomes infinitely precious. Whether we live or die, all that mattered to me was that we did it together! How utterly, utterly stupid and shortsighted was that?"

He took her in his arms. "Completely," he said. "Can't you see how much I hate you for it?" He tilted her chin back with one finger and kissed her upturned lips. She returned the kiss as if it were going to be their last.

And then there was a rattling at the door. Several guards presented themselves and walked directly toward Sheridan.

"No!" Delenn cried out.

They grabbed Sheridan by either arm, forestalling any chance he might have at trying to pull away. She cried out his name, and he called back, "No, Delenn! Don't show them any weakness!" before he was hauled out of the room.

The door remained open. For a moment, Delenn thought that somehow they had actually overlooked the fact that she was still in there. Or perhaps they were so confident that it never occurred to them that she might make a break for it.

But as quickly as those hopes went through her mind, they were dashed when she heard footsteps approaching the door. And then she took a step back, startled, when a figure in gleaming white appeared. He looked almost heaven-sent in that aspect.

"Hello, Delenn," he said. He turned to the guards at the door and indicated that the door should be shut behind them.

"Highness, are you sure?" one of the guards asked.

"No. But one of the perks of being a highness is that people must obey your orders, even when there's no certainty in your mind at all. Do it."

The door closed, and he turned to Delenn.

"I felt you would be able to talk more freely if we were alone. Now then," he said. "Let us chat."

*   *   *

G'Kar heard a noise at his door and stood. He was certain that this was going to be it. And he steeled himself for the escape attempt he knew he would have to make, no matter how hopeless it was. Whenever they entered his cell, they always did so with enough restraints, shock prods, and such to control a dozen Narn. But today he would have to display strength on a par with more than that, for he knew in his heart that he would not have another opportunity.

But then the door opened only slightly, and instead of someone coming in to pull him out, a body was shoved in. It stumbled and fell, and the door slammed shut.

G'Kar squinted with his one eye. Only a small bit of light filtered through the tiny window in the door. The sounds of the crowd were getting louder, reaching a fever pitch, it seemed, only to get louder still. And then his new cellmate stood, steadying himself a moment, then trying to make out the other person he sensed in the darkness. "Hello? Who's there?"

G'Kar heard that distinctive voice and, to his own surprise, laughed softly.

Sheridan took a step into the meager light and peered into the gloom. "G'Kar? Is that . . . you?"

The Narn thought about just the right thing to say, given the circumstances.

"Please tell me," he said finally, "that you brought a deck of cards."

Londo simply stood there, regarding her for a long moment. "No hug?" he asked.

"Have you come here to gloat, Londo?" she asked icily. "Or perhaps you would like me to thank you, after sixteen years, for the lovely present you gave David."

"That won't be necessary." To her surprise, it seemed as if he couldn't look her in the eye.

"Were you pleased with yourself when you did that?" she asked. She knew this was precisely the wrong tack to take. Anything from pleading to wheedling would probably serve her better, but she was so consumed with fury that she could not contain herself. "Dooming a child not yet born, to a monstrous fate . . . was that something you did routinely, or was it specially reserved just for us?"

"You were my friends," he said.

"Then may the gods have mercy on your enemies."

"They actually seem to, now that you mention it," he commented thoughtfully. "My enemies seem to fare much better than my friends. Everyone I have ever loved, or felt close to, has come to a bad end, whereas those who oppose me thrive. Perhaps the gods are already carrying through on your wishes, Delenn."

"If they are, then David would be free, we would be gone, and you would all be punished for what you have done."

"It may very well be . . . that that can be arranged. The first two, at least. The third, well," and he rolled his eyes, "we will have to leave that in the hands of others, I fear."

For a moment, just one blessed moment, she felt hope stirring. "Are you saying . . . that David, John, and I will be freed?"

"David . . . yes. I believe I can arrange that. You and your husband, however," and he shook his head gravely. "You desired to be gone. Well . . . dead is gone. It will, at least, end your torment. That is the most I can offer you."

"You're the emperor," she said. "I would have thought nothing beyond your abilities."

"I would have thought that, too. Odd how things do not always work out the way one hopes."

"You said David could be freed. How? What do you get out of it?"

"Information."

She snorted. It was a most un-Delenn-like sound. "I knew it. Well, you will have no more luck with—"

But he was waving his hands, endeavoring to quiet her. "This is information you will part with, I think. It will not, in any way, compromise the security of the Interstellar Alliance. I would suspect that what I desire to know is so old that it can be of no use to anyone but me."

"Old?" She looked with curiosity at him.

"I am interested . . . in the beginning," he said. "The beginning of all . . . this," and he gestured around himself as if to encompass the totality of existence. "It started with the Earth-Minbari War. It started with your people, really. Yours and the Humans. I know our side . . . I know the Humans' side . . . I would like to hear your side."

"Why?"

"Because, Delenn," he said with the air of someone who was releasing a great weight from himself, "when one does not see much of a future for himself, one becomes more and more intrigued by the past. I wish . . . to know these things. To fill in the gaps of my knowledge. My recollections of recent times fade in and out. I keep a journal from time to time, and that is all that preserves me, because I look at the entries several days later and cannot recall the incidents that prompted them. But my memory of times long past, ah . . ." and he waggled a finger at her, "that remains, clear and pure. But it is only partial knowledge. I desire to know the rest. And you can tell me."

"And if I do this thing . . . then David is free."

"I will see to it. His main importance was to get you here."

"That . . . thing on his neck. That will be removed from him?"

He hesitated. "I suspect," he said, "that if I tried to lie to you now, you would know. So I will be honest with you: I cannot guarantee that, no. I will try. I will present a case, plead for it. Say that he has suffered enough. All I can promise you, though, is that he will be free . . . and safe. It is the best I can offer you, Delenn."

She wanted to ask him to whom he would present such a case, but she suspected that she would not receive an answer. Her mind racing, she weighed her options . . . and discovered that, in truth, she had precious few.

"What do you want to know?" she said finally.

"Everything."

So she told him everything. It took some minutes, and it seemed as if she had to keep raising her voice as the cheers and shouts from outside grew louder still. He nodded, listening carefully, asking questions here and there. Finally she finished and there was silence for quite some time, punctuated only by the crowd's huzzahs.

"You . . . were responsible," he whispered. He seemed overwhelmed by the idea. "You were responsible for the Earth-Minbari War."

"Not solely. But . . . yes. Had I counseled differently . . . had I not been caught up in the moment . . . it would not have happened. Then again—" she shrugged "—perhaps had I voted differently, others of the Grey Council might have changed their vote. Or the military might have staged a holy war, unapproved by the Council, out of vengeance. It is possible that it might have occurred anyway. But . . . in this reality . . . yes. The stain is on my soul. I have spent much of my life endeavoring to cleanse it. I do not know, even now, how successful I have been."

"You did what you thought was right for your people . . . and millions died because of it."

"Yes."

To her surprise, he laughed softly. "It may very well be, Delenn . . . that we have more in common than either of us has thought . . . or is ready to admit."

And suddenly an explosion from overhead nearly deafened them.

Delenn looked up in the general direction of the sound, and the screams that were accompanying them. "In Valen's name," she whispered, "what's happening?"

Displaying remarkable sangfroid, as if nothing was capable of surprising him anymore, Londo speculated, "I would guess that we are under attack. This may be your lucky day, Delenn," he said grimly. "The punishment you desired may well be upon us. You could wind up getting all three of your wishes sooner than you anticipated."

— *chapter 20* —

Durla stood next to Vallko, amazed and impressed that the minister of spirituality was able to work up the crowd to this degree of ardor.

Vallko, Durla, and other ministers were standing on the steps that led into the temple. The courtyard and the streets nearby were absolutely packed. It might very well have been that every Centauri in the capital city was there, for word had spread that this was not going to be just another spiritual rally. Oh, those were exciting and uplifting enough, of course, but the rumors flying throughout the city implied that some special announcement would be made, one that was to be a culmination of years of effort. Probably the only Centauri who were not present were the permanent guards stationed around the Tower of Power, some of the palace staff . . . and, of course, the emperor himself. Durla had informed him of the plans for the day, and incredibly, the emperor had elected not to come. "It is your performance, Durla," he had said. "I would rather not be seen as simply your assistant." That was fine with Durla. The more the focus was on him, the more he liked it.

Durla could not have asked for a better day. The sky was pure blue, not a cloud disturbing the vista. In the near distance, the Tower of Power stretched toward the sky, proud and unbending, as if pointing the way to greatness.

He knew that in hyperspace, even as Vallko spoke of the proud destiny that awaited Centauri Prime, the ships were waiting. By this time, they were at their stations, awaiting only the go-ahead from Durla to start their assault. But Durla had time. Standing on the edge of history, he wanted to savor the moment a while longer, as one studies a particularly succulent meal and appreciates it before carving into it. A worldwide communications web was, even now, transmitting this rally on a narrow-cast beam into hyperspace. There, in front of all of Centauri Prime, Durla would give the codes that would signal the attack. Once and for all, the people would indisputably link with him the coming greatness that was the destiny of Centauri Prime.

"For many years now, we have taken back what was ours, bit by bit," Vallko proclaimed. "We have done so through the sweat and endeavors of true Centauri." Again, for about the thirtieth time since he had begun his speech an hour ago, cheers and chants interrupted him. He allowed them to build and die down before continuing, "We have worked together . . . we have fulfilled the desires of the Great Maker, and we have shaped the destiny that is, by rights, ours!" More cheers, more waiting. "Because our work is pure . . . because the Centauri way is the right way . . . because we have resisted the impurities that other races would bring to us . . . we have been lifted up, elevated to a position that is unrivaled in our history!"

Durla nodded, smiling, but feeling a bit impatient. As if sensing his thoughts, Vallko said, "I leave it now to your beloved prime minister, Durla, to bring you to the next step in our history. For remember that it is his visions of what we should be that have guided us to where we are . . . and what we will become."

This was the loudest cheer of all, the welcoming cheer for Durla. At least, that was how he perceived it. He stood at the top of the great steps, his arms outstretched the way they had been when he had witnessed the ships departing for their glorious quest. The cheering washed over him like a physical wave.

"My friends . . ." he began.

He got no further.

The massive explosion ripped through the air, startling and terrifying the entire crowd. Then another explosion, and a third, and everyone looked to the skies, screaming, convinced that death was being rained down upon them once again.

It was Lione who saw it first. "The Tower!" he shrieked, and pointed.

Sure enough, the Tower of Power was crumbling. Charges blasted up from beneath, enveloping it, the lack of windows causing the force of the explosion to be contained. Smoke blew out of newly formed cracks, rubble flew, and then the entire upper section began to tilt even as the lower half collapsed.

"Impossible! Impossible!" Lione clearly couldn't believe what he was seeing. "There are guards . . . no one could get close enough . . . no one—"

Another explosion ripped straight up the middle, and the entire upper section was blown apart. Debris hurtled everywhere. People screamed, trying to run, unable to move because they were so packed in. Vallko's and Durla's cries for calm did nothing to stem the tide.

Then the first of the bodies fell to the ground, having been hurled a great distance by the force of the blast. Impressively, it was mostly intact, but that lasted only until it landed on the temple stairs with a disgusting noise. At that point the body smashed apart like an overripe melon. But even in that condition, everyone could see that it was not a Centauri body.

And more started to plummet from overhead, and they weren't even close to intact. Heads, arms, legs, torsos, all grey and scaly, cloaked in shreds of black cloth, spewing down from the skies as if a gigantic pustule had been popped.

A hole gaped in the ceiling of the catacombs, exposing them to sunlight for the first time in their history. The area directly above had once been the foundation for the Tower of Power; now there was nothing but the tattered remains of the ground where Renegar's explosives had blasted apart the Tower from underneath.

Renegar clambered down from the surface and turned to Vir as the others held their collective breath. "Well?" Vir demanded. "What's happening?"

"It's raining Drakh," Renegar said.

"Good." Vir turned to Adi. "All right, Adi. Time for phase two. Tap into the broadcast web. Now."

What had seconds before been pure pandemonium had incredibly, eerily, fallen into silence, a silence that was even more deafening than the shouting had been. The Centauri were looking in wonder at the alien creatures who were suddenly in their midst, albeit in pieces.

"Wha—what is . . ." Kuto, the minister of information, couldn't comprehend what he was seeing.

Lione turned to Durla, kicking aside the remains of the body that had landed nearby. All the blood was draining from his face. "You . . . you said the upper portions of the tower were to be kept empty . . . for expansion . . . no one was to go up there, not even me . . . Were these . . . these . . ."

"Quiet!" Durla said urgently. "I have to think . . . I . . ."

That was when a gigantic hologram appeared before them, much like the one of Londo some fifteen years earlier, and Durla far more recently. But this was someone whom Durla had not remotely expected. Whom no one had expected.

"Cotto," Durla snarled.

"My fellow Centauri," the gigantic image of Vir boomed throughout the world. "I am Vir Cotto. I am the leader of a resistance movement called the Legions of Fire. We have known for some time that it is not the leaders—specifically, the prime minister—of Centauri Prime who have been shaping your destinies. It is these beings . . . the Drakh. Servants of the Shadows. Monstrous beings."

"This is broadcasting everywhere!" Durla practically howled at Kuto. "Shut it down! Find a way!"

"The people of Centauri Prime have been used. Duped. The Drakh played upon our nationalistic feelings in order to use you—to use us—as cat's-paws to strike against the Alliance. An Alliance that goes against everything they want to see happen in known space. They are a disease that has been slowly rotting us . . . and we did not even know that we were sick. But now you know. It has not been Centauri Prime for Centauri. It has not been the clear vision of a people, or even of the 'visionary' prime minister. He has been duped. You have all been duped.

"And to all the member worlds of the Alliance, know that the aggression you have seen from Centauri Prime has been nothing but the cold, manipulating tactics of an evil race. We are as much victims as you. We are—"

At that moment, the image of Vir Cotto blinked out. And then something monstrous came through the sky, something black and frightening, and—in the heads of everyone below—there seemed to be something akin to a scream as it flashed past.

The ship drove straight toward the vast hole that had been created by the explosion. Then, from the vessel, a small army of Drakh descended, heading right for the now-exposed tunnels.

*   *   *

The Drakh poured into the catacombs, weapons at the ready. And when they arrived, they found no one there. At least, no one at the point of entry.

"Spread out!" the order came down, and the Drakh moved every which way through the catacombs, searching for Vir Cotto and the others, certain they were facing a small force of people who could quickly be obliterated.

They were wrong.

For suddenly, from every discernible direction, Centauri came charging forward. They were servants and soldiers attached to the Houses. They were scholars. They were poets. They were subversives, philosophers, writers. But under the direction, planning, and supervision of Vir Cotto, they were warriors all. Moreover, they were warriors who had thoroughly familiarized themselves with every twist and turn of the catacombs.

The split troops of the Drakh were cut off from one another. In what could only be considered the height of irony, they were lost in the dark.

And then there was much screaming. Amazingly, little of it involved Centauri voices.

— *chapter 21* —

Mariel watched in amazement from the balcony. She had heard the explosions, the same as everyone else. She gaped in astonishment, watched the Tower of Power disintegrate. She saw distant, non-Centauri bodies falling through the air in assorted bits and pieces. Something smacked against the wall just to her left. It was a single small piece of grey flesh. She stared at it in wonderment as it hung there.

And then she heard the voice—that magnificent voice, that powerful voice—and the image, like a vision from the Great Maker himself. Vir—her Vir—speaking to the people of Centauri Prime, telling them what was happening, stepping forward into the position of leadership that she had always known he rightly deserved.

Then she saw the dark ship descending, and terror descended upon her, as well. Instinctively she knew who and what they were, and what they intended for Vir. She saw them stream down into the blast point.

There was no way to help Vir. Nothing she could do.

Then she realized that there was. She ran quickly into her bedroom, closed the door behind her, dropped to her knees.

"Please, Great Maker," she whispered, "I will give anything, do anything, sacrifice anything, but please let Vir be all right. Save him. And save Londo. I tried to do him ill and, in so doing, upset Vir, and I repent of that. I repent of it all, please . . ."

That, and similar sentiments were all she voiced for some minutes, until she heard shouting from the main room. First and foremost came Durla's voice, and then she heard others, as well. She heard the voices of Castig Lione, and Kuto, and there was Vallko, and Munphis, the minister of education. They were all talking at once, and it was difficult to make them out, until Durla shouted them down.

"This cannot be!" he bellowed. "It is a trick! A hideous trick!"

"You saw!" Lione shouted back. "We all saw! The Drakh. Great Maker, Durla, the Drakh!"

"You will address me as prime minister!"

"How can it be a trick?" It was Vallko, and he sounded like a broken man, someone whose faith had been shattered. "We saw . . . that ship, the Drakh, here in the heart of the city . . ."

"A trick, I tell you, put together by Cotto!"

"Prime Minister, it makes no sense!" That was Kuto speaking. "We saw them! We saw the Drakh attack! Drakh bodies falling from the Tower, Drakh warriors from the skies . . . it's . . ."

"Face it, Prime Minister . . . you've been used. We all have," Lione said.

Durla's voice was trembling with fury. "You will not stand there and tell me that my vision for Centauri Prime was something manufactured by an alien race!"

"Great Maker take your visions!" Lione snapped. "I'm telling you, we've been used!" There were mutters of agreement.

"I have trouble believing that you are my cabinet. My ministers, those I trusted." Durla's voice sounded like a mixture of disgust and sorrow. "That you would turn on me now, at our moment of greatest triumph . . ."

"Triumph! A war on the entire Alliance that was planned by a race who were servants of the Shadows!" That was the normally reticent Munphis speaking up. "Who knows what their long-term plans are! It could very well be that they're looking to us to smash the Alliance for them . . . and they, in turn, will conquer us!"

"We are Centauri Prime! We will never be conquered again! And I will not allow the trickery of the 'Legions of Fire,' and Cotto, and these imaginary Drakh to dissuade me from my course! I have planned this for far too long, done too much, to let it end here and now!"

She heard footsteps then, quick movements. "Durla, what are you doing?" It was Vallko's voice. He sounded as if he was starting to come out of his shock.

"This is my backup transmitter. We had to shut down the

world web to take Cotto's rants off-line, but this will still get me directly to the ships. The attack will go on as planned."

"You're insane! We can't! We have to wait, to get this sorted out—"

"That's what they want us to do, Lione! Wait! Because time is on the side of the Alliance! Cotto has convinced them, just as he has you, that we are the tools of a malevolent race! They will erect defenses against us! Be ready for us!" There was a tone of mounting desperation. "Besides, if the go-codes are not given within the next seventy-two hours, the fleet will stand down! They will think that something is wrong—"

"Something *is* wrong!" Vallko was getting more strident. "It may well be that nothing is what it has seemed! I have spent years, Durla, telling the people that the future of the Centauri people is in our own hands. We have seen evidence today that that may not be the case!"

"And how much of that did you know, eh?" Lione demanded. Their voices were moving around, making it clear that they were circling each other. "Why did you instruct that the upper floors of the Tower remain off limits? 'Reserved for future expansion.' You knew, didn't you. You knew that our symbol of destiny was . . . infested with those creatures!"

"I knew no such thing! It was part of my vision, I tell you—"

"A vision given you by the Drakh! Open your eyes and see the truth, Durla!" Lione shouted. "You've been used! Your power stems, not from any divine vision, but from notions planted in your skull by the Drakh! It's the only answer!"

And suddenly there was a deathly quiet. When Durla spoke again, it was with a soft and frightening conviction. "There is," he said, "another answer."

"Durla, put that down," Kuto said warningly, although Mariel had no idea what he was referring to.

"And that answer is that you're all in league with Cotto. I should have seen it earlier. All of you, trying to tear me down. Jealous of me. Planting those fake bodies, getting in league with those . . . 'Drakh' . . . to discredit me. Yes . . . jealous of me. And traitors, all of you."

As one, the ministers shouted out, and then Mariel heard the blasts. She clapped her hands to her ears, crying out, as the death screams and the sounds of weapon fire filled the air. It seemed to go on forever, although, in truth, it lasted only a few seconds. And then there was silence once more.

Very tentatively, afraid of what she would see, Mariel opened the door.

Durla was standing there, and contrary to what she had expected, he looked exceedingly calm. His hand was at his side, holding a plasma charge blaster. The floor was light red, thick with blood, and the bodies of the ministers were strewn about. Several of them had their eyes open, and they all seemed quite surprised, yet for all their astonishment they were no less dead.

Slowly Durla turned and saw Mariel standing there. Without a word he raised his weapon and aimed it at her. "Do you," he said steadily, "stand against me, too?"

She shook her head.

He smiled. "That's good. That's very good, my love. I would have hated if you had." He looked around at the carnage with a sort of distant sadness. "I was afraid this would happen. That's why I sent the guards away. I had hoped it would turn out differently but . . . not everything can. They didn't understand. None of them did."

She saw the transmitting equipment nearby. She stepped delicately over the fallen body of Lione, and said softly, "I understand. I didn't used to but . . . now I do." She was within six feet of him . . . five . . . walking slowly, almost slinking . . .

"That's good. That's very good. Would you like to watch, Mariel?"

"Watch?" She froze at four feet.

"Watch me transmit the codes that will launch the attack."

"Of course, my love."

He turned back to the transmitter and began to manipulate the controls.

Three feet . . . two . . .

Suddenly he turned and aimed his weapon at her. "I don't believe you," he said, and fired.

At point-blank range, he should not have missed. But Mariel twisted out of the way, the bolt barely grazing her hip, and then she was upon him. She grabbed at the gun with both hands, shoving it away from her, trying to shake it out of his hands, as Durla struggled against her. He shoved her away, tried to aim quickly, but slipped on the blood. Mariel leaped desperately, landed full on top of him, momentarily knocking the wind out of him, and they rolled across the floor. The gun fired wide, ricocheting harmlessly off the wall.

Durla managed to get to his feet, and Mariel clung on, like a spider holding on to a wind-tossed web. They were away from the blood, moving toward the balcony, and Mariel had a better grip on his gun hand this time. But Durla grabbed her trailing length of hair, twisting it around his free hand. She let out a howl of pain but did not let go.

"Stupid cow!" he howled as they staggered about. "I remade the world for you!"

"But I won't let you end it for me!" she cried out.

Her strength, her resolve, momentarily lessened, and then she thought of every time he'd struck her, every time she'd submitted to his abuse, and a fire of fury boiled through her veins. Mariel pushed back, as hard as she could, one desperate shove.

Durla's back hit the balcony railing, and he overbalanced, flipping over. An eight-story drop yawned beneath him. He let out a shriek of alarm, his fingers still firmly entangled in her hair. He dropped the gun and clawed at the air, and then he tumbled over the edge of the balcony. And Mariel, entangled in his grasp like some sort of perverse lovers' embrace, went with him.

As she fell, she felt some small degree of pleasure that he was screaming and she was not.

Londo . . . Vir . . . look! I'm flying at last was the final thought across her mind before the ground rushed up to meet them.

EXCERPTED FROM
THE CHRONICLES OF LONDO MOLLARI.
Excerpt dated (approximate Earth date)
January 1, 2278.

"Shiv'kala. Not dead, I see? Pity."

I have no idea what prompted me to sound quite as jovial as I did. It was probably the sight of the Tower of Power lying in ruin and rubble out in the town.

Shiv'kala, for his part, seemed positively disconcerted. How long I had waited to see him that way. He was covering it as best he could, to preserve what he fancied as his dignity and mysterious reserve. But we had been "together" too long. I could tell that he was trying not to panic, and only barely succeeding.

He had appeared, as always, out of the shadows in my inner sanctum. I still did not know how he had gotten there and, frankly, had stopped caring. "No, Londo . . . still not dead," he whispered. "And not for want of trying by your . . . associates."

"Are you implying that I had something to do with this?" I demanded. "How would you suggest I did that? Your little friend watches me at all times. If I were helping to run an underground rebellion, I think you would have known."

He advanced on me, his red eyes burning into me. "You always keep certain thoughts buried just below the surface, Londo. The keeper senses it, even if he can do nothing about it. I suspect they may have to do with your 'associates' . . ."

"Again that word. I am emperor. I work with any number of people. I remind you that your precious Durla is as much my associate as Vir."

"Not anymore. Durla is dead."

That brought me up short. "Dead?" I whispered. "When?"

"Moments ago. After he annihilated his ministry. He fell to his death off a balcony, locked in combat with his wife."

I had been standing, but suddenly the strength went from me. I sagged into a chair and for just a moment I had a mental picture of Mariel when I first saw her. Young and beautiful, and even though it was an arranged marriage and I wanted to

197

hate her out-of-hand, I was transfixed by her comeliness. I could not have known the future, of course. Could not have known what she would become . . . or what I would become. And now . . . now . . .

"Mariel," I whispered.

"She stopped Durla before he could issue the go-codes to launch the strike against the Alliance," Shiv'kala said, sounding rather bitter. "You must attend to it."

It took me a moment to focus on what he was saying. "I must attend to . . . what?"

"You must order the ships to launch against the Alliance worlds. The invasion can still go forward . . ."

"Are you mad? Yes, I think you must be. Shiv'kala . . . it is over." I managed to stand, because for this I wanted to be on my feet. I wanted to be eye to eye with him, not backing down. "Your involvement with our affairs, your manipulation . . . it is all out in the open now. The people of Centauri Prime will never support—"

"They will support what you tell them to support, Londo. With Durla gone, with the ministry gone, it is you to whom the people will turn. Rudderless, they will be looking for a captain to take control of the ship of state. You are the emperor. You are still sealed in their minds as the one who freed them from Cartagia, the one who subjugated the Narn, at least for a time. The people will follow you. The ships will attend to you. Even though you do not know the specific passwords and codes, the military will still respect your authority. You can order them to move and they will obey . . ."

"And what of the revelation of the Drakh involvement?" I said bitterly. "How do I explain that, on a world of Centauri Prime for Centauri?"

"We were your secret allies."

"You controlled us! Controlled me!"

"Lie, Mollari. It's what you're good at. Duplicity is the single most prevalent product that Centauri Prime exports. Say that you sought us out. Say that we offered our services. Say whatever you wish, but say something—"

"You want me to say something? Very well. I will say something," and I advanced on him. "Leave my world. You have done enough damage."

"Have we?" His eyes narrowed. "Have you forgotten the further damage we can do?"

It was at that point that my instincts as a card player kicked in. Because I knew precisely what he was referring to. I knew he was speaking of the bombs that he and his people had claimed to have planted throughout Centauri Prime. Bombs that they had been holding over my head to keep me in line all these years.

But I was certain at that point that Vir and his people had found them, defused them. He had been so thorough in so many other matters. Either that . . . or they had never existed in the first place. It was the latter that I was becoming more and more convinced of—for, as I said, my card-playing instincts told me Shiv'kala was bluffing.

"You must realize," I said carefully, "that it is indeed over. That this cannot continue. You can flood me with pain until I cannot stand, you can isolate me so that I cannot speak. You can use me as your public face and puppet ruler, but really . . . what is to be accomplished by this? It will not even work on the surface, for if you subsume my mind, turn me into nothing more than a shell who is your mouthpiece . . . the people will know.

"They know how I speak, how I carry myself. They will be alert to further Drakh manipulation. If I am not myself . . . either they will know, or at the very least they will be sufficiently suspicious that they will not heed me.

"And then there is your own presence. Knowing that you are here, at the very least the Humans will come for you all. Even as we speak, they may well be assembling a fleet for an assault. After all, you did introduce a plague into their Homeworld. The surviving Humans are not gently disposed toward you. And if you think that they will be worried about the prospect of some Centauri dying during an assault on a Drakh-held world, then you'd be well-advised to think again."

He actually looked away. He was unable to hold my gaze. I sounded conciliatory—an impressive feat—as I said, "You have always struck me as a race who does what needs to be done, but no more. You are not bloodthirsty. You are not barbarians. You have a purpose to serve, and you serve it. Annihilating my people simply out of a fit of pique, in the face of a hopeless cause . . . it makes no sense. It goes against the grain of the Drakh."

And he looked back at me with grim amusement in his eyes. "After all this time," he sighed, "how little you know us."

It was at that horrific moment, a moment that will always be frozen in time for me, that I knew I had badly miscalculated.

I was not even aware of the explosion when it actually occurred. All I knew was that one moment I was standing, and the next, I was on the floor. There was a ringing in my ears, and even though my eyes were wide open, all I saw was whiteness. I was flash-blinded.

Then a wave of heat swept over me, blasting in through my balcony, and wind so furious that it knocked everything off my walls and pushed me halfway across the floor.

I staggered to my feet, reaching out, trying to find something to hold on to so that I could get my bearings. A hand grasped mine. It was gray and scaly and cold to the touch, and I yanked it away quickly. I heard a low laugh, and I knew it was Shiv'kala's.

"You . . . you bastards . . ." I whispered.

My vision was starting to clear, and what I saw was beyond horrific. Fully half of the capital city was in flaming ruins. It was as bad as, if not worse than, when we had been attacked years earlier. A charnel smell wafted on the wind to me. The sky was already black with smoke, flames licking up toward the obscured clouds.

I reached out, as if somehow I could scoop up my people in my hand, preserve them, save them, turn back the hands of time and make it not have happened. And I heard voices crying out to me, *Londo, Londo, why have you forsaken us?* I could not tell if they were real or if they were imagined, but beyond question, they were my fault, my responsibility, on my head.

I had gambled with their lives, and I had lost.

"That," Shiv'kala said in a voice from beyond the grave, "was one third of the bombs we have planted. What you see here before you is merely representative of what has occurred throughout your world. Here is what you will do. Are you listening, Londo?"

"Yes," I whispered.

"You will bring Sheridan up here. You will show him the damage that was done, and you will make clear to him that these are crimes for which he and he alone bears responsibility . . . because he has been working in concert with the Legions of Fire."

"You intend . . . for me to blame this destruction on Vir?"

"Of course," said Shiv'kala. "He has already taken credit for destroying one monument. It is obvious that he will go to any lengths to satisfy his hatred of us, regardless of the cost. Next . . . are you listening, Londo?"

I nodded. I tried to hold my breath against the smell of burning flesh, and when I was unable to, I dry-heaved. Shiv'kala did not appear to notice, or care.

"After that, you will have Sheridan executed. Then you will have Delenn executed. I want the executions done separately, since I've no desire for people to see them drawing strength from each other in their last moments. Then you will find Vir Cotto, if he still lives, and execute him. And then you will inform the fleet that the assault against the Alliance is to be carried out.

"You are right about one thing, however: If we remain, there will doubtless be a strike launched against Centauri Prime. So we will make a show of departing, to put the Alliance off its guard. But once the Alliance is in disarray, we will return, to make Centauri Prime the cornerstone of the new Drakh Entire."

"Not Vir," I whispered.

He looked at me most oddly. "What?"

"I will not execute Vir. Nor will you. I will not stand in the way of what the people do, but he will not die by my hand, nor at the hands of the Drakh."

"Now you are the insane one, Londo." His voice rose. "Look at your city! Look at your world! It lies in ruins because you misjudged us, and you would still dictate terms?"

"You will grant me this," I said tightly, "or Mariel and Durla will not be the only ones who die off a balcony this day."

He seemed ready to argue it, but suddenly became impatient. "Very well," he said. "Do as you have been ordered, and Cotto will be spared. The odds are that he is dead anyway. And if he is not, well . . . the people will attend to him soon enough."

"Thank you," I said.

"You see, Londo? Even under such extreme circumstances . . . you cannot say that the Drakh are totally without compassion."

He said a few things more, but I was paying no attention. Instead my thoughts were elsewhere, nearly twenty years gone, to the words of the techno-mage, Elric. "I see a great hand reaching out of the stars. The hand is your hand. And I hear sounds . . . the sounds of billions of people calling your name."

"My followers," I had whispered in awe.

And in a voice like ice, he had replied, "Your victims."

I had always thought—always assumed—that he had been referring to the Narn. I now realized that he had not. That it was my own people, here and now, crying out for aid from an emperor whose misjudgment had resulted in widespread slaughter. I did not plant the bombs . . . I did not trigger the bombs . . . but, Great Maker, I did not stop them, and my people have paid for it.

I wanted to fly away. To be able to step to the balcony, change into a winged creature, and fly off to someplace where there was no death, no destruction. No voices calling my name, and no Drakh. I had waited sixteen years to feel fear and desperation from Shiv'kala, and I had managed it. But my people had paid a terrible, terrible price.

I had never wanted to be with Mariel at any given time as much as I did at that moment.

— *chapter 22* —

Vir gazed in horror at the smoking ruins of the city. A number of his followers stood at his side, likewise stunned by what they were seeing.

They had emerged from the far end of the catacombs, using as an exit the place where Renegar had first discovered the tunnels so many years ago, several hundred members of the Legions of Fire, looking ragged, exhausted, but also grimly triumphant. They had left a sizable number of dead Drakh below them, and with any luck those few that remained would wander hopelessly, lost in the maze.

But any satisfaction the rebels might have taken from their triumphs paled next to the aftermath they were seeing now.

"The Drakh," he whispered. "They must have done this. It could only have been them . . ."

"It certainly redefines the concept of 'sore losers,' " Renegar said.

"There may be more bombs," Finian said grimly. "If you'll excuse me, I'm going to go find them."

"Now? *Now* you're going to find them?" an incredulous Vir asked. "Why didn't you find them earlier, before this damage was done?"

"We'd always been seeking out Shadow technology. As near as I can tell, these explosives were of a more mundane nature. Even I cannot locate that which I do not know exists," Finian told him. "Leave it to me now."

"But—"

"I said leave it to me," he repeated firmly. And with that, he walked away.

"There may be bombs planted all over Centauri Prime," Renegar said. "How can he get to all of them . . ."

"He's a techno-mage," Gwynn said airily. "He may be a supremely annoying one, but he is a mage nonetheless. Don't underestimate us."

Vir stared off into the distance, and said, "Gwynn . . . I'm heading into the palace. You've got to get me in there."

A chorus of *"What?"* came from all around him.

"I have to see Londo. Have to speak to him. Make sure he's all right."

"Your concern for his safety is laudable," Gwynn said, "but ill-timed."

"No, it's the perfect time. Renegar, you'll be with me, too. You'll coordinate with Dunseny and help get David Sheridan the hell out of there. The rest of you," and he turned to his followers, "get to the city. Help where you can. Mount rescue operations, tend to the wounded, bury the dead. Gwynn . . . you're going to help us get inside."

"How?"

"You're a techno-mage. I don't underestimate you."

She smiled, but it looked more like a pained grimace.

The door to the cell opened, and the guards came in for Sheridan. He quickly got to his feet, and demanded, "What's going on out there? It sounds like a damned war zone!"

His only response was a quick club to the head, which caused him to sag in their grip. G'Kar took a step toward them threateningly, but half a dozen shock prods suddenly formed a barrier between him and the guards.

"Try it, Narn. Just try it," one of them said.

G'Kar didn't take him up on it, as Sheridan was dragged out of the cell. But while the door was open, just before it slammed, G'Kar could smell something wafting down the corridor, very faintly.

It was the distant aroma of burning flesh. It was a smell he knew all too well. It had hung in the air around Narn for months after the Centauri had attacked them with mass drivers.

"Do unto others," he said softly.

EXCERPTED FROM
THE CHRONICLES OF LONDO MOLLARI.
Excerpt dated (approximate Earth date)
January 2, 2278.

I had such dreams. Such dreams.

I dreamt of power and glory and followers. I dreamt of protecting my Home-world from dark invaders. I dreamt of restoring my great republic to its former glory. I dreamt of a noble death in battle, with my hands at the throat of my greatest enemy. I dreamt of love and I dreamt of redemption.

Such dreams. Such dreams.

Sheridan looked as if he were in a dream when they brought him before me some hours ago. I have known John Sheridan for longer than I would have thought possible . . . and never have I seen him with such an air of confusion.

The guards held him in front of me, bracing him firmly. He was shaking his head, as if he was uncertain of where he was. I looked to one of the guards and, my face a question, mimed a blow to the head to ask them if they had somehow beaten him severely, possibly concussing him. The Human skull is such a fragile thing. But the guard shook his head that he had not, and I had no reason to doubt him. I am, after all, such an infinitely trusting soul.

He looked up at me then and seemed quite surprised. I do not suppose that I can blame him. I have, of course, seen better days. Still, such a look of shock on his face. One would think he had not seen me for twenty years. The room was fairly dark, the only lighting provided mostly by the flames of my city dancing like ghouls outside.

". . . Londo? What . . . am I doing here . . . where . . ."

I smiled at him grimly. "Welcome back from the abyss, Sheridan. Just in time to die. Your timing, as always, is quite exceptional."

I did not think any single being could be as perplexed as that man. Then again, the Human capacity for bewilderment seems a virtually bottomless fountain.

"Londo . . . what am I doing here . . ." he said again. "What're you . . ."

It was necessary to be as forceful as possible. I needed everyone . . . and everything . . . to know of the certainty of my forthcoming actions. "What I'm doing is what someone should have done a long time ago," I told him. "Putting you out of my misery." I coughed slightly, mildly amused at my equally mild attempt at humor, and then growled, "Fitting punishment for your crimes."

Wide-eyed, he said, "What crimes? I don't—"

The man was beginning to annoy me. Naturally I understood his desire to avoid any sort of blame. Why not? I, who have been blamed throughout my life, whether justified or not, could easily comprehend a desire to avoid once, just once, recriminations being heaped upon me unjustly.

Nevertheless, I could not let such disingenuousness pass. I nodded to my men, and one of the guards punched Sheridan hard in the solar plexus. Sheridan went down on one knee, gasping. I stooped and looked into his eyes. I spoke as if I were playing to an audience, and in a way, I was . . . but it was none of the people in this room.

"The crime of neglect," I told him. "The crime of convenience. During your little war, you drove the Shadows away, oh yes, but you did not think to clean up your mess. If a few of their minions, their dark servants, came to Centauri Prime, well, where is the harm in that, yes? Hmm?"

He stared at me blankly. He seemed to have no idea what I was talking about. I began to comprehend just how this man, in becoming president of the Alliance, had formed himself into the most successful politician in the history of his race. Apparently his capability for self-denial knew no bounds. If I did not know better, I would think he had never heard of the Drakh, was unaware of the outcome of the Shadow War . . . that, indeed, everything I was saying was news to him.

And here I thought I was the foremost practitioner of self-delusion of our age.

"You want to see the harm? Do you?" I asked. Not waiting for an answer, I indicated to the guards that they should bring him to one of the windows. It used to be that I never had the curtains drawn. That I could not get enough of the view of the city that my station had afforded me. Now, of course, heavy drapes blocked the view. Drapes that the guards pushed aside so that Sheridan could see for himself the damage that had been wrought.

He stared in astonishment at the remains of Centauri Prime that flickered through the long, dark night. Ruined spires half thrown down, smoke rising from distant fires. Overhead a vehicle passed, dark and sinister, bristling with needlelike points. A Drakh escape ship; the last of their kind, one could only hope, making their way off the world that they had secretly run for so many years.

"There is the legacy of your war, the price we paid when you abandoned us to the enemies you managed to escape," I told him. "Forgive me if I do not share the view . . . I have seen it enough."

Sheridan was pulled back in front of me.

And he began to babble.

"But this couldn't happen, not in this amount of time . . . the time stabilizer . . . it was hit . . . what year is this?"

I stared at him incredulously. If he was trying to pretend that he had some sort of amnesia, then he was failing miserably. "It is the last year and the last day and the last hour of your life. Seventeen years since you began your great crusade . . . seventeen years since . . ."

And I faded.

My mind goes in and out. The moments of confusion, of depression, of total loss of where I am and what I am doing, become more and more frequent.

"I'm tired," I said. "Take him back to his cell." I fixed Sheridan with a glare, and said, "Make your peace with whatever gods you worship; you will meet them the next time I send for you. I cannot change what is . . . cannot recall my world from what it has become . . . but I can thank you . . . properly . . . for your role in it."

The guards pulled Sheridan out, half-dragging him as they went. For me, his presence was already a part of a distant past that I was anxious to forget, and would likely do so all too quickly. I walked back to my throne, touched it . . . not with pride, or possessiveness . . . but disdain. For this thing, this thing to which I would never have thought I could aspire, was something that had been tied around my neck, long ago, and was now crushing the life out of me.

I walked over to the window, glanced out in spite of myself. Then I drew the drapes closed.

I hear laughter as I write this . . . laughter from nearby. Who could laugh at such destruction?

Children. Yes, of course, children. At least two. I hear their rapid footsteps, their gleeful chortling, as they are running through the halls of the palace.

And then I hear an adult voice, a woman. She is calling with extreme urgency, "Luc? Lyssa! Where are you?" The voice—musical, softly accented—is unfamiliar to me . . .

No . . . wait . . .

I know . . . yes. Senta, was it? No . . . Senna, I think her name is. She is . . . a nurse or child attendant around here, I think. Or perhaps . . . yes . . . a retainer to one of our Houses . . .

I drink in the sound of their laughter, a man parched of emotion, with a soul as dry and shriveled as my skin. I hear them clattering about in the very next room.

Perhaps they will come in here. If they do, I will talk to them. I will tell them of how Centauri Prime used to be, of the greatness to which we aspired . . . in the beginning . . .

And then . . . then I will say my good-byes. To Sheridan and Delenn, to Vir and Londo . . .

Shiv'kala. He is the one to whom I would most want to say farewell. To be rid of him, quit of his influence, has been my fantasy for nearly fifteen years now. I suspect, however, it is not going to happen. Not only that, but his ego is so great that I fear—no matter what—that Centauri Prime will never rid itself of him or his influence. He fancies himself something more than a simple minion, a creature of darkness serving masters long-gone. He thinks himself a philosopher, a student of behavior. He thinks he is so much more than he is. Here, at the last . . . I pity him in a way. For he will never truly understand or know himself for the pathetic monstrosity that he is. Because of that, he is very predictable.

Whereas I know myself as that all too well. There is something to be said for self-awareness. It strips away your illusions and makes you unpredictable. That is the one great weakness that the Drakh have, and I am going to exploit it for all that I can . . .

— *chapter 23* —

Delenn sat in the dank cell, her legs curled up under her chin, rocking back and forth while softly chanting a prayer, and certain that she would never see her husband alive again.

"We're bringing him down," a guard had growled. "We know how much you'd like to have a last moment with him." From the tone of his voice, it seemed to suggest that there was some cruel surprise in store for her, and she was sure she suspected what it was.

When the door was yanked open, she was positive they were coming for her. That first they were going to bring in John's corpse as part of their perversity, allowing them "one last moment." Or perhaps they would present her with his head or some other identifiable body part—just so they could see her reaction. Perhaps they hoped that she would break down crying, sobbing, into a hopeless mess, wailing Sheridan's name and cursing her captors. If that was their plan, then they would be sorely disappointed.

Then, to her astonishment, Sheridan was thrown in, and the door slammed shut behind him. At first she could scarcely believe it was he. The fact that it was hard to see did not simplify matters, for the only illumination in the cell was a pale light coming in from a grated high window. Sheridan looked around as a man befuddled, leaning against the wall for support. Then he squinted into the darkness, and said, "Who . . . who's there?"

She could hardly speak. She was almost afraid that, if she said something, her own voice might break the spell of the moment. "John?" she managed to say.

She emerged from the shadows, and Sheridan turned and looked at her.

Every year she had dwelled on the dwindling time available to them. She had cursed it, cursed the fate that had given them so little time together. Now . . . now the three or four years that remained seemed an eternity. She would sell her soul just to have the opportunity to live out even one of those years by his side, instead of ending in this horrid cell. She rushed to him, embracing him with all the fervor of her passion for him.

"Delenn? What're you doing here?"

Yes, he was definitely confused. Perhaps a blow to the head had robbed him of some of his memory. But all she had to do was remind him of what was happening, and it would all come clear for him. "I didn't tell them anything. They tried to make me . . . but I didn't. There's nothing they can do to me. They know that now. They're allowing us one last moment together, before . . ."

She tried to finish the sentence, and couldn't. So instead, with determination to present a brave front, she managed a smile. "It's all right, John. I accepted this fate a long time ago. They cannot touch me. They cannot harm me. I'm not afraid. Not if you are with me. Our son is safe. That's all that matters. John . . . I love you."

And she kissed him.

He seemed startled, as if she had never kissed him before. But then he returned it, as if it was something that had always been meant to happen.

Then Sheridan gently pulled her away and looked earnestly into her eyes.

"Delenn . . . listen to me," he said intensely. "This may not make any sense . . . but I'm not supposed to be here . . . I'm not really here . . . the last thing I remember I was on Babylon 4, and my time stabilizer was hit, then suddenly I was here."

She was thunderstruck. Could this be? She stepped back further, studied him for a moment, and gradually the truth sank in. It was so absurd, and yet so obvious, that she almost wanted to laugh. Here she had been producing a tortured rationale as to why he seemed so disoriented . . . and yet she should have realized it instantly.

In the latter half of the year 2260, the lost space station, Babylon 4, had appeared like a gigantic phantom in space. Swept up in all manner of temporal flux and time anomalies, several people had braved that mysterious and ostensibly doomed station and found themselves caught in a bizarre unfolding vision of the future. Among those people had been Delenn, Sheridan . . . and Jeffrey Sinclair, the first commander of Babylon 5.

One dark night, long after they were married, and after Londo had risen to the post of emperor, Sheridan had told Delenn most of what he had experienced. He had been vague about the details of the encounter. Now she was beginning to understand why. How could he have told her that they would be trapped together in a Centauri prison, facing almost certain death?

In an amazed whisper, she said, "In Valen's name . . . it is true, isn't it? I can see it in your eyes. You told me, long ago, that you had seen this moment. But until now, I never really believed . . ." She was overwhelmed. There was so much she wanted to say to him. So many things . . . and her mind recoiled from the possibilities. One wrong word and her entire reality might come unraveled.

More than twenty years ago, she had held the fate of humanity in her hands. With the fallen body of her beloved mentor in her arms, and explosions of shorted circuitry all around her, it was she who had cried out in pain, *"They're animals! No mercy!"* Thus had the Earth-Minbari War begun. On her head. On hers.

Now, once again, the fates of untold millions were hers to do with as she wished.

Don't go to Z'ha'dum, she wanted to scream at him. He wouldn't know what she was talking about. *You'll die there! You'll come back, but changed, and your life will be reduced to but an instant!*

But she reined herself in, knowing that she did not dare.

"Oh, John . . . there is so much ahead of you, so many changes, so much pain and grief . . ." She shook her head, still finding it hard to believe. "I look in your eyes now, and I see the innocence that went away so many years ago. But then . . . you don't know any of what's happened, do you?"

Like a man trying to catch up with a play, though he had walked into the middle, Sheridan said, "From what Londo said, I get the impression that we won the war . . . but not completely."

She shook her head. "The war is never completely won. There are always new battles to be fought against the darkness. Only the names change." She saw that there was a bleak sense of despair creeping onto his face. She couldn't let him return, thinking that their grand endeavor had failed—*would* fail. "We achieved everything we set out to achieve . . . we created something that will endure for a thousand years . . ." she said proudly. "But the price, John, the terrible, terrible price . . ."

Don't go to Z'ha'dum!

She bit her tongue, kept the words in. "I didn't think I would see you again, before the end."

There were footsteps approaching briskly down the hall, moving with purpose. He pulled her close and spoke to her with a ferocious intensity that had within it hints of the man he would become. "Delenn . . . is there anything I can do to prevent this? There's still a chance . . ."

"No," she said forcefully. "No. This future can be changed only by surrendering to the Shadows, and that price is too high to pay."

The door opened. She knew that it was their time. She knew they were going to be brought to their execution.

"But we have a son . . ." Sheridan said. There was a touch of wonder in his voice.

"Yes. David . . ."

"Out!" the guard barked. "Now!"

She held him close, and then they faced the light. They walked to the door and through it, out into the hallway. Sheridan held her close . . .

. . . and staggered.

"John?" she said, and then more alarmed, "John!"

He collapsed, and at that moment, another guard—a more highly ranked one—strode down the hall and called out in annoyance, "New orders. The emperor said to wait an hour!"

"Why an hour?"

"Who knows?"

There was some muttering that Delenn couldn't quite make out, although the words "crazy old man" might have been bandied about. At that moment, though, she cared about nothing except her fallen husband. "Please . . . he needs help," she said.

"Why? You're both going to die soon anyway," one of the guards pointed out, but they helped Delenn and Sheridan back toward their cell.

At that moment, Sheridan suddenly roared, *"No!"* His eyes were wild; there was nothing but confusion in them. And for a moment she thought she actually saw some sort of glow around him. Instantly she realized what was happening; it was some sort of temporal backlash. The Sheridan of the past and the present were, in some way and on some level, colliding. They were struggling for possession of the one form.

And it was nearly tearing them apart.

Sheridan's knees gave out, and he collapsed to the floor of the cell. Delenn instantly fell at his side, pulling him to her, but he had passed out. "John . . . it will be all right . . . I swear to you, it will," she whispered over and over again as the cell door slammed behind them, their destiny postponed a short time longer. And as she kept assuring him that all would be fine, she thought bleakly, *Who says Minbari never lie?*

EXCERPTED FROM
THE CHRONICLES OF LONDO MOLLARI.
Excerpt dated (approximate Earth date)
January 2, 2278 (final entry).

Note to historians: This is the one entry of the emperor's chronicles that is not strictly from his physical chronicles. It is a combination of written notes he was making at the time that he dictated his history of Babylon 5, and audio records that were made secretly, by the emperor himself, at the time. It is believed that, knowing his final hours were upon him, he was taking extensive pains to leave as thorough an accounting as possible. That would be in keeping with the character of Londo Mollari, who—as anecdotal evidence indicates—had dreamt of this moment for so large a portion of his adult life that he likely considered it the defining moment of his existence. We of the Centauri Historical Institute believe that what follows is an accurate depiction of the emperor's state of mind. It has been approved by Emperor Vir Cotto for inclusion into the historical records, and we wish to believe that Londo Mollari himself would likewise have endorsed it as accurate.

I looked at the lady Senna, and in a low voice, a voice that might once have been alluring when spoken by a young and handsome man, I said to her, "Dear lady . . . I would love to walk with you on a beach . . . somewhere. For just five minutes." I felt tears welling in my eyes, and I fought them back. It was the single greatest battle of my life. "How strange . . . to have come this far, and to want so little."

I turned away from her, for I did not know how much longer I could keep my eyes dry. A dear, sweet woman. Two lovely children. They could have been mine. They are the life I turned away from—the life of a different man . . . a lucky man.

"Children." My voice was low and hoarse. "Will you remember this story? Will you remember me?"

"All my life, Majesty," Luc said in wonderment.

I nodded. It would have to suffice. "Then go."

213

But Luc suddenly seemed less than willing to depart. "What happened to Sheridan and Delenn?" he asked. "What about the end of the story?"

"Sheridan," I said slowly, "became the president of a great alliance, Delenn ever at his side. And the story . . . is not over yet. The story is never over. Now go."

Senna took one child in each hand, and she started to head out of the room. Then the girl, Lyssa, stopped, and inquired, "Did they live happily ever after?"

"Lyssa!" Senna said in surprise.

"Did they live happily ever after?" she repeated more insistently.

"That . . . remains to be seen," I said after a moment.

And as Senna ushered them out . . . I remembered her. For a brief moment, I remembered who Senna was . . . and then it was gone.

As was she.

I used a spy device to watch Delenn and Sheridan in a tearful reunion down in their cell. Very moving.

Not everything was in place, though. Not everything was ready. Everything had to be done just right.

I picked up a bell and rang it. Moments later, I said to the guard standing there in response to it, "I need another bottle. I will need several more bottles. Then wait one hour . . . and bring the prisoners here."

He nodded and left me alone . . . a state to which I have become accustomed. Sometimes I think I have been alone my entire life.

I had a bit of one bottle left, and I emptied the contents into a glass. I raised it and said, "To the future . . . my old friends." And I drained the contents.

I heard footsteps, and I recognized the stride. How could I not? After all these years, it was impossible for me not to. I looked up and there he was, holding several bottles on a tray. I waggled my fingers, and said, "Come here."

Vir approached me. He had obviously encountered the guard returning with the drinks and decided to bring them to me himself. Whether the guard had turned the drinks over willingly or not, I did not know . . . or particularly care at that moment.

There was so much to be said between us . . . but it was necessary to concentrate purely on matters of historical record. "You will drink with me, Vir?" I asked.

"No, if it's all the same to you," he said. I think of the old days, when his voice always seemed to have a slight tremor to it. No more. Now he speaks with confidence . . . and just a hint of perpetual sadness.

"I have decided to work on a history, Vir. And I have decided that you will write it with me."

"I will?" He seemed most surprised. Of all the things he probably thought we would discuss, I doubt this was listed among them.

"Oh, yes. It will be quite comprehensive. Unfortunately, I do not think I will have overmuch time to complete it. I would like your help in achieving that. You were there for most of it. I think you are fit to do the job. If you wish, you may put your name first in the credits. For I strongly suspect, you see, that it will be published posthumously."

"I see," he said.

"I shall spend the next hour," I told him, as I proceeded to pour a drink, "giving you some details . . . some highlights . . . for I have been discussing it at length recently, and it is all fresh in my mind. You may record it however you wish. Expand upon it, put it into chronological order at your convenience. Then you will leave me, for I will meet with Sheridan and Delenn."

"Are you . . . are you . . ." He could not even frame the words.

I shook my head. "I . . . do not wish to discuss it, Vir, for reasons I cannot explain at the moment. For I am watched, you see, all the time . . . even here. So let us instead discuss matters of scholarship . . . and let the rest sort itself out.

"And Vir . . . you will let the people know. Let them know there was to be more than a world in flames. That there was supposed to be . . . should have been . . . greatness. With all the sacrifices, with all the people who have died, you would think we were entitled to that.

"You will carry on for me, Vir. It will be among the last orders I give. You will carry on and tell the story to others. It will be uplifting . . . or a warning . . . or simply a rather Byzantine adventure, depending upon how it's told and who is listening, I would imagine. And in this way, the story will never end. You will do this thing for me, Vir?"

With true tragedy in his voice, he replied, "Of course I will."

"Thank you," I said. "Thank you, my old friend." I patted him on the hand and leaned back, feeling the warmth of the liquor already beginning to fill me.

I shall drink myself into oblivion . . . and shortly thereafter, my soul will follow.

Vir waited for me to speak. He had found a recording device, and held it in his hand. "Where . . . where do you wish to start?" he asked.

Where to start? Where else, of course? In the beginning . . .

I looked out upon the burning remains of Centauri Prime, steadied my hand so that I could permit the liquid to cascade down my throat . . .

. . . and I began to speak. "I was there, at the dawn of the Third Age of Mankind. It began in the Earth year 2257 with the founding of the last of the Babylon stations, located deep in neutral space. It was a port of call for refugees, smugglers, businessmen, diplomats, and travelers from a hundred worlds. It could be a dangerous place, but we accepted the risk because Babylon 5 was our last, best hope for peace . . . It became a dream given form . . . a dream of a galaxy without war, where species from different worlds could live side by side in mutual respect . . . a dream that was endangered as never before by the arrival of one man on a mission of destruction. Babylon 5 was the last of the Babylon stations. This is its story . . ."

I had such dreams. Such dreams . . .

— *chapter 24* —

His clothes were tattered . . . one eye was missing, replaced by a black cloth . . . and he had been beaten so thoroughly in recent days that almost every step was agony. And yet G'Kar carried himself so tall, so proudly, that one might have thought at first glance that the guards surrounding him were at his service, rather than acting as his captors.

But G'Kar was nothing short of astounded when the guards led him to the throne room . . . then stopped at the door. Under normal circumstances they would be flanking him, front and back, to make sure there was no way that he could spring at the emperor in some improbable fit of fury. But this time, it was not the case.

They were allowing him to go in unescorted.

One of the guards saw the puzzled look in G'Kar's good eye. "Emperor's orders," he said, matter-of-factly.

G'Kar nodded and stepped through the door. He had no idea what to expect. For some reason he thought that perhaps there was going to be a firing squad on the other side. The shooters would yell, "Surprise!" and then open fire, and that would be that.

He was, however, quite wrong. Instead there was the throne room, utterly devoid of retainers, guards, and such . . . except for two people. One of them he had expected to see. The other he had not.

There was a small table set up, and seated at it were Londo Mollari and Vir Cotto. There were several empty bottles and glasses on it. It seemed a phenomenal amount of alcohol to have ingested, even by Londo's standards. There was still a partially filled bottle. There was also a bowl of fruit, half consumed. Londo had just finished saying something about Delenn, and suddenly he was seized with a racking cough. Vir, for his part, didn't even seem to notice. Instead, he looked up at G'Kar and nodded slightly in greeting.

G'Kar hadn't quite recognized Vir at first. He looked so much older and so careworn. G'Kar made the traditional Narn gesture of greeting.

"That," Londo said, coughing, "is what we need."

Vir looked at him in confusion. "What is, Londo?"

"A way of saying hello. The Narn, they have that business with fist and chest . . . the Minbari, with their fingers as triangles . . . what do we do?" He waggled his fingers. Then he shook his head. "Pathetic. Truly. Perhaps we deserved our fate on that basis alone. Sit, G'Kar. Sit. Vir . . . I need you to do two final things for me."

"Whatever you need, Londo." G'Kar saw such sadness in Vir, he could barely conceive what it must have been like for him.

"I want you to go to my private chambers. There is a hidden place, behind my writing desk. In the wall. Volumes are stored there. Chronicles of my life as emperor. I think you will find them . . . illuminating. Combine them with what I have told you and . . ." He stopped and coughed for a full thirty seconds before he managed to pull himself together. His voice was hoarse and scratchy; he sounded as if he had been speaking for hours. Every word sounded as if it was taking effort. ". . . combine them . . . and tell others of me. Because otherwise I will be forgotten . . . and I do not think that I would like that."

"Because your heroic efforts deserve to be immortalized?" G'Kar could not resist asking.

But Londo looked up at him with a baleful stare that carried with it not a hint of irony. "No. Because stupidity as monumental as mine should be enshrined so that others may learn. Vir . . . the second thing . . ."

"Yes?"

"Once you have them . . . leave. Leave and do not look back. Do not return until it is safe . . . if ever. And watch the shadows . . . sometimes, when you're not watching . . . they move. I have struck a bargain of sorts to preserve your life. If I had not, you would have been dead moments after you set foot in my presence. But I do not expect that it will be honored beyond my death . . . which, I suspect, will come soon."

Vir nodded, and G'Kar wondered if he understood what Londo was talking about. Vir started to head out, and G'Kar wanted to say something, because he had the oddest feeling that he was never going to see Vir again. "Cotto," he called out.

Vir Cotto turned and waited politely for G'Kar to speak.

G'Kar gave it a moment's thought, and then said, "Never mind. It will come to me later."

Vir laughed softly at that.

And then he was gone.

It was just the two of them.

As Vir made his way hurriedly down the corridor toward Londo's private chambers, he ran into Senna coming in the opposite direction. They stopped, facing each other. For a moment, there seemed a gap between them that no amount of effort or emotion could possibly bridge.

And then, before either of them even realized it, they were in each other's arms, and he kissed her hungrily. He held her tightly, as if she were a lifeline.

"Come with me," he whispered. "At least for a little while. Until we know it's safe."

"I will . . ."

"The children . . . do you need to bring—"

Senna shook her head. "Luc and Lyssa's parents picked them up a few minutes ago. They have a bunker they built some time ago that they're taking the children to. They'll be perfectly safe."

"I have to make a quick stop at the emperor's private study . . ."

Her face was a question mark. "Why?"

"I have to get his legacy," he told her grimly.

Londo slowly leaned forward and clearly tried to focus on G'Kar. It seemed to the Narn that Londo was seeing less with two eyes than he, G'Kar, was seeing with one.

"Can you see it?" he whispered.

G'Kar made no effort to hide his confusion. "See what?"

"Ah. You have answered my question, thank you."

"Have I?"

"Oh yesss," Londo told him, slurring the words. "Because if you could see it, you would not have to ask what it is you are supposed to be seeing."

"I see."

"Sit, sit. You have become my regular dining companion, you know. I would not want to cheat you of a final meal."

"A final meal?" G'Kar sat opposite him and picked up a piece of fruit. He took a bite of it, wondering if it was going to be poisoned. If it was, it certainly tasted sweet. The juice ran down his face, and he made a token effort to clean it off with his sleeve. "Are you planning to kill me, then?"

"I? I make no plans. They require too much . . . planning." He took a deep swig of the contents of the bottle and, for some reason, glanced at his shoulder. "I have been giving matters . . . much thought. And I have decided . . . that all of this . . . was about me."

"All of what?" G'Kar was genuinely curious.

"Everything. Babylon 5 . . . the Shadow War . . . the fate of Centauri Prime . . . all about me."

"Very egocentric," G'Kar observed.

"That does not make it wrong," Londo pointed out. He seemed to be enjoying the effect that the alcohol was having on him. All his words were slurring, one into another, and it was with difficulty that G'Kar was able to understand what he was saying. "It was in her predictions, you know. The one about the man already dead . . . that was easy. That was Sheridan. She also told me that I had to save the eye that does not see. Until an hour ago, I thought that referred to you."

G'Kar was completely lost, but he was not about to admit it. "But now you no longer think that."

"No. I think I misheard her. I think she referred, not to the 'eye' as in orb, but rather 'I' as in 'I, myself.' Because I had all the hints, all the warnings that I needed. It was all there, right in front of me. Morella tried to warn me . . . and the techno-mage . . . and Vir, Great Maker knows, over and over again . . . they all tried to make me see. But I did not. I did not see where my path was taking me. In order to avoid the fire that awaits me at the end of my journey, I must first save . . . myself."

"It sounds like a bit of a tautology," G'Kar pointed out. "To save yourself, you must save yourself? Not very useful advice."

"It is useful if I put it to use . . . which is likely also a tautology, yes? But I am emperor, and so have that prerogative." He drank deeply again. Then he leaned forward, and said conspiratorially, "So . . . do you see it yet?"

"I suppose I do not," G'Kar admitted.

"Soon enough. Where was I?"

"Saving yourself."

"Ah, yes! Thank you, my good friend, G'Kar." He seemed to find that phrase rather amusing. "My good friend, G'Kar. Who would have thought such unlikely words would be paired, eh? Almost as unlikely as Emperor Mollari. No . . . not my good friend. My . . . greatest friend," and he clapped G'Kar on the shoulder. "And my greatest fear."

"I am flattered on both counts," G'Kar said, "that you—"

"You should be able to see it now," Londo suddenly said, sounding somewhat annoyed. "I don't understand why . . . oh. Oh, of course. I am still wearing my mantle. Naturally . . . naturally, you do not see it, because I am covering it. Here . . . hold on." He shrugged off his ceremonial cape. G'Kar leaned forward, confused. There seemed to be some kind of lump visible now, a tumor of some sort . . .

Then he gasped and tried to stand up so quickly that the chair he was sitting on tumbled back with a clatter. He almost stumbled, but righted himself at the last moment.

The creature situated on Londo's shoulder literally reeked of evil and foulness. It apparently had an eye of some sort, but the eye was just in the process of closing. G'Kar could barely make out tendrils that were extended down into the emperor's pure white clothes.

Londo was utterly unperturbed. "You see it, yes?"

G'Kar managed to nod, but just barely.

"Very stylish, eh? Soon everyone will be wanting one, I think."

"What . . . is it?"

"My conscience," Londo told him. His thick eyebrows knitted as he tried to pick up the thread of the conversation. "Ohhh . . . yes. Yes, I remember. All about me. That is what this has all been."

"Londo . . ." A stunned G'Kar was pointing at the creature on Londo's shoulder.

But Londo was paying it no mind at all. In his own mind, the conversation had moved on. "All of this . . . has been one great epic about the loss of a man's soul . . . and its eventual recovery and redemption, but only at a terrible price. As an epic story, it has potential . . . do you think?"

G'Kar managed a nod.

"The thing is, G'Kar . . . that at this point, the Drakh—believe it or not—need me. Even as some of their number depart this world, others desire to stay. They still see me as their instrument of revenge . . . their puppet, to be danced with for some time to come. Without me . . . they have nothing. And without Sheridan and Delenn . . . they do not even have revenge. They hate Sheridan and Delenn, you know. Because they told the Shadows to leave . . . and the Shadows did. In some ways, the Drakh are like . . ." He fished for a comparison and then smiled. ". . . they are like children. Children abandoned by their parents and taking out their anger on the world. I can almost find it within me not to hate them. Almost. But not quite."

"You said . . . 'without Sheridan and Delenn.' Are you saying that you intend to let them go?"

Slowly Londo managed to nod, though not without effort. "That is my intent. It will be . . . somewhat involved. The Drakh do not want them to leave. The Drakh want them dead. And in recent days, it has become rather important for me to do things . . . other than the way the Drakh desire."

Suddenly so much of everything that had happened became clear. How long had Londo not been responsible for his actions? How long had one of those creatures sat on his shoulder, watching him, manipulating his moves? All the way back to the beginning of the War? Had the creatures told him to bomb the Narn Homeworld? Betray G'Kar? Was Londo, after all this time, genuinely an innocent man?

"If Sheridan and Delenn can leave . . . so can you, Londo," G'Kar said with sudden urgency. "We all can. We can escape . . ."

But Londo shook his head. "No . . . no. Sooner or later, my small . . . associate . . . would awaken. The instant that happened, the Drakh vessels would come after us and blow us to hell."

"Then let me kill that thing . . ."

"If it dies, I die. Besides, G'Kar, some things are preordained. Trust me on that. This is the only way."

"But if that . . . thing . . . controlled your actions . . ."

"Ahhh . . . I see what you think. No, G'Kar, no. In the grand scheme of things, this," and he indicated the creature, "is only a recent acquisition." He leaned forward, coughed several times, and then said raggedly, "Would you like to know . . . what sort of person I was? After I arranged for the bombing of the Narn colony in Quadrant 14 . . . the emperor, Emperor Turhan, with his last breath, told me that my associates and I were damned. And I announced that instead he had condoned and applauded our actions. And do you know what else, G'Kar, old friend?" And he half smiled. "Given the exact same opportunity . . . I would do it again. I would figure out some way to spare my people this . . . this debacle," and he gestured to the smoking ruins of Centauri Prime. "But what I did to your people . . ." And he snapped his fingers. "Like that, once more, given the opportunity."

G'Kar bristled, his blood thudding in his temple, and it was all he could do not to leap for the smirking face right then . . .

And then he figured it out. He realized that Londo was just trying to get to him . . . to enrage him . . . to get him to . . .

Attack him? Kill him?

Of course. Kill him. That had to be it.

And then, before G'Kar could say or do anything further, there was the sound of voices approaching. Stern guards were saying, "Keep moving!"

Londo stood on uneven legs and, with more willpower than actual strength, thrust himself toward his throne. He caught himself on it and swung himself to a seated position, allowing the shadows to cloak him.

"Hide," he told G'Kar. "Now. Hurry. There is a small dressing chamber over there," and he pointed. Even that movement clearly pained him. "Go there."

"Why?"

"Because time is running short, and the minutes it would take me to explain to Sheridan and Delenn why things must be done, these lost minutes might well prevent our being able to do them. Do as I say."

"As you command," G'Kar said with a deep sense of mockery. He stepped into the room Londo had indicated and softly shut the door behind himself.

And then he waited . . . for his final instructions.

—— chapter 25 ——

Londo did not sit forward on his throne, because the pain was too great. His conversation with G'Kar had taken the last of his strength from him. He did not think he had any reserves left.

One of the guards came in first and walked toward the throne. He did so hesitantly, as if he wasn't sure if Londo was even there. That was how well hidden in the shadows Londo was. "Highness?"

"Yes."

Having affirmed for himself that Londo was there, the guard said, "Sheridan had passed out for a short time, but he seems to have recovered."

"Oh, good," Londo said dryly. "We wouldn't want him to be anything but awake for his final moments. Bring them in."

Sheridan and Delenn were ushered before his presence. They squinted in the dimness of the room; Londo preferred it dark these days. It was as if he had surrendered totally to it. The guards stepped out, leaving them alone. Sheridan and Delenn seemed puzzled, as if wondering whether they were alone.

Suddenly Londo's hand went numb. Even he had lost track of how much he had had to drink. The glass, which he had totally forgotten he was holding, slipped out of his grasp and clattered to the floor. Delenn jumped slightly. Sheridan did not. For some reason, Londo found that interesting.

Delenn and Sheridan slowly began to walk toward him, squinting.

"Close enough," Londo said softly. He spoke hardly above a whisper, and the words were slurred. He barely recognized his voice. He felt as if he were viewing the world through a haze.

He tried to stand and discovered that his legs and brain were no longer on speaking terms. If he did manage to get to his feet, he would most likely topple over, and how dignified would that be? It wasn't fit that he spend his last moments—and they were his last, he was quite convinced of that—flat on his face.

"You will excuse me if I do not stand," he managed to say. "You see, I have had considerable to drink . . . it is the only way we can be alone. We do not wish to wake it."

Sheridan looked at him in confusion. Technically, he looked twice as confused as he should be, because Londo was seeing two of him. "Wake what?"

Londo cocked an eyebrow, which was the only part of him capable of movement. "Ah, then you do not know. We all have our keepers, you see . . ." He chuckled softly. "Oh, they make us think we have free will, but it's a lie. I gave a very good performance, yes?"

He saw understanding beginning to dawn on Delenn's face. Sheridan still looked befuddled. That made sense to Londo. He had long suspected that Delenn was the true brains in the family. "It was satisfied," he continued. "It doesn't care why I do what I do as long as I do it . . . as long as you are dead."

He managed to find enough strength to lean forward. Delenn's face remained impassive. It was as if she was expecting to see the creature there. But Sheridan looked totally stunned, and that confused Londo even further. Londo knew that he had spotted the keeper on his son's shoulder, when he had endeavored to stop the boy from leaving Minbar. Now, though, Sheridan acted as if he'd never encountered one of them before.

"It cannot hold its liquor, you see," Londo explained. "I learned that if I drink just enough, I can put it to sleep for a few minutes . . . a few minutes where I am in charge of myself again . . ." He took a deep breath. Putting together understandable words, coherent sentences, was a tremendous effort for him. "But the minutes have been growing shorter and shorter . . . so we do not have much time."

He leaned back, once again at home in the shadows. And why not? He had been living within them for so long, he no longer had anything to fear.

"My life is almost over. My world, all I hoped for . . . gone. You two are my last chance . . . for this place, for my world . . .

for my own redemption." He steadied his voice, glad that the alcohol had so numbed him that he was no longer capable of feeling any emotion; merely observing it from a distance, as if in a dream. "You will find a ship hidden behind the palace. My personal guard will take you. In exchange for your lives, I ask that you and your allies help free my world. I can do nothing more for them."

Sheridan seemed touched, and still a bit bewildered. "Londo . . . if there's anything—"

Londo shook his head. "No. There is nothing. Now go, quickly. You don't have much time. I can . . . feel it starting to wake up. Hurry. Go," his voice got louder with the last words.

Sheridan and Delenn looked at one another, and then turned and left. He knew that Dunseny and Caso would be right outside, as they had been instructed. That they would carry out his final orders.

Alone, again, as always, Londo waited for the creaking of a door that he knew would come. "You are there, my old friend?"

G'Kar entered the room, watching him, looking at the keeper balefully. "Yes," he said.

"They will never make it out alive, unless . . ." He took another breath. "You see, my keeper will awaken any second. It will alert the others . . . and my only hope will die. And I will die soon after. They do not take betrayal lightly."

And at the last . . .

The words of Lady Morella floated to him across the years.

. . . you must surrender yourself to your greatest fear . . .

He wondered if that was strictly true anymore. Because in a way, his greatest fear was that he might continue to live.

. . . knowing that it will kill you.

He paused, an infinity of time passing in a second, and said the words that he had known, for as long as he could recall, that he was destined to say. "We have unfinished business between us, G'Kar. Let us have an end to it, quickly, before it stops me. I am as tired of my life as you are."

G'Kar came at him. His hands clamped around Londo's throat, and it did not seem right somehow, because in the vision he had always been fighting back. But he had no desire to do so. He just wanted it over, done, finished. He marveled at the Narn's strength, wondered what it would have been like to battle G'Kar hand to hand, man to man, back in his prime, back at a time when anything seemed possible.

And then the keeper awoke.

G'Kar could not count the number of times that he had thought of this moment. There were times when he had, for his amusement, speculated what it would be like to sink his fingers into Londo's fleshy throat, feel the pulse beneath his fingers, feel it slowing, feel it stopping. He had wondered how long he would actually stand there, once there was no life, and still keep squeezing, just enjoying the lifelessness.

And that day—that terrible day, when he had learned of Londo's duplicity, drinking with him in friendship while Londo sent ships to kill thousands, millions of innocent Narns—he had gone berserk that day. When he stormed down the corridors of Babylon 5, howling for Londo Mollari's blood, he would have done more than strangle him. He would have ripped his living hearts from his body, held up one, and consumed the other while the life flickered from Londo's eyes.

Now . . .

Now he had him. Londo wasn't putting up a fight. He was . . . he was sacrificing himself. Surrendering to G'Kar, telling him to get it over with, so Delenn and Sheridan could escape.

Sheridan. "The king." And he was the hand of the king, and those hands were wrapped with murderous intent around the throat of a true king, an emperor.

The Narn named G'Kar who had imagined this moment, the Narn named G'Kar who would have reveled in it, had died years ago, replaced by a philosopher who was revered throughout the Narn Homeworld as G'Kar the wise, G'Kar the thoughtful, G'Kar the scholarly. His writings were endlessly studied, examined for the slightest nuance. Students who sat at his feet repeated his teachings, statues had been built to him, songs sung, stories written. They worshipped him as a man of peace even more than they had revered him as a man of war. Some called his writings the most important since those of G'Quan himself—a claim he had always considered to be a tad overblown, but there it was, and he wasn't going to deny it.

G'Kar the wise had forgiven Londo his trespasses. Had come

to appreciate him, not for the man he was, but for the man he could have been . . . and might yet be.

The hand of the king was going to have the blood of the emperor on it, and G'Kar's will faltered. He saw Londo surrendering to what he recognized as his fate, and something in G'Kar recoiled at the very notion. There had to be some other way. Sheridan and Delenn had to escape, yes. But there had to be a way for Londo to escape as well, something that would not cost him his life. It couldn't simply end like this, with cold-blooded murder . . . even if it was at the request of the victim. He was not an executioner. He was G'Kar, son of G'Qarn, scribe, sage, both teacher and student of the universe, and he could not, would not, do this thing.

And in deciding this, he began to ease up, ever so slightly, on Londo's throat.

And then the keeper awoke . . .

We are threatened! We are being assaulted! It is trying to kill us!

The keeper howled in anguish and fear. It saw its host was in danger, saw its own life threatened, because they were bonded, one to the other. A keeper could disengage, but it was a lengthy process, one that took time . . . time the keeper did not have. It did, however, have defensive capabilities.

In the early years of their relationship, the keeper had simply been an observer. But as time had passed, the keeper had insinuated itself so thoroughly into Londo's nervous system that, in times of stress, it could take over the body entirely for short periods.

Stop them, Londo! We love you! We care for you! We will never leave you!

The creature had never been so terrified, not since its spawning. When Shiv'kala had removed it from its nourishment pouch, it had feared the Centauri. Feared it so much that it had trembled in Shiv'kala's keeping. But the Drakh had assured it that all would be well, and it had been.

And now it wasn't.

Protect us, Londo! Protect us! Save us! Love us!

And Londo's arms flew up, not of their own accord, but at the keeper's command. They grabbed on to G'Kar's throat, clamping in with ferocity.

— chapter 26 —

"I am Dunseny, and this is Caso," Dunseny said by way of hurried introduction as they proceeded down the corridor. "I tell you that so that, if this does not go well and we die, you will know whose name to curse with your final breath."

"Very considerate," Delenn said. She cast a worried glance at Sheridan, who was suddenly starting to look a little uncertain on his feet. Dunseny hurried on ahead, Caso behind him, leading the way for Sheridan and Delenn. His hand hovered near his weapon, just in case some sort of resistance might be met.

Suddenly Sheridan's legs began to buckle once again. He leaned against the wall, supporting himself. Delenn took his arm, her face a mask of worry. "What is it?"

Sheridan tried to fight off whatever had a hold of him, but was unable to. "I'm . . . being pulled back again. Go on, hurry, don't wait for me."

"No. I won't leave you," she said firmly, shaking her head.

He tried to take a few more steps, got halfway down another corridor, and then the pain overwhelmed him. "It's no good . . . I can feel time pulling at me . . ."

She held him tightly. "Then take these words back with you to the past: Treasure the moments you have. Savor them for as long as you can, for they will never come again."

She knew that was all she should say. That she could take no chance of disrupting the past. Who knew what she might change? If she said the wrong thing, David might never exist, or the Shadows might triumph, or . . . or anything. There was simply no way of knowing, and every instinct, every fragment of common sense she possessed, warned her to keep her mouth shut . . .

And then she heard her own voice blurt out, "John . . . listen to me, do not go to Z'ha'dum. Do you understand? Do not go to Z'ha'dum . . ."

She held him desperately, wishing she could shield him from harm with her own body, and suddenly Sheridan tore away from her, slamming against the wall as if in the grip of some vast invisible fist. He convulsed once more, his head snapping this way and that, and then with tremendous effort he focused on her.

"Delenn . . ." he whispered. "I . . . I blanked out, I . . ." He looked around the corridor in utter astonishment. "How did we get here? How did . . ."

Caso had stopped, and was standing there. He was looking around with barely controlled nervousness, clearly concerned that someone might show up. Realizing that they had halted, Dunseny came back to them and gestured urgently. "What are you waiting for?" he demanded.

Sheridan looked in confusion from one to the other. "Are you . . . taking us to Londo?"

"We were just there," Delenn told him. "John . . . we can't stop here and discuss this. Later. Later we can—"

Suddenly his hand clutched her arm so hard that pain shot up to her shoulder. Then he realized what he was doing, and eased up. "Babylon 4," he whispered. "The time flux . . . this was it . . ."

"Yes," she said, relieved that she wasn't going to have to explain.

"I *thought* I was suddenly having déjà vu," he said, looking around.

Urgently she suddenly inquired, "Z'ha'dum . . . did you—"

"Go?" He nodded. "Yes." He sounded almost apologetic, because obviously he remembered her breathless advice . . . and had felt constrained to disobey it anyway.

She felt an awful mixture of relief and pain, all at the same time. Relief because she had allowed a moment of weakness to jeopardize everything that was, or might ever be . . . and nothing had come from it. And pain because it meant that, in three years at the most, John would be lost to her. The time given him as a reprieve against death would be running out. If he had not gone to Z'ha'dum . . .

"Ifs," Sheridan had said to her, years before. With an amused grin he had explained, "My father used to say 'If ifs and ands were pots and pans, the world would be a kitchen.' " She hadn't been entirely certain she understood it, but the message was clear.

"Mr. President," Dunseny said with extremely forced politeness, and he indicated that the hallway awaited them.

Without any further discussion, Sheridan and Delenn bolted down the corridor. A series of quick turns and they emerged through a door of the palace. On a pad nearby, there was a shuttle waiting for them.

"It's the emperor's personal landing pad," Dunseny informed them. His attitude seemed to carry the message that for the emperor to provide such a service for them was a singular honor. They were, to Dunseny's mind, probably not acting with sufficient awe or gratitude. "He wished me to convey to you his hope that the shuttle will sufficiently accommodate you."

"What about David," Sheridan said urgently. He turned to Delenn. "Where is he?"

She rested a hand on his arm, and said firmly, "Londo assured me that David would be safe. That he would be gotten off-world. Londo said he himself would attend to it personally. Come." And she was pulling him toward the shuttle.

Had he not been so groggy and confused, Sheridan would have put up a greater struggle. As it was, he was arguing nevertheless, dragging his heels, not petulantly, but with determination. And each word or phrase was matched by a small stomp of a foot. "We aren't . . . leaving . . . without . . . David . . ."

"It has been attended to, sir," Caso offered. He led them over to the shuttle. "Now you have to leave . . ."

Clearly Sheridan was getting his usual fire and composure back, because standing just outside the shuttle, he rounded on the guard, and said, "Listen, sonny. We don't 'have' to do anything that gets in the way of what's important: namely, getting our son back." His hand was trembling, and he was shaking a finger at Caso. "If he doesn't turn up—"

"John!" Delenn's voice was a cry of alarm, flooded with relief. "Look!"

Sprawled in the center of the shuttle, like a large bag of produce, was David. Delenn ran to him, checked him over. She was relieved to see that his chest was rising and falling in a wonderfully normal manner. "David . . . David, wake up . . ."

"That would not be wise. Nor feasible," Dunseny said. "He's asleep because we drugged him."

"Drugged him!" Delenn said in alarm.

"Well . . . drugged his food, technically."

"What have you done to my son?" Sheridan demanded angrily.

If Sheridan's anger was intended to intimidate Dunseny, it didn't work. The faithful retainer looked at him with only the mildest of concern. "Nothing that wasn't necessary."

Suddenly Delenn understood. She pulled back the edge of his shirt, around the throat. The small mass of protoplasm—the thing called the keeper—was still attached, its single, fearsome eye closed. It slept as soundly as David.

"In Valen's name . . ." she whispered.

"As you see," Dunseny said mildly. "We did to him what the emperor did to himself, but on a far more extreme level. As I said, necessary. If his—associate—were to see the two of you, it would put an end to your escape." His face twisted in disgust. "The Drakh may be in the process of abandoning this world, thank the Great Maker. But if the keeper were in working order, you can rest assured that one of their vessels would still find the time to blow you out of the sky."

"He should be out for some time yet," Caso told them. "Perhaps not quite long enough for you to get to Minbar . . . but far enough, at least, to be safe in deep space, several jump points away."

"At that point, if he awakens, don't tell him your position. We're hoping even the keeper can't send information to the Drakh that his host doesn't possess." Dunseny looked around apprehensively once more. "Standing here talking is counter-productive. Leave. Now."

Sheridan quickly moved forward to the cockpit of the shuttle, Delenn staying by David's side, caressing his hair gently. Some part of her couldn't quite believe that he was with them again. She looked to Dunseny, standing outside the shuttle, looking in unflappably as the door irised shut. The skyline of the burning city was visible behind him, in the distance. Just before the closing door cut off her view of his face, he said—without the slightest trace of irony—"Thank you for visiting beautiful Centauri Prime. We do hope you've enjoyed your trip. Please come again." And then the door closed.

— chapter 27 —

Far, far away from it all . . .

The female Centauri lay on her deathbed.

The women who tended her were moving around like moths, flitting about, dabbing her head that was burning with fever, trying to keep liquids in her, and taking care of her needs. She did not pay attention to any of them, did not seem to know that any of them were there. She stared at the ceiling, although since her eyes were glassy, it was difficult to know just how much she actually saw.

In a way, it seemed that she was not looking at the ceiling . . . but through it. Through it to a place light-years away, to events that she could not see, could not possibly know about . . . and yet, somehow, she did . . .

The moment G'Kar felt the fingers tighten on his throat, he knew there was no backing out. He knew that he was in the fight of his life . . . a fight *for* his life. But he wasn't looking at Londo as he redoubled his efforts to crush the emperor's throat. His focus was entirely on the eye that was peering back at him . . . the single, unblinking eye.

He saw terror in it, and from that terror, he drew strength.

Harder, Londo! Save us! Save us! We do not want to die!

Londo saw the fearsome red eye of G'Kar, and it was looking to his side. He realized that, at the last, G'Kar's battle was not with him, but with the thing on his shoulder. Londo's mind was almost detached from what was happening. In a way, it was symbolic. The keeper was the incarnation of all the dark, back-

232

ground forces that had made Londo their puppet for so many years.

And even as he thought that, his efforts increased, his death grip on G'Kar's throat redoubled. Strength flowed from the panic that the keeper fed into him, and he wanted to scream *Faster, G'Kar! Faster! End it before it's too late!* But he could say nothing, for his windpipe was already crushed. He had no chance, and still he fought on.

Londo! You can stop him! You can kill the Narn and we can live on, and it will be much better, you will have more time for yourself, we can do this thing for you, we will treat you better, and the Drakh will make things better, love us, Londo, stop him!

Londo had heard that, when one is dying, one's life flashes before one's eyes . . .

As G'Kar's fingers burrowed deeper, his mind further disassociated, and he waited, and saw nothing . . . and there was still nothing, and time stretched out and continued to warp around him and there was nothing . . .

Nothing . . .

Londo . . . fight . . . fight . . . help us . . . Shiv'kala . . . Drakh, masters of shadow, help us . . . do not flee, do not run, help us, help your servants . . .

Words . . . so many words . . .

It was incredible to G'Kar. He had been a warrior, with no patience for words, and yet words had become his weapon, cutting more deeply than any blade, smashing down more doors than any strength of arm. Words, words came floating back to him . . .

No one here is exactly what they seem . . .

I did not fight to remove one dictator just to become another myself . . .

There's someone else out there, Na'Toth . . .

The future isn't what it used to be . . .

These and hundreds of others tumbled around, fighting to be noticed, to be remembered and treasured and cherished one final time, one final moment before sliding off into oblivion.

He shoved forward, tumbling to the floor, his hands still wrapped around Londo's throat, his eye still fixed on the malevolent creature staring back at him. He desperately wanted to hear the mouthless creature scream. He thought, in some way, he actually heard it doing so. Not hear it . . . feel it . . .

Feel it . . . feel it all . . .

Feel the agony of seeing his father hanging from a tree, telling his son with his dying breath that he was proud of him . . .

Feel the warmth of the blood splattering on him . . . the blood of the first Centauri he killed . . .

Feel the pain of Delenn's gravity rings crushing him . . .

Feel the loss, the humiliation, the betrayal of his people at the hands of Londo Mollari . . .

Feel the ignominy of being forced from the council after the Narn had fallen . . . and the swell of desperate pride as he made his exit speech . . .

Feel the agony of the eye being torn from his face . . . that was as nothing compared to Cartagia's lash upon his back . . .

Feel the momentary glory of triumph, breaking free of his bonds in Cartagia's throne room, seeing the shock of his Centauri captors as they realized just what it was they were facing . . .

Feel the serenity of his writings . . .

Feel the friendship for Londo that he never thought could occur . . .

Feel the pride in accomplishment . . . the softness of a woman's skin pressed against him . . . the smell of fresh air . . . the warmth of a sunrise . . . the coolness of a sunset . . . *the hands around his throat . . . the pain . . . receding . . . the job . . . not done . . . not quitting . . . wetness . . . on his hands, Londo's tears flowing, sobbing at his fate, tears on G'Kar's hands . . . the hand . . . of the king . . . saving the king . . . saving the realm . . . saving . . .*

Londo! Do not stop! You can save us! The darkness . . . there are things in it . . . I am afraid of the darkness . . . Londo . . . love us . . . Londo . . . Londo . . .

* * *

Nothing . . . there was nothing . . . he was . . .

I saw nothing . . . not a thing . . .

When Kosh emerged from the encounter suit . . . to save Sheridan that time . . . Londo had been standing there . . . and the words, the whispered wonderment . . .

Valeria . . . Droshalla . . . G'Lan . . .

They all saw . . . something . . . and Londo, squinting against the light . . . saw . . .

I saw nothing . . . not a thing . . .

Nothing . . . the nothingness of an empty soul . . . the nothingness of the damned . . . the nothing . . .

Londo! Save us . . . save . . . save . . .

Save . . . save us . . .

Save me . . .

And then . . .

. . . then the mental picture that he had snapped of that moment, buried in his head for all these years . . . suddenly developed . . . the detail fleshing in, and he saw . . . he saw . . .

. . . a being . . . a great being, with wings outstretched, looking up . . . no, down . . . down at him, smiling, and the face, a female face, flickering, shifting, and it was Adira, smiling at him, telling him that there was nothing to fear, and she stretched her hand out to him . . . he reached for it . . . and tears began to flow, tears of joy . . . and behind her, a beach seemed to shimmer . . .

Black tendrils, snared around his arm, pulling him back . . .

. . . he fought against them, the final fight, the only fight, the only one that mattered, and his fingers were almost brushing against hers . . .

Londo . . . you cannot get away . . . you will always be ours . . . you . . .

I will be my own man, *he howled in his mind, and he lunged for her, for the warmth, for the beauty of that winged and glorious creature, and his fingers brushed against hers. The moment they did there was a crackle of energy, and it filled him, and exploded within him, and then the world turned to pure white . . .*

*   *   *

Far, far away from it all . . .

The female Centauri focused, for the first time in a long time, on those who were tending her. And in a voice surprisingly strong and firm, she said, "Oho. *Now* he needs me. Typical . . ."

. . . and then her eyes closed in repose, and Timov, daughter of Algul, empress-in-exile of Centauri Prime, passed away . . .

— *chapter 28* —

Renegar and Gwynn were standing at Vir's shuttle, gesturing frantically for him to come aboard. Gwynn seemed to be assessing Senna, casting a critical eye up and down. Senna didn't seem to meet with her approval. Then again, very little did. So instead she turned her attention to the skies, obviously anticipating the possibility that one of the Drakh might detect them somehow and take their revenge. But as Vir approached, he suddenly slowed, then stopped.

"What the hell are you doing?" Renegar demanded.

Senna turned to look back at him in confusion. "Vir?"

Vir was holding a large satchel clutched in his arms, like a child. Suddenly he shoved it into Senna's arms, kissed her quickly on the cheek, turned, and headed back for the palace.

"I'm going back to help Londo."

"You can't help him," Gwynn said flatly. "You can only destroy yourself."

"Destroy myself?" There was a flat, disbelieving tone in Vir's voice. "You still don't get it, do you, Gwynn. Everything that was good about me is long gone. Everything that I used to despise about myself, I now realize was the best of me. I can't destroy myself; Vir Cotto was destroyed long ago. I can only end myself, and believe me, at this point, I don't much care about that."

He turned and bolted for the castle. Behind him, Renegar shouted, "You're being a fool!"

"Long practice," Vir shouted back.

Renegar watched him go in disbelief, and then shaking his head, he turned to the techno-mages. "Do we wait for him to come back?"

"Only if we are as great fools as he is," Gwynn shot back.

"Come." She headed for the shuttle, then stopped at the door . . . knowing without even needing to look that Renegar hadn't budged from the spot. Neither had Senna.

"Leave without me if you want. I'm waiting here," Renegar informed her.

"As am I," Senna echoed.

Gwynn let out a long, frustrated sigh, and then said, "No. We're not. We're taking off, right now."

Renegar turned away from her and then felt her hand on his arm. The other hand touched Senna's arm. They tried to pull away, and Gwynn muttered some words, and they each felt a tingling sensation that quickly moved up into their heads. Then just like that, Gwynn was pulling them along and they were unable to prevent her from guiding them into the shuttle.

There was deathly silence in the throne room when Vir entered. Somehow, before he even walked in, he knew what he would find. They were lying there, G'Kar and Londo, hands wrapped around each other's throats. There was, to the scene, a sense of completion, of closure, as if this was somehow always meant to be.

The great seal of the emperor lay nearby. Slowly Vir crouched and picked it up. He turned it over and over, felt the weight of it, shaking his head as he did so. He felt as if he held the entire weight of all the expectations of Centauri Prime, all the dashed hopes, all the shattered promises of the future.

His eyes were dry. He had no more tears to shed.

He looked down at Londo, the life gone from him. His final expression, incredibly, was a smile.

He looked over to G'Kar, into his eye . . .

The burning red eye . . . which moved. Twitched ever so infinitesimally.

"Great Maker," Vir breathed, scarcely able to believe it. "G'Kar . . ."

G'Kar's eye focused momentarily on Vir, then glanced away . . . glanced . . . at something . . . toward Vir's feet.

Vir reflexively looked to see what G'Kar was looking at . . . and took a step back, gasping in horror.

The creature appeared to be in extreme pain. Its tendrils were whipping about noiselessly, its single, hideous eye crusting over.

There was a gaping hole in its side, like a hornet having torn its stinger away to pull itself free. But it was inches away from Vir, and it was not done yet, hanging on with determination that bordered on the supernatural.

The keeper looked up at Vir, although it might not have seen him so much as sensed him.

And Vir screamed, but it wasn't a sound of terror. Instead it was blind fury, such as he had never known. And gripping the seal of the emperor, he smashed it down upon the keeper. It made a vomitous squishing sound, and he was certain that somehow he heard a screech in his head ... impossible, certainly, since the thing had no mouth, but he heard it just the same. He was positive it wasn't his imagination. Even as he raised the great seal up, he saw the mass on the floor still twitching. It wouldn't have mattered if it had been moving or not, for he was so seized in a fit of fury that he would have brought the seal crashing down again even if the creature hadn't been moving so much as a centimeter.

And then a third time, and a fourth and a fifth. He lost count. He lost track of time and lost all reason. He was astounded to realize that he was sobbing, the tears that he hadn't thought he possessed opening up. He hurled every invective he could think of at the creature and all that it represented, every profanity in his vocabulary, words that he had never uttered and never thought he would. The empty throne room rang with the clanging of the great seal of the emperor, which became more dented and twisted with every impact.

Finally, his fury expended, he backed up and assessed the damage he had done. The keeper was nothing but an indistinguishable pile of goo on the floor. He tossed aside the seal, not caring about its tradition or sacred meaning. It lay on the floor like some worthless piece of scrap metal, which—as far as Vir was concerned—was all it was.

He looked over at G'Kar, and he knew instantly that the life was gone from the great Narn. Indeed, he wondered whether he had even been alive at the last. Whether that twitch of his scarlet orb was deliberate, a mute warning ... or just some after-death spasm simulating a last act of heroism. He couldn't know, nor would he ever.

"Tell your masters," Vir snarled at the smear on the floor that had once been alive, "that their time is over. Centauri Prime for Centauri."

"Tell us yourself."

The words were a hoarse whisper that came from behind. He whirled and saw half a dozen Drakh directly behind him. One of them he recognized instantly.

"Shiv'kala," he said.

"Vir Cotto," Shiv'kala replied. "Finally . . . we are face-to-face . . . true enemies revealed at last."

"You won't control me," Vir shot back.

"You know so little," the Drakh snarled. "But you will learn."

They advanced on him, and Vir backed up as fast as he could. They were coming in from all sides, circling him, and the only avenue left was the window, facing out onto a drop that would kill a hundred Virs.

Vir did not hesitate. He clambered up onto the window, poised in the sill. The night air, heated from the flames in the distance, swept around him.

"I've nothing to learn from you," he said defiantly, "except the lengths that someone should be willing to go to, just to live free in mind and spirit."

He took a look down, getting ready to make his fatal plunge. And then his eyes widened as he saw . . . a shuttle. No, not just any shuttle: his shuttle. It was approaching rapidly from below, coming straight toward him with a roar of engines.

The Drakh came at him, and he was out of time and options. Vir leaped through the air, feeling anything except graceful, and he landed atop the shuttle. He cried out, having landed badly, pain shooting through his right knee. He thought he might have torn a ligament, and then he started to slide off the top. It was smooth, giving his desperate fingers no purchase upon which to grab. But then the doors irised open, and Renegar was there, catching Vir as he slid by. "Hang on, I've got you!" he shouted, and hauled the flailing Cotto into the shuttle as if he weighed absolutely nothing.

Vir heard a screech of rage from the Drakh even as he tumbled into the shuttle.

Then he heard the sound of weapons fire.

He scrambled to his feet and what he saw through the window was enough to make his hearts sing. Guards, led by Caso, had come pouring into the room, heavily armed. The Drakh had turned to face them, a dark and fearsome last stand against the rather unexpected forces of light. The guards were opening fire on the Drakh. The grey servants of the Shadows were putting up a struggle, but it didn't seem likely they were going to survive for long. In a city reduced to smoking ruins thanks to their evil, at least one group of Drakh was undergoing what could only be described as a desperate last stand. He envisioned a throne room littered with Drakh bodies . . .

. . . and then couldn't help but remember that one of the bodies littering that throne room was that of he who should, by all rights, be sitting in that throne.

"Are you all right, Vir?" Senna asked. She was by his side, and he realized she was checking him over to ascertain whether he had sustained any sort of damage. "Are you unhurt?"

"That's . . . two different questions, really," Vir said ruefully. "I'm unhurt, yes. As for my being all right, though . . . I don't think I'll be all right ever again."

"Londo . . . were you able to help him?" Renegar asked . . . and then he saw the expression on Vir's face.

Senna did as well. "You mean . . . he's . . ."

"He died at G'Kar's hands, as did G'Kar at his."

"But why?" Senna asked desperately. "I don't understand. I don't understand any of it. Why would they kill each other?"

"I have some guesses on the matter," Vir said thoughtfully. "I don't know that we'll ever know for sure."

Senna began to sob. She seemed unable to find words to express the grief she was feeling. Vir reached for her and held her close to him.

"He tried. He tried so hard to be the best emperor he could," Senna managed to say.

"He did the most that anyone could—"

"Excuse me," Gwynn cut in, sounding a bit annoyed. "Can we save the maudlin eulogizing for a more appropriate time? There are other matters to be attended to."

"Shut up, Gwynn," Vir shot back. "You're a techno-mage, and I know perfectly well that there's a huge amount of things that you know about that I couldn't even begin to understand. But there are some things that you know absolutely nothing about, and this is one of them, so I'm telling you again, especially when it comes to Londo: Shut the hell up. Got that?"

Dripping with sarcasm, Gwynn bowed slightly, and said, "Of course, Vir Cotto. After all, I'm only the one who brought this vessel around, using my skills to find you, and saved your life. It's not as if you owe me the slightest bit of gratitude."

Vir allowed the remark to pass, partly from disdain and partly from the fact that he knew, deep down, that she was right. But she was so damned annoying that he couldn't quite bring himself to show his appreciation. So instead he changed the subject. "The remaining bombs . . . are we sure we've got them all?"

Renegar nodded. "Once we knew they existed—although it would have been great if we could have discovered it through some other method than having them be set off—Finian was able to tap into their energy signatures and locate them quickly enough. They were cloaked, but you can't cloak something from a techno-mage if they know what to look for."

"He never told anyone," Vir said in amazement. "Never trusted anyone . . . trusted me . . . enough to tell me . . ."

"Can you blame him?" Senna asked. "He must have thought that you would find them on your own. And he must have been afraid that, if he did say something, the Drakh would detonate the bombs as punishment. Afraid." She said the word again as if she could not quite digest its full meaning. "How many years must he have spent living in fear."

"I don't know that you can exactly call that living," Vir said. "Where are the bombs now?"

"Finian has them," Gwynn said immediately. "He was anxious to get them off-world, away from possible Drakh influence. He's defused them, but he felt it best that the Drakh be given no opportunity to use them for further mischief."

"Where is he now?"

"In another vessel."

"Can you communicate with him somehow?"

Gwynn nodded. "Absolutely. Where do you want them brought? Truth to tell, he'd be more than happy to be rid of them, sooner rather than later."

Vir didn't even hesitate. "To Minbar. I'm going to turn them over to Sheridan. A little gift in advance . . . for the help he's going to give us."

"What help are you talking about?"

"I suspect," Vir said, patting the satchel that was lying on the floor—the satchel that held Londo's memoirs—"that these words of Londo's are going to be very instrumental in letting the Alliance know just how involved the Drakh were in much of what has been blamed on Centauri Prime. The Alliance isn't going to appreciate being played for fools, and as for Sheridan . . ." He shook his head. "Let's just say that he has the most finely tuned sense of moral outrage I've ever seen in a Human. Now that the Drakh are in disarray, it shouldn't be too difficult to convince the Alliance to join forces with the Centauri fleet. Right now our ships are all sitting on station, waiting for someone to gather them in . . ."

"And that's going to be you?"

Vir nodded.

"How do you figure that?" Gwynn asked.

"For starters," Vir said slowly, "the fleet commanders have now been made to understand that what was supposed to be an initiative of Centauri origin was actually a massive manipulation at the hands of the Drakh . . . including the manipulation of the much-beloved, much-attended-to Prime Minister Durla. Durla's vision was actually Drakh vision, and that's not going to sit too well for men whose mission once seemed so clear-cut.

"I can guess that, even as we speak, there are counsels going on among the military leaders, trying to figure out what will happen next. Some will struggle for dominance. The ships may even be fighting each other. As soon as a new leader is announced and affirmed, the chances are that the fleet will fall into line eagerly, just so it can have a genuine purpose, for the first time in its existence."

"And you still think that leader will be you?" Renegar asked. "How do you figure that?"

"For starters, my connection with unveiling the Drakh is well known. And second, Londo once moved heaven and earth to try to get an endorsement from a techno-mage, because he felt that such an action would be a tremendous boost for his own chances at the throne. I know, because he enlisted my aid in trying to make things happen. Me . . . I'm going to have the endorsements of *two* techno-mages. That can be arranged, can't it, Gwynn?"

Gwynn was at the controls of the shuttle, guiding the vessel with speed and certainty away from the burning world below. She grunted in response. "Don't bet on it."

Without hesitation, he continued, "I'm also going to have the influence of the extremely influential General Rhys. I contacted him shortly before the revelation of the Drakh, informing him of what was going to happen. That was a gamble on my part, but the interaction I'd had with Rhys told me that he, of all people, would be the most outraged over the pervasive Drakh influence. He was loyal to Durla; when Durla proved less than trustworthy, Rhys needed someone to whom he could switch allegiance. I suspect that I will be that individual, and when that occurs, he'll bring the rest of the key military personnel along."

"Unless Rhys chooses to grab power for himself."

Vir shook his head. "Not Rhys. Believe it or not, he's not the type. He's old school, and believes that his allegiance is, and always must be, to the emperor. But the title of emperor is one that has traditionally always passed to those of higher birth. Rhys is lowborn, and proud of it. He's not going to want to reorder all of Centauri society just to accommodate some sort of power play.

"Now I . . . I'm of higher birth . . . no matter how much my parents would have liked to deny it," he added as a witheringly accurate self-portrayal. "Also, I believe that John Sheridan, president of the Alliance, will support my claim as well, as will most of the remaining Centauri nobility."

"You've been giving this a great deal of thought," Renegar observed.

"I learned from the best," Vir replied.

"But why?" Senna asked.

He looked to her, not quite understanding. "Why what?"

"Why would you want to be emperor? The responsibility, the danger, the—"

"The need," Vir said. "I see . . . a need. I've been doing that for years now, Senna. I see a need that has to be filled, and I . . . well . . . I just do it. Ever since I first came to Babylon 5, really. Londo needed an aide, I was his aide. He needed a conscience, and I was that, too . . . although I don't know that I did such a good job of it. The Narns needed someone to help them get to safety, and I was there for them. Centauri Prime needed someone to—"

"I need you to be quiet," Gwynn said tartly. "Am I going to get my wish?"

"Am I going to get the endorsement I need?"

"Anything for you, Your Highness."

Vir nodded in exaggerated gratitude. But despite the moment of levity, he still couldn't erase the image of the fallen Londo from his mind.

And on some level, he didn't want to.

EXCERPTED FROM
THE CHRONICLES OF VIR COTTO.
Excerpt dated (approximate Earth date)
January 12, 2278.

I should be trying to figure out some sort of memorable opening words to this, but nothing's really coming.

Londo had such a way with words. Him and G'Kar. When I think of the two of them lying there, hands around each other's throats, I'm kind of struck by the irony of it. Two people who had the greatest gifts for words of anyone I've ever met, aside from John Sheridan. And the source of that strength, their words . . . cut off. What were their last thoughts, their last feelings? G'Kar . . . well, in many ways, I never really understood him, even at the end.

As for Londo, I can only think that it was probably something like relief.

I should introduce myself, I suppose. I am Vir Cotto, once the embarrassment of my family. I was considered to be such a joke that I was basically "exiled" to a station called Babylon 5.

It's a funny thing about that space station. In order to generate artificial gravity, it turned, like the center spoke of a great wheel. Sometimes I think that Babylon 5 was the hub of our universe, turning in the center of it while the rest of events circled around it.

That's good. I like that. Deep thoughts, descriptive phrasing . . . yes. Yes, that's definitely the type of thing that these journals should be filled with. I don't know if that's really me . . . but it's what people have come to expect. And every so often, you just have to knuckle down and give the people what they want.

In any event, I was packed off to Babylon 5, to serve as the aide to a lower-level politician named Londo Mollari. No one could possibly have known that the association would wind up leaving me in the highest position of power in all of Centauri Prime. Selfishly, I wish my family had survived the bombs to see it. Then again— and I know this will sound cold, but it's also true—if my family had lived to see me attain this height, they would have been perfectly capable of planting their own bombs outside the palace, to blow the whole thing into orbit. Anything would have been preferable to allowing such a humiliating joke of a person as myself to assume power.

What can I say? That's just the kind of loyalty I inspired in my family.

Following the escape from Centauri Prime, my arrival on Minbar was greeted with some suspicion by the local residents. I can't entirely say I blame them. After all, the Centauri had been painted as mad-dog killers for so long, the Minbari probably couldn't help but think that I had some sort of sinister motive planned. Sheridan and Delenn, who arrived at roughly the same time, however, intervened in this potentially sticky situation. They paved the way for my setting up a temporary "exile headquarters" on Minbar.

From that point on, the rest was simply a matter of organization. Word was sent out to the remaining heads of the Centauri Houses. Some came to Minbar curious, others came in anger, still others came seeking answers, while still others desired power. The point was . . . those who survived, came.

I managed to keep the debate under control. There was some initial resistance, but I was backed up by the techno-mages, the Alliance in the person of John Sheridan, and the awareness on the part of the House heads that the fleet was still floating around out there, looking for a target. If matters continued in a disorganized fashion for too long, someone in the military might have taken it into their head that Centauri Prime itself was ripe for military rule. Either that, or we might have had various leaders go rogue and decide to start attacking the Alliance on their own initiative. That, of course, would have been suicidal. What little of Centauri Prime was still standing wouldn't have remained standing for long, once the Alliance started fighting back.

Thanks to the agreement that has come to be known as the Minbar Accord, the following was worked out:

The House heads have recognized my claim as emperor.

The military is being recalled to Centauri Prime, with new instructions and directions being given them. They will have the target they so desperately need to validate their fleet's existence. That target is the Drakh. Many of the escape vessels were tracked and targeted. A number of Drakh were also captured and were . . . shall we say, forthcoming . . . about certain Drakh interests and strongholds. The Centauri fleet, in tandem with the resources of the Alliance, is going after the Drakh with a vengeance.

Sheridan has been good enough to put telepaths at the disposal of the Centauri and Alliance fleets. Telepaths capable of detecting both the Drakh and their keepers, should any more of those vile little creatures try to spread their influence.

What has been most impressive during all of this, I must admit, is Senna. As if she has been watching, waiting, and preparing for this her entire life, she has been dealing with the House heads, the remaining ministers . . . all of them. They are surprisingly—even to themselves, I think—comfortable discussing such things as military, financial, and governmental matters with her. It's unusual, considering that women are held, if not in low esteem, at least in less-than-impressive regard in our society. Perhaps it is because she has been around for so long that many of them know her and feel at ease.

Perhaps, as the daughter of Lord Refa, the ward of Londo Mollari, and the beloved—yes, I'm afraid it's that evident—of the next emperor, they see her as a connection to the far and near past and to the future. It would be premature, maybe even absurd, to think that she could one day hold a position of authority in our government. Then again, this is a time of possibilities, and why shouldn't something such as that be possible? Such things do not happen overnight.

Sheridan and Delenn have been remarkably supportive. At one point, Delenn looked me straight in the eye, and said, "Vir . . . you're a living symbol of everything that is positive about Centauri culture." Hard not to be flattered over something like that. Sheridan has likewise been forthcoming with his help, support, and insight. I very much doubt whether I could have held matters together in the initial stages if his presence had not sent a very distinct message.

Their son, David, on the other hand . . . well . . . that is another matter . . .

— *chapter 29* —

David pulled once more against the restraints, his face twisted in fury. For Delenn, watching from the edge of the room, it took every amount of strength and self-control she possessed not to let her grief be displayed. Those monsters might be watching her at this very moment, peering through the hideous eye that sat unblinkingly upon her son's shoulder, at the base of his neck.

Nude from the waist up, David had absolutely no chance of tearing free of the straps that held him firmly to the chair. That did not, however, stop him from trying.

The keeper remained inscrutable, but it was his actions they were viewing. Delenn was quite sure of that.

A score of Minbari doctors and scientists had been through the medical facility, studying the situation from every possible angle. They were the best that the Minbari had to offer. Yet the man next to whom John Sheridan was now standing, the man who had just gotten done examining David—he was someone whose medical expertise Delenn trusted above all others, including that of her own kind.

"What do you think, Stephen?" Sheridan asked.

As dire as the situation was, Stephen Franklin would not be rushed. He put up a hand to quiet Sheridan as he finished studying readings he had taken.

Delenn looked at her son once more, her heart aching for her inability to help him. She knew that if anyone could, it would be Dr. Stephen Franklin. David, after all, was a unique hybrid: mostly human, but with a few Minbari traits. And he had a creature spawned from the black pit of Shadow and Drakh technology bonded to him.

Franklin's knowledge covered all the bases. He had been an expert on Minbari physiology at a time when the Minbari were busy trying to exterminate Humans altogether. He had been squarely in the middle of the Shadow War, and his detailed research into Drakh capability during the time of the Great Plague gave him insight into the bio-organics that that insidious race was capable of.

"If anyone can help, he can."

The hushed voice next to her, verbalizing the words in her head, startled her. She turned and let out an automatic sigh of relief when she saw Michael Garibaldi standing beside her. He had barely slept since David's return. If he had not been consoling or giving moral support to Delenn and Sheridan, he had been by David's side, trying to reach the boy, help him, as if he could get the teen to rid himself of the Drakh influence by willpower alone. He had been awake for so long that Sheridan had personally threatened to knock him cold just to make sure he got some sleep. Reluctantly, Garibaldi had gone off to bed, promising he'd sleep until he felt rested. That had been forty-seven minutes ago, yet she couldn't find it in her to scold him.

"I know," she said softly, patting him on the cheek. His three days' growth of beard was scratchy.

Sheridan started to say "Well?" again, almost out of reflex, and then stopped himself with visible effort and waited.

As for David, he said nothing, as he hadn't for some time. It was as if the creature had some sort of lock on his speech center. In a way, Delenn was grateful for that. What if the keeper had so subsumed his personality that he began spitting out curses and defiance, like some demon-possessed shell? Or worse . . . what if his own personality held sway, and he was crying out for her help? The prospect of standing there, listening to his cries, knowing she could not aid him . . . it would have been beyond excruciating.

Franklin finally looked up and indicated with a gesture of his head that they should reconvene outside the room. They walked out, Delenn bringing up the rear and casting one last, sad look at her son. It was hard to tell whether he was even aware of it.

"Look," Franklin said slowly, "I have to admit, my ego, if nothing else, would love to be able to come in here, take one look at the situation, and say that there's some simple answer that everyone else has overlooked. But there's not. That thing is like . . . it's like a parasite that's literally eaten into him on a neurological basis. It didn't happen overnight, either. The . . . keeper, you said it's called?" Sheridan nodded. "The keeper, as near as I can tell, has been establishing a psychic bond with him for a number of years now. It had the opportunity to intertwine itself with him on a far more comprehensive and profound basis than it could have with an adult, because it connected with him at such a young age. For all I know, it's been influencing him on a low-level basis of some kind since birth."

Delenn let out a choked sob but managed to pull herself together quickly. Coming apart now wasn't going to benefit anything. Instead she let the cold, burning fury that she felt for the monsters that had done this come to the fore.

"The creature's tendrils have wrapped themselves around David on a basic neurological level," Franklin continued. "If we tried to remove the thing by force, it would be the equivalent of tearing out his central nervous system with a chain saw."

"We can put it to sleep," Delenn suggested. "Londo told us that alcohol numbed its awareness."

"It's awareness, yes, but not its influence. If its life is threatened, no matter how incapacitated it is, it will fight back, and David will likely be the battleground. The chances are that, even if David manages to live, there will be nerve and brain damage so extensive that whatever is left won't really be David anymore."

"There has to be a way."

Franklin took a deep breath. "As near as I can tell—based on brain-wave readings I've gotten off the keeper—it draws a sort of strength from its point of origin."

"Point of origin?" Garibaldi sounded confused.

But Delenn understood instantly. "The Drakh that made it."

"Made it, nourished it, sustained it . . . however you want to describe it," Franklin agreed. "That Drakh, whoever and wherever it is, is the keeper's foundation. As with any house, remove the foundation, and the structure collapses."

"Is there a way to generate some sort of scrambling field so it can't communicate with the Drakh?" Sheridan asked.

Franklin shook his head. "Even if we could manage it, it would just trigger the keeper's self-defense mechanisms, and David would suffer for it. The only thing I can suggest is finding a way to terminate the signal from the other end, as it were."

"You're saying we have to find the Drakh who did this . . . and kill it," Sheridan said grimly.

"In essence . . . yes."

"How in Valen's name can we possibly do that?" Delenn demanded.

"I wish I had an answer for you . . . but I don't."

Slowly, Garibaldi walked toward David. His determination to struggle against his bonds seemed endless. During every waking hour he kept it up; only when he slept did he cease his struggles, and he only slept because he had exhausted himself so thoroughly that he couldn't move anymore.

Garibaldi focused all his attention on the keeper, staring straight into that hideous eye. "Whoever . . . wherever you are," he said intently, "if you're seeing me . . . sensing me, whatever . . . I'm telling you right now: I will find you. And when I do, the only thing that's going to be on your side is that you'll die quick and easy. Trust me: I'd rather prolong it. Make you feel every second of agony, for as long as possible. But I don't want you influencing this boy for an instant longer than necessary. You got that, you disease-ridden piece of filth? I . . . am coming . . . for you."

The keeper didn't seem especially perturbed by the prospect.

Dinner that evening was a less-than-festive affair. Vir and Senna had joined Delenn, Sheridan, Franklin, and Garibaldi around a table that had more than enough food to accommodate everyone. Unfortunately, much of it was left uneaten, since no one seemed particularly hungry.

Franklin, in short order, brought the two Centauri up to speed with what he had already told the others. Vir didn't seem especially shocked to hear it. "I can't say I'm surprised," he told them. "You know of how I found G'Kar and Londo . . ."

"With their hands at each other's throats," Sheridan said grimly.

"There was no way . . . *no way* . . . Londo was trying to fight G'Kar off on his own. He wanted to make certain that the two of you escaped, and he was willing to sacrifice his life to make sure that happened. Any resistance given to that end was entirely at the keeper's control."

"Is that supposed to make us feel better about the guy?" Garibaldi demanded.

"Michael . . ." Sheridan tried to rein him in.

But Garibaldi wasn't listening. He put down the fork that he hadn't used to pick up any food for twenty minutes, and leaned forward. "You're sitting here telling me that, after he was responsible for the deaths of millions, all long before the Drakh got their hooks into him, we're all now supposed to feel sorry for Londo Mollari and take pride in him because he sacrificed himself to save three people? Granted, three people whom I myself would crawl through hell over broken glass to help, but three people nevertheless? Is that somehow supposed to balance the scales?"

"No," Vir answered softly.

"Then don't try to make him out to be some sort of grand hero, at least not while I'm around."

Once upon a time, Delenn thought, Vir would have been intimidated by the ferocity and intensity of Garibaldi's outburst. Instead he just looked a bit tired, and said, "You know, Mr. Garibaldi . . . Londo was endlessly fascinated by Earth and its inhabitants. He stepped in whenever he could to help you. Did things behind the scenes, positive things, which your people never knew anything about. He read over Earth culture endlessly, always researching, always trying to understand. I asked him occasionally why he was so intrigued by all of you, and he never really managed to give me any sort of satisfactory answer. But you know what? I think I've figured it out. I think that, in many ways . . . he was far closer spiritually to any of you than he was to any of us. He had a clear vision of what he wanted, a vision that exceeded his grasp at every level, but he never stopped reaching, despite the inherent character flaws that pulled him down. Londo Mollari was not a hero, Mr. Garibaldi. What he was . . . was all too Human."

There was a long moment of silence, and then Sheridan turned to Vir. "Well spoken," he said.

Garibaldi rolled his eyes. "Sometimes I don't get any of you people."

"That's quite all right, sir," Senna spoke up. "I don't 'get' any of you, either. And I'm speaking largely as an outsider. But what I do see," and she looked around the table and actually smiled, "is a group of people who would very much prefer to like each other . . . but have been through so much, they don't know if they can."

"This is quite a perceptive young woman you have here, Vir," Delenn remarked. "You would do well not to let her get too far."

"Thank you," Vir said. "I'll see that she doesn't. Oh . . . Senna. Do you have the drawings?"

"Drawings?" Sheridan asked.

"Senna's been busy," Vir said, by way of explanation. "She has untapped talents."

Senna had unrolled several large sheets of paper, and she handed them to Garibaldi. He endeavored to maintain his surly attitude, but in spite of himself, he raised an eyebrow upon seeing the illustrations. "Fairly decent likenesses of Londo and G'Kar," he said. "I like the way they're standing there, with their backs to each other. Seems symbolic."

"It's quite rough," she said.

"What's this area between them?"

"That's the city. I told you it was rough."

"The city?" Then he understood. "These are statues. Designs for statues. My God, they're huge."

"Statues?" Sheridan leaned over, as did Delenn. Franklin got up and came around the table to get a better look. "You're thinking about building statues to Londo and G'Kar."

Vir nodded. "At either gate of the main city. Part of the rebuilding of Centauri Prime." He shook his head. "Hard to believe. It seems that just yesterday we had to rebuild from the Alliance attack. Now we're looking to the Alliance to help us recover again."

"The Alliance will be there to help," Sheridan assured him. "That much I can promise you. And this . . ." He shook his head and tapped the drawings. "If you'd told me twenty years ago that there would be a statue of G'Kar . . . of any Narn, for that matter . . . built right on the edge of the city . . ."

"It is a most perceptive concept," Delenn said. She tapped the paper. "I am curious, though. Why are they both faced away from the city? It almost seems to say that they have turned their backs on the Centauri people."

"No, Delenn, not at all," Garibaldi told her. "Takes an old security warhorse to understand: they're standing guard. You can't stand guard if your back is to your enemies."

"That's exactly right," Senna said. "Although it's also more than that. Londo . . ." She seemed to know what she wanted to say, but had trouble putting it into words.

Vir stepped in. "We have Londo facing away from the capital that he inhabited for so long . . . obsessed over for so long . . . that it was all he could see. He didn't look to the long-range results of his decisions, because he was so blinded by his poor decisions."

"So instead," Senna said, "we're positioning him the way I think he would have wished he had been. He's looking away from the city and, instead, to the horizon."

"Very nice," Sheridan said. "And something tells me that G'Kar would have appreciated the irony of protecting the capital city of what were once his enemies."

Garibaldi commented, "And the way that you have them positioned . . . they're really watching each other's backs."

"As they did in life," Delenn said. "It has a symmetry to it. Well done, Vir and Senna . . . very well done."

"I just wish they could have lived to see it," Sheridan said.

She put her arm through his, linking them. "You know, John . . . I think, in a way that we'll never understand . . . they did."

EXCERPTED FROM
THE CHRONICLES OF VIR COTTO.
Excerpt dated (approximate Earth date)
January 20, 2278.

Senna and I returned to Centauri Prime today. The reception was muted, which is to be expected. We are still burying our dead, and naturally it's a little difficult to get all worked up over the arrival of the man who has been promised to be the next emperor.

The fires have long been put out, but the damage remains. The smell of burned flesh still hangs in the air; if I take a deep breath, my gag reflex kicks in. Upon my arrival, the first thing I did was walk through the streets of Centauri Prime, surveying the damage. It was as if I were wandering through a ghost town, except the ghosts were out and about. People looked at me with haunted, almost vacant expressions. Despite my brief holographic appearance, they likely didn't know who I was. I have not yet taken to wearing the white. I don't know when I will. I think there's a long way for our world, our people, to go before we start assuming the outward vestments of the past.

The palace, of course, remains untouched. Naturally. For the Drakh, it was a symbolic stronghold of their influence, second only to the Tower of Power they engineered. Sheridan showed me a picture of a tower on an Earth desert, constructed by insects and swarming with them. That's what the Tower of Power was: an infestation. We exterminated that infestation. But, like any number of insects, the inhabitants of the Tower turned around and stung us. It will take us a long time to recover from such a severe stinging.

On the shuttle from Minbar to here, I brought some acquisitions that Sheridan and Delenn were generous enough to give me. Books and some assorted pieces of furniture, including several tables, chairs, and a large wardrobe. All very old and crafted in the Minbari style. Their generosity is amazing.

I have had initial discussions with my ministers. I intend to make General Rhys minister of Internal Security. He told me he didn't want the job. That's more than enough reason to give it to him.

When I arrived at the palace, Dunseny was waiting for me, as were Caso and Renegar. Renegar handed me a crystal that, when I played it, revealed a communication from Gwynn and Finian on it. Both of them looked . . . tired. As if the events that had transpired had taken a lot out of them. I couldn't really blame them, I guess. I think we all felt that way. But the fact that they were techno-mages should have . . . I don't know . . . protected them somehow.

"It's over, Vir," Finian told me. "But it's also just started. And Gwynn and I both want you to know . . . that if an emergency ever presents itself . . . if there is ever some catastrophe facing you as you proceed on your path as emperor of Centauri Prime, trying to pull together the shattered remains of your republic . . . in short, if there's ever a situation in which the talents of the techno-mages are required . . . then both Gwynn and I want you to know . . ."

"That you can forget it," Gwynn completed.

I actually laughed out loud at that as the picture blinked out. One had to credit them: techno-mages habitually spoke in a manner so oblique, so indecipherable, that it was a pleasure to see that they could say exactly what they meant when they put their minds to it.

As the day drew to a close, I held Senna close to me and watched the sun turning red on the horizon. So much to do. So many things that needed attending to. And I found my thoughts turning to Timov, the former wife of Londo. Word had reached us that she had passed away quietly, of illness. Apparently she had hung on for far longer than the doctors had believed possible. She died on the exact same day that Londo did. On the one hand, there is certainly no reasonable way she could have known. On the other hand, considering the formidable woman she was, it might be that she was simply so stubborn that she felt she had to outlast Londo, no matter what.

And naturally, thoughts of Timov turned me to Mariel.

We all carry our sins upon us. Mariel will always be mine. I was working to save a people . . . and in doing it, destroyed one woman. I can justify it as much as I want. I can make myself believe that she had it coming. That it was necessary. That it was any one of a hundred things. But what I keep coming back around to is that it was wrong, and it's something that I can never, ever fix. Not ever.

I felt a frost upon my spine, feeling as if a shadow had touched me, and held Senna closer as the night chill began to fill the air.

— *chapter 30* —

"Do you want me to sleep with you tonight?" Senna asked.

Vir considered it a moment, but then shook his head. "The time . . . isn't right." He sighed. "I don't . . . I can't . . . I . . ."

She put a finger to his lips and hushed him. "When the time is right, then." Her lips brushed lightly against his. "Good night then, Vir."

"Good night."

He went to his quarters then. He had selected something simple for himself, nothing ostentatious. He couldn't bring himself to take over the private quarters that had once belonged to Londo. Too many ghosts that had not been laid to rest, and quite possibly never would be.

As the door slid shut behind him, he glanced around the room approvingly. The things he'd transported from Minbar had been brought there and set up just as he had specified. There was the desk, and the chairs. And the wardrobe, polished and ornate, big as a man and twice as wide.

It was late; he'd had a long day, and he had a series of meetings scheduled for tomorrow that were going to be pivotal in his decisions as to what direction Centauri Prime should go. Yet with all that, he could not bring himself to sleep. Instead he sat down at a computer and recorded another entry in his chronicles. There were many ways in which he had no intention of following Londo's example, but the concept of keeping a journal was a good idea. For an emperor owed it to more than himself to try to keep his thoughts orderly, try to maintain a record of his achievements, or lack thereof. An emperor owed it to whoever followed him in the office. A blueprint, a template, for what to do right . . . and what to avoid.

"I felt a frost upon my spine, feeling as if a shadow had

touched me, and held Senna closer as the night chill began to fill the air," he said, and was about to continue when another chill struck him. That was odd, however, because when he'd been with Senna, they'd been standing on a balcony. Here, however, he was in a room that had been warm only moments before.

The room also seemed darker somehow, and the shadows were—impossibly—starting to lengthen.

Slowly Vir rose from his chair. He appeared for all the world as if he wanted to cry out, but he could not.

A form separated itself from the shadows and stood facing him in the middle of the room.

"Shiv'kala," Vir managed to say. "You're . . . not dead."

"In that ambush? No." When he'd encountered Shiv'kala in the past, he'd always been struck by the calm, level tone of the Drakh. Now, however, Shiv'kala sounded as if every word from his mouth was laced with rage. He couldn't be sure, but it looked as if Shiv'kala was actually trembling. "No, I was able to make my escape . . . for all the good it did me."

"Good?"

"I," the Drakh growled, "have been shunned. Shunned by the Drakh Entire. Because of Londo. Because of you."

"I . . . don't understand . . ."

"Of course you do not," he snarled. "You cannot understand. Cannot know what it was to commune with the Entire. But our hold on Centauri Prime has disintegrated, my people are in retreat. The mighty fleet we helped construct now seeks us out to destroy us . . . and they blame it on me. They say I did not treat Londo harshly enough. I attempted to educate him, you see." He was circling Vir, exuding anger. Vir was rooted to the spot. "Tried to teach him our purpose. Our reason for existence. Tried to get him to understand the rightness of our cause. Instead he mistook compassion for weakness, and betrayed us in a way that he never would have if I had treated him appropriately. I did not break him sufficiently. I will not make that mistake again.

"My people have abandoned me along with this world . . . but I will get them to understand. I will show them just what I am capable of. I will bend this world to the way of the Shadows, single-handedly if I must. And the Drakh will see my accomplishment, and return. If it takes a century, it will not matter, for we have nothing but time, despite all your ships' pathetic attempts to track us down and annihilate us. But it will start with you, Vir Cotto."

"You mean . . . you . . ." Vir gulped. "You're going to try to break me the way you didn't with Londo?"

"No," the Drakh said, speaking so softly that Vir could barely hear him. "You . . . I am simply going to kill. I will deal with whoever follows you . . . but you I will not suffer to live."

Vir licked his lips, seeming to summon his courage. "No. You won't kill me. Instead . . . you're going to tell me where I can find the Drakh that spawned the keeper on David Sheridan."

It was hard to believe that a Drakh could look surprised, much less as surprised as Shiv'kala did just then. "I had thought," he said slowly, "that you simply acted the fool, in order to throw suspicion from yourself. But I was wrong. You truly are a fool."

"Tell me," Vir said, as if somehow he had the upper hand.

"You want the Drakh who produced David Sheridan's keeper?" He spread his arms wide. "He stands before you." And then his hands came together, and he advanced on Vir.

Vir didn't budge. "Thank you. I figured as much. And it's all I wanted to know."

Shiv'kala had taken only two steps toward Vir when the door of the Minbari wardrobe cabinet banged open. He spun, staring in confusion.

Standing inside the cabinet, a PPG clenched securely in both hands, was Michael Garibaldi. There was a lopsided, wolfish grin on his face and a glitter of death in his eyes.

"What's up, Drakh?" he asked.

Shiv'kala let out the howl of a damned soul, and his arm moved with a blur. But Garibaldi didn't give him any time. He squeezed off two quick shots, and both struck home, one in the Drakh's stomach, the second in his chest. The impact lifted him off his feet and slammed him against the far wall, even as a pointed steel rod flew from Shiv'kala's sleeve. It thunked into the wood six inches to the right of Garibaldi's head. He didn't even flinch, or seem to notice.

Shiv'kala flopped about on the floor like a beached whale. The only sound issuing from his mouth was a sort of incoherent grunting, and his chest made a wheezing, sucking noise that Garibaldi knew all too well. The floor beneath him became dark and stained with the awful liquid that passed for the creature's blood.

Garibaldi stood over him, aiming the PPG squarely between Shiv'kala's eyes. "The first one was for David . . . and the second was for Lou Welch. And this . . ."

"Mr. Garibaldi," Vir said sharply. Garibaldi looked to him, and Vir extended his hand, a stern expression on his face. "I can't let you do that. Give it here. Now."

Slowly, reluctantly, Garibaldi handed it over. Vir held it delicately, hefted the weight, clearly impressed by the lightness of it. Then he looked down at the fallen Drakh. "In the end . . . Londo had you pegged," he told the Drakh. "He said you were predictable. And you were. Your ego had to bring you back here, make you vulnerable. To get away, all you had to do was leave. We'd probably never have found you. But you had to stay around, to have your vengeance. You refused to admit that the time of the Drakh on Centauri Prime is over. A lot of creatures that walked or swam or flew this world's surface didn't realize when their moment passed. But it's strange: Nature doesn't care whether they knew it or not. Nature just got rid of them. Turned them extinct. Oh . . . and by the way," he added, almost as an afterthought, ". . . this is for Londo and G'Kar." And with that, he blew Shiv'kala's head off.

David Sheridan's shriek was so loud that many Minbari within a mile radius claimed to have been able to hear it.

Sheridan and Delenn were there in seconds, neither of them having even bothered to pull on robes. They had no idea what they were going to find when they entered the room, although neither of them would have been surprised to discover their son's corpse.

Even faster on the scene, amazingly, had been Stephen Franklin, who had opted to stay on Minbar for a time, to monitor the boy's condition as best he could. He was already there when Sheridan and Delenn arrived, and his body blocked their view of their son. "Stephen!" Sheridan cried out. "David! What's wrong with David?"

Franklin turned around, and said with an absolutely unreadable expression, "Wrong?" Then he stepped aside.

They saw with astonishment that Franklin had just finished

unstrapping the teen, who wore a pale and wan expression. Sheridan immediately looked to the keeper . . . except it was no longer there. There was a severe reddish mark indicating where the creature had been, but it was gone. Instead he saw Franklin crouching and picking it up with a pair of forceps. Its tendrils were hanging limply. Its eye lay wide open, but was glassily blind. It seemed about as threatening as a clump of seaweed. Clearly the creature was dead or dying. Franklin opened a large specimen jar and dropped the thing in, and it landed with a sickening little *plop*.

Delenn and Sheridan moved instantly to their son's side. Delenn was running her fingers over the area where the keeper had been, shaking her head in wonderment.

"Lemme guess," David said, in a voice that was hoarse and croaking. "Uncle Mikey?"

"I suspect so," Sheridan told him. "He volunteered to go on 'stakeout,' as he called it, on Centauri Prime. Something tells me he hit pay dirt far more quickly than we could have hoped."

"Oh, David," Delenn said, stroking his face repeatedly as if unable to believe it was him.

"It's okay, Ma . . . really. I just . . . I'd like to know one thing . . ."

"Anything, son. Just name it," Sheridan said.

"Okay." He took a deep breath. "Can I have that second piece of birthday cake now?"

Sheridan and Delenn looked at each other, then burst into joyous laughter, holding their son tight.

"More than that, David," Sheridan said fiercely. "If there's one thing I've learned, it's that hiding you here can't protect you from the galaxy. So we might as well go out there and take it on. When you recover, I'm taking a break from the presidency . . . Michael goes on vacation from his business . . . and Michael and I are going to take you on a tour of known space. Hitch some rides, grab some freighters, go down and dirty—the real worm's-eye view. Just us guys."

"Really?" David looked in amazement at Delenn. "Mom . . . that's . . . that's okay with you? You won't feel left out or—"

She laughed. "*Someone* has to run things while your father and godfather are gallivanting about in the throes of their second childhood."

He embraced both of them, and as he did, Delenn breathed silent prayers of thanks to Vir, to Garibaldi, to Valen, to Lorien. To whoever and whatever beings, real, spiritual, or imagined, had given her back her son. She would never again bewail the dwindling amount of time she had left with her husband, because at least they would all be able to enjoy it.

"So . . . Vir . . . well done," Londo's voice growled in my ear. "Look where you've come, eh? Who would have thought?"

We sat drinking together on a beach, the wave washing up along the shore. The sun shone down upon us, bathing me in a pleasant warmth. I had read in his final memoirs how he would have given anything to walk upon a beach for a brief time . . . and here it appeared he was going to have an eternity of time to do so. He looked just as I remembered him when we first met. I never realized how young he was. Great Maker, how young we all were.

"Who would have thought," I echoed.

"Look at you. Remember the days when you would get drunk on one glass alone?" He chortled at the thought. "I'll be honest with you, Vir. When you first came to Babylon 5, I gave you three months. Six months at the outside. I didn't think you'd last. Who could know that you would last . . . and I wouldn't?"

"You lasted a good long time, Londo," I assured him. "You had a good run."

"Did I?" He laughed softly. "I suppose I did. A low-level ambassador assigned to a space station that was considered a joke. They called it 'Sinclair's Folly,' you know. It wasn't exactly a stepping-stone to greatness. It was considered more a dead end. Who knew that it would lead to the throne."

"It didn't lead there, Londo. The path was very crooked, and you cut it yourself."

"I was led," Londo said firmly. "The Shadows and their agents, and their agents' agents, led me. But make no mistake. I'm not tossing aside responsibility. It was I who walked that path, and walked it willingly. Perhaps . . . perhaps at the end, that was what mattered. I took that final responsibility . . . and preserved a future that didn't include me. Does that make sense?"

"I suppose it does." I looked around. "Too bad G'Kar couldn't join us."

"He had another engagement in Na'Toth's dream. Even he can't be everywhere. On the other hand, there are always unwelcome visitors. Hold on a moment, please . . ."

Suddenly there was a sword in his hand. I flinched automatically, but he turned away from me and, in one smooth motion, threw the blade with unerring accuracy. It thudded into a grove of bushes nearby. There was a grunt, and then the impaled body of a Drakh fell from darkness into the red-tinted sunlight that was just filtering through from the sun on the horizon. The moment the rays struck it, it evaporated into dust.

"If he had been expecting that," Londo said mildly, "he could have stopped it. That's what you always have to do with forces of darkness, Vir. You have to catch them by surprise. Emissaries of evil tend to think very far, and very deep, but not very fast. Are you writing this down, Vir? That was a good one. You should remember that."

"I will."

"And never stop watching the shadows. You never know."

"But the Drakh are gone from Centauri Prime, Londo. In full retreat. Our people are safe, they—"

"Vir," he said patiently. "You started out as an aide to a low-level ambassador and you wound up emperor. What does that say to you?"

"You never know."

"Exactly."

"I'll watch the shadows, Londo, just in case they decide to watch me back."

"That is good. That is very good." He took a deep, final drink. "I think, Vir, it is time for deep, thoughtful, and profound words of wisdom that will explain the entire purpose of the universe and guarantee a life of accomplishment and prosperity."

"And they would be . . . ?"

Londo rose and walked across the sands. Standing there was Adira, smiling, her arms open to meet him.

Then I heard a steady, measured tread, a "splish splish." And there came Timov . . . walking across the surface of the water. "Londo!" she called sternly with a smile. "It's getting late."

Londo saw her, rolled his eyes, and, inclining his head, said, "She always has to show off."

She stepped out of the surf and they regarded me warmly, although Timov was watching Londo with the patient air of someone who had evaluated all of Londo's flaws and simply decided to find them charming.

"The words of wisdom, Londo?" I prompted.

"Oh, yes. Of course." And in a booming voice, Londo said, "Make love as often as possible." And with that, Londo and his women, one of passion, one of conscience, walked away, leaving no prints on the sand. His deep laughter echoed down the palace halls and carried me into wakefulness.

The sunlight of the new morning beamed through the window at me. I glanced at the corners of the room, but the light was thorough and revealed nothing of any threat hiding there.

I shrugged on my robe and left my quarters to find Senna and heed Londo's advice. I think he would have wanted it that way.

Book 4, **NO SURRENDER, NO RETREAT**, sums up the spellbinding fourth season: Captain Sheridan being pronounced missing and presumed dead on Z'ha'dum, Delenn feverishly rallying support for an all-out offensive against the Shadows, internal strife among the Centauri erupting in a shocking and violent betrayal, and Garibaldi resigning as security chief and plotting against his comrades. From "The Hour of the Wolf" to the shattering finale, "The Deconstruction of Falling Stars," Jane Killick's summaries and analyses capture all the action and intrigue of Babylon 5 circa 2261—"the year everything changed."

Book 5, **THE WHEEL OF FIRE**, covers the last season of the history-making show as the action reaches the boiling point and the stage is set for the new follow-up series, *Crusade*. Episode by episode, Jane Killick looks at Byron and his rogue telepaths' demand for a homeworld, Elizabeth Lochley's assignment as head of Babylon 5, Sheridan's inauguration as president of the new Alliance, G'Kar's unwilling ascension to the role of messiah, and the clandestine political intrigue on Centauri Prime.

Babylon 5:
Season by Season

Published by Del Rey Books.
Available wherever books are sold.